Dance of Death

By Edward Marston

THE HOME FRONT DETECTIVE SERIES

A Bespoke Murder • Instrument of Slaughter
Five Dead Canaries • Deeds of Darkness • Dance of Death

THE RAILWAY DETECTIVE SERIES

The Railway Detective • The Excursion Train
The Railway Viaduct • The Iron Horse
Murder on the Brighton Express • The Silver Locomotive Mystery
Railway to the Grave • Blood on the Line
The Stationmaster's Farewell • Peril on the Royal Train
A Ticket to Oblivion • Timetable of Death
Inspector Colbeck's Casebook:
Thirteen Tales from the Railway Detective
The Railway Detective Omnibus:
The Railway Detective, The Excursion Train, The Railway Viaduct

THE CAPTAIN RAWSON SERIES

Soldier of Fortune • Drums of War • Fire and Sword
Under Siege • A Very Murdering Battle

THE RESTORATION SERIES

The King's Evil • The Amorous Nightingale • The Repentant Rake
The Frost Fair • The Parliament House • The Painted Lady

THE BRACEWELL MYSTERIES

The Queen's Head • The Merry Devils • The Trip to Jerusalem
The Nine Giants • The Mad Courtesan • The Silent Woman
The Roaring Boy • The Laughing Hangman • The Fair Maid of Bohemia
The Wanton Angel • The Devil's Apprentice • The Bawdy Basket
The Vagabond Clown • The Counterfeit Crank
The Malevolent Comedy • The Princess of Denmark

THE BOW STREET RIVALS SERIES

Shadow of the Hangman • Steps to the Gallows

Dance of Death

EDWARD MARSTON

Allison & Busby Limited
12 Fitzroy Mews
London W1T 6DW
allisonandbusby.com

First published in Great Britain by Allison & Busby in 2015.

A CIP catalogue record for this book is available from
the British Library.

First Edition

ISBN 978-0-7490-1839-9

Typeset in 12/18 pt Adobe Garamond Pro by
Allison & Busby Ltd.

The paper used for this Allison & Busby publication
has been produced from trees that have been legally sourced
from well-managed and credibly certified forests.

Printed and bound by
CPI Group (UK) Ltd, Croydon, CR0 4YY

To
Elaine's Dance School in Gloucester
with love and thanks for countless happy hours of
Ballroom, Latin and Sequence Dancing

CHAPTER ONE

It was perfect Zeppelin weather – a dry, moonlit night without a breath of wind. When the fleet had crossed the British coastline, it was guided towards London by winding rivers and glistening railway lines. There was a blackout in the capital but the enemy could see the beckoning searchlights illuminating the sky. A Zeppelin raid created a terror that was completely out of proportion with the actual damage it could cause. Trains and buses stopped in their tracks, lights were dimmed, fires were drawn and some people huddled throughout the whole night in underground stations. Bolder and more curious inhabitants, however, came out into the street and tried to catch a glimpse of the monsters of death some 20,000 feet above their heads. They could hear the distinctive throb of the engines, punctuated by a series of small explosions from incendiary bombs dropped with indiscriminate malice by the German crews.

Simon Wilder was not at first aware of the raid. When he slipped out of the house and began the walk home, his mind was on other things. He'd gone a hundred yards before he heard the whirr of the engines and the successive blasts of the bombs. Farther down the road, a small crowd had gathered on a corner to gaze up with a mixture of fear and wonder. Many of them had watched raids before but nothing like this one. The Zeppelins were not given the freedom of the sky. Fighter pilots of the Royal Flying Corps were already in action, soaring up to confront the enemy. Anti-aircraft guns were booming gamely from below but their shells were falling well short of the target. The Zeppelins cruised on with menacing indestructibility, dropping their bombs over a constantly widening area and spreading panic.

Something extraordinary then happened. One of the fighter planes, which had taken the best part of half an hour to climb to the requisite altitude, launched an attack with its guns blazing. The pilot's aim was lethally accurate. A Zeppelin suddenly burst into flame and lit up the night sky with spectacular effect. All over London, people were able to watch an unexpected firework display as an enemy aircraft was destroyed over British soil for the very first time. It was a turning point. The capital no longer simply had to endure a raid and pray for survival. Evidently, it was possible to fight back at last. A huge but unwieldy Zeppelin could, after all, be reduced to a gigantic fireball. Those watching from below were so elated that they cheered and embraced each other. Seized by patriotic fervour, some even broke into the national anthem. It had been a night to remember.

Simon Wilder did not take part in the celebrations.

Stabbed to death, he lay in a blood-soaked heap on the ground.

CHAPTER TWO

The telephone was a mixed blessing. When it was first installed in his house, Harvey Marmion had been delighted. It meant that he had direct contact with Scotland Yard and – when he was at work – he and his wife, Ellen, had a means of getting in touch with each other in the event of an emergency. On the debit side was the fact that Superintendent Claude Chatfield could wake him at will at any ungodly hour and the last voice that Marmion wanted to hear when hauled out of bed was Chatfield's. It was like the yapping of an angry dog. Having padded downstairs in his pyjamas, Marmion held the instrument inches away from his ear to deaden the superintendent's stridency.

'Is that you, Inspector?'

Marmion yawned. 'Yes, sir.'

'I know you're tired but I make no apology. Thanks to that Zeppelin raid, I was trapped in a train outside Paddington for three hours. It was maddening. I didn't get to bed until well after midnight.'

'Did you want something, Superintendent?'

'Of course I do,' snapped Chatfield. 'I didn't ring you up to talk about the weather. We have another murder on our hands. A car is on the way to pick you up.'

'Very good, sir.' Marmion yawned again.

'Wake up, man. You're on duty now.'

Marmion shook his head to clear it then took a deep breath before speaking.

'Where did the incident occur?'

'Chingford.'

'Is the victim still there?'

'No,' said Chatfield. 'I gave orders for him to be moved.'

'I've told you before, sir. I prefer to see a body at the scene of a crime. You can learn so much from it.'

'I saw the victim. I can tell you all you need to know.'

'I'd rather have seen everything for myself.'

'You can look at police photographs.'

'Do we know anything about the man?'

'Very little, I fear – he was in his late thirties, at a guess, and smartly dressed. There were no documents on him to indicate his identity. That's really all I can say at this stage. Make a note of the address and get over there at once.'

'I'll have to collect Sergeant Keedy first.'

'Oh, he's probably still up, carousing. He's a bachelor – at the moment, anyway. Young, single men have more energy than weary old husbands like you and me. Talking of which, have the sergeant and your daughter set a date yet?'

'No, sir, they haven't,' said Marmion uneasily.

'Marriage will slow him down. Wait until he becomes a father. Although,' he added with a hollow laugh, 'he might already have achieved that feat. Rumour has it that Sergeant Keedy did not live the life of a monk.'

'You were about to give me an address. I have a pencil in my hand.'

As the superintendent gave him the details, Marmion wrote them down but his mind was elsewhere. The reference to his future son-in-law was deliberately intended to needle him. On the subject of his daughter's engagement, Marmion was still sensitive, not least because the developing relationship between Alice Marmion and her father's closest colleague had been kept hidden from him. It was not just the secrecy that hurt Marmion. Where young women were concerned, Joe Keedy had a reputation for loving and leaving them. Marmion did not want his daughter to be the latest casualty of a fractured romance.

'I'll get over there as soon as the car arrives, sir,' he said.

'Do that.'

'Who raised the alarm?'

'Someone who works as a postman,' replied Chatfield. 'He was leaving early for work when he found the body in an alleyway beside his house. It was probably just as well that it was still dark. He didn't see exactly what had been done to the victim. It's the reason I had the body moved so quickly. It was an indescribably hideous sight. That kind of thing always brings the ghouls running.'

'You said that he was stabbed to death.'

'He was also badly mutilated, Inspector.'

'In what way?'

'To begin with,' said Chatfield, 'someone gouged out both eyes.'

It took only one beep on the car horn to rouse Joe Keedy from his sleep. Jumping out of bed, he pulled back the curtain and waved to the car below. Then he dressed with speed. Since he was habituated to an early morning summons, he always shaved last thing at night so that he did not have to worry about a full day's growth of beard when he awoke. Murder took precedence over grooming. When he had a

11

free moment, he could shave later on at Scotland Yard. Four minutes after the call, Keedy was leaving his digs and straightening his tie as he hurried towards the waiting vehicle. He was a tall, wiry, handsome man in his early thirties who took pains with his appearance. Marmion, by contrast, always contrived to look slightly shabby even when he wore his best suit.

Keedy opened the door and climbed into the back seat beside him.

'Good morning,' he said as the car set off.

'Good morning, Joe.'

'Where are we going?'

'Chat is sending us on a little visit.'

'That sounds ominous.'

'A phone call from our beloved superintendent is never an occasion for pleasure. When he drags me out of bed, he always makes it sound as if I was in breach of police regulations by daring to go to sleep.'

'What has he got for us this time?'

Marmion passed on the information he'd been given. He was a solid man in his forties with the physique of a labourer. It was allied to a quick brain, an ability to work long hours without flagging and a tenacity that meant he would pursue any killer relentlessly until he was able to make an arrest. Keedy had the same sense of commitment. He'd joined the police force in search of action and found plenty of it. Having listened to his companion's recitation, he grimaced.

'Why would anyone gouge out the man's eyes?'

Marmion shrugged. 'I can't help you there, Joe.'

'I suppose that we have no idea when the murder occurred?'

'We don't have a precise time,' said Marmion, 'but it was obviously during the night. The blackout is a boon to criminals. They work best in darkness.'

'It wasn't that dark,' recalled Keedy. 'When I walked Alice back to her digs, there was an air raid on and we saw the most amazing thing. One of our planes shot down a Zeppelin. There was a massive explosion and night turned to day for what seemed like minutes.'

'You and Alice should have taken shelter.'

'I don't think the Zeppelins had *us* on their targets list.'

'I'm serious, Joe,' scolded Marmion. 'It's a question of safety first. *You* may want to take risks but I'd rather you didn't force my daughter to do the same. Look at the constant reports we've read of people being hit by fallen masonry from buildings that are bombed. You can't be too careful.'

'I wouldn't have missed seeing that fireball for anything. It was marvellous.'

'This is a war – not a sideshow.'

'We were in no danger, honestly. We felt perfectly safe out there in the street.'

'So did the murder victim.'

Word of the killing had spread like wildfire. When the police had first arrived at the scene of the crime, a number of people came out of their homes to see what was going on, then flinched at the sight of the corpse in the alleyway. Lights had been rigged up so that photographs could be taken. After making a preliminary examination, the pathologist said that the cause of death was all too apparent but that full details would only emerge at the post-mortem. The body had been duly removed.

By the time that Marmion and Keedy got there, it was light enough to see clearly. A uniformed policeman was guarding the spot where the victim had fallen. The paving stones were stained with blood. Passers-by tried to stand and stare but the policeman moved them on. As soon as he saw the detectives, he recognised both men because their reputations went before them. During a series of murder investigations, their photographs had appeared regularly in the newspapers and their record of success was unrivalled. The policeman was a big, chunky man in his forties with a bulbous nose and rubicund cheeks. He stepped forward to greet the newcomers.

'Good morning, Inspector,' he said in a gravelly voice, 'and good morning to you, Sergeant.'

The detectives nodded in acknowledgement.

'What's your name?' asked Marmion.

'PC Alec Bench, sir.'

'How long have you been here, PC Bench?'

'I was the first person on the scene,' said the other, proudly. 'Well, not exactly the first, of course. That would be Mr Parry, the postman.' He indicated the adjacent house. 'He actually found the body and came looking for us at once. This is our beat, you see. Everyone round here knows us.'

'We'll need to speak to Mr Parry. Is he at home?'

'No, sir, he went off to work – but not before I took a full statement from him,' he went on, patting the notebook in his top pocket. 'Some people would have been very upset by what they'd seen but not Denzil Parry. It's not the first dead body he's stumbled on. Postmen see all kinds of nasty things in the early hours. Denzil has discovered two corpses,' he confided, 'though both were of poor, homeless wretches who'd simply frozen to death.' He nodded towards the house. 'Mrs Parry is the problem. When she heard about the blood, she came out here with a bucket of water and a mop. I told her that she couldn't tamper with a crime scene.'

'Quite right,' said Keedy, eyeing the dark stain on the ground. 'What happened from the moment that you got here?'

Alec Bench knew how to deliver a report succinctly. His account was so smooth and coherent that it was almost as if he'd been rehearsing it. When he described the arrival on the scene of Claude Chatfield, his face was impassive but there was a glint in his eye that suggested he was not overly impressed by the superintendent's officiousness. Marmion and Keedy exchanged a knowing glance.

'So you've met the superintendent, have you?' said Keedy.

'He didn't stay long, sir. Once the photographer and the pathologist had done their jobs, the superintendent wanted the body moved at once so that the crowd would disperse. The neighbours were a blooming nuisance but you can't arrest someone for being curious.'

'I suppose that there were no witnesses.'

'None that I know of, Sergeant.'

'Yet someone might have been out and about last night. Air raids always bring out the braver souls.'

'They may be brave,' said Marmion, pointedly, 'but they're also foolhardy.'

'If the constable was on duty during the raid, he'll have seen what happened up there in the sky.'

'Oh, yes,' said Bench with a chuckle, 'there was a Zeppelin raid. I saw one of them shot down.'

'It was thrilling, wasn't it?'

'I can't wait to get home to tell the wife.'

'The Zeppelin was blown to bits.'

'I just couldn't resist clapping my hands.'

'Let's concentrate on the murder victim,' insisted Marmion, terminating their reminiscences of the event. 'He deserves all our attention.'

He walked around the spot where the body had been found,

wondering how and when the attack had been made. Patently, the killer had chosen the alleyway in order to delay the discovery of the body. Nobody walking past in the dark would have been able to spot it there. Denzil Parry, the postman, had turned into the alleyway on his way to work and almost tripped over the corpse.

'Right,' said Marmion after a long pause, 'I'm satisfied that there's nothing else to see here. I'd like to interview Mrs Parry first. I'll speak to her husband when he returns home. In due course, we'll deploy our men to knock on every door in the vicinity. We may be lucky – but somehow I doubt it. Any witnesses would surely have come forward before now.'

'What about me, sir?' asked Bench.

'When do you come off duty?'

'I reckon it will be in just over an hour.'

'You can leave well before then,' said Marmion. 'When I've finished with Mrs Parry, I daresay the lady would like to clear up the mess out here. This is a nice area to live in. Residents don't want ugly bloodstains like that. When Mrs Parry does come out and wash away the stain,' he went on, 'I'd like to hear the statement you took from her husband. After that, you can go.'

'Thank you, Inspector.'

'When you get home, remember that, first and foremost, you're a policeman.'

Bench was nonplussed. 'What do you mean, Inspector?'

'I mean that a brutal murder took place here and that it's of more importance to us than the air raid, however remarkable it may have been. Tell your wife what happened down here on the ground – not about events up there in the sky. A burning Zeppelin may have given you some entertainment but you should focus on the plight of the victim discovered by Mr Parry. He deserves our sympathy and so does his family.'

'Yes, sir,' said Bench, accepting the reprimand.

Marmion's voice softened. 'There's something else you can say to Mrs Bench,' he added.

'What's that, Inspector?'

'Tell her that you did your job well and that I said so.'

Bench rallied and straightened his shoulders.

'Thank you, sir.'

CHAPTER THREE

War had come as a rude interruption to Alice Marmion's career in education. Having trained as a teacher, and found a school she loved working at, she began to feel guilty that she was doing so little to help the war effort. As the conflict wore on, and as British casualties reached frightening numbers, Alice decided to abandon her pupils in order to join the Women's Emergency Corps, one of the many organisations that had been formed in response to the national crisis. It was hard work that demanded long hours and confronted her with all manner of challenges. Instead of teaching young children in the safety and comfort of a classroom, Alice was out and about in all weathers, driving a lorry, repairing the engine when it broke down, unloading supplies or finding accommodation for the Belgian refugees who flooded into the country. Satisfying as it was, the work lacked a component that she sought and the only place she believed that she could find it was in the Women's Police Service. Accordingly, she followed her father – and Joe Keedy – into uniform and, even though women were not involved in detective work, she at least had the illusion of carrying on the family tradition established by Harvey Marmion and his own father before him.

Keedy had often complained to her about the frustration of being at the beck and call of an overbearing superintendent and she understood his predicament only too well because she had her own version of Claude Chatfield to endure. Inspector Thelma Gale was a stout woman in her forties, with short hair brushed back from her forehead and held in a tight bun and defiantly plain features routinely distorted by a frown of disapproval. She seemed to take offence at the fact that Alice was slim, lithe, above average height and decidedly pretty. The inspector made no attempt to hide her resentment at the younger woman's privileged position with regard to Scotland Yard. While the duties of the Women's Police Force were strictly limited in scope, Alice had easy access to two detectives engaged in major investigations. It was a sore point with Thelma Gale.

'What's your father working on at the moment?' she asked.

'I don't know, Inspector. I haven't seen him for days.'

'Sergeant Keedy will have kept you abreast of developments, surely.'

'You're quite wrong,' said Alice, firmly. 'We spend so little time together that we never waste it talking about a case he may be working on. Apart from anything else, it's none of my business.'

'That's certainly true.'

'I never ask and I'm never told.'

'Come, come,' teased the other, 'you don't expect me to believe that, do you?'

'You can believe what you wish, Inspector,' said Alice, anxious to get off a subject that cropped up so regularly. 'I concentrate on my own duties. They keep me fully occupied.'

'And so they should.'

It was strange. The inspector was seated behind the desk in her office yet Alice had the feeling that the other woman was somehow looming over her. Such was the force of her personality that Thelma Gale seemed to fill the room. Alice was eager to get well out of her reach.

'With whom will I be working today, Inspector?' she asked.

'I've assigned a new recruit to you.'

'Oh, I see.'

'Though I have grave reservations about your abilities,' said the other, getting in one of her customary digs at Alice, 'I have no choice but to put you in charge of her. Show her the ropes and make sure that you don't pass on any of your bad habits.'

Alice bit back a reply. It was her usual response to the inspector's goading. There was, in any case, no time for her to defend herself against the undeserved criticism because there was a timid knock on the door and it opened to reveal a chubby young woman with a hopeful smile.

'Good morning, Inspector,' she said.

'You'll be on duty with Constable Marmion,' Gale told her, indicating Alice. 'If she can manage to remember it, she'll tell you all you need to know.'

'Thank you.' The newcomer turned to Alice. 'Hello, I'm Iris Goodliffe.'

'I'm pleased to meet you,' said Alice, pleasantly.

'I've heard about you.'

'Have you?'

'Well, don't just stand there,' ordered the inspector with a flick of a hand. 'Get out and start doing something useful.'

Grateful to be dismissed, the two women made a quick exit. Outside in the corridor, they were able to introduce themselves properly. While Alice contrived to look poised and comfortable in the unbecoming uniform, Iris Goodliffe had been given an ill-fitting jacket that only accentuated her bulging anatomy. She kept tugging at it self-consciously.

When she saw the slight angle at which Alice wore her hat, Iris adjusted her own into a similar position then gave the nervous giggle that was to become her trademark. She stared at Alice through eyes brimming with admiration.

'They say that your father is a famous detective inspector.'

'He'd never think of himself as famous.'

'Police work must be in your blood.'

'Not exactly, Iris,' said Alice. 'What we do is very mundane but nonetheless important for that, mark you. We leave serious crime to Scotland Yard. That's their territory. I could never follow in my father's footsteps.'

'You must have picked up *some* tips from him.'

'I preferred to find my own feet in this job. I was a teacher before I came here. I suppose that involves asserting a certain amount of authority. That's what we have to do when we put on these uniforms.' She appraised the other woman. 'Where have you come from Iris?'

'I used to work in the family shop. It was a pharmacy. One day was much like every other one. I wanted some real excitement.' She pulled down her jacket again. 'And I'm hoping that exercise will help me lose weight.'

Alice warmed to her. Iris seemed keen to learn and would be agreeable company on the long trudge around the streets of London. The new recruit had an air of innocence about her that was offset by a quiet determination to succeed in her new role. In Iris Goodliffe, Alice sensed, she had acquired a new friend.

'What's the trick, Joe?' asked Marmion.

'There isn't one.'

'Then why is it that, as soon as we get anywhere near the morgue, my stomach starts to heave like the North Sea while you stay as cool as a cucumber?'

'It's a simple case of self-control.'

'Yes, but how did you *get* that self-control?'

'I got paid for looking at dead bodies,' said Keedy with a grin. 'When it comes down to money, you very quickly learn to be detached.'

'Even you can't be that cynical.'

'I was only joking. The truth is that . . . well, I just got used to it.'

Keedy came from a family of undertakers and worked in the family business for some years before joining the police force. Marmion always argued that looking at a murder victim was very different from studying the corpse of someone who died a natural death, but all dead bodies were the same to Keedy. He could look at the most grotesque injuries without turning a hair whereas Marmion's heart began to pound the moment they entered the morgue. It was doing so all over again. When they walked into the room, he began to perspire slightly even though the atmosphere was chill. The abiding aroma of disinfectant unsettled him even more.

Chatfield had warned him that the victim had been badly mutilated but that was in the nature of an understatement. When the shroud was drawn back to expose the naked man to view, Marmion had to turn away for a moment in disgust. Keedy, however, looked with professional calm at the multiple wounds, starting with the head and working his way along the body. Both eyes had been removed, leaving two ugly craters, and both cheeks had been slashed open. The whole torso bore the marks of repeated stabbing. There was a final indignity. When Marmion found the courage to look again, he saw that the victim had been castrated.

'Dear God!' he exclaimed. 'It must have been a frenzied attack.'

23

'Why go to all that trouble?' wondered Keedy. 'One thrust through the heart would have killed him.'

'Someone wanted to do more than simply end his life.'

'His face is unrecognisable. Nobody would be able to identify him.'

'We can only hazard a guess at his age.'

'Before it was attacked, his body was in good condition,' observed Keedy. 'The musculature is good and there's not an ounce of superfluous weight.'

'Yes – until today, he was fit and healthy.'

'Who on earth is he?'

'We'll soon find out, I suspect.'

'I can't, for the life of me, see how.'

'I can.'

Keedy had shown great interest in the injuries but Marmion's queasiness wouldn't allow him to do that. He had instead been looking at the man's left hand. On the third finger was the telltale mark of a missing ring.

'I think he was married. His wife will probably be searching for him.'

The woman was tall and slender with a fading beauty. Even though concern was etched into her face, she looked a decade younger than her forty-five years. The duty sergeant noticed how elegant she was. Pen in hand, he was ready to take down all the details of her missing husband.

'Let's start with his name, shall we?' he suggested.

'Simon Wilder,' she replied.

He wrote it down with care, then looked up as a memory stirred.

'I've seen that name somewhere before, Mrs Wilder.'

'It's on the poster outside our dance studio.'

'Yes, of course, I remember now. There's a photograph of him, isn't there?'

'It's a photograph of *both* of us, actually, holding the cup we won at a national competition. It was one of many triumphs we shared. I was my husband's dancing partner until . . .'

Her voice died away. The sergeant waited for an explanation that never came. At length, he broke the silence.

'What's your address?'

'We live around the corner from the hall.'

She gave him the address, then explained why she was so worried. Her husband had been away all evening the previous day but had assured her that he would return home. Catherine Wilder didn't know exactly where he'd been or with whom. He had commitments in the West End. He was often out late. The one thing on which she could count, however, was that – if he'd promised to do so – he always came home.

'Where could he possibly be?' she asked, worriedly.

'Let's not jump to conclusions, Mrs Wilder,' he said in an attempt to soothe her. 'There may be a perfectly reasonable explanation why he didn't turn up. In fact, he may be sitting at home this very minute.'

'He's not there, I tell you. If he was anywhere, he'd be at the studio. He had an early appointment. I went there on the way here. The place was locked and the woman expecting an hour's private tuition from my husband was standing outside.'

Rubbing his chin meditatively, the sergeant changed his tack.

'What time did you go to bed last night?'

She was affronted. 'I can't see that that has anything to do with it.'

'Answer my question, please, and you'll understand.'

'As it happened, I went to bed early – around ten o'clock.'

'Are you a heavy sleeper, Mrs Wilder?' Seeing the protest hovering on her lips, he carried on quickly before she could voice it. 'If you were, you'll have missed the air raid. London was attacked by a whole fleet of Zeppelins. It brought the city to a standstill. If your husband was on a train or a bus, he might have been held up for hours somewhere.'

'He would have been back by now,' she said, speaking very slowly and emphasising each word. 'Can you hear me, Sergeant?'

'Yes, I can, Mrs Wilder.'

'Then please accept the fact that my husband is definitely missing.'

The sergeant manufactured a conciliatory smile that only served to irritate her. Torn between impatience and anxiety, Catherine Wilder stared at him as if demanding action. He gestured an apology.

'Before I raise the alarm,' he said, pen poised, 'I need a few more details about the gentleman . . .'

Superintendent Claude Chatfield was a tall, thin, angular man with a centre parting separating what little remained of his hair. As Marmion delivered his report, his superior looked at him through bulging eyes. But for a change of heart on the part of the inspector, their positions could have been reversed. Both had applied for the vacant post of superintendent and Marmion had been the slight favourite. When he realised that he would spend most of his time behind a desk, however, he had second thoughts about promotion and deliberately failed the interview, allowing Chatfield to believe that he had become superintendent purely on merit. There was an underlying tension between the two men that would never be resolved.

'You seem to have done everything needful,' said Chatfield, grudgingly.

'The victim's injuries were horrendous.'

'Now you see the wisdom of my decision to move the body from the scene of the crime. One woman fainted when she saw what had been done to his face.'

'You are – as always – right, sir,' said Marmion, feigning deference.

'What is your immediate reaction?'

'I think that the victim was known to the killer. This was no random attack. There was something very specific about the mutilation. The killer was making a statement of sorts. When we've identified the victim, we should start looking within his social circle.'

'That could prove difficult, Inspector.'

'Why is that, sir?'

'He may turn out to have an extremely large social circle,' said Chatfield, reaching for a sheet of paper and glancing at it. 'We've had three reports of missing persons but this is far and away the most likely. A lady walked into the police station in Chingford – a quarter of a mile from the scene of the crime, please note – and reported the disappearance of her husband. He was due back home in the early hours but never arrived.'

'What's the gentleman's name, sir?'

'Mr Simon Wilder.'

'Is there a description of him?'

'We've got something better than that.' Chatfield picked up a photograph. 'It could well be the man on a slab in our morgue. In fact, I'd go so far as to say that it certainly is. Mr Wilder was a handsome devil, no question about that.' He handed the photograph to the inspector. 'What puzzles me is the name on the back.'

Marmion turned the photograph over and read out the inscription.

'The new Vernon Castle.'

'That means nothing to me.'

'Then you obviously have no interest in ballroom dancing, sir,' said

Marmion. 'Vernon and Irene Castle are American dancers – the best in the world, in fact, or so it is claimed. They've created all kinds of new dances, including the Castle Walk. Their book on modern dance is a bible for anyone interested in the subject.'

Chatfield sniffed. 'That excludes me, I can assure you. Mrs Chatfield and I have no predilection for dancing of any kind. I'm surprised to find that you do.'

'My wife and I are very fond of dancing,' said Marmion, wistfully. 'The problem is that I chose a job that leaves us very little time to enjoy it. There's an irony in that, isn't there?' He studied the photograph then turned it over again. 'But you're right about the extent of his social circle. This was taken at the Wilder Dance Studio. If he's good enough to be compared to Vernon Castle, he's going to have a vast number of pupils. But that shouldn't deter us, Superintendent.'

'Why not?'

'The overwhelming majority of them will be female.' He gave the photograph back to Chatfield. 'And we're looking for a man.'

CHAPTER FOUR

Ellen Marmion never knew what time her son would get out of bed in the morning. Sometimes he didn't come downstairs until well into the afternoon, yet, on other occasions, she'd heard him get up in the middle of the night and raid the kitchen in search of food. Paul's unpredictability was only one of the problems she faced. Chief among the many others was his sudden change of moods. He would shuttle freely between hope and despair, making ambitious plans for his future before deciding that he might not actually have one. It was dispiriting. Glad to have him home again, with no serious wounds to his body, Ellen struggled to cope with his capriciousness. When he'd joined the army with the rest of his football team, Paul had been a bright, lively, determined, extrovert character with unassailable buoyancy. That was the young man his mother had sent off to France. What she got back from the battle of the Somme was a blinded soldier obsessed with war and tortured by guilt that he'd survived when so many of his friends had perished. His liveliness had given way to inertia and his optimism had, more often than not, been replaced by a sense of desolation.

As he chewed his way through breakfast that morning, he was in a world of his own. Ellen knew better than to interrupt him. She waited until he was ready to initiate conversation.

'Oh, hello,' he said, looking up as if aware of her for the first time. 'I heard the phone go off in the night.'

'It was for your father.'

'That means only one thing.'

'Yes,' said Ellen resignedly, 'there's been another murder.'

Paul was bitter. 'One person gets killed over here,' he argued, 'and the whole of the Metropolitan Police are after the person responsible. Thousands of British soldiers are murdered every day in France yet all we can do is to send thousands more to their deaths. It's not fair.'

'No, Paul, it isn't.'

'Somebody ought to do something about it.'

Ellen nodded in agreement because it was the safest thing to do. On the previous day, convinced that he would regain his sight completely, Paul had talked about going back to the front to join his regiment. He was pursuing a different theme now. As he ranted on about the folly of war, his mother gave him free rein, trying to humour him, afraid to contradict. It was only when he finally came to the end of his tirade that she dared to speak again.

'How are you feeling today?' she asked.

'I feel fine in myself, Mummy.'

'What about your eyes?'

'If anything,' he replied, producing a semblance of a smile, 'there's been a slight improvement. I can shave without cutting myself now. The doctors did say that I might recover full sight one day. I'm sure they're right. I'm counting on it. I'll be able to go back, after all.'

'No, Paul,' she said in alarm, 'you mustn't do that.'

'It's my duty.'

'You've already done that by volunteering.'

'I can't let my friends down, Mummy. They'd expect it of me.'

'Remember what they told you at the hospital. Shell shock can stay almost indefinitely. You're in no state even to think about going back to France.'

'I'm not a coward,' he declared, stiffening.

'Nobody says that you are, Paul. You're a wounded hero and you must accept that. You've done more than your bit. You're entitled to stay out of the war.'

'I could never do that. I think of nothing else.'

'You mustn't let it prey on your mind.'

'I can't just forget it,' he said with mounting anger. 'You saw what the Germans did to me. I was lucky to survive. I feel that I was kept alive for a purpose and I know what that purpose is. When I can see perfectly well, I'm going back to get my revenge on those bastards.'

Ellen flinched. 'Mind your language, please!'

'Well, that's what they are.'

'I'm sure it's what you call them when you're with your friends,' she said, raising her voice, 'but you're not in the trenches now, so we don't want words like that in the house, thank you very much.'

Paul looked bemused. 'What did I say?'

'You know full well what you said. Your father is dealing with criminals all the time so he probably hears foul language every day but he never brings that language home. If you must swear, do it somewhere else.'

'I'm sorry,' he mumbled.

'We've had to make a lot of allowances since you came back but there are some things we just won't put up with. Do you understand?'

While Paul was surprised at the admonition in her voice, Ellen was even more so. She hadn't realised how much anger had been bottled up inside her. Before she could stop herself, it had come gushing out. She was a motherly woman of middle years with a spreading midriff and greying hair. Ellen was not sure if she should apologise for her outburst or wait to see its effect on her son. As it was, Paul seemed too stunned to speak. His mother had been so amazingly tolerant since his return that he'd been taken unawares by her sharpness.

Each of them was still wondering what to do or say when they heard the letter box click open and shut. Ellen was glad of the excuse to leave the kitchen.

'There's the post,' she said.

She rushed to the front door, picked up the mail and brought it back into the room. There were only two letters. One was addressed to her husband and the other one was for Paul.

'It's for you,' she said, holding it out.

He snatched it from her. 'It must be from my regiment.'

'I don't think so, Paul. That looks like a woman's handwriting.'

He tore the letter open and peered at it through narrowed lids. After struggling to make out the words, he eventually gave up and slapped it down on the table. Ellen was sympathetic. She sat down beside him and picked up the letter.

'Shall I read it to you?'

Paul was frustrated. 'My eyesight should be better by now!'

'It will be – in due course.'

'I ought to be able to read properly.' He took a deep breath to compose himself, then gave a nod. 'Yes, please – if you would.'

'It's from someone called Mavis Tandy.'

'Why is she writing to me?'

'I daresay that she'll tell you in the letter.'

'How did Mavis know that I'd be here?'

'Perhaps she'll explain. You know who she is, then?'

'Oh, yes,' he said, 'I heard about Mavis.'

'You've never mentioned her before, Paul.'

'Why should I? I haven't even met her. Mavis was *his* friend.'

It was Marmion's turn to take the lead. Whenever they viewed a body at the morgue, he drew strength from the sergeant's experience of dealing with death. The breaking of bad news was a different matter. The inspector was infinitely better at dealing with bereaved families, more sensitive, more soothing and less likely to say anything out of place. As they stood outside the house in Chingford, Keedy was glad to hand over the task of passing on the sad tidings to the victim's wife. After ringing the bell, they were kept waiting for a full minute and wondered if nobody was at home. The door was then opened by a short, skinny woman in her fifties with spectacles perched on her nose. After the detectives had introduced themselves, she explained that she was Grace Chambers, next-door neighbour of the Wilders.

'It's bad news, isn't it?' she whispered.

Marmion's expression was blank. 'Is Mrs Wilder at home?'

'Yes, I've been sitting with her since she got back from the police station.' She stood aside to admit them. 'You'd better come in.'

They entered the house and were conducted to the living room, a large, well-furnished and well-proportioned space. They had no chance to notice the plethora of framed photographs and the collection of silver cups in the glass-fronted cabinet because Catherine Wilder leapt up from the sofa in alarm. After performing introductions, Marmion spoke softly.

'Perhaps you'd like to sit down again, Mrs Wilder.'

'Yes,' said Grace, taking her cue and easing the other woman back down on the sofa. 'I'll sit with you, Catherine.'

Holding their hats in their hands, the detectives sat in the armchairs opposite. Marmion made a swift assessment of the victim's widow. She had the frightened eyes of someone expecting to hear something terrible. For his part, Keedy was looking at Grace Chambers, clearly nervous but exuding sympathy. He was grateful that the neighbour was there.

'When you reported that your husband was missing,' said Marmion, 'the information was passed on to Scotland Yard. As it happens, we had an unidentified body . . .' He paused as Catherine tensed and Grace put a consoling arm around her. 'It's my sad duty to tell you that the photograph you sent has convinced us that the deceased is almost certainly Mr Wilder.'

'Simon is *dead*?' gasped Catherine.

'I'm afraid so, Mrs Wilder.'

'But how did he die – and where did it happen? Was he knocked over by a car or a bus? It couldn't have been a heart attack or anything like that. Simon was in the best of health. How was he killed?'

Marmion traded a glance with Keedy then lowered his voice even more.

'I regret to say that your husband was . . . murdered.'

'Murdered!' exclaimed Catherine, one hand to her throat. 'There must be some mistake, Inspector. Who could possibly want to murder Simon?'

'It will be our job to find out, Mrs Wilder.'

'Are you absolutely *sure* that it was my husband?'

'All the evidence points that way, I'm afraid.'

'Did you find the business cards he carried in his wallet or see his

34

name on the watch I had engraved for him?' He shook his head. 'Then it can't have been him,' she decided. 'Simon had documents with him. Each one of them bore his name.'

'They were deliberately stolen by the killer, Mrs Wilder. There was no form of identification on him. Even his wedding ring had been removed.'

The spark of hope that had momentarily ignited her face was cruelly snuffed out. As she sagged back on the sofa, Catherine didn't even feel her neighbour's arm tighten around her. She was still reeling from the impact of the news. The detectives waited in silence. It gave them the opportunity to look around the room and see how many of the photographs featured Simon Wilder and his wife on a dance floor. After a couple of minutes, Catherine gathered up enough strength to speak.

'I want to see him,' she said. 'I want to be certain that it's Simon.'

'I wouldn't advise that, Mrs Wilder,' said Marmion.

'Why not? He's my husband. I have a right.'

'Indeed, you do, and a positive identification from a family member would be very helpful to us. But there are distressing circumstances here. I would hate you to see your husband in that condition.'

'What do you mean?'

'He suffered appalling injuries, Mrs Wilder.'

Grace was curious. 'What sort of injuries, Inspector?'

'He was not simply stabbed to death . . .'

There was a long and very awkward pause. Keedy broke the silence.

'He was not simply stabbed to death,' he said, quietly. 'Mr Wilder was badly mutilated.'

Catherine heard no more. Mouth agape, she fainted.

* * *

'Why do they call her Gale Force?' asked Iris Goodliffe.

'You'll soon find that out.'

'She was very nice to me when I first met her.'

'Wait until you step out of line,' warned Alice Marmion. 'Then you'll find yourself in the middle of a howling gale. When the inspector loses her temper, we all run for cover.'

'Oh dear, is she that much of a tyrant?'

'Not really, Iris. She's a good-hearted woman who does a difficult job very well but she doesn't suffer fools gladly. Watch your step. That's my advice.'

'Thank you, Alice.'

Out on patrol, they were walking side by side down a long street. It was Alice who collected the few curious glances from passing men. A window cleaner even winked at her and lifted his cap. To her dismay, Iris didn't attract any attention. She was there to learn from her companion and found her a mine of information. After being plied with dozens of questions, Alice asked one of her own.

'Why did you choose the police?' she asked. 'With your background in pharmacy, the obvious place for you to go was into nursing.'

'I was tempted.'

'What changed your mind?'

'It was what happened to my father,' explained the other. 'We lived above the shop, you see. Someone broke in one night and tried to steal drugs of some kind. My father went down to confront him. Instead of just running away, the thief gave my father a terrible beating. He was off work for a month. I had this terrible sense of helplessness, Alice,' she went on. 'I should have been able to go to my father's aid but I was just cowering upstairs. That's the real reason I joined the police. I want to learn how to cope with situations like that. To put it more bluntly,

I suppose I want to be toughened up.' She turned to Alice. 'Does that make sense to you?'

'It makes a lot of sense – and it reminds me of my own father.'

'Oh – why is that?'

'Daddy never intended to become a policeman,' said Alice. 'He was happy working in the civil service. He and Mummy had a very different life in those days. But my grandfather was in the Metropolitan Police. Then he was murdered on duty one night and it changed Daddy's life. He wouldn't rest until the man was caught. When the police were unable to find the killer, my father pursued him across the Channel and caught up with him in France. He dragged him back here to face justice and he's been a copper ever since.'

'You must be very proud of him, Alice.'

'I am.'

'What did your mother think when he joined the force?'

'I think she preferred living with a civil servant.'

'But that would be so dull and uneventful.'

'Mummy always says that it would be better than having a husband who's on call twenty-four hours of the day and who has to court danger every time he goes in pursuit of a killer. Daddy makes light of the dangers. It's all part of the job to him and he accepts that without complaint.'

'Are you an only child?'

'No, I have a brother. Paul is at home at the moment.'

'Hasn't he been conscripted?'

'He and his friends were among the first to sign up when the war broke out. Unfortunately, my brother was injured at the Battle of the Somme and invalided out. He keeps talking about going back to the front again one day,' said Alice with a sigh, 'but that's another story . . .'

* * *

37

Holding the letter to catch the best of the light, Paul tried to make out the words again. The handwriting was neat and, by screwing up his eyes, he could read most of the letter. Replying to it, however, was a more taxing assignment. Crouched over the kitchen table, he worked slowly and laboriously. His first two attempts were so bad that he scrunched up the pieces of paper and threw them hard into the bin. Paul gave up all hope of writing properly. Through his blurred vision, the words looked like childish squiggles. As a last resort, he began to use large, decisive capital letters, explaining the problem with his eyesight. The words came much more easily.

It never occurred to him that he would live to regret writing them.

CHAPTER FIVE

Because he was tetchy at the best of times, it took very little to provoke Claude Chatfield's ire. He was always simmering. When he found something that really annoyed him, he became uncomfortably loud and extremely animated. All that Marmion could do was to stand there and listen.

'It's disgraceful!' cried the superintendent, pacing his office to work up a head of steam. 'As if the police don't have enough to do, we've had to rush men over to a village near Enfield to guard the remains of that Zeppelin. Sightseers have descended on the place in thousands by bus, train and car, and they all want souvenirs from the wreck. It's repulsive. Human beings died in that crash but people show no respect. According to one report I've had, they tried to lift the tarpaulin to gloat over the charred bodies. Can you imagine that?' he howled. 'In the end, soldiers had to remove the corpses to a tiny corrugated iron church and stand guard over them. If they hadn't been stopped, I dare swear that some of the vultures would have hacked off parts of the bodies and carried *those* away as souvenirs.'

'To some extent, sir,' ventured Marmion, 'it's understandable.'

Chatfield rounded on him. 'Don't tell me that you *approve*.'

'Far from it – but you have to look at the circumstances. We've suffered any number of air raids in London but this is the first time we've been able to strike back. The Zeppelin is no longer invincible. That's something to celebrate. No wonder people want to get their hands on a piece of the wreckage.'

'Well, I think it's deplorable.'

'It's an enemy aircraft, sir. They feel entitled to revel in its destruction.'

'They shouldn't revel in the death of the crew.'

'That's human nature, I'm afraid,' said Marmion. 'War has coarsened all of us. The public loves to hear about German casualties. Suddenly, they have a chance to *see* some of them. It's dreadful, I know. Like you, I deplore what's happening near Enfield,' he went on, 'but, with respect, the fate of the Zeppelin crew is not really our concern. The murder of Simon Wilder should be our priority.'

Chatfield came to a halt. 'Don't presume to lecture me, Inspector.'

'I was just giving you a gentle reminder, sir.'

'Well, it's a totally unnecessary one.'

'Then I take it back.'

'It's too late for that.'

After shooting him a look of displeasure, Chatfield walked behind his desk and lifted up the report that Marmion had brought. As he read through it, his anger slowly abated and he even managed a grunt of admiration. At length, he put the paper aside and turned his gaze on his visitor.

'You always did know how to dress up a report,' he said.

'I wanted you to have enough detail for the press conference, sir.'

'Are you absolutely *certain* that the victim is Simon Wilder?'

'We are.'

'When he was butchered in that alleyway, he was less than half a

40

mile from his home. What was he doing there?'

'That's something of great interest to us, sir. Even as we speak, our men are calling on every house in a wide circle around the scene of the crime. *Somebody* must know why he happened to be in that part of Chingford at that late hour.'

Chatfield glanced at the report again then fired an unexpected question.

'How would your son react?'

Marmion was taken aback. 'Paul? What do you mean, sir?'

'He's a soldier. He'll have been coarsened more than any of us. What will be his response to the shooting down of the Zeppelin?'

'He'll be very glad.'

'Won't he be rushing over to Cuffley? That's the place where it actually came down. Doesn't he want to be part of the grisly crowd that's keen to wash their hands in the blood of the enemy?'

'My son has seen enough dead bodies already, Superintendent, and he's watched how degraded men can become by war. The hordes over at Cuffley are not the only souvenir-hunters. German soldiers have collected the most macabre trophies from fallen British soldiers.'

'I know. I've heard the stories.'

'They're horribly true.'

'How *is* Paul?'

Marmion was surprised by the considerate tone in which he spoke. Ordinarily, Chatfield only mentioned the inspector's family in order to discomfit him. There was genuine interest in his question this time and Marmion was touched. He was reminded that the superintendent was a family man himself and had four children, though he had no son of an age that made him liable to conscription.

'He's . . . getting better, sir,' said Marmion, guardedly.

'One reads terrible things about shell shock.'

'Paul is learning to cope.'

'I wish him well.'

'Thank you, sir.'

After a brief foray into Marmion's private life, Chatfield reverted to being the peppery superintendent who was always respected but never liked by those of lower rank. The return to normality pleased Marmion. He always felt uneasy when Chatfield talked to him as a human being rather than as a colleague who needed to be kept firmly in his place. They discussed the report line by line and the superintendent made a few small adjustments.

'I like to face the press well prepared,' he said.

'That's to your credit, sir.'

'Unfortunately, I don't expect to get the publicity we need. We have sixteen newspapers in London alone and details of this murder should be on the front pages of every one of them. But it's not going to happen, is it?'

'No, sir, the shooting-down of that Zeppelin will be the main news.'

'I hope they pour contempt on those ghastly souvenir-hunters.'

'We're dealing with one ourselves,' said Marmion, grimly.

Chatfield was checked. 'Are we?'

'Yes, sir – the killer wanted keepsakes from his victim and I'm not just talking about his wallet, watch and wedding ring.'

'Quite so,' said the other, face darkening. 'You were right to give no details of the mutilation in your report. There are times when information is best held back from the press. Apart from anything else, it would distress the widow beyond bearing. Thank heaven that Mrs Wilder doesn't have to view the body.'

'But she's eager to do so.'

Chatfield was startled. 'I can't believe that.'

'She more or less insisted, sir.'

'When she heard what had actually happened, I thought she fainted.'

'It's true,' replied Marmion, 'but she recovered very quickly. Mrs Wilder wanted proof that it really was her husband who was murdered. She's clinging on to a pathetic hope that it might just be someone else.'

'And she really wants to put herself through that ordeal?'

'I advised against it, sir, but to no avail.'

'She's going to have the most awful shock.'

'A neighbour will be with her to offer support.'

'I saw the corpse, remember. That face of his was like something out of a nightmare. I strongly urge Mrs Wilder to reconsider her decision.'

'It's too late, Superintendent,' said Marmion, looking at his watch. 'My guess is that the lady will be arriving at the morgue with Sergeant Keedy at any moment.'

Joe Keedy had lost count of the number of times he'd had to catch people who collapsed when they viewed the corpse of a loved one. It was not only women who let out a shriek of horror and lost consciousness. Apparently strong men had also been overcome by emotion. Keedy had once had to catch a vicar whose wife was the victim of a hit-and-run road accident. A person who'd seen many dead bodies in the course of his work fell into Keedy's arms when confronted with the corpse of the woman he'd married. The sergeant felt that he would need to be alert yet again. Having recovered from the initial shock, Catherine Wilder had revealed an inner steeliness that was quite at variance with her appearance. She had not merely asked to see the body of her husband, she had demanded it as next of kin. The arguments put to her by Marmion and Keedy had been swept aside.

As they entered the morgue, Keedy had the consolation of knowing that most of the wounds would be kept hidden from her. All that she would see was the eyeless face of her husband. The worst excesses of the attack would remain beneath the shroud. It was a source of relief to him. He was then struck by an idea that might lessen the torment even more. It brought him to an abrupt halt. Catherine Wilder was impatient. Arm in arm with Grace Chambers, she fretted at the slight delay.

'Don't stop on my account, Sergeant,' she said.

'I thought you'd like a moment to prepare yourself.'

'I'm as ready as I'll ever be.'

'Then let me make a suggestion,' he said, indicating a door to his left. 'Your husband's effects are in here. It's only his clothing, I'm afraid. Anything of value was taken away.' When she gave a nod, he opened the door. 'This way, ladies . . .'

He let them go into the room before following. When he spoke to the man on duty behind the counter, the latter disappeared for a short while. He returned with a large metal box, placing it on the counter and waiting for an order. Catherine hesitated. Grace had to squeeze her arm to produce a request.

'Please open it,' said Catherine.

The man spoke gently. 'I'd better warn you what to expect.'

'Just open it.'

'Do as Mrs Wilder asks,' added Keedy.

The man lifted the lid of the box to expose the blood-soaked suit, shirt, tie and underwear of the deceased. When he lifted the items out, they could see that even the shoes and socks had been dyed red. But it was the coat that upset Catherine the most. It was the stylish jacket of a suit made by an expensive bespoke tailor. Worn by her husband, it

44

had fitted him perfectly and given him a slightly raffish appearance. It was the suit he wore for special occasions but he would never put it on again. There were so many slits and holes in it that it was little more than a pile of rags. As Catherine tottered, Keedy moved in closer to her but she somehow found the strength to remain standing. It was Grace who averted her eyes and began the retch.

'Do you recognise it as your husband's clothing, Mrs Wilder?' asked Keedy.

'Yes, I do,' she croaked.

'I'm so sorry that you had to see it in this condition.'

'My husband was not merely killed, he was . . . slaughtered.'

'The attack was indeed very severe,' he said, nodding to the man to put everything back in the box. 'Shall we continue?'

'No,' said Catherine, raising a palm.

'But you came to see the body.'

'I've seen what was done to it, Sergeant, and that's more than enough. I can identify my husband by his clothing. I can't bear to see anything else.' She took a deep breath. 'Take me home, please.'

Keedy was content. His strategy had worked.

Ellen Marmion walked slowly along the pavement with her son beside her. Paul could see just well enough to be able to go out alone now and to dispense with the white stick with which he'd first been issued. When he learnt that his mother had to visit the shops, however, he took advantage of her company so that he could go to the post office. It meant that he could keep his arm in contact with hers as they strolled along. His confidence was boosted by the fact that he was, in effect, walking normally.

'I never thought that Colin was interested in girlfriends,' she said.

'He wasn't until we went abroad,' he replied. 'But the rest of us all had someone back home who wrote to us and who sent us her photograph. Colin was the odd man out. He met Mavis on his last leave and, suddenly, he couldn't stop talking about her. He realised what he'd been missing.'

'I'm glad that he met someone but I do feel sorry for her.'

'Mavis will miss him badly – and so will I.'

Colin Fryatt had been Paul's best friend. They'd been inseparable at school and in the years beyond it. They'd played in the same football team, sharing the same excitements and disappointments. Driven by a collective surge of bravado, all eleven of them had enlisted together because it meant that they could serve in the same regiment. Paul had watched the rest of the players dying off one by one. When Colin was killed in action, Paul was not far away from him on the battlefield. Blinded by the explosion, he'd crawled under fire to his friend, relieved him of his beloved mouth organ then blown it with all his might to attract attention. He was eventually rescued by stretcher-bearers. The instrument had saved Paul's life.

'I'm so glad you were able to reply to the letter,' said his mother.

'I made myself do it. The only thing I couldn't manage was her name and address on the envelope. You put that on – thanks, Mum.'

'It was no trouble.'

'I'll be able to do things like that for myself soon.'

'Yes, Paul, I'm sure you will.'

It was a fervent hope rather than a statement of belief but Ellen hid her doubts from him. She'd been told how important it was to keep up his spirits. Mavis Tandy had written to ask if she could meet Paul and, in his reply, he'd agreed. Ellen had reservations about the idea. When her son had first gone off to war, he left behind a girlfriend who

46

was devoted to him. She and Paul seemed an ideal couple. On his first leave home, they'd even talked of getting engaged. He then returned to France and saw action at last. It had a searing effect on him. On his second visit home, he was a different person, surly, uncommunicative and prone to drunkenness. He kept picking arguments. All of the tenderness vanished from his romance and it quickly turned sour. Instead of getting engaged to him, his girlfriend had been frightened away. Ellen had been deeply hurt.

'Do you think you did the right thing, Paul?'

'What do you mean?'

'You don't *have* to see her.'

'Why not?'

'Well, she's a complete stranger.'

'She was Colin's girlfriend. I feel that I already know her.'

'Perhaps you should wait until you're . . . properly on the mend.'

'Mavis knows what happened to me,' he said. 'She said how sorry she was. All that she wants to do is to talk about Colin. What's wrong with that?'

His mother could not find the words to tell him. Her worry was that a visit from Mavis Tandy might bring back all the things that haunted him. She and Marmion had done everything to take his mind off the war and, in particular, off the death of his close friend. It would all be brought vividly back to life now. Ellen was also concerned for the young woman. Paul was so changeable and liable to such explosions of anger that she didn't want Mavis to see her son in that state.

'What's wrong with that?' he repeated, voice rising dangerously.

'Nothing,' said Ellen, 'nothing at all.'

'Yes, there is. You're holding something back. What is it?'

'Forget that I spoke.'

47

'You want to *stop* her coming, don't you?'

'No, I don't.'

'Yes, you do,' he went on, stopping in his tracks and pointing an accusatory finger. 'I'm old enough to make my own decisions. I want to see Mavis and nobody's going to stop me so you can mind your own bloody business!'

'Paul!'

Pushing his mother away, he lurched off down the street. Fuelled by anger and forgetting how limited his eyesight was, he blundered on until his shoulder collided with a lamp post. Ellen winced as a stream of expletives poured out of him.

The ride back to Chingford was conducted in silence. Stunned by what they'd seen at the morgue, both women were lost in thought. They were seated in the rear of the car while Keedy occupied the front passenger seat. When they got to the house, however, he had to speak. He waited until all three of them entered the living room.

'I'm sorry to put you through that, Mrs Wilder,' he said.

'I had to be certain that it was Simon,' she murmured.

'I'll look after her now,' said Grace, dismissively. 'Thank you, Sergeant.'

'There's something I need before I go,' said Keedy with quiet firmness. 'In due course, we'll have to talk to Mrs Wilder at length about her husband. This is clearly not the best time. What would be helpful to us is to borrow Mr Wilder's appointments book.'

Catherine looked up at him. 'You won't find the killer in there, Sergeant. My husband's pupils worshipped him. Why do you want the book?'

'It will give us some idea of his routine.'

'I can tell you what that was. He gave lessons on a daily basis and, from time to time, organised a dance at the hall. It was always well attended. My husband and I built up a thriving business.'

'They were like Vernon and Irene Castle,' Grace interjected. 'That's what they were called in one of the newspapers.' Her gesture took in the whole room. 'Look at any of these photographs. You can see what a wonderful couple they were on the dance floor.'

'Who provided the music?' asked Keedy.

'We hired a small band for the dances,' replied Catherine. 'If it was a case of private lessons, we either used a gramophone or an accompanist.' She brought both hands up to her cheeks. 'Dear me!' she cried, 'I'd forgotten Mrs Pattinson.'

'She's their pianist,' explained Grace.

'Wait until *she* hears the news. It will be a crushing blow.'

'Why is that?' asked Keedy.

'Mrs Pattinson has been with us from the start. She idolised my husband. When she learns that he was murdered, it will destroy her.'

CHAPTER SIX

The more time she spent with Iris Goodliffe, the more Alice liked her. Proud to be wearing a police uniform – albeit a rather tight one – Iris felt a sense of importance as she strolled along with her new friend. To the casual observer, they presented a stark contrast and, when they saw their reflections in shop windows, they realised what an odd couple they looked. The Women's Police Service had been founded two years earlier yet there were still people who refused to accept it as a necessary organisation. While they fielded warm smiles of encouragement, therefore, they were also given the occasional hostile glance by those who felt that women had no place whatsoever in law enforcement. Alice took it all in her stride and Iris followed suit.

'What's the worst thing you've had to do?' asked Iris.

'It was being on night duty in central London.'

'Was it rowdy?'

'The noise was deafening.'

'Did you have to make any arrests?'

'We had a policeman with us to do that. He also gave us welcome protection, of course. I wouldn't have liked to walk those streets on my own.'

'Neither would I.'

'Drunks were the big problem,' recalled Alice. 'They were often soldiers on leave, either spoiling for a fight or looking for women.'

'You mean women who . . . ?'

'Yes, I do.'

'I've never met . . . one of those.'

Alice grinned. 'You probably have without even realising it, Iris. They lead normal lives when they're "off duty", so to speak. Some of them are forced into it because they lost their husbands at the front and can't make ends meet. Gale Force thinks that we should clean up the city by getting rid of all the prostitutes but that's impossible. There are thousands of them. And there's always a demand.'

'Is that all soldiers do when they're on leave – get drunk or . . . ?'

'It's what some of them do, Iris. They drink to forget the horrors they've seen at the front and they snatch at pleasure because they think it may be their last chance. In some cases, I'm afraid, it probably is.'

'I can't believe your brother is like that.'

'No,' said Alice, defensively, 'Paul is . . . above that sort of thing.'

And yet, she admitted to herself, her brother had gone off to a pub with friends whenever he was on leave. Until he was invalided out of the army, he'd been a typical soldier. When he'd broken up with his girlfriend, there'd been nobody else waiting for his return. Alice realised that she'd never even considered the possibility that he might have paid for the services of a prostitute. It had seemed so unlikely that she'd pushed it to the back of her mind. Thanks to Iris, she found herself thinking about it for the first time and she was troubled. What if Paul was not the decent, clean-living young man she believed him to be? He would not be the first soldier whose moral standards had crumbled under the pressures of war. The thought was unnerving.

'I always wanted a brother,' said Iris, brightly. 'Instead of that, I had an older sister who used to make fun of me and pull my hair.'

'Paul did that to me sometimes but we had so much fun together.'

'I had very little.'

'What does your sister do?'

'She works in one of the other shops. We own three altogether. You'll find a Goodliffe Pharmacy in Camden Town, East Finchley and Walthamstow. Actually, Evelyn – that's my sister – has been so much nicer to me since she got married.'

'Is her husband in the army?'

'No, Alice, he's in a reserved occupation. He's a doctor.'

'I see.'

'I doubt if I'll ever get married,' said Iris, pulling a face.

'Why not?'

'Who'd look twice at me? My sister was always the pretty one. You're a bit like her, really. You must have had offers.'

Alice smiled. 'I got the one I really wanted.'

As they came round a corner, they saw a news vendor selling copies of the lunchtime edition. On the board propped up against his stand, two headlines had been scrawled in large capitals. The first was ZEPPELIN SHOT DOWN.

'I heard about that,' said Iris, excitedly.

'We actually saw it.'

'Did you? What was it like?'

Alice didn't even hear the question. Her eye had been caught by the second news story – BRUTAL MURDER IN CHINGFORD.

In all likelihood, she guessed, her father would be involved in the investigation and so would Joe Keedy. She bit her lip in disappointment.

The detectives were going to be busier than ever now, putting their social lives aside. Alice feared that she might not see Keedy for some time.

Though it was early afternoon when he got back to Scotland Yard, Keedy had already been up for well over eight hours. His body was reminding him of the fact. He felt tired and sluggish. He went straight to Marmion's office and found him poring over a street map of London.

'What are you looking for?' he asked.

'Inspiration.'

'Well, I can't help you there. I ran out of it years ago.'

Marmion stood up. 'How did you get on at the morgue?'

'I was in luck. I managed to keep Mrs Wilder away from the slab itself.'

He explained how he'd let her see her husband's effects and how that had deterred her from wanting to view his corpse. He then described the return to the Wilder house and held up a large leather-bound appointments book.

'I had a real job getting this out of her.'

'It's vital to the investigation, Joe.'

'I just couldn't convince her of that. According to Mrs Wilder, every name in here belongs to someone who thought that Simon Wilder was a kind of god. I had a closer look at some of those photographs in their living room,' said Keedy. 'He really was a striking figure in tails. It turns out that he and his wife beat all-comers on the dance floor. That was before the accident, of course.'

'What accident?'

'It was something the next-door neighbour told me when she let me out. Simon and Catherine Wilder won every competition they entered until she had a fall and did something to her back. It ruined her career. Mrs Wilder had to give up something she loved dearly. It's made her very bitter.'

'I'm not surprised,' said Marmion. 'It must have been a cruel blow. What about her husband? Has he withdrawn from competitive dancing as well?'

'Oh, no – he's found himself another partner.'

'And who's that?'

'I've no idea but her name will be in this appointments book somewhere.' He put it on the desk and opened it at the page that referred to the previous day. 'I had a look at this on the drive back here. It's the list of classes he had yesterday.'

Marmion studied the page. 'There were six of them in all.'

'Two involved couples but four ladies came for individual tuition.'

'So he was dancing for all of six hours. I could never do that.'

'He always kept himself very fit, apparently,' said Keedy. 'I wondered how he'd managed to avoid conscription but Mrs Chambers, the neighbour, explained that as well. Wilder was forty-two when it was brought in earlier this year. If he'd been twelve months younger, he'd have been in uniform at the front.'

'That might have saved his life.'

'Or it might have shortened it just as brutally.'

'Too true!'

Marmion picked up the book and flicked through it. He was impressed both by the number of would-be dancers who'd come for instruction and by the amount of money they were prepared to pay out.

'Four pounds an hour! No wonder he could afford a lovely house like that.'

'That's almost as much as we get,' joked Keedy.

'I wish it was.' They shared a hollow laugh. 'I reckon that Mrs Wilder looked after this,' he went on, tapping the book. 'It's so meticulously kept. She was his secretary as well as his dance partner.'

'Do we have to interview *everyone* named in there?'

'That's how we're most likely to pick up valuable clues.'

'But the murder may have nothing to do with his occupation.'

'He didn't *have* an occupation, Joe. He had a way of life. Artistes are not the same as lesser mortals like us. They dedicate themselves to their calling.'

'Isn't that what *we* do?'

'Not in quite the same way,' argued Marmion. 'Simon Wilder lived and breathed dancing twenty-four hours a day. That's why his death has to be connected to something that happened in the course of his work.' He looked at the page in front of him. 'I wonder what this means.'

Keedy looked over his shoulder. 'What are you talking about?'

'There's a letter beside each name. It's either a "p" or a "g". Does that indicate the grade each dancer has reached?'

'Do you mean they're either poor or good?'

'It's a possibility.'

'Well, I can make a better guess than that.'

'Go on, then.'

'Wilder sometimes used an accompanist and sometimes he didn't. I think we're looking at "p" for piano and "g" for gramophone. How does that sound?'

'It sounds very convincing to me, Joe.'

'His pianist was a woman named Mrs Pattinson who adored him.'

'He seems to have surrounded himself with adoring women. What's more,' said Marmion, rolling his eyes, 'he made them pay four pounds an hour for the privilege. What does that tell you about him?'

'He was a lucky devil!'

'Why did his luck run out?' He turned to the page listing the most recent pupils. 'We'll start with these last two names.'

'Why pick on them?'

'The first four sessions of the day had piano accompaniment whereas the last two – both of them ladies – danced to music from a gramophone. That may not be an accident. If you took an interest in a woman, would you rather have a third person in the dance studio with you or would you prefer to keep it more private?'

'It may be that the pianist was not available for those sessions.'

'A moment ago, you told me that she adored Wilder. I reckon that she'd have played for him until her hands dropped off. What was her name?'

'Mrs Pattinson – Audrey Pattinson.'

Marmion closed the book. 'Let's have a word with her, shall we?'

She knew that something had happened. When she got to the studio that morning, Audrey Pattinson had found Catherine Wilder in an agitated state, explaining to the woman who'd come for a dance lesson that her husband had gone missing and that the class would have to be cancelled. Having gone there to provide accompaniment, Audrey instead found herself pinning a notice on the door, warning those due for a class later in the day that all instruction had been suspended until further notice. She then returned home in a complete daze. Her husband, Martin, had made her a cup of tea and tried to stop her speculating on Wilder's disappearance. It took him hours to calm her down. When he felt able to leave her, he went off in search of information.

Audrey sat there in utter dismay, holding the framed photograph of Wilder that he'd given her as a Christmas present. He was leaning on a piano with her beside him. Audrey felt a thrill whenever she looked at the photograph. Wilder was a brilliant dancer and she felt that it was an honour to play for him. The notion that their partnership might somehow have come to an end was terrifying. Audrey was a shapeless, grey-haired lady in her fifties with the kind of nondescript face that made her almost invisible. After leading a largely anonymous life, she'd been employed by Wilder and suddenly blossomed. Her name was printed on the poster outside the studio and she was mentioned in all of his publicity. Wilder had given her an identity and purpose in life she'd hitherto lacked.

When her husband had returned, she'd risen from her chair and rushed into the hall. One look at his face confirmed her worst fears. Martin Pattinson was a tall, straight-backed, sharp-featured man in his sixties with well-groomed white hair and a neat moustache. He'd shrugged helplessly. Then he'd simply taken his wife into his arms and held her close. Audrey had sobbed until there were no more tears left.

Simon Wilder had gone for ever. Her life was empty once again.

Marmion and Keedy sat in the rear of a car that took them in the direction of Chingford. The inspector was engrossed in the appointments book, going through page after page in the search for patterns that might yield clues. Having bought a copy of the lunchtime edition as they left Scotland Yard, the sergeant was holding it open and looking for a mention of the murder. He found it on an inside page.

'There's not very much,' he complained. 'All that it says is that the body of a man was found in Chingford in the early hours and that the police have launched a murder inquiry. They don't even give Wilder's name.'

'The paper was printed too early for that, Joe. By the time Chat held his press conference, that edition was already finished. And it doesn't worry me that we've been overshadowed by the Zeppelin story,' he continued. 'I'd always prefer to give newspapers too little information than too much.'

'Tomorrow will be even worse. There'll be photos galore of the wreckage. The papers will really make a meal of that. Simon Wilder is going to be hidden away on an inside page once again.' The car slowed to a halt in thickening traffic. 'We can't be shuttling to and fro all the time,' he went on. 'It's the best part of a ten-mile drive. We lose valuable time darting to Chingford and back.'

'I disagree,' said Marmion. 'Time in transit is never wasted. We have a chance to discuss the case and read through any documents we have – such as this.' He held up the appointments book. 'It's fascinating, Joe. It's a far better read than any of those novels Ellen takes out of the library.'

'I still think we should establish a base in Chingford.'

'The idea is appealing, I grant you that. It would be wonderful to put ten miles between us and Chat. I hate it when he's breathing down our necks.'

'I hate it when the old so-and-so is breathing.'

Marmion laughed. 'Don't wish him dead. Chat has his faults and there are plenty of them but it could have been worse.'

'I don't see how.'

'What if *I'd* become superintendent? I might have turned into a real tyrant and you'd have been working hand-in-glove with Inspector Chatfield instead of with me.'

Keedy groaned. 'I'd sooner be back in uniform.'

The traffic cleared, the car picked up speed and they eventually got near their destination. Since he was a stranger to the area, the driver stopped to ask directions from a passer-by. Two minutes later, the vehicle was turning into a tree-lined avenue with a series of detached houses down each side. Audrey Pattinson's address had been found in the appointment book along with the addresses of everyone else connected to the dance studio. Marmion could see why Catherine Wilder had been so loath to part with the book. It was a detailed record of the life she'd shared with her husband and, as such, would be a treasured memento.

'There's one thing I couldn't find in here, Joe,' he said.

'What was that?'

'There's no record of payment to the accompanist.'

'Perhaps she played for nothing.'

'I can't believe that he'd exploit her like that.'

'You have to be ruthless in business.'

The car stopped at the kerb and they got out. Marmion led the way up the little path and rang the doorbell. A moment later, Martin Pattinson opened the door and identified them from press photographs.

'I've seen you two gentlemen before, I fancy,' he said.

'Then you'll know our names, sir. Are you Mr Pattinson?'

'I am, indeed. You must have come to interview my wife.'

'Is she aware that . . . ?'

'I'm afraid so, Inspector Marmion. Be gentle with her, please. She's in a very delicate state. Working with Mr Wilder meant a great deal to her.' He ushered them into the living room. Audrey was in a chair, staring blankly ahead of her. 'There are some detectives from Scotland Yard who wish to speak to you, my dear.'

'What?' She came out of her reverie. Seeing the visitors, she became flustered. 'Oh, I wasn't expecting anyone to call.'

'We were hoping you might be able to help us, Mrs Pattinson.'

'I'm sure that she will, Inspector,' said her husband. 'May I stay or would you rather not have me in the way?'

'The choice is yours, sir. I suspect that Mrs Pattinson would prefer you to remain and we're very happy with that.'

Audrey nodded and beckoned for her husband to sit beside her. Marmion and Keedy were waved to an armchair apiece. While the inspector held the appointments book in his hand, Keedy took out his notebook and pencil. As they settled down, they each stole a quick look around the room. A third of the space was taken up by a grand piano. On the mantelpiece was a large, framed photograph taken at the Pattinsons' wedding. He was wearing an army uniform and his wife was in a white bridal dress. Both of them looked to be well into their thirties.

'What would you like to know, Inspector?' prompted Pattinson.

'Well, we really want to find out where Mr Wilder went yesterday evening. That's our starting point. When did you last see him, Mrs Pattinson?'

Audrey leant forward. 'I played for him at a class in the afternoon and left there about three o'clock. That was the last time I . . .' Tears threatened but she made an effort and kept them at bay. 'That was the last time I saw him alive.'

'Do you have any idea where he went after that?'

'Well, he had two more classes, of course, and that would have taken him on to five o'clock. Mr Wilder used music from the gramophone for those.'

'Why did he do that, Mrs Pattinson?' asked Keedy. 'Were you too exhausted after playing the piano for four hours?'

'Not at all,' she replied, huffily. 'I've played for five or six hours on many occasions. It's not continuous accompaniment, you see. Mr

Wilder gives instruction first. It's only when certain figures are perfected that he's ready to dance to music. When some of the beginners come to a class, I sit on my hands most of the time.'

'Did Mr Wilder tell you where he was going that evening?' asked Marmion.

'No, Inspector, and it wasn't my place to ask.'

'His wife said that he'd gone off on business somewhere.'

'Then that's what he did.'

'He was an extraordinary man,' said Pattinson. 'I've never met anyone with that amount of energy. He was indefatigable.'

'We've gathered that, sir.' Marmion tapped the book then switched his gaze to Audrey. 'I see that you've had a long association with him, Mrs Pattinson.'

'Audrey joined him soon after he opened the dance studio,' said her husband on her behalf. 'He tried another accompanist before her but the man could not compete with my wife.'

'How would you describe him?'

'He was a man of the utmost charm and had a good business sense.'

'Actually, sir,' said Marmion, pleasantly, 'the question was for your wife.'

'I do beg your pardon.'

'Mrs Pattinson?'

After a considered pause, she began to speak, measuring her words carefully. It was almost as if she'd been gathering material for a biography of Simon Wilder because she knew so much about him. The detectives were not surprised to find out that, before he turned to dancing, he was an actor. He'd had a fairly successful career onstage but there were inevitable lulls. During periods of unemployment, it transpired, he had a second string to his bow. As the son of a photographer, he'd learnt the trade at his father's knee and become so proficient that he was able to make a good income by taking photographs.

'They were mostly of other actors,' said Audrey. 'A lot of them still choose Mr Wilder's portrait of them to put on display at the theatre in which they're working. That shows how good they are.'

'Actors are very vain,' added her husband. 'Look at those photographs and you'll see that they were usually taken years ago. Oh, I'm sorry,' he said, drawing back, 'I didn't mean to interrupt.'

Audrey continued her monologue, explaining that Simon Wilder was a stage name. He'd been christened Stanley Hogg but felt that it was not the ideal name for an ambitious young actor. He'd met Catherine when they appeared together in a play by Bernard Shaw. She'd been trained in ballet and the couple shared a love of dance. Once married, they devoted all their spare time to dancing until they reached a level where they began to win competitions and garner good publicity. Abandoning the stage, Audrey told them, they bought the hall and converted it into a dance studio.

'That must have cost a lot,' observed Marmion.

'Mrs Wilder had private wealth,' said Pattinson, butting in again. 'Not that I'm suggesting Wilder married her for her money. Heaven forbid! No, they're very well matched. They worked around the clock to get where they are now and deserve every ounce of success.' He touched his wife's hand. 'I do apologise, Audrey. You know far more about them than I do. Please go on.'

But the interruption had served to stem the flow of her reminiscences. After a few more sentences, she sat back and folded her arms to show that she'd finished.

'Thank you, Mrs Pattinson,' said Marmion. 'That was enlightening.'

She smiled for the first time. 'He and his wife were the personification of grace on the dance floor.'

'But I was told that she is no longer able to partner him,' said Keedy. 'Since her accident, she's had persistent back problems.'

'Fate was so cruel to the poor woman. She can't even take classes.'

'Who replaced her as Mr Wilder's dancing partner?'

'Odele Thompson.'

'She was the person in the final class yesterday afternoon,' said Marmion, remembering the name he'd seen in the appointments book.

'That was usually the case, Inspector. They wanted practice time. Mr Wilder didn't need to instruct Miss Thompson. She's a professional dancer, you see. After a day with less talented dancers, he loved to work with someone who was his match on the dance floor.'

'Yet he didn't make use of you as an accompanist.'

'He had the gramophone. They were able to dance to a full orchestra. Is that all?' she asked, wearily. 'I'm very, very tired.'

'Then we won't tax you any more, Mrs Pattinson,' said Marmion, getting to his feet. 'I'm sorry to intrude at a time like this. We'll leave you in peace.'

'One last question,' said Keedy, rising from his chair. 'When the inspector went through that book earlier on, he couldn't find any mention of payment for the accompanist. How do you explain that?'

Audrey was so shocked by the question that she began to tremble. It was almost as if Keedy had hurled an insult at her. Pattinson glared at him with something akin to outrage. He crossed to the door and held it wide open.

'Good day, gentlemen,' he said. 'I'll show you out.'

CHAPTER SEVEN

Since she knew how busy her brother-in-law was, Ellen was very grateful that he'd been able to make time to call at the house. She gave him a kiss of welcome and took him into the living room. Raymond Marmion was a few years younger than his brother but he had the same solid frame and the same pleasant features. What set them apart was that Harvey Marmion had far more hair and an almost permanent look of concentration. His brother, on the other hand, had a spiritual quality that seemed to shine out of him like a beam of goodness. He had a big, friendly, open face and a high, domed forehead. In his Salvation Army uniform, with its silver crest denoting his seniority, he was an imposing figure. As he sat on the sofa, he put his peaked hat down beside him.

'It's wonderful to see you again, Raymond,' she said.

'Your telephone call worried us.'

'I didn't mean to burden you with our problems. It's just that Paul is behaving strangely and – without Harvey here – I'm having difficulty handling him.'

'Where is he now?'

'He's upstairs in his room.'

'What exactly is the trouble, Ellen?'

'Before I tell you,' she said, perching on the edge of an armchair, 'let me first ask after you and the family. How are you all?'

'We're much as usual,' he replied. 'We could do with less work and more sleep but that's impossible in the life we've chosen. Lily sends her love, by the way.'

'Take ours back to her.'

Ellen had always liked him. Raymond Marmion was kind, compassionate and trustworthy. She felt able to confide her innermost secrets to him, knowing that she would always get a fair hearing and good advice.

'I do feel something of a fraud,' she began.

'Why is that?'

'Helping people in distress or in dire circumstances is what you do for a living. Our problems are nothing beside those of people who are on the verge of starvation or simply have nowhere to live.'

'It's nonetheless real, Ellen.'

'And we're so much better off than other parents of wounded soldiers.'

'Forget about them. Let's talk about Paul.'

She heaved a sigh. 'I'm not quite sure where to start . . .'

It was as if a tap had been turned on inside Ellen. One after the other, her woes and fears poured out in quick succession. She listed a whole a series of incidents that ended in friction with her son. When she told him about the letter from Mavis Tandy, he held up both palms to stop the surge.

'Hold on a moment,' he said. 'Why were you so unhappy when he agreed to meet this person?'

'She wants to talk about Paul's best friend. She wants to know exactly what happened to Colin Fryatt. I read her letter out to him. It seemed so . . . well, morbid. She's obviously grieving – and she has my sympathy for her loss – but she's trying to draw memories out of Paul that are best left hidden.'

'There are some things you just can't bury, Ellen. This may be one of them.'

'I don't want him to suffer that torment all over again.'

'In the end, it's his choice.'

'He should put it all behind him.'

'That's easier said than done. What do you know of Mavis Tandy?'

'She lives in Gillingham.'

'How did she come to meet Paul's friend?'

'Oh, it was quite by chance,' said Ellen. 'Colin had relatives in Gillingham and called on them during his last leave. He met Mavis at the tea shop where she worked. When she realised he was a soldier, she said that she was thinking of volunteering to become a nurse and asked what conditions were like in France. They liked each other on sight, apparently. That's how it started.'

'Then it sounds very much like the way Lily and I got together,' he said with an affectionate smile. 'I saw her walking down the street and I was captivated. She was not just beautiful, she was so self-possessed. I'd never met a woman like her.'

She gave a dry laugh. 'It was different for Harvey and me. We took a long time to decide if we really had found the person we'd like to share our lives with. The trouble was that we spent so little time alone. My father was very strict. He watched us like hawks.'

He chuckled. 'I remember my brother complaining about it.'

'He always said that if *we* ever had a daughter, he'd allow her more freedom.'

'And is that what he did with Alice?'

'Well, no, Harvey was almost as bad as my father at first. When she had her first boyfriend, he told her the exact time she had to be back at home.'

'I can't imagine Alice putting up with that attitude.'

'She challenged her father. I was too meek and mild to do that with mine.'

'You never struck me as meek and mild, Ellen. You've got real spirit.'

'I've only been able to show it since I was married.' She reached out to touch his arm. 'Will you speak to Paul for me, please?'

'I haven't come all this way to miss seeing my nephew.'

'Thank you, Raymond. I knew I could rely on you.'

'I can't promise I'll achieve the result you want.'

'That's part of the problem,' she confessed. 'Where Paul is concerned, I'm not absolutely sure what I *do* want.'

On the drive to the next house, the detectives were able to discuss the visit to the Pattinson household. Both of them had reached the same conclusions.

'Mrs Pattinson is smitten with Wilder,' said Marmion, 'and her husband is not entirely happy about that.'

'No,' agreed Keedy, 'if he hadn't been there, his wife would have been able to talk much more freely.'

'She filled in a lot of blank spaces for us, Joe. I'm grateful to her for that.'

'So am I. Did you notice that photograph on the mantelpiece?'

'Yes, Pattinson was wearing the uniform of a major.'

'A lot of retired soldiers use their rank to impress people. I wonder why he doesn't do that.'

'He must have his reasons.'

They were both mystified by the response they got to their inquiry about payment. Since Wilder had been running a business, they'd assumed that he would pay his accompanist accordingly but she was insulted by the very suggestion, and so was her husband. Marmion took a practical view.

'She's obviously a good pianist,' he said, 'and deserves some sort of wage.'

'Maybe she's happy with rewards of the heart.'

'Would *you* be happy in her situation?'

'No, I certainly wouldn't. I've got too many bills to pay. Anyway,' admitted Keedy, 'I haven't got a musical bone in my body. Alice says that I can't even whistle in tune. She's always complaining about it.'

'Alice had piano lessons when she was younger. She used to practise all hours. When she was a teacher, she sometimes played for the children. But the real surprise is Paul,' he continued. 'He's turning into the family musician.'

'Is he still playing his friend's mouth organ?'

'Yes,' said Marmion, 'but it's not any old mouth organ with a limited range of notes. His friend, Colin Fryatt, used to belong to a harmonica band. From time to time, they earned a few bob playing in pubs.'

'Is that what Paul wants to do?'

'No, Joe, I think it just helps him pass the time. But he's got a good ear for music and loves playing the songs they sing at the front. Ellen gets a bit fed up when she hears "It's a Long Way to Tipperary" a hundred times a day but playing the mouth organ seems to be his only interest.'

Paul Marmion shook hands with his uncle. Though pleased to see him – if only in hazy outline – he had no illusions about the purpose of Raymond Marmion's visit. When his mother went off to make some tea, Paul sat down opposite him.

'How are Auntie Lily and the boys?' he asked.

'They're keeping busy. Your aunt is in charge of the soup kitchen. We sell it at a penny a bowl. We're always short of helpers.'

'Don't look at me.'

'You don't need much training to dole out soup.'

'It's not the work that worries me. It's the uniform.'

'You wouldn't have to wear one.'

'No, but I'd be surrounded by people who do.'

Raymond laughed. 'Is that what worries you – guilt by association?'

Without warning, Paul's manner changed in a flash. Having been relaxed and friendly, he suddenly became tense and hostile.

'The Salvation Army uniform has always annoyed me,' he complained.

'It's something I wear with great pride, Paul.'

'But it gives the wrong impression.'

'What do you mean?'

'You put on a uniform in the name of peace. I put it on to kill people.'

'We're soldiers of the cross,' said his uncle. 'We fight a different battle.'

'You should try fighting a real one. Nobody at the Somme was thinking about salvation. The only thing on our minds was survival.'

'The two are closely linked.'

'I don't think so.'

Raymond tried appeasement. 'Well, I don't want to preach at you,' he said, affably. 'After all this time, you know where we stand as an organisation. I only called in to see how you were getting on.'

'You were sent for,' said Paul, resentfully. 'You came to change my mind.'

'I'd certainly like to change your mind about the Salvation Army.

70

We're not skulking over here while the soldiers are at the front. We've set up canteens in France close to the trenches. You fought the enemy with bullets. Our ammunition is cups of tea and doughnuts. When British troops are half-dead with exhaustion, we help to revive them. We offer them physical and spiritual assistance and I won't have anyone disparaging us when they don't realise what we're doing for the war effort.'

Paul was momentarily checked by his uncle's passionate response. He then got to his feet, wagged his finger and spoke earnestly.

'I want to see her, Uncle Raymond, and nobody can stop me.'

'I couldn't agree more.'

'Colin was a good friend. He'd expect it of me.'

'Of course he would.'

'And, whatever you say, I still think the Salvation Army looks silly, dressing up in uniform and playing at being soldiers.'

'Come and see us at the hostel. We might shatter a few illusions for you.'

'No, thanks – I've got much better things to do.'

On that disagreeable note, he turned on his heel, stalked off to the door and let himself out. A couple of minutes later, Ellen entered with the tea on a tray.

She looked round. 'Where's Paul?'

'He walked out on me.'

'That was very rude of him.'

'I didn't take it personally, Ellen,' he said with a tolerant smile. 'For some reason, this uniform often upsets people. I didn't realise that my nephew was one of them. But if you want my opinion,' he went on, glancing upward, 'it's this. You're right to be very concerned about Paul. He's undergoing some sort of crisis.'

* * *

The news did not come entirely as a surprise to Odele Thompson. She'd heard rumours of a murder and, when she walked past the dance studio, she'd seen the notice pinned to the door. When the detectives called on her, therefore, they were only confirming what she'd feared. Her reaction was strange. Instead of being shocked like Catherine Wilder, or distraught like Audrey Pattinson, she thought only of herself.

'That means I'll miss the British Dance Championships.'

'Mr Wilder will miss them as well,' Marmion pointed out, 'and his loss, if I may say so, is a great deal more serious than yours.'

'We've worked so hard these past few months.'

'That's beside the point, Miss Thompson.'

'And we had a good chance of winning. I feel so *cheated*.'

'How do you think Mr Wilder feels?' asked Keedy.

'I find that remark in bad taste, Sergeant.'

Odele Thompson was a thin, animated woman in her late twenties with dark, curly hair, high cheekbones and darting eyes. She rented a flat in a large house in Wood Green. Everything about the room suggested that she lived there alone. On the mantelpiece and on every shelf was a framed photograph, mostly of her dancing on her own. Simon Wilder partnered her in the large photograph that hung on a wall. Also on the walls were framed theatre posters bearing her name. Marmion found her unattractive and self-centred, yet Keedy was struck by her brittle beauty. Neither of them could believe that they were dealing with someone who ought to feel bereaved. Odele seemed more irritated than heartbroken.

'Who killed him?' she asked.

'We're hoping that you might help us find the man,' said Marmion.

'What can I possibly do?'

'Well, for a start, you can tell us about what happened yesterday. You and Mr Wilder had a practice session, I believe.'

'That's right, Inspector.'

'What sort of a mood was he in?'

'We were both optimistic. For once, everything went right. We danced like the Castles and never put a foot out of place.'

'Have you ever *seen* the Castles dance?'

'As a matter of fact, I have,' she said, airily. 'I was working in Paris when they came there a few years ago. What they did was amazing. They took the Café de Paris by storm – that's where I saw them doing the famous Castle Walk. As for their foxtrot, it was a revelation.'

'What time did you part company with Mr Wilder yesterday?' asked Keedy.

'It must have been well after five o'clock. When you have such a strenuous rehearsal, you need to get your breath back.'

'And what happened when you parted?'

'Simon went his way and so did I.'

'Do you have any idea where he went?'

'He said that he was going home first.'

'And after that?'

'You'll have to ask Catherine.'

'We already have,' said Marmion. 'She has no idea where he went.'

Odele smiled. 'Simon did rather like to cover his tracks.'

'Why was that, Miss Thompson?'

'Are you married, Inspector?'

'Yes, I am.'

'Then you'll know why men sometimes prefer to keep their wives in the dark.'

Marmion was nettled. 'I'm always very honest with my wife.'

'Honesty can be a dangerous thing, Inspector.'

'Are you telling me that you're *dishonest*?'

'I live in the real world.'

'Miss Thompson,' he said, close to exasperation, 'I must say that you surprise me. When most people hear of a friend being murdered, they at least express some kind of sympathy. And they also want to know exactly what happened.'

'Simon is dead. That's what happened. I have to suffer the consequences.'

'Don't you feel *sorry* that he's dead?' asked Keedy.

'Yes, I do, naturally. I'm very sorry. He taught me a lot. But you must understand that I have my career to consider.'

Judging by the size and comfort of the room, her career had brought her an appreciative income. Expensive ornaments stood on every surface. A silk dressing gown was draped over the back of a chair. On a table in the corner was the largest gramophone either of them had ever seen. There was a sizeable collection of records stacked neatly underneath it.

She looked from one to the other. 'You don't understand, do you?'

'I'm afraid that we don't,' replied Marmion.

'I first danced on stage when I was only five years old, Inspector. My parents both performed in music halls, you see. I was born to it. But I always found those audiences a trifle vulgar. What I really wanted to do was to appear in stage musicals that gave me a chance to sing and dance. Have you ever heard of *Gaiety Girl*?' She sailed on before they could respond. 'I had my big chance in that. I understudied the female lead and went on for five performances. Simon Wilder was at one of them. He was an actor in those days and we . . . knew each other.'

'We didn't ask for your life story, Miss Thompson,' said Keedy.

'But it explains the way I behave.'

'Does it?'

'Live theatre is a long succession of hazards. So many things can go wrong. I rehearsed for three weeks for one show and it was postponed because the principal dancer broke her leg in a fall. When I auditioned for the second production, I didn't get a part. In another stage musical, the leading man had a heart attack and collapsed. They brought the curtain down and sent everyone home. I never even got to show the audience what I could do as a dancer. And there are dozens of other examples,' she went on. 'I'm inured to calamities. I've been the victim of so many.'

'It's Mr Wilder who's the victim here,' said Marmion with asperity.

'I'll write to Catherine.'

'Have you always been so heartless?'

'You have to develop a thick skin in my profession, Inspector.' She sized up Keedy. 'Have you ever thought of taking up dancing, Sergeant? You have the body and the looks for it.'

'The only body that interests me at the moment,' he said, levelly, 'is that of Mr Wilder. We need to find his killer.'

'We all want that.'

'Did he have any enemies?'

'He had a lot of rivals,' she said, 'but that's in the nature of things. He turned the dance studio into a small gold mine and he gave lots of ladies an experience that they will treasure. Speak to Audrey Pattinson. She was his accompanist.'

'We already have spoken to her.'

'When she first met Simon, she was a sad, dried-up little creature who'd never had any real joy in her life. Her father had been a cathedral organist and she'd learnt to play organ and piano. But her real yearning was for dance music,' said Odele. 'Simon showed her a whole new world. In a sense, he resurrected her.'

'Let's go back to the question the inspector asked you,' suggested Keedy. 'If he didn't have enemies, did he have any rivals who might go to extremes?'

She suddenly twitched and sat bolt upright in her chair. Her mouth fell open, her eyes glazed over and she began to shiver. It was as if the news of the murder had finally penetrated her consciousness. It was no longer an inconvenience to her dancing ambitions. She realised that she'd lost a dear friend and was aghast. Having been appalled at her earlier reaction, they now felt sorry for her.

'I'll tell you something,' she said, querulously.

'What's that Miss Thompson?' asked Keedy.

'I was with Simon a couple of weeks ago in Shaftesbury Avenue . . .'

'Go on.'

'Well, he came to an abrupt halt and swung round sharply.'

'Why did he do that?'

'He thought that someone was following him.'

A working day in the company of Iris Goodliffe had cemented their friendship. Alice got on well with all her colleagues in the Women's Police Force but had never really found a close friend. She wondered if Iris might be able to fill that gap in her life. As they came off duty, they were about to go their separate ways.

'Will you be seeing your fiancé tonight?' asked Iris.

'I doubt it very much.'

'You don't *know* that he's involved in that murder investigation.'

'Yes, I do,' said Alice. 'When I saw that mention in the newspaper, I felt my heart sink. That's an infallible sign.'

'So you won't see much of Joe *or* of your father.'

'They'll be working flat out, Iris.'

'Don't you wish that you could be helping them?'

'No, I don't. I know my limitations.'

'We're bound to have female detectives one day.'

'That's still a very long way off,' said Alice with regret. 'War has given us the chance to show that we can do most things as well as men but confronting desperate killers is not one of them. Joe has had a lot of injuries and so has my father. When someone is facing the prospect of execution, they fight like mad to resist arrest.'

Iris sighed. 'There's so much violence in the world.'

'You'll see some of it yourself if you're ever on night duty. That's when you realise how dangerous policing can be. Mind you,' she went on, 'I'd sooner take on a drunken hooligan than face Gale Force when she's in a bad mood.'

They came out of the building and into the street. The sense of being off duty was invigorating. Both of them felt it. Iris was sad to part with her friend.

'What are you doing this evening?' she asked.

'I need to go back home.'

'Oh, I see.'

'I promised my mother I'd call in when I had the chance. And I haven't seen my brother for weeks.'

'I'd like to meet him some time,' said Iris, angling for an invitation.

But Alice was not yet ready to introduce her to the family. Though she and Iris had passed a pleasant day together, she felt that she had to keep some space between them. Iris was very needy. Alice didn't wish her friend to become too dependent on her. That would limit her freedom. And there was something else that made her draw back from taking Iris home with her.

'Paul is not very hospitable at the moment,' she explained.

'Oh – what's wrong with him?'

'He prefers his own company.'

Holding the letter beside the window in his bedroom, Paul read it yet again, searching for something between the lines that was not actually there. After all this time, he knew the words off by heart but he still wanted to see Mavis Tandy's neat, looping handwriting and take pleasure from the sentiments expressed. It was a letter primarily about his friend, Colin Fryatt, but he was slowly persuading himself that she really wanted an excuse to see him. The thought was exciting. When he'd finished reading it, he slipped it back into the envelope and put it under the pillow.

Then he reached for the mouth organ and started to play.

CHAPTER EIGHT

Sir Edward Henry had planned to retire in 1914 as Commissioner of the Metropolitan Police Force but the outbreak of war prompted his innate patriotism and he agreed to continue in his extremely demanding role. While he had a wide range of duties and responsibilities, he always showed especial interest in the progress of any murder investigation. It was the reason he summoned Claude Chatfield to his office. The superintendent delivered his report crisply.

'Thank you,' said Sir Edward. 'It seems that we have a monster in our midst.'

'We'll catch him.'

'That's why it was important to assign the case to Inspector Marmion. He and Sergeant Keedy have an uncanny knack of getting their man.'

'Marmion also has an uncanny knack of holding things back from me,' said Chatfield, testily. 'That's why I don't approve of his request to establish his headquarters in Chingford. I prefer him where I can see him, Sir Edward.'

'You have the use of a telephone.'

'It's not the same thing.'

'You should learn to trust your officers.'

'I want them to trust *me* enough to pass on all relevant information as soon as it's available. Marmion hides things from me.'

'Come now, Superintendent,' said the other with a smile. 'Let's not be melodramatic. Marmion may seem slow and methodical but that's only because he doesn't want to make any mistakes. I can't believe that he'd deliberately *conceal* anything from you.'

The commissioner's gaze shifted to the newspaper on his desk. He was a tall, slim, immaculately dressed man with wavy grey hair and a twirling moustache.

'You've seen the lunchtime edition, I take it.'

'Yes, Sir Edward.'

'The Zeppelin raid is on the front page.'

'I was bewailing the fact earlier. Of far more concern to me is the public reaction to the shooting down of an aircraft. It's induced a collective madness. People are descending on the crash site in thousands.'

'It's reprehensible, I know, but one can't arrest mobs like that.'

'The army should be deployed in larger numbers.'

'They're somewhat preoccupied by the small matter of a war,' said the older man, drily. 'Army and police alike lack resources for something on this scale.'

'From what I hear, they've been fighting over souvenirs.'

'A piece of a Zeppelin is a rare trophy for any collector.'

'It shouldn't be allowed, Sir Edward.'

'How can we stop it? Besides, souvenirs are not in themselves bad things. I have several of my own, as it happens. Oddly enough,' said the commissioner, opening a drawer in his desk, 'I came across one only this morning. It's in the nature of an historic document now.'

'What exactly is it?'

'You can see for yourself, Superintendent.'

Taking the notice from the drawer, he passed it over. Chatfield was quick to recognise its significance. Issued by the Great Western Railway, it was the timetable for a train journey made by His Royal Highness, the Archduke Ferdinand of Austria from Windsor and Eton to Paddington.

'According to this,' said Chatfield, 'it took exactly thirty minutes.'

'I can vouch for its punctuality because I had the privilege of being on the train at the time. It was one of the perquisites of office.' He took the notice back and looked at it. 'Friday, 21st November, 1913,' he said, mournfully. 'The poor man had less than a year to live.'

'Given what later happened, that souvenir has great significance.'

'I'd never dream of parting with it.'

'What I'd enjoy,' said Chatfield, fussily, 'is a souvenir from Marmion about the current investigation. Why doesn't he get in touch? What on earth is he *doing*?'

'He's doing what he always does – patiently gathering evidence.'

'Well, I wish he'd pass it on to me, Sir Edward.'

'He'll do so in due course, Superintendent. And when he does, you can tell him that I endorse his suggestion. He must, of course, operate from somewhere in Chingford. It would be foolish to have him popping back here all the time.'

Chatfield spluttered. 'But I like to question him face-to-face.'

'The decision has been made. Please pass it on to the inspector.' He put his souvenir away and closed the drawer. 'Was there anything else?'

Having started his shift early that morning, Denzil Parry went back home while most of London was still at work. He was surprised to see a car parked outside his house and even more surprised to find two men enjoying a cup of tea with his wife. When he learnt that they were from Scotland Yard, he was delighted. Once he had his own cup of tea, he told his story. Having done so many times at work, he'd embellished it a great deal and had to be warned to restrict himself to the facts. Parry was a fleshy man in his fifties with a bald pate and a weather-beaten face. Like his wife, Megan, he had a sing-song Welsh accident.

'Strong drink is the devil's brew!' he said with puritanical zeal. 'That's why I signed the pledge years ago. When I see a man stretched out on the pavement, more often than not he's drunk. That's what I thought when I tripped over the corpse. Then I tried to shake him awake and found my hand covered in blood.'

'He came straight back in here to wash it off,' said Megan, a roly-poly woman with a practical air about her. 'I told him to go looking for Constable Bench.'

'We've heard *your* version of events earlier, Mrs Parry,' Marmion reminded her. 'We'd like to hear what your husband has to say. He, after all, discovered the body.'

Keeping to the facts, Parry gave his statement with due solemnity and Keedy took notes. When it was all over, the postman drank his tea and thanked his wife with a sly wink of the eye. Marmion then told him the name of the victim. The postman's eyebrows rose in surprise.

'Simon Wilder, the *dancer*?'

'That's him, I'm afraid.'

'But he's quite famous in these parts, Inspector.'

'Did you know him?'

'Well, no, but I've delivered letters to his house. He has a very pretty wife, I can tell you that. But then,' he added quickly, 'so do I.' Megan beamed. 'Simon Wilder's name was always in the local papers.'

'It's going to be in the national newspapers now,' said Keedy. 'You must know this district very well, Mr Parry.'

'I know it like the back of my hand.'

'Is there much crime in Chingford?'

'We don't have all that many dead bodies, if that's what you mean, Sergeant. Most people around here are decent and law-abiding. We have our share of crime but it's gone down a bit since the war because most of the young men who committed it are now in the army.'

'It's the same everywhere,' said Keedy.

'Adult crime may have gone down,' Marmion pointed out, 'but juvenile crime is on the rise. Lots of fathers signed up. Without a strong man in the house, children can sometimes get out of control.'

'Our boys are both in the navy,' said Megan. 'We were living in Swansea when they were born. The smell of the sea got in their nostrils.'

'Tell us about this area, Mr Parry.'

The postman seized on the invitation. He gave them a lilting lecture on the history of Chingford and listed all buildings of note. He and his wife, it emerged, were keen walkers so they visited Epping Forest on a regular basis. By walking the streets of the area for ten years or more, Parry had got to know it intimately. He began to reel off the names of the public houses where most trouble occurred.

'Thank you, sir,' said Marmion, politely interrupting. 'We can get all those details from the local police station. We may be camped there for some while.'

'Drop in for a chat any time you wish,' urged Megan. 'There's always a cup of tea and a biscuit waiting for you here.'

The detectives thanked her and got up to leave. Keedy remembered someone.

'Have you ever delivered mail to the home of Mr and Mrs Pattinson?'

'Oh, yes,' replied Parry. 'I certainly have.'

'How do you get on with them?'

'Mrs Pattinson is a very nice woman. She plays piano at the dance studio so the news about Mr Wilder will come as a bombshell.'

'What about her husband?'

Parry emitted a grunt. 'He's a different person altogether.'

'You sound as if you don't particularly like him.'

'I don't like him one little bit, Sergeant,' said the other. 'There's something odd about that man. Don't ask me what it is because I don't rightly know. All I can tell you is that . . . well, he's a bit weird.'

Ellen was so pleased to see her daughter that she hugged Alice for a full minute. There was no need for the visitor to ask where her brother was. Strains of 'The Long, Long Trail', as played on the mouth organ, came wafting downstairs. There was a haunting note to the music.

'How is he, Mummy?' asked Alice.

'The truth is that he's getting worse.'

'Oh dear – I'm sorry to hear that.'

'He even managed to be rude to your Uncle Raymond.'

'Has *he* been here?'

'I rang Lily and told her what was happening. She said that Raymond would come over as soon as he could.'

'What exactly did Paul say to him?'

'They had a row about the Salvation Army uniform.'

'Why ever did that happen? He's always liked Uncle Raymond in the past.'

'Things have changed for the worst. Paul takes against any and everybody. It was *my* turn earlier on. I found it very hurtful.'

Ellen went on to describe what had happened when she and her son were walking to the post office. Alice was upset on her mother's behalf. She pressed for more details of her brother's aggressive behaviour. The two of them were so deep in discussion that they didn't notice the music had stopped. The next moment, Paul came into the living room.

'I thought I heard voices,' he mumbled.

'Paul,' said Alice, planting a kiss on his cheek, 'it's lovely to see you again.'

'Is it?'

'We heard you playing the mouth organ earlier. You're a real musician.'

'I'll never be as good as Colin.'

'Why don't we all sit down?' said Ellen, moving to the sofa. 'Come on, Paul,' she went on as she saw his reluctance. 'You don't get to see your sister that often.'

'Oh, all right, then,' he said as if making a major concession.

When they were all seated, Alice conjured up a friendly smile.

'How *are* you, Paul?'

'I'm no better and no worse,' he replied.

'There must be some improvement.'

'I can see at last. That's the main thing. Being in the dark was frightening.' He squinted at her. 'You're in uniform.'

'I came straight from work.'

'Have you had a good day?' asked Ellen.

'Yes, I did, Mummy. We had very few incidents to deal with and it was a lovely day to be out on patrol. I had to shepherd a new recruit.'

'That shows how much the inspector trusts you.'

'I wouldn't go that far.'

'Are you still having trouble with that woman you call Gale Force?' said Paul.

'I've learnt to live with it.'

'That's what we had to do with this pig of a sergeant. He was always throwing his weight around and nobody was allowed to answer back. That's one thing I *don't* miss about the army – all that blooming discipline.'

'Those days are over, Paul.'

'No, they're not. You never know what might happen.'

'That's true,' said Ellen, relieved that her son was in such a subdued mood.

In spite of their bickering during childhood, Paul and Alice had always got on well together. Each had taken a pride in the other's achievements. As the two of them chatted away about old times, Ellen relaxed for the first time that day. Alice's visit was turning out to be a tonic for her and for her son. A sense of family had returned. She only wished that her daughter would live at home so that she could help her cope with Paul's outbursts but Alice had her own life now.

Just as the conversation was flowing easily, a sour note intruded.

'Why did you want to go into the police?' he asked his sister.

'I felt drawn towards it, Paul.'

'We don't need two coppers in the family.'

'Learn to count. We've got three now. There's Joe as well, remember.'

'I've been meaning to speak to you about him, Alice.'

'Why?'

'You're making a big mistake in marrying him.'

'Paul!' exclaimed Ellen.

'Let him give his opinion, Mummy,' said Alice, calmly.

'He's not the right man for you,' he resumed. 'Joe Keedy is too old and too fond of women. He's not the marrying type.'

'Well, I think he is.'

'And so do I,' added Ellen, stoutly. 'Now let's talk about something else.'

'But I'm trying to help Alice,' he argued.

'All that you're doing is upsetting her.'

'No, he isn't,' she said. 'Paul's only saying what others have said behind my back. Joe *is* much older but that's made him more mature. He really wants to settle down. In any case,' she went on, pointing a finger at her brother, 'you were all in favour of it when I first wrote to you to say that we were getting engaged.'

'I only told you that,' he said, 'so that I didn't hurt your feelings.'

'Then why are you hurting Alice's feelings now?' demanded Ellen.

'I'm just telling her the truth.'

'You always liked Joe Keedy.'

'Yes, I did and I still do. He's just not the right man for Alice.'

'It's my choice,' said his sister, anger rising.

'Then it's a bad one.'

'It's the best one I ever made in my life.'

'Don't blame me if he never even gets as far as the altar,' he said, almost taunting her. 'I've met dozens of happy-go-lucky lads in the army. They just want to have their fun and move on to the next girl.'

'I won't hear any more of this,' said Ellen, jumping to her feet.

'What am I supposed to do – button my lip and let Alice suffer? What kind of brother would I be if I did that? She needs to be warned.'

'I'm grateful for the warning,' said his sister, icily, 'but that's all I want to hear on the subject. Do you understand, Paul?'

'Oh yes, of course,' he said, cheerily, getting up and walking to the door. 'I can't see most things, Alice, but I can see when you're about to walk into disaster.'

He went quickly out of the room and slammed the door behind him.

'Oh, I'm so sorry,' said Ellen, arms around her daughter.

'I feel pity for *you*, Mummy,' she said hugging her. 'There was real malice in his eyes as he goaded me. If that's how Paul behaves, it must be murder living under the same roof with him.'

'It is, Alice. Every day is an ordeal.' Above their heads, the mouth organ tackled 'Goodbye, Dolly Gray'. 'It's a sinful thought for any mother,' she added with unaccustomed bitterness, 'but I'm starting to wish that I could say goodbye, Paul Marmion.'

Late evening found Claude Chatfield still at his desk, working his way through a mound of paperwork that seemed to be self-generating because it never reduced in size. He was still checking a document when Marmion and Keedy finally appeared.

'Ah, you're back, are you?' said Chatfield, sarcastically. 'It's so kind of you to remember that you do actually work at Scotland Yard!'

'We've been busy, sir,' said Marmion.

'All I've been doing is twiddling my thumbs for the last ten or twelve hours.'

'There was a lot to do in Chingford.'

'Yes,' said Keedy in support, 'it's not so long ago that you were an inspector yourself. You'll recall only too well how difficult the first day of an investigation can be. You have to get the lie of the land, search for witnesses, speak to interested parties and try to identify suspects.'

'You don't need to tell me that, Sergeant.'

'I'm just asking for some understanding, sir.'

'A little sympathy would not go amiss,' said Marmion, producing a glare of disapproval from the superintendent, 'but I can see that it's in short supply at the moment. Very well, sir,' he continued, 'this is how we've been occupying our time.'

After handing him the appointments book, Marmion launched into his report. Though it was concise and briskly delivered, it contained all the relevant facts and left Chatfield with no room for criticism. They had followed procedure dutifully. The superintendent flicked through the pages of the appointments book then passed it back to Marmion.

'When we introduced ourselves at the police station in Chingford,' said Keedy, 'they were only too willing to give us the use of a room and a telephone. All we need is your permission to accept their offer.'

'I'm not convinced it's necessary.'

'What about the commissioner? Should we refer the decision to him?'

'No, Sergeant,' said Chatfield, making no mention of his conversation with Sir Edward Henry. '*I* will make it.'

'Does that mean we operate from here?'

'You may remain in Chingford on the condition that you keep in regular contact with me.'

'That goes without saying, sir.'

'Unfortunately, it doesn't. I haven't forgotten when the pair of you led the investigation into the deaths of those five munitions workers in Hayes. I was being hounded by the press for information and you failed to provide it.'

'We did actually *solve* the crime,' said Marmion.

'Let me in on the secret of how you're doing it this time,' warned Chatfield. 'I'm not just here as a conduit between you and the press. Believe it or not, I may be able to *help* you.'

By way of proof, he listed a number of things they could do on the following day. Many of them had already been decided by Marmion and Keedy but the superintendent did suggest a couple of useful initiatives that had not occurred to them. They were reminded that, beneath his bluster and his idiosyncrasies, Chatfield was an experienced detective

89

who had more than justified his promotion. He already had a firm grasp of details of the case.

'That appointments book is a wellspring of information,' he said. 'It should be your bedside reading tonight, Inspector. Like you, I believe it will contain names that are highly relevant to this investigation but we must not rely solely on it. Pay a second visit to the widow,' he advised. 'Wilder must have had a study or something of that kind. Ask for permission to search it. That remark made by Miss Thompson could be significant,' he argued. 'If Wilder thought that he was being followed, he might have received a threatening letter.'

'Wouldn't he have told his wife about it, sir?' asked Keedy.

'She might be the last person in whom he'd confide.'

'I agree,' said Marmion. 'Mrs Wilder was not told where he was going on the night of the murder and that seems to have been a normal practice between them. She was used to him climbing into bed beside her after midnight.'

'You're assuming that they did still sleep together.'

'Mrs Wilder is a very handsome woman,' said Keedy. 'I can't imagine any husband unwilling to share a bed with her.'

'If I may say so,' said Chatfield, 'that's the observation of a bachelor.'

'Is it?'

'There are lots of reasons why married couples don't sleep together. You may find that out in due course. Illness or disability might be a factor. Didn't I hear that Mrs Wilder has a bad back? It might be uncomfortable for her to have her husband beside her at night.'

'In that case, he might well look elsewhere for pleasure.'

Chatfield bristled. 'Marriage is not entirely about pleasure, Sergeant. That's something else you're destined to find out.'

'I think it's time to go,' said Marmion, jumping in before Keedy could reply. 'We have to make an early start in the morning.'

There was a flurry of farewells, then the detectives withdrew from the office.

Keedy was peevish. 'Why did you interrupt like that?'

'I was only trying to rescue you, Joe.'

'He was taunting me. You should have let me challenge him.'

'I've just saved you from a sermon on the purpose of holy matrimony. Chat is a devout Roman Catholic. He sees things differently from you. Cheer up,' he went on, patting Keedy's shoulder. 'We've got what we wanted. From now on, we'll be based in Chingford. That's ten miles away from the superintendent. Savour that thought.'

'I was only saying what's obvious to anyone,' complained Keedy. 'There's definitely another woman in this case.'

'I agree, Joe. I suspect that we may find more than one.'

Catherine Wilder was about to retire to bed when she heard the doorbell. Pulling her dressing gown around her, she went to the door and unlocked it cautiously. She was surprised to see Audrey Pattinson standing there.

'I know it's late,' said Audrey, nervously, 'but I simply had to come.'

CHAPTER NINE

Ellen Marmion didn't even think about going to bed. No matter how late he was, she was determined to stay up to speak to her husband. The day had left her thoroughly jangled. After a row with Paul, she'd had the embarrassment of hearing that her brother-in-law had been rudely treated by him, then had watched helplessly as her son had hounded his sister unmercifully before going up to his room. With Paul in such a mood, she felt as if she was walking through a minefield. One wrong step was liable to set off a small explosion. What made it worse was the fact that her son offered no apology whatsoever afterwards, reserving the right to feel that *he* was the injured party. Ellen didn't know how much more of his tantrums she could endure.

When she heard the sound of a car pulling up outside, she was on her feet at once. Marmion didn't need to insert his key in the lock because she opened the door for him. Seeing the state that his wife was in, he embraced her and held her for a long time. After closing the door, he took her into the living room. As they sat on the sofa, he listened intently as she poured out her woes. When she'd at last finished, he looked ruefully upwards.

'What time did he go to bed?' he asked.

'It was well before ten. He wants to be up early tomorrow.'

'Has he invited Mavis Tandy here?'

'No,' she replied. 'He's arranged to meet her somewhere but didn't tell me where it was. I didn't feel able to ask him. He's so touchy.'

'He should still remember his manners.'

'I was horrified when he rounded on your brother. Raymond is a saint. He just shrugged it off. Anybody else would have been very offended.'

'I didn't see any signs of sainthood when we were growing up,' recalled Marmion with a grin. 'Raymond could be a mischievous little so-and-so.' His face hardened. 'But he didn't deserve what Paul did to him – and neither did Alice.'

'I just hope that he doesn't say anything like that to Joe.'

'So do I, Ellen. He'll get a flea in his ear if he does. I had my doubts about this engagement at the start but I'm coming to accept it now. Joe has put his past behind him. He really loves Alice and he won't stand for anyone telling her that she's chosen the wrong man. He'll strike back on her behalf.'

'She's not sure if she should tell him what Paul said.'

'I hope that she doesn't.'

'I told her you'd say that. Alice has to do what I've been forced to do – forgive and forget.' She shook her head in dismay. 'I find it very hard to forgive some of the things he's done, Harvey, and I don't think I'll ever forget.'

'I'm sorry that you're in the firing line.'

'I love Paul as a son but I hate what he's turning into.'

'It's not a permanent condition, Ellen. The doctor warned us that there'd be problems during this period of adjustment. He may improve in time.'

'If anything, he's been getting worse.'

Marmion ran a hand through his hair. 'By rights, I really ought to have a stern word with Paul but I have to be off at the crack of dawn.'

'Oh, I'm so sorry,' she said, a palm on her chest. 'Here am I, telling you *my* troubles without even asking what you've been up to. Is it another murder?'

'Yes – and a particularly nasty one at that.'

'Where did it happen?'

He was careful to give her only the outline details of the case. Ellen did not ask for anything more. She was converting what he'd told her into one cold, hard, menacing fact. At a time when she needed him to confront their son, Marmion would be out of the house all the time. She'd be left alone to cope with any further discord.

Ellen made a conscious effort to shake off the sense of dread.

'I shouldn't be so selfish,' she said, apologetically. 'What you've just told me has put everything in a different light. All that I'm upset about are some harsh words and a display of bad temper. A man was stabbed to death in Chingford. I should bear that in mind. His widow will now be mourning his death.'

'That's not a fair comparison, love.'

'It makes me feel so selfish.'

'It shouldn't, Ellen. You're in mourning as well, remember. There's no murder involved maybe but the suffering is still acute. You're grieving over the death of our son. The Paul who went off so blithely to war is not the one who came back.'

'I realise that every time I speak to him.'

Marmion brightened. 'Perhaps this new friend will lift his spirits.'

'I doubt that, Harvey. Her letter was depressing. My fear is that she'll drag Paul down into an even deeper despair. Frankly,' she went on, gripping his arm, 'I wish he'd never even heard of Mavis Tandy.'

Mavis Tandy got to the bus stop long before it was necessary. It was a blustery day but she didn't even feel the wind tugging at her clothing and trying to dislodge her hat. All she could think about was the letter inside her pocket. It was a lifeline to her. Having feared that he wouldn't wish to meet her, she had instead got a warm response, even if it was couched in spidery capital letters. That endeared her to him even more. Paul Marmion was a wounded hero. She'd heard so much about him from Colin Fryatt that she felt she already knew him. He was the strongest link between her and her dead boyfriend. That made him very special.

She was a tall, gawky, freckled-faced young woman with frizzy red hair poking out from beneath her hat. She was wearing her best dress and a smile that combined hope, sadness and excitement. Through Paul Marmion, she would learn the truth about the death in action of the man she'd loved. It was a huge consolation to her. When the bus came, she hopped onto it and found a seat beside the window.

Then she took out his letter and read it through yet again.

Marmion had anticipated awkwardness but it never materialised. Since they'd had such difficulty prising the appointments book out of Catherine Wilder, he thought that she was unlikely to give him ready access to any private papers. In the event, he was pleasantly surprised. She was happy to let him search through her husband's desk. Catherine was much more in control of her emotions that morning. Marmion had noticed it at once. The main reason was that she had now someone on whom she could lean for advice. Grace Chambers, the next-door neighbour, had been supplanted in every sense by Catherine's elder brother, Nathan Clissold, a flabby man in a well-cut dark suit and gleaming black shoes. Marmion could see no resemblance between the siblings. When told that Clissold was a solicitor, Marmion's initial assessment of the man was confirmed. As they were introduced, he noticed Clissold's rather clammy handshake.

'I'll need to be there, of course,' Clissold stipulated.

'Don't you trust me, sir?' asked Marmion.

'It's not a question of trust, Inspector. I'm curious, that's all. I happen to be pathologically tidy whereas my brother-in-law had a Bohemian streak. To put it another way, his study – I'd prefer to call it a lair – is in a complete mess.'

'Simon always was a bit disorganised,' said Catherine with a forlorn smile. 'That's why *I* took charge of his appointments.'

Marmion nodded. 'We thought we recognised your handwriting, Mrs Wilder. By the way, I noticed that the last person with whom he danced was a Miss Odele Thompson.'

'He and Odele had regular rehearsals, Inspector. That was vital.'

'We spoke to the lady. She told us of an incident in Shaftesbury Avenue.'

'That was Simon's spiritual home. He loved to hang around dressings rooms with friends. Whether it was a play or a stage musical, he always knew someone in almost any cast.'

'Tell us about this incident,' said Clissold.

'Oh, it was something and nothing, sir,' replied Marmion. 'It's just that he turned around suddenly as if aware that someone was following him.'

'And were they?'

'Miss Thompson saw nobody.'

'Then there was nobody there,' said Catherine, dismissively. 'That's why he never mentioned the incident to me. Besides,' she added, waspishly, 'I wouldn't trust everything that Odele says. She is inclined to dramatise.'

Clissold took charge. 'Shall we start work, Inspector?'

They followed the same route as on the previous day. Iris Goodliffe was glad to be back at work, having spent a long, dull, lonely evening in her flat, trying to mend a dress in poor light and managing to draw blood from a finger. Much as she enjoyed her new job, she foresaw a number of similarly arid evenings ahead of her and she said as much in blunt terms. The hint was too large to be ignored but Alice was still not ready to spend leisure time with her after work.

'You could always pop back to see your parents,' she suggested.

'I became a policewoman to escape them.'

'What about your sister?'

'Evelyn and her husband are still too wrapped up in each other to want me there. You may not believe this, Alice, but their idea of fun is to play chess together.'

'And your sister actually *enjoys* it?'

'She loves it – but only because she usually wins. I can just about play draughts. Chess is well beyond me.'

'It's only a case of application, Iris.'

'Can *you* play it?'

'Strangely enough, I can. Daddy taught me when I was much younger. We had a holiday in Torquay and it rained every day so we played cards most of the time. We also had this little chess set.'

'Do you think you could teach *me* to play?'

'Oh, no – I'm nowhere near good enough to do that.'

'We could learn together, Alice.'

'I just don't have the time.'

'What a pity!'

'That's the way it is, I fear.'

It was a paradox. Alice was desperate to speak to someone about the argument she'd had with her brother and she had a friend beside her who would be a highly sympathetic confidante. Yet she simply could not let Iris into her family somehow. The woman's urge for a closer relationship was bordering on desperation. Her fervent desire to be included was the very thing that excluded her. Alice had to suppress sad thoughts about her visit home and concentrate on her duties. Inspector Gale would expect a report when they returned. There were some incidents early on to divert them. They had to stop some children from throwing stones at each other, help an old man to his feet when he tripped up and speak to a woman who accosted them. Smart, shapely, well spoken and in her thirties, she turned to Alice.

'You don't remember me, do you?' she said.

'I can't say that I do.'

'It was a couple of weeks ago, dear. You and that policeman moved me on.'

'Oh, yes,' said Alice, looking at her more closely. 'I recognise you now.'

The woman smiled. 'As soon as you'd gone, I went straight back.'

After a cheerful wave, she strode off down the street. Iris looked after her.

'Who was that, Alice?'

'I never knew her name.'

'She seemed to know you.'

Alice grinned. 'Let's just say that you've had a new experience, Iris.

99

You won't be able to claim that you've never met a prostitute now.'

Iris was flabbergasted. 'So you mean . . . ?'

'We moved her on from her pitch.'

'But she looked so respectable and . . . so healthy.'

'She looks very different at night when she's searching for customers.'

'Goodness me!' exclaimed Iris. 'And there she was, right in front of me.'

Alice was amused by her naivety. Iris continued to talk about the woman for the next five minutes. It was only when they paused to cross the road that she changed the subject.

'What sort of evening did *you* have last night?'

It was a question that Alice had feared because it revived some unpleasant memories. She found it impossible to give an honest answer.

'We had a lovely time,' she heard herself saying.

'How was your brother?'

'Oh, Paul was starting to behave like his old self. It was a joy to see him.'

Paul had suggested the park because the bus stopped right outside the gate. All that he had to do was to walk down a gravel pathway for a couple of minutes to one of the benches. He was relying on the fact that his letter had actually been delivered that morning and that Mavis would comply with his wishes. It never crossed his mind that she wouldn't turn up. He was also counting on good weather but, in the event of rain, he hoped that the wrought iron bandstand would give them some protection. As it was, bright sunshine had dispelled the gusting wind and was now lighting up the park, bringing out the birds in profusion. He could hear them twittering merrily away. Paul felt better than he'd been for weeks. Inhaling deeply, he thrust out his chest. Because of his poor eyesight, he made slow, deliberate progress until he saw the vague outline of the bandstand looming up before him. In younger days, he and Colin Fryatt had played on it many times, daring each other to climb to the very top of its ornate ironwork. It was another reason why he'd selected that particular spot for the meeting. It kindled rich boyhood memories. He and his best friend had enjoyed so many wonderful adventures in the park. A different one now beckoned. Choosing an empty bench, he sat down to wait. Within minutes, he felt a soft hand on his shoulder.

Mavis Tandy had a gentle voice with a trace of a Kentish accent.

'You must be Paul,' she said.

Simon Wilder had taken over one of the bedrooms as his study. Marmion was glad that it was so large and had such a high ceiling. He would not have enjoyed spending time with Clissold in a confined space. Although the solicitor claimed that he was there out of curiosity, he was watching Marmion carefully and asking to examine anything that the inspector found. It was inhibiting. Wilder's threefold passions – dance, theatre and photography – were on display in abundance. The walls were plastered with overlapping posters of dances and plays in which he'd been involved. Marmion noticed the framed poster of Bernard Shaw's comedy, *You Never Can Tell*. Listed among the cast were the names of Simon Wilder and Catherine Clissold. It was during the run of that play, Marmion remembered, that the couple had first met. Clissold looked over his shoulder.

'You can see why my sister was happy to change her name to Wilder,' he said. 'Her given name does not exactly have a theatrical ring to it, alas. Both of them were committed to a career onstage at that point. Their mutual love of dance took them in another direction.'

'So I understand, sir.'

'It was a big decision to make but . . . it was what they wanted.'

'Did you ever see Mr and Mrs Wilder dance?'

'No, Inspector. My taste runs to opera and orchestral music.'

'But they were described as the nearest thing to Vernon and Irene Castle.'

'To this day,' said Clissold, as if taking pride in the fact, 'those names are meaningless to me. Very little about America has a purchase on my attention.'

The roll-top desk was littered with letters and bills, some of the latter as yet unpaid. Marmion searched the drawers and found each one crammed with theatre programmes, dance advertisements or correspondence with a solicitor.

'I assumed that *you* would handle any legal matters,' said Marmion.

'Clients in the family are never a good idea,' returned the other, loftily. 'Besides, I'm not a low-grade lawyer dealing with the more mundane issues of life. I specialise in criminal law, Inspector. I'm on *your* side.'

'I see,' said Marmion, concealing his dislike of the man.

He turned his attention to the two large cameras that stood on a small cabinet in a corner. Both were of good quality and partnered with a tripod. Several books on photography were piled carelessly on an oak bookcase. There were also books on dancing, one of which, Marmion noted, had been written by Vernon and Irene Castle. He could not resist thumbing through it.

'I doubt that it's an enthralling read,' said Clissold with disdain. 'I'm a Trollope man myself. You get a good story, engaging characters and some priceless humour all rolled into one.'

'Given the circumstances,' said Marmion, putting the volume aside, 'you'll understand why I'm more interested in Mr Wilder's reading habits than in yours. Everything in this study helps to define the man. That's why it's important to see every bit of it.' He reached out to take a photograph album from the bottom shelf of the bookcase. 'Are these photographs that *he* took, I wonder?'

'I daresay that they are. Simon was a very gifted photographer.'

Marmion opened the album and found himself looking at a photograph of Simon and Catherine Wilder at a dance contest. Striking an imperious pose, they were standing in front of a dance band. There were several other photographs of the couple and they clearly had elegance and glamour when dressed in their finery. Marmion then came to a collection of photographs taken by Wilder himself. Featuring a series of female dancers – and the occasional male – they were of noticeably better quality. The women were of varying age and build. What they shared was an obvious delight in facing a camera with Wilder behind it.

'There's your answer, Inspector,' said Clissold, wrinkling his nose. 'Look at the way they're smiling at Simon. They're infatuated with him. Imagine what their husbands must think. My brother-in-law was a handsome man who danced with their wives to suggestive music and had a licence for bodily contact with them. That's enough to arouse anyone's jealousy. Search among the husbands of Simon's pupils. That's where your killer is lurking.'

'Thank you for your advice, sir,' said Marmion, coolly. 'I had already made that deduction but, in my case, it was tempered by caution. I never jump to hasty conclusions. They're invariably wrong.'

They'd spent a long time searching the study and tidying it as they went along. During the remaining ten minutes, Clissold maintained a resentful silence. When they'd sifted through other albums and the last pile of correspondence, he rubbed his beefy hands together.

'Right,' he said, 'that's everything, I fancy.'

'Not quite,' argued Marmion, gazing around, 'there's one last item.'

'What are you talking about?'

'I've been through Mr Wilder's appointments book and had a long talk to his accompanist, Mrs Pattinson. Both sources told the same story. The dance studio was very profitable. Money changed hands on a daily basis. Your brother-in-law may have been very casual with regards to everything else but he'd surely protect the day's takings. I sense that there's a safe in the house somewhere – most likely, in here.'

'You only have to ask my sister. Catherine will tell you.'

'That would be cheating, Mr Clissold. I'd rather sniff it out myself, if you don't mind.' He walked across to a large and rather garish painting of Spanish dancers at some kind of festival. Lifting it gently from its hook, he swung it aside to reveal a safe set into the wall. Marmion smiled at his companion.

'You didn't know *that* was there, sir, did you?'

Though he would have preferred to accompany the inspector, Keedy accepted that someone had to stay at the police station for the routine task of taking statements from potential witnesses. The murder had been given a measure of prominence on the inside pages of the newspapers and there was an appeal for people to come forward if they had any information that might be of value to the police. As was so often the case, Keedy had to put up with spurious witnesses who invented stories in order to feel a sense of importance they lacked in their normal lives. Keedy was brusque with them and threatened to make an arrest for wasting police time. The duty sergeant at Chingford police station saw three or four people scuttling out of the room with their tails between their legs. Keedy had seen through them at once.

A team of detectives had been going from house to house in the area where the murder had taken place but none of them had found any useful intelligence. Those who had been out late that night had been watching the Zeppelin raid and it had been an irresistible distraction. Keedy was realistic. Nobody was going to walk into the police station with positive evidence regarding the killer's identity because the crime had taken place in a dark alley. He and Marmion would have to beaver away until the clues began to emerge. During a long gap when he was left alone, Keedy was pleased when a young police constable brought in a cup of tea.

'Thanks,' he said. 'It's much appreciated.'

'There's a lady outside, sir. She's asking to see you.'

'Is she drunk or sober?'

'Oh, she's very sober, Sergeant.'

'That will be a welcome change. Two of the so-called "witnesses" I had the misfortune to interview came in here stinking of beer.'

'This lady wears perfume, sir – a very nice one, actually.'

'Did she give a name?'

'Yes, sir – it's Miss Thompson. She claims to have met you.'

'Send her in, Constable.'

When the man went out, Keedy forgot about his tea and rose to his feet. He smoothed down his hair with the flat of his hand and straightened his jacket. Odele Thompson was then shown in and the door was closed behind her. She seemed pleased that Keedy was alone. For his part, he noticed how much attention she'd paid to her appearance. When they'd called on her the previous day, she'd worn little make-up and was dressed in a blouse and a loose skirt. Odele had now used her cosmetics liberally and put on a navy-blue suit that accentuated her figure. On one lapel was a gold brooch in the shape of a dancing couple.

After an exchange of greetings, she accepted the seat he offered her and adjusted her skirt. Keedy sat down again. She held his gaze for a moment and, before he could stop it happening, he felt a frisson of pleasure.

'What can I do for you, Miss Thompson?' he asked, politely.

'To begin with, you can call me Odele.'

'If that's what you prefer.'

'What's *your* first name, Sergeant?'

'I'd rather you call me by my rank.'

'At least I can know your Christian name, can't I?'

'It's Joseph, actually, but I'm Joe to most people.'

'I'm not most people,' she said, tossing her hair. 'Joseph is a nice name. And it's about as Christian as it could be.' She laughed, then became businesslike. 'But I didn't come here to discuss names. I've thought of something that may be relevant to the investigation.'

'Oh – what was that?'

'I was too dazed even to consider it at the time but it hit me this morning as I was looking through the programme for the British Dance Championships.'

'I'm listening, Miss Thompson . . .' He corrected himself. 'Odele, I should say.'

'Well, that's it – the championships.'

He was bewildered. 'What about them?'

'Don't you see?'

'Frankly, I don't.'

'That's because you don't know what a cut-throat business the world of dance can be. We may look graceful as we glide around the dance floor but most of us are intensely competitive. We have to be, in order to survive.'

'Is there a big reward for the winner of this dance championship?'

'It's not the money that matters, Joseph, and it's not the gold medal or the cup. It's the kudos. To be able to say that you are British Champions lifts you above the herd. Simon won the title on two occasions with Catherine,' she said, 'and he promised me that our turn would be next.'

'I'm sorry that Fate robbed you of it, Odele.'

'It wasn't fate who stabbed him to death. It was someone who'd stop at nothing to prevent us winning the title.'

'Do you have any particular person in mind?'

'I have two possible suspects to offer you.'

'Which of the two is the prime suspect?'

'That would have to be Allan Redmond. No, no,' she went on as he started to write the name down, 'there's no need for that.' She opened her bag to extract a piece of paper. 'I have both names here and the addresses where you'll find them.' She gave him the paper then clasped his hand before he could move it away. 'Don't tell them that I put you on to them, will you?'

'There's no need for you to be mentioned at all.'

'If it's known that I'm behind this, there could be repercussions.'

'In that event, you'll be offered complete protection.'

'Thank you.' Realising that she was still holding his hand, she let it go. Keedy was a trifle disappointed. 'I could be wrong, of course, but I've seen the lengths people will go to. Both of the people I've named there were close rivals of ours. Question them, Joe.'

'We will, don't worry.' He glanced down at the first name. 'Do you really believe that Allan Redmond is capable of a savage attack?'

'I know only too well that he is.'

'Why is that?'

She rose from her chair. 'Let's just say that we used to be . . . acquaintances,' she said, evasively. 'Please keep me informed of any developments.' She held his gaze once more. 'You know where I live.'

CHAPTER TEN

Paul Marmion had only ever seen her through the prism of Colin Fryatt's eyes. His friend had described her in glowing terms and – because of his impaired sight – that was how Paul now viewed her. He truly believed that Mavis Tandy was beautiful. Through his milky vision, he couldn't see that she was, in fact, a rather plain, thin-lipped young woman with an ugly mole on her cheek. She, however, had been given a far more accurate description of Paul and had been able to pick him out instantly. Until she got close to him, he seemed to have survived action at the front without any visible injury. It was only when she sat beside him on the bench that she saw the telltale scars on his face and the constant fluttering of his eyelids.

'What happened, then?' she asked.

'I don't know, Mavis. The explosion knocked me senseless. I've no idea how long I must have been there. I felt like death. I had shrapnel wounds all over.'

'Where was Colin?'

'He was quite close. I was able to crawl to him.'

'In his last letter, he told me that the two of you had agreed that, if you had to die, you'd rather do it together.'

'That's true,' said Paul, 'we did agree that. To be honest, there've been

109

times when I wish I *had* been killed alongside him at the Somme.'

'No!' she exclaimed. 'That's a terrible thing to wish for.'

'It's like hell some days.'

'Why is that?'

'You wouldn't understand, Mavis.'

'Do you feel guilty?'

'That's part of it.'

'What else is there?'

'It doesn't matter.'

'Yes, it does. You can tell me, Paul.'

Some children were playing with a ball nearby and making a lot of noise. One of them kicked the ball and it bounced off Paul's shin. He flinched slightly.

'Can we go somewhere else?' he suggested.

'Yes, of course.'

'There's a cafe not far away. We can have a cup of tea.'

'I'd like that, Paul.'

'I don't want to hold you up.'

'You're not.'

'If you've got somewhere to go . . .'

'I want to stay with you as long as I can,' she said, taking him by the arm and easing him off the bench. 'I can't tell you how much this means to me. Let's have that cup of tea, shall we? I want to hear a lot more about Colin.' She squeezed his arm. 'Can you manage?'

'It's easier if you hold me, Mavis,' he said, relishing her touch and warming to her with each second. 'It's very kind of you.'

When Marmion returned to the police station, he found that Keedy was interviewing a man. He did not have to wait long. The door soon opened and Keedy more or less propelled his visitor towards the exit, thrusting him out into the street.

'Who was that?' asked Marmion.

'It was someone who came to confess to the murder.'

'That was obliging of him.'

'All he had was a ridiculous cock-and-bull story.'

'We usually get one or two fantasists.'

'This idiot gave himself away completely,' said Keedy. 'He claimed to have stabbed the victim once in the chest because of an unpaid gambling debt. *You* saw him. A skinny little runt like that wouldn't have the strength to do what the real killer did. That's why I threw him out.'

'Did I catch a whiff of alcohol as he went past?'

'He was reeking of it.'

In order to compare notes, they went into the room that had been set aside for them. After hanging his hat on the back of the door, Marmion sat down and talked about his search of the victim's study.

'Mrs Wilder's brother stood over me all the time,' he said, bitterly. 'I'm surprised he didn't give me a bill for his services afterwards. You know what solicitors are like.'

'I avoid them like the plague.'

'We uncovered some interesting things but nothing that gave me an idea of who the killer could possibly be. My hopes rose when I discovered the safe but we were unable to open it. Mrs Wilder didn't know what the combination was or where her husband kept it hidden.'

'In the safe, perhaps?' joked Keedy.

'In the end, I had to send for a locksmith. He'll be there this afternoon so I'll go back then. All in all,' he added, 'it was rather disappointing. I expected to get some kind of lead.'

'But the cupboard was bare.'

'And I had Nathan Clissold breathing down my neck. He was worse than Chat. The result is that we still have no suspects.'

'Yes, we do,' said Keedy with a grin. 'In fact, we have two.'

'Where did they come from?'

'I had a visit from a helpful member of the public – Miss Thompson, though she asked me to call her by her first name.'

'Be careful, Joe. You've been warned about that. Keep her at a distance.'

'I will, I promise you.'

'What did she have to say for herself?'

Keedy gave him a brief account of the conversation with Odele Thompson, omitting any mention of the pleasure he'd taken in her company. He was confident that she might have opened up a productive new avenue in the investigation. Marmion was more sceptical.

'I'm not convinced, Joe.'

'It all sounded very plausible to me.'

'Why kill a man when he could easily have been disabled in some way? The level of violence was quite unnecessary.'

'Both of the men hold grudges against Wilder, apparently.'

'You and I hold grudges against our dear superintendent. Does that mean we feel impelled to stab him repeatedly?'

'I have been tempted, Harv.'

'Seriously, you have to remember the nature of the injuries. They were put there by someone with more than a desire to win a dance competition.'

'It's the British Championship.'

'I never even knew that such a thing exists.'

'According to Odele – Miss Thompson, that is – dancers would kill to win it.'

'She was speaking metaphorically.'

'I don't think so,' said Keedy. 'These men are worth talking to, especially Allan Redmond. He and Miss Thompson obviously knew each other at one time and she regrets it.'

'So she's getting her own back by naming him as a murder suspect.'

'There's more to it than that.'

Marmion sat back in his chair and thought about the new development. It aroused his curiosity more than his suspicion. Talking to the two men would at least give them insight into the world of dance and that would be helpful.

'Very well,' he decided. 'Speak to them.'

'Who will man the barricades here?'

'One of our lads can do that. They'd much rather be sitting in here, meeting exotic dancers like Miss Thompson – Odele to you – than pounding the pavements and knocking on doors. You talk to Redmond and this other chap. What's his name?'

'Tom Atterbury.'

'See if there's any substance in what she told you.'

'Meanwhile,' said Keedy, 'you could do something for me.'

'What's that?'

'When you go back to Wilder's house this afternoon, mention those two names to his wife. She's bound to know them. I'd be interested in her reaction.'

'Prepare to be disappointed.'

'Why?'

'Mrs Wilder has had time to absorb the shock of her husband's death by now. If she thought for one moment that Redmond or Atterbury had anything to do with it, don't you think she'd have been urging us to go after them? I'm sorry, Joe,' he went on. 'When two suspects pop up

113

out of nowhere, then it's usually too good to be true. I fancy that Odele may be leading you up the garden path.'

Keedy came dangerously close to blushing.

Seated on the sofa, Catherine Wilder looked down the list of things that had to be done in preparation for the funeral. It had been prepared by her brother and typed out carefully by his secretary. Since her husband had died an unnatural death, there would be a post-mortem and an inquest. She had no idea when the body would be released to her. Meanwhile, there were lots of people who had to be informed of the tragedy. Some might find out about it reading the newspapers, but others would not. Catherine and her brother had never been close but she valued his presence now, even though he'd disapproved of her marriage to Wilder.

He watched her intently and saw more resignation in her face than evidence of bereavement. She had always been a strong-willed woman with a tendency to ignore the advice of others. Nathan Clissold was pleased that she was now in a position where she was prepared to rely on his counsel.

'What did you think of Inspector Marmion?' he asked.

'He seems very competent.'

'It's not his competence that's in question, Catherine. I took exception to his manner. He came within inches of being sarcastic.'

'Did you provoke him in some way?'

'Of course I didn't. You know better than to ask such a thing.' He sat forward in his armchair, corrugating his jacket and waistcoat. 'Why didn't Simon give you the combination to that safe?'

'It was his. Why would I need to look in it?'

'Didn't you keep your jewellery in there?'

'No,' she said, 'I have an even larger safe in the bedroom. It needs a key as well as a combination. Simon wasn't able to unlock it. We guarded our privacy, you see.'

'I find that strange in a married couple who always showed a front of mutual dependence to the general public. What they saw were two people who appeared to live in each other's pockets.'

'They saw what we wanted them to see, Nathan.'

'You mean that you were both playing a part?'

'Isn't that what we all do to some extent?'

'Not in my case,' he said, frostily. 'I don't take on any role. I am exactly what you see – a highly successful solicitor with a wonderful wife and family.'

'Children were out of the question for us. Dancing always came first.'

'Those days are past,' he said.

There was a long silence until she was nudged by a memory.

'I had a visitor last night,' she said.

'Was it that lady from next-door?'

'No, Grace had already given me far too much of her time. I sent her home. To be honest, her sympathy was a trifle oppressive.'

'So who was this visitor?'

'It was Audrey Pattinson, our accompanist. I was just about to go to bed when she turned up.'

'What did she want?'

'Comfort, that's all. She just wanted to *be* with someone.'

'Isn't she married?'

'Oh, yes. Her husband is a retired estate agent. After a career in the army, he turned his hand to selling property.'

'Why couldn't he provide the comfort?'

'Martin Pattinson is not that kind of husband, Nathan. As a matter of fact, he wasn't even there. It was his night for going to his club. He doesn't come back until after midnight, apparently.'

'He left his wife *alone* when she was in need of sympathy?'

'That's what she said.'

Martin Pattinson returned to find that the house was empty. Since his wife had not spoken about going out that morning, he wondered where she was. It did not take him long to work out where she might be. As a result, he lifted the lid of the piano stool and saw that several sheets of music were missing. It was decisive proof. Pattinson went straight out and walked the short distance to the dance studio. The door was closed but unlocked. As he eased it open, he could hear the sound of the piano playing a slow waltz. At the far end of the hall, filling it with lilting music, was his wife, seated at the piano up on the stage. Oblivious to the fact that he was there, she played beautifully and imagined couples circling the floor at a dance. She took immense pleasure from her work, striking the keys hard to produce more volume than she usually achieved. Tears were streaming down her face as she played a melodious requiem for a lost friend. When she finished the waltz, she needed a handkerchief to dab at her face. Only then did she become aware of her husband's presence.

He strolled meaningfully down the hall.

'You never told me that you were coming here,' he said, quietly.

'I felt the need to play the piano, Martin.'

'You could have done that at home on a much better instrument.'

'It's not the same.'

'I think you should finish now.'

Audrey was given no choice in the matter. With great reluctance, she gathered up the music she'd brought and put it into her satchel. After closing the lid of the piano, she caressed it with her hand as if bidding farewell to a favourite pet. When she came down the steps from the stage, Pattinson was waiting for her with hand outstretched.

'I'll have the key, please,' he said. 'You won't be coming here again.'

Mavis Tandy never tired of asking questions and Paul Marmion never tired of answering them. Though they were ostensibly talking about Colin Fryatt, they were also getting to know each other. Paul was finding out things about her that his friend had not bothered to tell him. A vicar's daughter, she'd had a better schooling than Paul and spoke with an educated voice. When she first met Fryatt, Mavis had only been helping out in a tea shop because a friend who normally worked there had been taken ill. Since she'd got to know a soldier, she'd felt an even stronger urge to go to the front as a nurse. Hoping it would bring her closer to him, Fryatt had encouraged her to go to France.

She kept repeating one question as if she'd forgotten his answer to it.

'Did Colin ever talk about me?'

'He never stopped, Mavis.'

'What did he say?'

'He said that you meant everything to him.' Her face lit up. 'In fact, he said it so often that some of the other lads teased him.'

'Did you tell him about *your* girlfriend, Paul?'

'Ah, well . . .'

She was immediately apologetic. 'Oh, have I said the wrong thing? I'm sorry. I thought that every soldier had someone back home. That's what Colin told me, anyway. Until he met me, he claimed he was the odd man out.'

'Yes, he was.'

'So . . .'

If their friendship was going to develop into something more serious, Paul decided that he had to let her know that he was available. He therefore admitted that he'd had a girlfriend when he went off to war but that she was terrified that he would either die or come home with horrific wounds. Unable to cope with the prospect, she'd stopped writing to him. When he came home on leave, she told him that they were better apart. The picture he painted was very different from the truth. In fact, it was he who'd driven away a loyal, loving young woman by his fits of anger, his drinking and the coarse language he'd picked up in the trenches.

'That's dreadful, Paul. She should have stood by you.'

'I was banking on that, but it never happened.'

'Are you still in touch with her?'

'No, Mavis, we've drifted apart completely.'

'So you're on your own.'

'I can manage.'

'It's so unfair to let you down like that.'

'I'm not complaining. The past is past.'

He smiled bravely in the hope that she would say something affectionate to him. In the event, there was a long silence. A waitress came to clear away the things on their table in order to remind them how long they'd been sitting there over a pot of tea and a couple of scones. Minutes later, Mavis revived the conversation.

'Did Colin ever talk about *me*?'

It took the locksmith a considerable time to open the safe in the study but he eventually managed it. Marmion thanked him and moved forward to inspect the contents. As before, he was accompanied by

Nathan Clissold, who peered over his shoulder as if expecting some dark secret to emerge. In the event, the only surprise was that a substantial amount of cash had built up in the safe. For the rest, they found Simon Wilder's will and a series of legal documents. While Clissold went through the latter, Marmion counted the money then called Catherine into the study.

'There are hundreds of pounds here, Mrs Wilder.'

She was taken aback. 'Are you *sure*?'

'Count it for yourself, if you wish.'

'No, no, I'll take your word for it, Inspector.'

'You obviously didn't anticipate an amount as large as this.'

'It's true,' she said. 'Since you have the appointments book, you can see that money came in on a daily basis. I checked it carefully. Simon always kept it in his safe until the end of the week then took it to the bank.'

'How do you explain the fact that so much money is still here?'

'To be honest, I'm at a loss to do so.'

'Did he have another source of income?' asked her brother.

'No, he didn't, Nathan.'

'Then he was obviously not banking the income from the dance studio.'

'But he was,' she insisted, 'because he gave me the bank statements at the end of each month to file away.' She turned to Marmion. 'In case you don't know, Inspector, the dance studio is in *my* name. When Simon and I first married, he had some difficulty raising a loan to buy the hall. I stepped in to provide the funding.'

'My advice was that she shouldn't risk her own money,' said Clissold, firmly. 'I couldn't see that the studio was commercially viable. As it happens, I was wrong about that and I admit it freely. It actually flourished. On one thing, however, I was right,' he continued. 'I urged Catherine to retain sole ownership of the place. That annoyed Simon intensely but it was the sensible thing to do. In the event of a divorce, I wanted Catherine to have a property that was hers by right.'

'I never even considered the possibility of divorce,' she protested.

'*I* did.'

'That was an irrelevance to me, Nathan. I just wanted what I actually paid for.'

As the two of them bickered away for a couple of minutes, Marmion could see that there were similarities between them, after all. Both had independent wealth and a determination to safeguard it. Each of them was upset to discover that Wilder had an apparent source of income about which they knew nothing. Clissold chided his sister for not being vigilant enough and she countered by saying that he was happy to keep his own wife in the dark about family financial affairs.

Marmion cut the argument short by changing the subject completely.

'I'm sorry to interrupt,' he said, 'but I have a question for Mrs Wilder.'

'My apologies, Inspector,' she returned. 'Our differences of opinion should have been kept to ourselves.'

'I'll leave you alone,' said Clissold, peevishly.

Still seething about the reference to his wife, he went out of the room.

'You must excuse my brother,' she said. 'He hates to be challenged. More to the point, he and Simon did not see eye to eye. It caused . . . complications. However,' she went on, 'you said that you have a question for me.'

'What can you tell me about a man named Allan Redmond?'

She blinked in surprise. 'Why do you ask that?'

'You do know him, I assume.'

'Everyone in the dance world knows Allan. He's a brilliant dancer.'

'And I believe he's a leading contender in the British Dance Championships.'

'He's a leading contender in *any* competition.'

'So he and your husband were fierce rivals.'

'Oh,' she said, shaking her head, 'I can see what you're getting at and you're quite wrong, Inspector. Allan Redmond is a ferocious competitor but he'd never stoop to murder.'

'I gather that he's unlikely to mourn Mr Wilder's death.'

'That's true.'

'Did they ever lock horns?'

'They did so many times. They were natural adversaries. You must know what it's like to have an adversary, Inspector.'

Marmion thought of Claude Chatfield. 'Yes, I do.'

'It's just a fact of life. You can forget about Allan Redmond.'

'We'll have a word with him, that's all.'

'Then you'll be wasting your time.'

'What about Tom Atterbury?'

Catherine tensed. 'I never thought of him,' she said. 'Now that I do, I can see that he would be well worth looking at closely. He's the person to go after, Inspector. Tom Atterbury is a sly, calculating man. More to the point, he has a few scores to settle with Simon – and he's quite capable of doing it in a dark alley.'

Since the house was much closer to Chingford than the one in which Allan Redmond lived, Keedy decided to interview Tom Atterbury first. When he set out from the police station, he had no idea what to expect but he was quite undaunted by Marmion's opinion that he was being misled by Odele Thompson. He had more faith in her instincts. Atterbury, he discovered, lived in a large but crumbling house in Islington, overlooking Regent's Canal. The property had been divided up into flats and Atterbury occupied the ground floor. The rooms were spacious and filled with tasteful decoration. There was a piano in the bay window. Arranged on top of it was an array of silver cups and other trophies from dance contests.

Atterbury was a tall, lean, slightly sinister individual in his early forties with prominent cheekbones and watchful eyes. When Keedy explained the reason for his visit, the other man pretended that he was hearing the news for the first time.

'Simon was *murdered*?' he gasped. 'That's incredible.'

'I assumed that you'd already know, sir.'

'How could I, Sergeant? I rarely read the newspapers. They're always full of such dispiriting news. When and where did it happen?'

'Mr Wilder was stabbed to death two nights ago in Chingford.'

'Poor Catherine – I must write to express my condolences.'

'How well do you know Mrs Wilder?'

'I admire her as a dancer but we were never really on visiting terms.'

Keedy saw an opportunity to learn something about Odele Thompson.

'How did she compare to Mr Wilder's other dancing partner?'

'Oh, she was far superior in my view,' said Atterbury. 'Catherine was a natural dancer whereas Odele is a manufactured one, if you understand my meaning. That's not to say she isn't extremely competent – but you need more than competence to excel on a dance floor. Catherine could float. Odele will never do that.' His eyelids narrowed. 'Why exactly are you here, Sergeant?'

'I'd like to put a few routine questions to you, sir.'

'Ask anything you like.'

'Thank you, sir.'

'I'm not a suspect, surely?'

'Where were you two nights ago?'

Atterbury was stung by the implication. 'What's that got to do with it?' he demanded. 'Look, who gave you my name in the first place? Is someone trying to make trouble for me?'

'A moment ago,' Keedy reminded him, 'you said that I could ask anything I liked. And what I'd like to know is what you were doing two nights ago.'

'I was not killing Simon Wilder, I can assure you.'

'Then what *were* you doing, sir?'

'That's my business.'

'In the circumstances, we have to make it *our* business as well.'

Atterbury glared at him but Keedy remained calm and absorbed his hostility with ease. He'd already taken a dislike to the man, not least because Atterbury wore a much more expensive suit than he could afford. The dancer wore accessories – spats, a cravat, a carnation in his buttonhole – that would have looked absurd on a detective. On Atterbury, however, they reinforced the impression of a vain man with an eye for the latest fashion. He was impatient.

'I hope that this won't take long, Sergeant,' he said, irritably. 'I was just about to go out when you called. In answer to your question, I dined with some friends and got back here around midnight. And yes, I will happily give you the name of those friends if you refuse to take my word for it.' He spat out his question. 'Is that a sufficient alibi for you?'

'I'm afraid that it isn't, sir.'

'Why not, damn you?'

'Can anyone vouch for your return here?'

'Don't you believe me?'

'We always like corroboration, sir.'

'I've given you my word as a gentleman – isn't that enough?'

'To be candid,' said Keedy, 'it isn't. I've met too many gentlemen who've committed unspeakable crimes, so I take nobody's word at face value.'

'You're being very offensive, Sergeant.'

'And you're evading my question.'

After an attempt at bluster, Atterbury controlled his temper.

'I came back here around midnight,' he said, slowly, 'so it's more than possible that one of the other residents will have heard me letting myself into the building. My wife is away at the moment, visiting sick parents, so I can't ask her to confirm that I went to bed shortly after my return. What she will tell you, however, is that I'm a heavy sleeper. Once my head hits the pillow, I drift off into oblivion very quickly.'

'When did you last see Simon Wilder?'

'It was certainly not two nights ago, Sergeant.'

'Was it at some kind of dance competition?'

'No,' replied Atterbury, 'it was at the theatre, actually. I bumped into him as he was coming out of the stage door at the Haymarket. We exchanged a few words and that was that.'

'Were any of the words spoken in anger?'

'They were icily cold. We've never been friends.'

'Why was that, sir?'

'I'd rather not speak ill of the dead.'

'I daresay you spoke ill of him when he was alive. Did you accept that he was a better dancer than you?'

Atterbury blenched. 'He was not better,' he retorted. 'He was just very clever at persuading people that he was. Simon was a flashy dancer.

He favoured style over substance and I deplore that.'

It was a strange remark for a man to whom style clearly meant so much but Keedy didn't point that out to him. He kept on prodding until Atterbury let out some of the bile simmering inside him. For all sorts of reasons, he had despised Wilder. Having said he would not disparage his dead rival, he summed him up in a way that showed his deep dislike of the man.

'The truth about Simon Wilder is this,' he declared. 'He was ruthless, selfish, single-minded, disloyal, dishonest, prone to steal ideas from others like myself and thoroughly loathsome. Does that answer your question, Sergeant?'

Keedy took out his notepad. 'Could I have the names of those friends with whom you dined two nights ago, sir?'

CHAPTER ELEVEN

When he left Catherine Wilder and her obnoxious brother, Marmion only had to go a few hundred yards before he reached his next destination. He was calling at the home of Colette Orme, the woman who'd had the dance lesson immediately prior to Odele Thompson two days earlier. In answer to his knock on the door, he heard someone coming slowly along the passageway. The door was then opened by a fresh-faced young man leaning heavily on a walking stick. When Marmion introduced himself, the man smiled with relief.

'Thank heavens you've come, Inspector!' he said. 'Colette has been in despair since we heard the news. I'm her brother, Dennis, by the way. Come in.'

He stood aside to let Marmion into the house. As they went into the cramped living room, he could see how awkwardly Orme moved and how his left arm hung limply by his side. He indicated a chair for his visitor.

'I'll fetch my sister,' he said. 'I may be a little while.'

Left alone, Marmion was able to take his bearings. The house was much smaller than the one he'd just left and it had none of the comforts of the Wilder residence. But it was clean, tidy and relatively cosy. Either side of the clock on the mantelpiece were two framed photographs. One was of Colette Orme, taken at a dance, looking radiant in a long taffeta dress and beaming at the camera as she stood beside Simon Wilder. He had his arm around her waist and wore an almost proprietary smile. Yet it was the other photograph that interested Marmion because it showed Dennis Orme in uniform somewhere at the front. Tall, proud and with a touch of arrogance in his expression, he looked very different from the wounded soldier who'd let Marmion into the house.

Colette had also changed from the slim, attractive and happy young woman in the photograph. When her brother showed her into the room, she was morose and stooping. After he'd introduced her to their visitor, Orme lowered himself gingerly onto the sofa and she sat beside him.

'How could something so terrible happen, Inspector?' she wailed.

'It's our job to find out,' said Marmion.

'Simon was the most wonderful person in the world. He believed in me.'

'Quite right,' said her brother, loyally. 'You're very talented.'

'What use is that *now*?'

She snatched a handkerchief from her sleeve and held it to her eyes to stem the tears that gushed out. After consoling her, Orme looked across at Marmion.

'Mr Wilder changed my sister's life,' he said. 'In fact, he changed all our lives because Dad and I were both part of it.'

It had all begun, he explained, when Simon Wilder had attended an amateur production of a play that featured young female dancers. He'd been so impressed by Colette's talent that he'd spoken to her afterwards and recommended that she took instruction at his studio. At first it had seemed an impossible dream because the cost of the lessons was too high.

Her widowed father earned only a modest wage as a plumber and her brother was not well paid as a store man in a factory. Yet both of them were determined to help her afford the lessons because they'd been told that Colette might one day be good enough to be a professional dancer. To help the family finances, Wilder found her a job selling programmes at a West End theatre. The lessons started and she learnt quickly. Her talent burgeoned accordingly.

'Then I joined up,' continued Orme, 'but I made sure that some of the money went to Colette. She took on all sorts of other jobs in order to buy the right dresses and shoes. Mr Wilder said that *he'd* had to make the same sort of sacrifices when he first started.' He chuckled. 'Not that he had to buy dresses, mind you. Anyway, he never stopped encouraging my sister.'

'He told me that I could be as good as Miss Thompson one day,' she said, reviving slightly. 'That's his dancing partner.'

'Yes,' Marmion told her. 'We interviewed the lady.'

'She's a *wonderful* dancer, Inspector.'

'So are you, Colette,' insisted her brother. 'That's why you must go on.'

'I couldn't do that without Mr Wilder.'

'There are other dance teachers.'

'Nobody could compare with him.'

Marmion was touched by the tragedy of her situation. Bolstered by her father and brother – both men of limited means – she'd worked hard to develop her skills on the dance floor. Having been through the appointments book, Marmion knew how often she'd had lessons with her mentor. Clearly, she was dedicated to her art. The high hopes of the whole family had now been more or less extinguished. Wilder was dead, Colette was distraught and her brother, once an army corporal, was now a limping shadow of his former self. It was impossible not to feel sympathy for them.

'The inspector has come to ask questions, Colette,' said Orme, a steadying hand on her arm. 'You must help him all you can.'

She was despondent. 'What can *I* do, Dennis?'

'You may be able to do more than you think,' said Marmion, taking over. 'First of all, tell me what happened the last time you saw Mr Wilder.'

'It was magical,' she said. 'He put on some records and we danced for a whole hour. From time to time, he'd stop and adjust my posture or explain what I was doing wrong but I felt as if I was . . . well, as if I was getting somewhere.'

'Did you leave when Miss Thompson arrived?'

'No, Inspector, she came a little early and watched us. When we finished dancing a tango, she actually applauded me. A tango is a very difficult dance, you see, and a lot of people frown on it. They say it's too . . . indecent to be seen in public.'

'They're narrow-minded,' said Marmion. 'The same people condemned the waltz when it was first introduced because they thought dancers got too close to each other. I've heard of the tango, Miss Orme, but I've never had the opportunity to see it performed. I expect I'm far too old ever to dance it.'

'I'll never get the chance either, Inspector,' said Orme, sadly. 'My dancing days are over. But I did see Colette and Mr Wilder give a demonstration of it once. It was very dramatic.'

'And so it should be, Dennis,' she said. 'It's telling a story.'

Marmion let her ramble on, throwing in the occasional question whenever she flagged. He was learning a great deal about her and about Wilder's teaching methods. As he looked at Colette, he was bound to contrast her with Odele Thompson. One was a talented amateur while the other was a seasoned professional, able to cope with the pressures and disappointments that such a life would inevitably bring. There was still a faint air of innocence about Colette and he was not at all sure that she'd be able to cope with the rough and tumble of a precarious profession.

'You said earlier,' Marmion recalled, 'that you and Mr Wilder danced to gramophone records. Was that always the case?'

'Oh, no – at the start, when I was learning, we had a pianist, Mrs Pattinson.'

'We've spoken to her.'

'She was very kind to Colette,' said Orme.

'Dennis!' scolded his sister. 'There's no need to mention that.'

'It doesn't matter now. He'll never find out, will he?'

'That's not the point.'

'He probably knew, anyway. Audrey told him everything.'

'But she didn't – it was our secret.' She looked balefully at Marmion. 'We weren't doing anything wrong, Inspector.' After a silent conversation with her brother, she decided to confess. 'Mrs Pattinson is a good friend, you see. She knew that I didn't have any money so she let me into the studio for free when there were no lessons. She even played the piano for me. If you want to be a *real* dancer, Mr Wilder told me, you have to practise every day.'

'That was very kind of Mrs Pattinson.'

'She's a dear old lady,' said Orme. 'And I think she liked to get out of the house to escape that husband of hers. I didn't like him at all.'

Marmion was curious. 'Why not?'

'It was the way he treated her, Inspector. He made all the decisions in the house. And he was nasty to me as well,' he went on. 'Since he'd been in the army, you'd have expected him to take pity on someone wounded in action but he looked straight through me as if I wasn't there. I've met other officers like that.'

'Let's go back to Mr Wilder,' said Marmion. 'Did he ever talk about his professional rivals?' he asked.

'He did mention one or two,' she replied. 'He said that they'd try any trick to win a dance competition. Allan Redmond was one of them, I think. I never met him but I've seen an article about him in the paper. It said he's a very good dancer. Mr Wilder always complained that Mr Redmond had an advantage because was so much younger than him.'

'Why wasn't he conscripted?'

'I asked him that once. Mr Wilder said that he had connections.'

'What did he mean by that?' asked Orme.

'Friends in high places,' said Marmion, disapprovingly. 'If you know the right people, you can always get an exemption. It's very unfair because it lets able-bodied young men evade their duty. But let me ask you one last question, Miss Orme,' he continued. 'Was there any occasion when Mr Wilder seemed to think that someone might be following him?'

'Why, yes,' she said. 'There *was* one time. He picked me up one night at the theatre where I'd been working. As we strolled towards the bus stop, he swung round sharply as if someone was directly behind him.' She hunched her shoulders. 'But nobody was there.'

'Thank you for being so helpful, Miss Orme,' he said. 'I won't press you any further. If you can think of anything else that Mr Wilder said about his rivals, you can get in touch with me at the local police station.' As he rose to his feet, he glanced at one of the photographs on the mantelpiece. 'What was your regiment?'

'East Surrey,' replied Orme, proudly. '8th Battalion. I was glad to fight for my country, Inspector. It cost me a shattered knee at the Somme but I have no regrets. I'll be able to go back to work in time.'

Marmion felt a pang of envy. His son, Paul, had also been a casualty of the Battle of the Somme. Rather than adapting to his disability, he was instead causing the family huge problems. Dennis Orme had set a good example. Marmion wished that Paul could follow it.

'My son was in the Middlesex Regiment,' he said. 'He's back home now, suffering from shell shock. But,' he went on, trying to cheer himself up, 'there's every chance that he may make a complete recovery one day.'

A cup of tea turned into a meal then evanesced into a stroll around the park. Paul Marmion and Mavis Tandy walked arm in arm and continued their discussion. When he finally prised her away from the subject of her dead boyfriend, he asked her about the sort of home life she enjoyed.

'Do you *mind* having a vicar for a father?'

'Not at all,' she said. 'Daddy's very sweet and he works so hard. I help out in the church sometimes.'

'What do you do?'

'Oh, it's nothing important. I'm on the cleaning rota and the flower rota, that's all. And I do house visits sometimes.'

'House visits?'

'Some of our parishioners are too ill or decrepit to get to any of the services. Daddy likes them to feel that they're not forgotten so we give them small gifts now and again – things that other members of the congregation have donated.' She looked at him. 'Do you ever go to church, Paul?'

'Not really.'

'Didn't you want to thank God for letting you survive a fierce battle?'

'I was lucky, that's all.'

'Yes, but who *provided* that luck?'

Paul felt embarrassed. Religion had never played a large role in his life and his years in the army had considerably weakened his belief in the existence of God. He was not about to admit as much to Mavis. If he wished to get closer to her – and the desire to do so had been getting stronger all the time – he would have to find some way of reconciling her faith with his lack of it.

'We had a chaplain at the front,' he said. 'He talked a lot of sense.'

'It was very brave of him to join the army.'

'He heard a call – that's what he told us.'

'What did you learn from him?'

'I can tell you the main thing,' he said with a laugh. 'I learnt never to play cards with him for money because he had the luck of the devil. Either that or God was dealing the cards for him. Anyway, he was always there if you wanted a chat and, when some of the lads made fun of him, he just put up with it.'

'Christians are taught to turn the other cheek, Paul.'

'Yes, I suppose so.'

'Colin told me that he loved attending services on a Sunday.'

'Did he?'

Paul was surprised. His friend had been even less of a believer than he was but he was clearly ready to invent a faith that he didn't, in fact, hold. Paul didn't want to upset Mavis by telling her the truth. He simply followed his friend's example.

'Colin loved music of all kinds – especially hymns.'

'He played one for me on his mouth organ.'

'I've still got it,' he said, taking it from his pocket. 'I get hours of pleasure with it. We learnt so many songs in the trenches.'

'It was "Onward, Christian Soldiers".'

'My uncle's band plays that all the time. Uncle Raymond is in the Salvation Army. They've adopted that hymn as their own. My uncle says that it's a rousing piece to march to. Before I went in the army, he was always trying to get me to join his band but I was like Colin. When we did have some spare time, we always wanted to go to the park and kick a football about.'

They'd reached a bench and, almost without thinking, they sat down on it. Mavis released his arm but stayed close. Paul appreciated that. However, he was still very much aware that there were three of them there. No matter how much Paul nestled up against her shoulder, Colin Fryatt remained between them. It would take time to move him gently out of the way.

'I ought to go home,' she said.

'Don't leave just yet,' he pleaded.

'I've been here for hours, Paul.'

'It's been such a treat for me to talk to you about Colin.'

'We can do it again some time.'

His heart lifted. 'Can we?'

'Yes,' she said. 'In fact, I've got an idea . . .'

Having taken an immediate dislike to Tom Atterbury, he had a good first impression of Allan Redmond. Keedy met him outside a rambling house in Wimbledon. He was just about to ring the bell when he was hailed by a sprightly man in his late twenties. It was Redmond, returning from the common where he'd just taken his Labrador for a walk. When he learnt why Keedy was there, he invited him in at once and offered him refreshment. It was waved away with polite thanks. Allan Redmond was a handsome man of medium height who held himself so rigidly upright that he seemed taller. His face radiated intelligence and his voice was the product of a leading public school. Keedy found it a little intimidating at first.

'Yes,' said Redmond, picking up a newspaper, 'I read the report in *The Times* this morning. Simon Wilder, of all people – I mean, everyone liked Simon. He was a delightful chap when you got to know him.'

'I understood that you and he didn't exactly get on.'

'We fought tooth and nail on the dance floor, if that's what you mean, but there was no real animosity on either side. Simon was a true professional. I take my hat off to him. He'll be a loss to the world of ballroom dancing and it's already sustained far too many losses.'

'Oh?'

'The war, dear fellow,' said the other. 'It's played havoc with us. We've lost so many marvellous ballroom dancers to the army. Many of them have been killed or maimed by the Boche. In a sense, of course, it's helped people like Simon and Tom Atterbury, both of them in their forties. They've dominated the scene now that younger men have deserted it to go to the front, and it's to their credit. At their age, they have to make extra efforts to keep a high standard of fitness, whereas young Turks like me can keep themselves in trim by taking the dog for a walk each day.'

Keedy didn't believe him for a second. Redmond had the glowing health of a man who took pains to keep himself fit. They were in the living room of what Keedy learnt was the parental home. At that moment, Redmond's father and mother were visiting relatives in Scotland, leaving their only son in charge. The place was redolent of people who belonged to the Victorian age, dark, dated and hopelessly cluttered. Redmond seemed quite out of place there.

'Oh, I have a cottage of my own in the country,' he explained, 'and that is furnished more to my taste but this is a useful base whenever I'm in town. Anyway, ask what you have to, Sergeant. You don't want to hear me burbling on.'

'Where were you two nights ago, sir?'

'I was at a restaurant in Mayfair, dining with a friend.'

'May I know his name?'

'No, you may not,' said Redmond, smiling, 'because it was a young lady. You can have her name and address, by all means. When I left her, it was very late. I got back here in time to see the most extraordinary air raid.'

'Yes,' said Keedy, 'I saw it as well, sir. It was astonishing.'

'That damned Zeppelin got what it jolly well deserved.'

'I agree, Mr Redmond.'

'Anyway, that will give you a more or less accurate time of my return here. But there were witnesses. Most of our neighbours were hiding under their bed with their fingers in their ears but a few intrepid souls came out to watch. I can give you their names, if you like.'

'Thank you, sir.'

'I've always been an obliging cove.'

'When did you and Mr Wilder last see each other?'

'That would be a month or so ago . . .'

Redmond recalled a chance meeting and what he described as an enjoyable chat. He went on to talk about the professional rivalry he and Wilder had shared over the years. There was no hint of the antagonism towards the murder victim that Atterbury had shown. Redmond appeared to be genuinely sad.

'I'll be at his funeral,' he said, solemnly. 'All of us will.'

'There may be one exception, sir.'

'Ah, you're talking about Tom Atterbury, I take it.'

'I met him earlier.'

'Don't take him too seriously. Tom is always rather spiky. My feeling is that there's room for all of us to live together harmoniously in our chosen walk of life but Tom is not a devotee of harmony. Strife is his natural habitat. He divides people into friends and enemies.'

'Then I suspect that the enemies vastly outweigh the friends.'

Redmond brayed. 'You judge him aright, Sergeant.'

'I was cast firmly into the ranks of the enemy,' said Keedy, 'because I had the gall to question his honesty. Mr Atterbury was very upset when I treated him as a potential suspect whereas you, Mr Redmond, have not turned a hair.'

'I'm only too glad to be of assistance, old chap.'

'Don't you object to being questioned like this?'

'Why should I?'

'Nobody likes to be thought of as a possible killer.'

'But that's not what's happening here,' said Redmond, amiably. 'We're just playing a little game, aren't we? And I know full well who instigated it.'

'Do you, sir?'

'Yes – you didn't come here because you believe I committed a foul crime. You were sent here, out of spite, by Odele, dear girl that she is.' He put his face close to Keedy's. 'Did she tell you why she mentioned my name?'

'I'm not prepared to discuss sources, sir.'

'I bet that she didn't.'

'Don't assume anything.'

'It was because she once got hold of the preposterous notion that she and I were engaged to be married. That's how my name came to be whispered into your ear. Let me give you a warning, Sergeant,' he said, clapping him familiarly on the shoulder and lowering his voice to a conspiratorial whisper. 'Hell hath no fury like a woman scorned.'

Odele Thompson poured two glasses of gin, added soda from a siphon then offered one of the glasses to her visitor.

'Oh, I daren't,' said Audrey Pattinson, shrinking back in alarm. 'I couldn't go home with the smell of alcohol on my breath.'

'That's why I chose gin. It leaves none.'

'Even so . . .'

'Take it, for heaven's sake,' said Odele, thrusting it into her hand. 'You need it as much as I do.' She raised her glass. 'Let's drink to Simon.'

'Well, yes, that's a toast I won't refuse.'

While Audrey took a small sip from her glass, Odele gulped down a lot more.

'This is my secret weapon,' she confessed. 'You've no idea how many stage shows and dance competitions I've got through because I had a nip of gin. Simon preferred a tot of rum to get him in the mood but this is my tipple.'

'The one time we drink at home is at Christmas, and then it's only a glass of cooking sherry. Martin won't have strong drink in the house.'

'An army officer who doesn't drink – I don't believe it.'

'Martin has always been abstemious.'

'What about that club he goes to?'

'He always says that he sticks to water.'

Odele doubted that. She'd only had a few brief meetings with Audrey's husband but it had been enough to convince her that she disliked him intensely. He'd seemed cold, judgemental and detached. Odele had also noticed that Audrey was always on edge in his presence.

'Is he helping you to cope?' she asked.

'Yes, Martin has been wonderful.'

'I get my comfort from the gin bottle.'

Audrey gave a pale smile. She and Odele lived in different worlds that happened to collide occasionally in a dance studio. Having been their accompanist when Odele and Wilder first got together as a team, she had been replaced by the gramophone, but she'd seen enough of them as dancers to form an opinion of their standard. Though it was extremely high, it did not match that achieved by Wilder and his wife. In Audrey's view, they had been the perfect couple.

'I went to see Catherine yesterday,' she said.

'That was kind of you. I didn't really feel that it was my place to drop in on her. There's always been a slight awkwardness between us. Catherine feels a natural resentment that I took over from her so I keep out of her way.'

'She always speaks well of you, Odele. She thinks you have every quality a ballroom dancer ought to have.'

'Except one, that is.'

'What's that?'

'I don't have a partner.' She took another drink. 'How was she?'

'We didn't really talk but she's bearing up much better than I am. Every time I remember what happened, I want to burst into tears. I actually went to the house to console Catherine but she finished up consoling me.'

'What did she think of those two detectives?'

'She thought they handled a delicate situation very well, especially that Inspector Marmion. He inspires confidence.'

'I was more impressed by Sergeant Keedy. The inspector was far too staid for me. When I went to the police station, I was glad that the sergeant was there.'

'Why?'

'I had a feeling that he was more likely to take me seriously.'

Odele told her about the visit and how she'd named two possible suspects. Dubious at first, Audrey slowly came round to the idea that someone was so jealous of Wilder's success that they wanted to bring it to an abrupt halt.

'But I can't believe that it was Mr Redmond,' she said. 'I met him once. He was quite charming.'

'Oh, Allan can charm a bird out of a tree,' said Odele, harshly. 'If they gave prizes for charm, he'd be a clear winner. When it comes to honesty, however, it wouldn't be the same at all. He never honours his promises.'

'Have you ever danced with him, Odele?'

'To my eternal regret, I once did.'

'Mr Wilder said that he was a worthy rival.'

'I won't offend you by giving *my* estimation of Allan Redmond. Suffice it to say that he's ambitious enough to brush away anyone who stands in his path. That's why I gave his name to the sergeant.'

'But he seems far too nice and well educated to be a killer.'

'You don't know him as I do.'

'What about Mr Atterbury?'

'Oh, you wouldn't like him at all, Audrey, I promise you. He's neither nice nor well educated. As for charm, he was at the back of the queue when that was doled out. Tom Atterbury has a cruel streak,' said Odele. 'Allan would murder a rival who stood between him and success, whereas Tom would murder for the sheer pleasure of it. He's that kind of man. You'd be far too scared to play the piano for *him*. Tom would frighten the daylights out of you.'

It was Audrey's turn to take a long gulp of gin this time.

* * *

When he eventually got back to the police station, Keedy found Marmion sitting at the desk as he sifted through some sheets of paper. The inspector put them aside.

'Very little happened in our absence, Joe,' he said. 'Detective Constable Gibbs was hoping that the killer would pop in and give himself up but all he got were some people who thought they *might* have seen someone who answered the description of Simon Wilder on the night in question. "Might" is not good enough. We need someone who actually did.'

'What happened to Gibbs?'

'I gave him a pat on the back and said we'd call on him again tomorrow.' He swung round in the chair. 'Take a seat and I'll tell you what I've been doing.'

Keedy sat down and listened to an abbreviated report about the inspector's day. Like Marmion, he was disappointed that the safe in Wilder's study had not yielded any clues as to the identity of his killer. He was interested to hear how calm and composed the widow had been.

'She must prefer to do her crying in private,' he said.

'Mrs Wilder certainly wouldn't do it in front of her brother. Sympathy is in short supply there. Clissold is more likely to tell her to pull herself together than show any human emotion.'

'Did you mention the two names I gave you?'

'Yes, I did, Joe.'

'And?'

'They obviously hadn't occurred to Mrs Wilder.'

'How did she react?'

'She said that we could forget the name of Allan Redmond completely. Yes, I know,' he said before Keedy could interrupt, 'Redmond was the one picked out by Miss Thompson.'

'Her money was fairly and squarely on him.'

'Then she stands to lose it. Mrs Wilder warned me not to listen to any more of Miss Thompson's suggestions. She claims the woman makes things up for effect.'

'That wasn't my impression of her,' asserted Keedy. 'What about Atterbury?'

'Now he *is* worth a close look. Mrs Wilder was certain about that. Before you give me *your* judgement of the two men,' said Marmion, 'let me finish my tale.'

He told Keedy about his visit to Colette Orme's house and how struck he'd been by the way that her father and her brother had supported her ambitions to be a dancer. When he talked about Dennis Orme's acceptance of his lot as a disabled soldier, he didn't need to draw a parallel with his own son. Keedy could do that for himself. He was touched by the revelation that Audrey Pattinson had given the young dancer free access to the studio so that she could practise on her own.

'She seems to have treated the girl like a daughter,' he remarked.

'I wonder if her husband knew what was going on.'

'I can't see her defying Pattinson, somehow.'

'Maybe not, Joe, but I can imagine her seizing the opportunity to have as much time away from him as possible. Dennis Orme didn't like Pattinson at all.'

'You'd have thought they'd have a bond, both being soldiers.'

'Well, they didn't.'

'Why is that?'

'Pattinson became very lordly, apparently. He treated Orme as if he was the lowest form of humanity. Paul complained about people like that in *his* battalion. They ooze superiority.'

'Just like our superintendent,' said Keedy.

'Nobody is like Chat. He's beyond compare.'

Laughing aloud, the sergeant took out his notebook and described what he'd been doing. Although it was the second of his two visits, he began with Allan Redmond, whom he found both pleasant and plausible.

'I don't usually like toffs but Redmond was different somehow. You couldn't take offence at him. Mind you, I did wonder why he wasn't fighting in France.'

'Colette Orme had the answer to that – friends who can pull strings.'

'It's a pity her brother didn't have the same friends or he'd still have two good legs. I hate the whiff of privilege.'

'From what you're saying, Allan Redmond stank of it.'

'Yet it didn't upset me in the way it usually does,' said Keedy, perplexed. 'Everything he told me was true. I spoke to the young woman with whom he dined and the manager of the restaurant told me exactly when they'd left. Redmond was seen returning home by neighbours and stayed out with them to watch the air raid.'

'That lets him off the hook, then. What about Atterbury?'

'He was a nasty piece of work. Also, he's a barefaced liar.'

'How do you know?'

'I spoke to the other residents in the house and to the neighbours. A couple of them came out to watch the fireworks as well. They saw the Zeppelin shot down but not a single one of them remembers seeing Tom Atterbury come back home.'

'Do you think he's our man?'

'Possibly – though we'd need a lot more evidence before we arrest him.'

'Can we eliminate Allan Redmond as a suspect?'

'He's already done that himself,' said Keedy. 'He wasn't at all upset that Miss Thompson had given us his name. Redmond said that she was getting her revenge because he once jilted her – or, at least, that's what she believed.'

'There can't be any doubt about it, can there?'

'Redmond implied that there was.' Keedy shrugged. 'I was disappointed, really. After the way that Miss Thompson talked about him, I was convinced that he was the killer.'

Marmion smiled complacently. 'I won't remind you what I said.'

'You thought I was on a wild goose chase,' retorted Keedy, 'and I wasn't. Atterbury had all the signs of a man who nurses resentments until they turn into something more dangerous. My journey was not in vain. We have a suspect.'

'I rather think that we have two, Joe.'

'You can discount Redmond altogether.'

'I wasn't thinking about him.'

'Then who is this other suspect?'

'Martin Pattinson.'

He kept the room locked because nobody else – not even his wife – was allowed inside it. When he went in, Pattinson locked the door behind him then he surveyed his little museum. Neatly arranged on shelves or tables was a display of militaria. Medals were set out in a glass cabinet. A tattered Union Jack was hanging above the fireplace. The collection of weapons occupied most of the available space. Guns covered the largest of the tables but the weapon that he picked up was a gleaming bayonet. Taking a cloth from a drawer, Pattinson began to clean it with slow deliberation.

CHAPTER TWELVE

Sir Edward Henry had earlier complained that the air raid on London would dominate the newspaper headlines, pushing details of the murder that same night to the inside pages. Yet, in effect, that was exactly what he was doing himself. When Claude Chatfield went to see the commissioner about the investigation, he had to listen instead to information about the pilot who'd shot down the Zeppelin.

'His name is Lieutenant William Leefe Robinson.'

'So I understand, Sir Edward.'

'He'd been in the air for two hours, it seems, and had already attacked another airship. When he went for a second Zeppelin, he shot it to pieces.'

'It was very commendable,' said Chatfield, impatiently.

'People are already talking about awarding him a VC.'

'That might be going too far.'

'I disagree, Superintendent. He risked his life to achieve what nobody else has managed to do. That deserves recognition. And there's more to come, of course.'

'Yes, he'll receive public adulation.'

'He also stands to claim £500 from a shipbuilder who offered the money to the first British pilot to knock a Zeppelin out of the sky. And don't I remember reading somewhere that the *Newcastle Daily Chronicle* was offering three or four times that amount for the feat?'

'Lieutenant Robinson was not motivated by money,' said Chatfield, piously. 'He was simply doing his duty. However . . .'

'Ah,' said the other, sensing his irritation, 'I do apologise. You've come to talk about a murder inquiry and my head is still, so to speak, in the clouds. What's happened?'

Chatfield waved some sheaves of paper.

'First of all, you should see this, Sir Edward. It's the post-mortem report.'

He handed over the document then waited a couple of minutes while the commissioner read through it, clicking his tongue in disgust as he did so.

'This is revolting,' he said, returning the report to the superintendent. 'The press must not get to see this and neither, on any account, must the widow.'

'The salient point is that the victim was first knocked unconscious with a blow to the back of the head by a blunt instrument. He was then dragged into the alley where the butchery took place.'

'And all the while, people were gazing up at the Zeppelins.'

'The killer was able to slip away quietly in the darkness with his . . . trophies.' Chatfield grimaced. 'It's barbarity on a medieval scale.'

'The Middle Ages are still with us in some places, Superintendent. I found that out during my years in India.' He stroked his moustache absent-mindedly. 'Has any progress been made so far?'

'I spoke on the telephone to Inspector Marmion a short while ago. He and Sergeant Keedy have interviewed a number of people and feel that they may – just may, mark you – have identified two suspects.'

'That's cheering news.'

'It's too early to call it that, Sir Edward. Marmion has made mistakes before.'

'Are these suspects being brought in for questioning?'

'We haven't reached that stage yet,' said Chatfield. 'All we have are two men who've aroused our interest. They'll have to be watched while further evidence is gathered. Naturally, neither of their names must be released because both may turn out to be completely innocent.'

'More pertinently, if one of them *is* guilty, we don't want to forewarn him that we are on his tail.'

'Exactly – he must not know that he's under suspicion.'

'How confident was the inspector that these men were potential killers?'

'Marmion always errs on the side of caution, Sir Edward. That's something I've drummed into him. Over-hasty arrests can have embarrassing consequences.'

'I can't recall that Marmion ever made an over-hasty arrest.'

'That's because I've kept him on a short leash.'

'Though we did end up with red faces a few years ago,' said the commissioner with a wry smile. 'Someone arrested a gang on a charge of obtaining money by false pretences. It turned out to be a case of mistaken identity. Every one of them had to be released. The press ridiculed us over that.' His eyes twinkled. 'I can't remember who was responsible for the faux pas but we suffered as a result.'

Chatfield gritted his teeth. The commissioner knew only too well who the culprit had been. It was Chatfield who'd ordered the arrests in the first place and who had been pilloried in the newspapers. It was an event in his past that he tried hard to live down. Since then his record had been spotless and it had led to his promotion.

'Who are these suspects?' asked Sir Edward.

'One is a professional dancer and the other is a retired estate agent who was formerly in the army.'

'What motive could they possibly have to commit such a detestable crime?'

'Marmion and Keedy are endeavouring to unearth one.'

Marmion had heard more than enough about Tom Atterbury to arouse his curiosity. He therefore decided to visit him that evening in order to make his own appraisal of the dancer. When he called at the Islington house, he was given a very different reception from Keedy. Atterbury made a visible effort to be pleasant to him. Since he had no natural charm, he instead relied on a kind of battered politeness. During introductions, he pumped Marmion's arm.

'I had a feeling that you'd come, Inspector,' he said.

'Why did you feel that, sir?'

'Because I could see that your sergeant was an efficient man. After he'd taken my statement, he doubtless went off to check my alibi. He found . . . discrepancies.'

'He found that you were not entirely honest with him, Mr Atterbury.'

'Put that down to the effects of too much alcohol.' He peered at Marmion. 'You have the look of a married man.'

'And what kind of look is that?'

'It's the one that Sergeant Keedy did *not* have.'

Marmion smiled. 'That's a fair comment. And yes, I am married.'

'Then you'll know how lonely you feel returning to an empty house when your wife is away somewhere. The demon drink beckons.'

'I can't say that it's ever beckoned me in those circumstances because my wife never goes away. Even if she did, I'd never get hopelessly drunk on a regular basis. One reason is that an inspector's income could never sustain the cost, and there are other reasons.' He took out a notebook. 'Why don't you give me a revised statement, Mr Atterbury?'

'I'd be happy to do so.'

Marmion could see why Keedy had taken against the man. Beneath the forced affability was a surliness fringed by a lack of respect for the police. Though Atterbury had arranged his features into something resembling a smile, his eyes remained cold. His story introduced a new element. After leaving the friends with whom he'd dined, he now claimed, he was keenly aware that his wife would not be warming the bed for him. He therefore popped into his club for a nightcap that became a long series of drinks. Atterbury could not remember the exact time when he tumbled out of there and made his way home. What he did remember rather hazily was that there was an air raid and that he sought the first shelter he could find.

'It was an underground station, Inspector,' he said. 'We were packed in like sardines. There was the most unwholesome stink, I can tell you. I fell fast asleep. When I finally woke up, the air raid was over and people were going back to their homes. That's when *I* turned my steps in this direction. In other words,' he concluded, 'I didn't lie to Sergeant Keedy. I simply forgot one element in the chain of events.'

'I'm glad we've cleared that up, sir,' said Marmion.

'You'll want the address of my club, of course, and you'll need to speak to the steward. I can assure you that he'll support what I've told you.'

'I never doubted it for a second.'

Marmion wrote down the name and address of the club but did not expect the steward to contradict Atterbury's revised story. Stewards of gentleman's clubs were notoriously loyal to members, protecting them from inquisitive wives, drawing a veil over their peccadilloes and saying what they'd been paid to say. While they would not tell outright lies during a murder investigation, they would be parsimonious with the truth. Closing his notebook, Marmion made ready to leave.

'You do believe me, don't you, Inspector?' said Atterbury.

'I've no reason *not* to believe you, sir.'

'Obviously, I can't give you the names of anyone in the underground station that night. We were just one seething mass of humanity, praying that London would still be standing when we went back up into the street.'

'What you've told me is perfectly adequate,' said Marmion, blandly. 'We'll not be disturbing you again, sir.'

'Thank you for being so understanding. It means a lot to me.' Atterbury's face hardened. 'Your sergeant took a more abrasive tone.'

'I'll speak to him about it.'

'I hold no malice against him. He was only doing his job, I daresay.'

'We don't like to upset members of the public, sir. If we do that, they have no incentive to help us, whereas you have been extremely cooperative.'

After another handshake, Marmion took his leave, certain that he'd just been told a pack of lies but careful not to reveal the fact. He could feel Atterbury's eyes following him all the way to the waiting car.

Ellen Marmion's anxiety about her son's long absence was compounded by the fact that she had no idea where he was. Though she knew that he'd gone to meet Mavis Tandy, he made no mention of time and place. He'd now been out of the house for several hours and she began to fear that he might have been involved in an accident of sorts. Equally disturbing was the thought that he'd spent the whole day with his new friend. Ellen did not want him to wallow once again in the mud of the Somme. He'd done that so many times at home and his maudlin reminiscences always ended in rage and recrimination.

When he did finally return, however, Paul was in an unusually pleasant mood. He even gave his mother a token kiss on the cheek. All he would say was that he'd had an enjoyable day. Refusing the offer of a meal, he went straight off to his bedroom, leaving Ellen to wonder what had happened to transform his manner so completely. A minute later she heard 'Onward, Christian Soldiers' being played on the mouth organ.

Colette Orme was delighted when she had a visitor. Her father and her brother were endlessly kind and sympathetic but she really yearned for the company of another woman. When Audrey Pattinson arrived at the house, therefore, Colette was relieved. She not only had a true friend, she had someone who had been very close to Simon Wilder. The two men went off into the kitchen, leaving them alone. After a tearful embrace, the women sat side by side on the sofa, drawn together by their mutual bereavement. Audrey was able to say the things that her friend really wanted to hear.

'You were always his favourite, Colette.'

'Thank you, Mrs Pattinson.'

'Mr Wilder predicted a great future for you.'

'It's in tatters now,' said Colette with a sigh.

'You may think that at the moment – it's only natural – but in time you'll have the urge to go on without him. You have to develop your talent. It's what Mr Wilder would have wanted.'

'Do you really believe that?'

'Yes, I do. Think of all the time and effort you put in.'

'It didn't seem like an effort, Mrs Pattinson. I loved it.'

'You don't need to tell me that, Colette. I've never known such enthusiasm. We've had good dancers before – male and female – but somehow they couldn't stand the pace. You did. Mr Wilder said that that was the sign of a professional.'

Overcome with grief, Colette burst into tears and Audrey enfolded her in her arms. Having to comfort someone else helped her to cope with her own anguish. When the weeping finally stopped, Colette apologised profusely and wiped her eyes with a handkerchief.

'Thank you so much for coming, Mrs Pattinson.'

'I knew how you'd be feeling.'

'I just can't stop thinking about . . . what happened to him.'

'Have the police been to see you?'

'Yes – an Inspector Marmion called earlier.'

'We met him as well.'

'He was very nice to me, though he did ask some odd questions.'

'What sort of questions?'

'He wanted to know about Mr Wilder's rivals. The only one I knew anything about was Mr Redmond but there were others, I expect. The inspector also asked me if I'd ever been with Mr Wilder when he behaved as if he thought someone was following him.'

'That *is* an odd question,' said Audrey.

'The funny thing is that it *did* happen once,' admitted Colette.

She told Audrey about the incident and how Wilder had dismissed it with a laugh. It was the only occasion when she'd seen even the slightest fear in him. Audrey was disturbed. The fact that neither Colette nor Wilder saw anybody at the time did not mean that a stalker was not there. It could be that he was simply clever enough to remain out of sight. It made Audrey wonder if, on one of the many occasions when she and Wilder had walked together, *they'd* been under surveillance. It was an unnerving thought.

Colette was contrite. 'There's something I have to own up to, Mrs Pattinson.'

'Is there?'

'It wasn't my fault, really. Dennis blurted it out before I could stop him.'

'What did he say?'

'He told the inspector that you were kind enough to let me into the studio on my own so that I could practise with you on the piano. It was supposed to be our secret but Dennis let the cat out of the bag.' She saw Audrey's dismay. 'I hope that Mrs Wilder doesn't find out. She'd want to charge us for every session.'

'Is Inspector Marmion likely to tell her?'

'I don't think so.'

'Then – with luck – we may have got away with it.'

'The only people who know are you, me and Dennis. Oh, I was forgetting,' she went on, 'there's your husband as well.'

Audrey grabbed her wrist. 'He knew nothing about it, Colette.'

'But I thought—'

'Well, he didn't and he must never know. Do you understand?'

'Yes,' said Colette, wincing, 'but you're hurting my wrist, Mrs Pattinson.' Audrey released her. 'Thank you . . . what will happen now?'

'My guess is that the studio will close and the hall will be put up for sale. I can't believe that Mrs Wilder will have the interest or the energy to continue.'

'But it *must* stay open. Think of all the people who depend on it. I'm not the only person who lives to dance. There are dozens and dozens of us. When we hold a dance there, we get almost a hundred couples.'

'With luck,' said Audrey, 'someone may take it over and run it in much the same way. In the meantime, you need to find yourself a new dancing partner.'

'There'll never be anyone as good as Mr Wilder.'

'He taught you very well but you must find someone closer to your own age. A pretty girl like you should be able to do that.'

'All the young men have been called up,' complained the other.

'Not all of them. Look at Mr Redmond, for instance,' advised Audrey. 'He's still in his twenties. I'm not suggesting that you're ready to partner him, of course, because he already has someone to dance with. But there must be other young men who have somehow escaped conscription. Search for another Allan Redmond.'

The death of Simon Wilder preyed on her mind. Whatever she did, Odele Thompson could not stop reflecting on it and on its implications for her. Deprived of a chance to win a national dance championship, she would have to tell her agent to get her an audition for the next available stage musical. Even if she succeeded in finding work, she would be one dancer in a company rather than someone with an award that lifted her above the herd. She went for a walk in the park to clear her head. Wilder had been an irreplaceable part of her life. The only thing that could bring any solace was the arrest and conviction of his killer. As she eventually headed for home, she was thinking about all the things she'd like to do to the man before he was executed.

When she let herself into her flat, she was still musing on a suitably drastic punishment for the killer. Odele was quite unaware that she had a visitor.

'Hello, darling,' said a man's voice.

She let out a squeal of surprise and backed away in alarm. Perched nonchalantly on the arm of the sofa, Allan Redmond drew on his cigarette then exhaled the smoke.

'How on earth did you get here?' she demanded.

He held up a key. 'Before I returned the other one,' he explained, 'I had a duplicate made. I had a feeling that it might come in useful one day.'

'Get out!'

'We need to talk first, Odele.'

'Get out or I'll call the police.'

'That's exactly what I wanted to discuss with you,' he said, getting up and crossing over to her. 'Thanks to you, I had a Sergeant Keedy treating me as a murder suspect. What exactly did you tell him?'

Though he doubted if he would hear a contradiction of Tom Atterbury's alibi, Marmion went to the man's club and sought out the head steward. Dressed in a smart uniform, he was a short, stubby, middle-aged man with a gleaming bald pate and a face of permanent impassivity. Since he had been on duty on the night of the air raid, he was in a position to confirm what Marmion had been told.

'Yes, Inspector, Mr Atterbury was here that evening.'

'At what time did he depart?'

'I couldn't be specific about that, sir.'

'Just give me a rough time. Was it early or late?'

'Mr Atterbury is the best person to ask.'

'I'm asking you,' said Marmion, forcefully, 'and I'm sure that you're aware that withholding information from the police is an offence.'

'I've given you all the information I can,' said the steward, politely.

'How long has Mr Atterbury been a member here?'

'He joined the club in 1907.'

'And how often does he come here?'

'On average, he calls in at least twice a week.'

'Your membership, I fancy, is exclusive. Did he need a sponsor to join?'

'Yes,' replied the man, 'the club is not open to any Tom, Dick or Harry. As it happens, the person who proposed Mr Atterbury was the club president, Sir Howard Legge.' A smile threatened but never actually came. 'Is there anything else you'd like to ask me, Inspector?'

'There is,' said Marmion, acidly. 'Why is it that you can remember the exact details of Mr Atterbury's membership from nine years ago whereas you can't tell me what time he left the premises earlier this week?'

'I can't account for that, sir.'

The steward's stony expression infuriated Marmion but he knew that his anger was futile. The man's first duty was to the membership. Even though he was dealing with a murder investigation, his memory was deliberately selective. The visit, however, was not without its reward. When Marmion left the club, he crossed the road and looked in the window of a bookshop for a few minutes, wishing that he had the leisure to read. It was a luxury that his profession would never give him.

As he turned from the shop, he glanced across at the club and was just in time to see one of the members going in through the door. Marmion only caught a glimpse of the man but he recognised him instantly.

It was Martin Pattinson.

Alice Marmion was always ready to learn something new. When it came to police matters, she was very much the senior of the two but Iris Goodliffe had expertise that Alice could never hope to match. Her years of working in the family pharmacy had given her a knowledge of medicines and herbal remedies that was impressive.

'What would you recommend for someone like Paul?'

'He's already getting medical attention, isn't he?'

'The army can only do so much. He's been discharged from hospital and they're calling him in for regular check-ups. But they can't do anything about his black depression, Iris, or about his shifting moods. One minute, he boasts that he's going back to fight at the front; the next minute, he's saying that life isn't worth living.'

'It must be very trying,' said Iris, 'but there's no easy cure.'

'It's put Mummy under terrible stress.'

'Ah, now there are pills to relieve that, Alice.'

'We want a pill to get rid of the *cause* of the problem – my brother's despair.'

'He may get better in time.'

'Then again, he may not. There's one thing that would help, though.'

'What's that?'

'An end to this terrible war.'

'That's too much to hope, I'm afraid.'

They were enjoying a cup of tea together in the canteen. One of the reasons that Alice was questioning her about her previous job was that she wanted to keep Iris from asking her what was happening that evening. Though nothing had so far been arranged, Alice was still reluctant to let their relationship spill over into her private life. Once her new colleague was allowed to feel that she had a true friend, Iris, she suspected, would expect to spend more and more time with her.

The awkward question, however, could not be fended off indefinitely.

'What are you doing this evening?' asked Iris, artlessly.

'I'm seeing a friend, actually.'

The lie popped out so easily that Alice almost believed it herself.

'Is it someone from the Women's Police Force?'

'No, Iris, I try to keep my work and social life quite separate. Ideally, of course, I'd like to spend the evening with Joe but that's not possible.'

'How is the investigation going?'

'I don't know but there's usually slow progress at the start. There's so much information to gather and to collate. That's the bit Daddy is so good at.'

'What about your fiancé?'

'Joe thrives on action. Arresting the killer is always the best part for him.'

'Do they always manage to solve a murder, then?'

'They've been lucky so far, Iris.'

'It takes more than luck, surely.'

'Yes, it does,' agreed Alice. 'Joe always says that it's ninety-nine per cent hard work and one per cent luck.'

'There's another element, isn't there?'

'Is there?'

'I think so,' said Iris. 'He's spurred on by the thought that he won't spend any time with you until the killer is behind bars. *You're* one of the reasons he's so good at his job, Alice. You inspire him.'

Alone at the police station, Keedy went through the list of alleged sightings of Simon Wilder on the night before he died. Some of the statements had been given at Scotland Yard then phoned through to Chingford. By putting them all together, he was able to establish that Wilder had been seen in Shaftesbury Avenue around ten o'clock at night by three different people. How he'd got back to Chingford, nobody was able to say. Nor could anyone explain how he came to be in the particular part of the district where he was murdered. Keedy spied a possible explanation. Before he became a dancer, Wilder had been an actor, a man used to putting on disguises. Having gone to the West End where he was well known, he might – Keedy surmised – have changed his appearance so that he was unrecognisable then gone back to Chingford to see someone. Secrecy was involved. That suggested a tryst.

He was still poring over a street map when there was a tap on the door. A uniformed policeman entered to say that Miss Thompson had come to see him again. Keedy was on his feet in a flash, crossing to the door to invite her in, then closing it behind her. Odele was close to tears.

'I prayed that I'd catch you alone, Joe!' she said.

'Why is that?'

'I need your help.'

'Inspector Marmion could offer that just as well as me.'

'I prefer to see you.'

Without warning, she flung herself into his arms and he tried to soothe her with soft words while patting her back. Eventually, he lowered her into a chair and sat opposite her, making sure that there was some distance between them. Her fear was genuine and he had to resist the temptation to comfort her again.

'As calmly as possible,' he said, 'tell me what happened.'

'He threatened me.'

'Who did?'

'Allan, of course,' she replied. 'He was so angry that I'd mentioned his name to you that he came to frighten me.'

'He obviously succeeded,' said Keedy. 'Why did you let him in?' She lowered her head. 'All you had to do was to refuse to speak to him.'

'Allan Redmond doesn't take refusal seriously. But the main reason I couldn't shut the door in his face was that . . .'

Odele paused and searched his eyes as she tried to decide if he'd be shocked or sympathetic. Sensing that he was a man of the world, she pressed on.

'He was already *inside* the flat,' she explained. 'There was a time – a very brief time, I should add – when he had a key. Before he gave it back to me, he had a duplicate made.'

'Is that why you gave us his name?' asked Keedy in annoyance. 'Did you simply want to cause him embarrassment?'

'No,' she cried, 'I'd hate you to think that. I mentioned Allan because I really thought – and still think – that he has to be a possible suspect. He loathed Simon and, by nature, he's a violent man.'

'He didn't seem very violent when I met him, Odele.'

'That's because he pulled the wool over your eyes.'

'I've had a lot of experience at sizing people up.'

'And what was your opinion of Allan?'

'I thought he was one of those privileged young men who get the kind of chances that never come near the rest of us. He's as glib and self-assured as any confidence trickster but I didn't sense that he'd resort to violence.'

'Then how did I get this?' she asked.

Thrusting out an arm, she pulled up her sleeve to reveal an ugly bruise. Keedy was taken aback. When she displayed a matching bruise on the other arm, he accepted that she'd been held exceptionally hard.

'Do you want him charged for assault?'

'No, I want him arrested for murder.'

'We have no evidence that he was anywhere near the scene at the time.'

'Find it.'

'Mr Redmond has an alibi. I checked it myself.'

'Someone is lying on his behalf.'

'There's no proof of that.'

'Find it,' she demanded, on her feet. 'Find it, find it, find it!'

'What I can do,' he conceded, getting up from his chair, 'is to make sure that he's arrested and charged with assault.'

'That's not enough.'

'It's all I can do at the moment, Odele.'

'The charge will be denied.'

'How can it be? You have visible signs of the attack.'

'So does Allan,' she confessed.

'Are you saying that you provoked him?'

'That's what he'd argue in court and I don't want my name in the newspapers. If you get into trouble with the police, theatre managers won't touch you with a barge pole. Dancers are ten a penny. If I'm seen as a difficult woman who'd resort to violence, my reputation will turn to dust.'

He took a step closer. 'What exactly did you do?'

'It doesn't matter now.'

'I need to know, Odele.'

She tried to brush the question aside but Keedy insisted on an answer. In the end, she took a deep breath and told him the truth.

'I hit him with a flower vase.' He gaped in astonishment. 'But it was only in self-defence. Allan was trying to molest me, Joe. I had to do *something*.'

'Did you draw blood?'

'Only a little – that's what upset him. He grabbed me by the arms and shook me like a rag doll. I thought he was going to kill me.'

163

'What is it that you actually want?' he asked, torn between impatience and a growing attraction towards her. 'If I can't arrest him for assault, do you wish me to issue a warning? Is that why you're here?'

'No,' she replied, 'it isn't. Allan and I have . . . known each other in the past, though it was always on his terms, unfortunately. In order for you to understand, I'd have to explain what actually went on and I'm not sure that I can rely on your discretion.'

'Anything you tell me of a private nature will remain private.'

'I'm afraid that you'd tell the inspector.'

'I'd only tell him things that are related to the murder.'

'Allan Redmond is related to the murder,' she insisted. 'How many times do I have to tell you that? If you knew what he'd done to me in the past, you might start to believe me.'

'I do believe you, Odele,' he said, glancing at the bruises on her arms. 'You have my sympathy.'

She stepped forward and put both hands on his shoulders.

'I want more than that.'

'Do you?'

'I need police protection. Allan could come back. I need police protection,' she repeated with emphasis, 'and I want *you* to provide it, Joe. I want you to stay overnight in my flat to look after me.'

Before he could stop her, Odele kissed him full on the mouth.

CHAPTER THIRTEEN

Ellen Marmion felt completely isolated. Though her son was upstairs, it was as if she were the only person in the house. Her husband was still at work and her daughter was either with a friend or on her way back to her flat. Ellen did have the option of inviting one of her neighbours in but, when she'd done that before, Paul had been so unpleasant to the visitor that it had become a positive embarrassment. It was rather like having an uncontrollable dog that kept barking at anyone who crossed the threshold. At least for the moment, the dog was quiet and that afforded Ellen some relief. Adjourning to the living room, she tried to escape into the latest romantic novel she'd borrowed from the library but it failed to hold her interest for more than a few minutes. All she could do was to sit there in a daze.

Sounds from above eventually told her that Paul was on the move and she soon heard him coming downstairs and going into the kitchen. Unsure whether to join him or leave him alone, Ellen dithered. In the end, her son made the decision for her.

'Would you like a cup of tea?' he called.

'Yes, please,' she answered, getting up. 'I'd love one.'

She got to the kitchen in time to see him lighting the gas under the kettle.

'You still haven't eaten anything, Paul,' she said.

'I'm not hungry.'

'At least, let me make you a sandwich.'

'I had a big meal earlier on. I'm fine.'

'What about a biscuit?'

'I'm *fine*, Mum.'

He spoke with enough force to bring the conversation to an end for a couple of minutes. Ellen put the crockery on the table then reached for the milk and sugar. She eventually plucked up enough courage to ask him how he'd spent his day.

'Did you see Mavis?'

'Yes.'

'Where did you meet?'

'It doesn't matter,' he mumbled.

'What was she like?'

'Mavis was just as Colin said she'd be.'

'Did she talk about him at all?'

'Yes.'

'Did she ask you about . . . ?'

'That's private.'

'I just didn't want you to dwell too much on . . .'

Paul fell silent and she was afraid to say anything else. She watched while he made the tea then poured two cups before adding milk and sugar to one of them and stirring it. Without a word, he headed for the door. Ellen found her voice again.

'Paul . . .'

'Yes?'

'Bring your tea into the living room.'

'Why?'

'We could have a proper talk.'

'What about?'

He looked at her as if she'd just made the most ridiculous suggestion. Ellen felt utterly rejected. She made one last attempt to engage him in conversation.

'I heard you playing the mouth organ earlier on.'

'So?'

'It was "Onward, Christian Soldiers".'

'What about it?'

'Your Uncle Raymond would love to hear you play that.'

'It wasn't for *him*,' he said, disdainfully. 'It was for her.'

Turning his back on his mother, Paul went quickly upstairs.

It was uncanny. As soon as they got back to Scotland Yard and entered the building, Claude Chatfield knew they were there. When they reached Marmion's office, the superintendent was waiting for them. After an exchange of niceties with the two detectives, Chatfield demanded the latest intelligence. Marmion went first, describing his visit to Tom Atterbury and his subsequent discovery that the man was a member of the same club as Martin Pattinson.

'So we can put the two suspects under the same roof,' said Chatfield.

'It could just be a coincidence, sir.'

'I think you've stumbled on an important link, Inspector.'

'The club has a large membership,' argued Marmion. 'Atterbury and Pattinson may not even know each other. Having met both men, I can't see that they'd have much in common.'

'I'd endorse that,' said Keedy. 'They're unlikely friends.'

'You're both missing the obvious,' scolded Chatfield.

'Are we?'

'Yes, Sergeant, you are. They may have different personalities but what unites them is a mutual hatred of Mr Wilder. Since they have a common enemy, they might have come together to get rid of him.'

'I can see that Atterbury is a likely suspect,' said Keedy, 'because he was so shifty when I interviewed him, and the inspector had the same feeling about him. But I'm still not persuaded that Pattinson is in any way involved.'

'He has a motive,' Marmion pointed out. 'Although he appeared to approve of his wife's slavish devotion to Wilder, I fancy that he was seething with envy. You must remember those photographs of Wilder we saw at his house. Compare him to Pattinson. He's younger, more handsome and more attractive in every way. He could bring an excitement into Mrs Pattinson's life that her husband could never do.'

'Then why didn't he just stop her playing the piano for Wilder?'

'I don't know.'

'I fancy that that he rules the roost at home. If he hated Wilder that much, he could have forbidden his wife to have anything to do with him.'

'Separating them was not enough,' said Marmion, thinking it through. 'His hatred went deeper than that. Pattinson wanted revenge.'

'Yet on the night *of* the murder, he didn't go to his club,' said Chatfield, shrewdly. 'That was in one of your reports, Inspector. It wasn't his regular night there. How could he kill someone when he was lying beside his wife in bed?'

'He couldn't, sir. He needed someone else to stab Wilder to death. That brings us back to the curious fact that he and Atterbury belong to the same club and share the same loathing of Wilder.'

'In short, they're in this together. It was a conspiracy.'

'That's possible, Superintendent.'

'It's beginning to seem probable to me,' said Chatfield, imagination roaming. 'Atterbury did the deed but Pattinson helped to plan it. *That's* why he let his wife continue to work with Wilder. She would be aware of his movements. When he wanted to know where Wilder was likely to be on any given day, Pattinson simply had to ask his wife. Unbeknownst to her, she helped to set up a heinous crime.'

'With respect, sir,' said Marmion, 'you're confusing facts with guesswork. *Nobody* knew where Wilder was on the night of his murder, Mrs Pattinson least of all. Her only contact with him was at the studio.'

'He might have let slip where he'd be going that night.'

'Then why didn't she mention it to us?'

'The poor woman was grief-stricken. She couldn't think properly.'

'No,' said Marmion, firmly, 'if she'd had the slightest clue where he went, Mrs Pattinson would have told us by now. She's had time to get over the initial horror of what happened. Nobody is keener to see the killer found and arrested than her. She's desperate to help us without quite knowing how.'

Chatfield was adamant. 'I rely on instinct. Pattinson is implicated somehow.'

'There's something I'd question, sir.'

'What's that?'

'Earlier on, you said that on the night of the murder he was lying in bed beside his wife. You're assuming that they actually sleep together.'

'It's what married couples do, Inspector.'

'That's not true,' Keedy interjected. 'I have an uncle and aunt who don't sleep together even though they've been married for thirty years. Uncle Ben snores so much that Auntie Frances refuses to share the same bed.'

'And – as was pointed out once before – there are lots of other reasons why people sleep apart,' said Marmion.

'I agree with the inspector, sir. The Pattinsons did not strike me as a couple who were particularly close in any way. They could well have separate bedrooms.'

'That being the case,' said Chatfield, seizing on the suggestion, 'he *could* have committed the murder, after all. Pattinson could have waited until his wife dozed off then slipped quietly out of the house.'

Marmion was unconvinced but he held his tongue. After further speculation, Chatfield turned his attention to Keedy. It was a moment the sergeant had been dreading because he would have to describe his second meeting with Odele Thompson, an event that still caused him unease. He licked his lips before speaking. As Keedy recounted the incident, Marmion noted how nervous he seemed and wondered if they were hearing a full and unedited version of what had actually happened. When Keedy had first told him about Odele's visit, his account had been unusually concise. Marmion was now hearing additional details. Among them was the fact that Odele had demanded police protection.

'There's no question of that,' snapped Chatfield. 'We don't have the manpower to assign a bodyguard to her. Besides, I find it hard to have sympathy for the woman.'

'She was definitely attacked, sir,' said Keedy. 'I saw the bruises.'

'Redmond was retaliating after her assault.'

'He obviously terrified her.'

'To some extent, she asked for it. We're not talking about a vestal virgin here, Sergeant. Miss Thompson admitted that she and Redmond had been lovers – she even gave him a key to her flat. Intercourse outside marriage is a sin,' insisted Chatfield, 'and she paid the penalty for it.'

'That's a very harsh judgement, sir,' said Marmion.

'She struck the fellow with a flower vase and he hit her back. To my mind, that comes under the heading of a domestic incident. There's no need for police involvement. They both got what they deserved.'

'You're missing the point, sir,' ventured Keedy.

Chatfield glared. 'I *never* miss the point, Sergeant.'

'Redmond came to see her because she'd named him as a potential suspect. In doing so, he behaved in a way that I'd never have thought possible.'

'Nor me,' added Marmion. 'He was, by report, such a personable character. I couldn't envisage him threatening a woman, still less actually striking one.'

'We have another suspect, Superintendent,' said Keedy. 'Miss Thompson may have been right all along. Redmond was her first choice as the killer.'

'She was acting out of malice when she named him,' argued Chatfield. 'It's often the way with discarded lovers. They're driven by spite.'

'But Odele – Miss Thompson, I should say – was not discarded. She led me to believe that she got rid of *him*. She demanded the key back then threw him out of the flat. If anyone nursed resentment, it was Redmond.'

'It looks as if we now have three possible killers,' said Marmion, thoughtfully. 'To the names of Atterbury and Pattinson, we have to add that of Allan Redmond.'

'I favour the first two,' asserted Chatfield, 'acting together.'

Keedy shook his head. 'My preference would be for Redmond.'

'What's your opinion, Inspector?'

'So far,' said Marmion, 'we have three persons of interest. My opinion is that – before long – we may well have one or two more. Let me introduce a possibility that we haven't yet considered. The killer may not be a man, after all. Simon Wilder might have been murdered by a woman.'

* * *

Catherine Wilder was so full of anger that she wielded the knife with real venom. She was simply slicing a cucumber yet she might have been hacking away at her worst enemy. Not having been able to eat anything for several hours, she felt hungry but the only thing that tempted her palate was a cucumber and tomato sandwich. When she'd finished making it, she put it on the kitchen table and sank down into a chair. The doorbell then rang. Catherine's first impulse was to ignore it but she had second thoughts. Although it was quite late, she decided that it might be the police or even her brother, Nathan, returning for something he forgot to take with him. Reluctantly, she got up and went to the door. An unlikely caller awaited her.

'Colette!' she said in surprise.

'Hello, Mrs Wilder.'

'What are *you* doing here?'

'I was hoping for a few words with you,' said Colette, tentatively. 'If it's a bad time, I can always come back in the morning.'

'No, no – you might as well come in.'

Catherine let her visitor in and took her into the living room. Pointedly, she didn't offer Colette a seat. When she studied her, Catherine could see that she'd been crying. Like her husband, she'd been quick to identify her talent as a dancer but had grown tired of Wilder's endless praise of the girl. Whenever they'd met, there'd been a slight tension between them. Catherine resented the amount of time her husband lavished on the young dancer while Colette felt that she was being judged and found wanting by the older woman. The tension was now stronger than ever.

'I'm so sorry about what happened,' said Colette, trying to break it.

'We all are.'

'Yes, but it must be so much worse for you, Mrs Wilder. I only saw your husband for lessons. You shared your whole life with him.'

'I did have outside interests as well,' said Catherine, defensively.

'It was such a shame that you had to give up dancing. You were marvellous.'

'Thank you, Colette.'

'I'll always remember the two of you at the Dance Championships. You were wonderful to watch.'

Catherine was bitter. 'My career was cut short by a bad accident,' she said. 'Bear that in mind and be very careful at all times. You have to be in perfect health to dance well.'

'Mr Wilder kept telling me that.'

There was a lengthy pause. Colette shifted her feet uneasily while Catherine tossed a glance in the direction of the sandwich. Envious of her visitor's youth and lithe body, she just wanted her to go. Dispensing with politeness, she indicated the door.

'It was good of you to pass on your condolences,' she said, curtly, 'but I'm very tired and would like to be left alone.'

'Yes, yes, of course, Mrs Wilder. It's just that . . .'

'Well?'

'It's just that . . .'

'Go on, Colette – don't keep me waiting.'

'The thing is . . .' said the other, chewing her lip, 'the thing is . . .' Losing her nerve, she blurted out something she hadn't even intended to say. 'I was wondering what was going to happen to the dance studio.'

'It's closed down.'

'Are you going to sell it?'

'I haven't made any decision yet. The one thing I won't be doing is to reopen it. When we started, it was an exciting new project. Now . . . well, to be honest, it's just a burden, so it may well have to go.'

'That's very sad.' Seeing that Catherine wanted to usher her out,

Colette moved on to the real purpose of her visit. 'Did Mr Wilder *leave* anything for me?'

'What a strange question!'

'Did he?'

'I haven't really looked at his will.'

'I'm not talking about his will, Mrs Wilder. I just thought that . . . there might be something for me in an envelope.'

Catherine's voice tightened. 'Are you talking about money?'

'No, no, it's nothing like that.'

'I hope not.'

'Then forget I even came. It was wrong of me to interrupt you when . . . and it's not that important, anyway. If it had been, Mr Wilder would have left it for me. Clearly, he didn't. Goodbye,' said Colette, turning away, 'I'll let myself out.'

Before Catherine could move, her visitor hurried to the front door and opened it before charging out into the night. Fear and remorse etched deeply into her face, Colette ran all the way home.

When she got back to her flat, Alice Marmion began to regret that she'd been so intent on guarding her privacy. As a result, she would spend the rest of the evening alone. There were other female tenants in the house and they sometimes gathered in a room downstairs but there was no sign of them now. All that Alice could do was to return to her room and wonder what it was that made her want to keep Iris Goodliffe at a slight distance rather than seeing her as a potential true friend. Throughout the murder investigation, she would have to work her way through a whole litany of excuses because Iris would not be easily shaken off. There would come a time when Alice gave in out of exhaustion. Why not spare herself all the deceit, she asked?

As she sat beside the window, she gazed unseeingly down at the street. There was enough moonlight to pick out an old man with a dog on a lead. He walked past the house without looking up. A bus then drove past noisily. Alice didn't even hear the sound. It was only when a car drew up in her direct line of vision that she took notice. The door of the front passenger seat opened, someone got out and waved a thank you to the driver, then the vehicle pulled away. Alice was on her feet in an instant. Though she could not make him out clearly, she was certain that Keedy had come for her. She raced down the stairs and let herself out of the building.

Flinging herself into his arms, she kissed away the time they'd been apart.

'I never *dared* to expect you, Joe,' she said.

'I've always been full of surprises.'

'How did you get hold of that police car?'

'The driver was an old friend. I asked for a favour.'

'Well, I'm the one who got the favour,' said Alice, squeezing his arm. 'Let's go for a walk.'

'You could always invite me in,' he teased.

'If I did that, my landlady would throw me straight out again. You know the rules, Joe. Men are only allowed in at certain times and under controlled conditions.'

'What did your landlady used to be – a prison wardress?'

'She's very old-fashioned, that's all.'

He fell in beside her and she took his arm. They strolled on down the street. For the first few minutes, they said nothing at all, simply enjoying the pleasure of being together again. Then he glanced upwards.

'Who knows? We might get to see another Zeppelin being shot down.'

'It was an amazing sight, wasn't it?'

'Yes, Alice, the problem was that it got me into trouble with your father.'

'What did Daddy say?'

'He wasn't happy that I kept you out so late,' said Keedy. 'You didn't get back to bed until the dead of night and neither did I. Not that I need have bothered, mind you. No sooner had I fallen asleep than I was awakened again. Your father was outside in a car. On the drive to Scotland Yard, I told him we'd actually seen the air raid and he went off into that disapproving silence of his. Anyway,' he added, 'that's enough about me. What have you been getting up to?'

Alice told her about the new recruit and how she somehow had reservations about Iris Goodliffe. Though she liked her immensely, she felt unable to take their friendship to another level.

'I can explain that,' he said, airily.

'Can you?'

'It's deep-seated jealousy. If you let her into your social life, you're afraid that she'll fall madly in love with me and want to scratch your eyes out.' He recoiled from the punch she gave him in the ribs. 'It's one explanation.'

'Believe it or not, Joe Keedy, not every young woman is standing there with her tongue out, waiting for you to come along. As it happens, Iris doesn't seem that interested in men. She's never had a boyfriend and never taken steps to find one.'

'Is she attractive?'

'She could be.'

'So what's the problem?'

'Iris thinks she'd too podgy to interest men.'

'Then let her lose weight. Take her out running somewhere.'

'I don't like running.'

'That's not true at all. You ran after me for years. Aouw!' he yelled as she landed another punch. 'All right, maybe *I* was the one doing the chasing but that's what men are supposed to do, isn't it?'

'You can be very annoying sometimes, Joe.'

'It's one of my many irresistible features.' She laughed and he slipped an arm around her shoulders. 'So what are you going to do with Iris?'

'I haven't decided.'

'That's unlike you, Alice. You're very decisive as a rule.'

'I don't want her to take over my social life completely.'

'Then tell her that in so many words. I'm sure that she'd appreciate a bit of leisure time with you even if it's strictly limited.'

'I don't want to be unkind to her.'

'Find out what she's like off duty. There's no harm in that, is there?'

Alice was pensive. 'I suppose not . . .'

'Right,' he said, 'that's your problem solved. Let me tell you about one that I have. In the course of our investigation, we've met a middle-aged pianist and her somewhat older husband. Answer me this: how do we find out if the pair of them sleep together?' When she began to giggle, Keedy was upset. 'Don't laugh, Alice,' he remonstrated. 'It's a serious question.'

Seated at the grand piano in an empty house, Audrey Pattinson was in her element, playing a medley of waltzes, quicksteps and foxtrots as if trying to evoke the spirit of Simon Wilder. As her fingers moved deftly over the keys, she remembered him dancing with his wife, circling the floor in such perfect harmony that they might have been joined mysteriously together. Odele Thompson came next to mind, working hard to master every new figure she was taught and always ready to take the rehearsal on beyond its allotted time. Other female dancers came to mind, some much older than Wilder but feeling rejuvenated when they were being instructed by him. Finally, Audrey recalled the way that Colette Orme had been introduced to the dance studio by her mentor. She arrived as a wide-eyed young woman with a lack of confidence and been taken on a magical journey, honing her raw talent into something that was a delight to behold and that would – in time, perhaps – have commercial viability.

Simon Wilder had made such a difference to so many lives. Men had profited from his instruction just as well as women. One couple who first met at the dance studio went on to get married and Audrey had played the organ at their wedding. Lost in her love of dance music and the memories it kindled, she nevertheless realised that she was no longer alone. While she didn't hear her husband's key being inserted in the lock, she was very much aware of his presence. Moments later, Pattinson opened the door of the living room and looked in.

'You'll have to stop playing now,' he said.

She closed the lid of the piano at once. 'Yes, yes, of course I will, Martin.'

'I'm going to bed. It's time that you did as well.'

'You're right,' she said, submissively. 'It is rather late.'

There was an exchange of muted farewells, then Pattinson climbed the stairs. Audrey heard him go along the corridor using a key to unlock the door of his bedroom. As on every other night, she heard her husband lock it again from within.

Since their father went off to work early that morning, Colette and her brother were left to have breakfast together. Orme spoke through a mouthful of toast.

'Dad says that you went out last night.'

'Yes, I did.'

'Where did you go?'

'I just went for a walk.'

He smiled sadly. 'And I daresay that walk took you past the studio, didn't it?' She nodded. 'There are other places to learn, Colette.'

'Nobody could teach me like Mr Wilder.'

'Then you've got to accept that and live with it. Look at me,' he went on, indicating his leg. 'Nothing will ever be the same for me either, will it? I'm never going to play football or do any of the things I loved to do. So I simply put it all behind me and start afresh.'

'That's different, Dennis.'

'The difference is that you still *can* carry on as before. Inside your head, you've got all those dances and figures that Mr Wilder taught you. Find a new partner and you can blossom even more.'

'I don't feel like dancing ever again,' she confessed.

'You will, Colette.'

'I don't see how.'

'Dad believes in you,' he said, earnestly, 'and so do I. That's why we scrimped and saved to pay for the lessons. Don't let us down, please. And don't let Mrs Pattinson down either,' he went on. 'She believes in you as well.'

Colette ate her toast and retreated into silence. She still regretted the decision to go to the Wilder house. She'd been given a tepid welcome and left in turmoil. There was no way that she could explain to Catherine what she was really after. All that she did was to feel extreme embarrassment. It was only when her brother offered to make some more tea that she realised he was there.

'No, thank you,' she said. 'I've had enough.'

'So have I, then. I drink too much tea as it is.' Orme grinned. 'Last night, I drank far too much beer.'

'I was in bed when you got back.'

'They had to carry me most of the way.'

'Daddy said that he'd always fetch you.'

'I hate to call on him, Colette. Besides, what else are friends for?'

Dennis Orme was a sociable character. As soon as he was released from hospital, he set about finding other injured soldiers from his regiment so that they could meet in a pub once or twice a week to share their experiences at the front. They were important meetings for him, getting him out of the house and talking to the only people who really understood what he'd been through. Colette was proud that her brother was the unofficial leader of the group but she did worry that he drank far too much.

'It's not good for you, Dennis.'

'You can't turn down a pint from a friend – and the beer is watered, anyway.'

'I worry about you.'

'The only thing you need to worry about is a career as a dancer,' he said. 'It's what we've all worked for, Colette. I can't wait for the time when I walk past a theatre and see your name up in lights.'

'I'd prefer to be known as a ballroom dancer.'

'Then I'll polish every cup you win until it dazzles your eyes.' She laughed and reached out to touch his hand. 'It won't be long before I earn a proper wage again. My leg doesn't hurt any more and I'm getting more and more movement in this other arm of mine. Can you hear what I'm saying, Colette?'

'I think so.'

'I'll soon be able to pay for *more* lessons for you.'

Harvey Marmion was already missing the amenities of his office at Scotland Yard. While it was serviceable, the room allotted to them at Chingford Police Station had few comforts and, even in the warm weather, had a lingering dankness. What both he and Keedy had noticed was the reliance on special constables. They were always flitting in and out. Some of them were in their fifties and sixties. War had depleted the Metropolitan Police Force. The thousands of officers who'd left to join the army had been replaced by untrained volunteers who learnt as they went along. At a time when the scope of police duties had widened considerably, the force was distinctly understaffed and overburdened.

'We could do with another twenty detectives at least, Joe,' said Marmion.

'Make it thirty. We need to knock on every door in Chingford.'

'*Somebody* must have been with Wilder that night.'

'I agree,' said Keedy. 'The trouble is that she probably has a husband. The last thing she wants to admit is that she was enjoying some hanky-panky with another man. She must be panic-stricken at the thought that she was one of the last people to see him alive.'

'We can't assume that a lover is involved.'

'Wilder was a ladies' man.'

'You're forgetting that he had a beautiful wife.'

'I still think that he strayed and I fancy that Mrs Wilder reached the same conclusion. It would explain why she didn't exactly behave like most wives of murder victims. You said how controlled she seemed.'

'That was because her brother was there.'

'I think there was another reason. Deep down, she doesn't really *care*.'

'Some people don't wear their hearts on their sleeve. Catherine Wilder could be one of them – unlike Miss Thompson, for instance.'

Mention of Odele Thompson made the sergeant recall his meeting with her on the previous day. He could still taste her kiss and felt guilty at doing so. It was one of the reasons he made the effort to see Alice that night.

'Right,' he said, getting up, 'if you want me to tackle Allan Redmond again, I'll be on my way. What will *you* be doing this morning?'

'I'll be speaking to Wilder's bank manager. As soon as Gibbs turns up to take over here, I'll be off. Bank managers are like priests taking confession. They tend to know their clients' darkest secrets.'

'My guess is that Wilder's were darker than most.'

'Leave me to find that out, Joe. Your job is to plumb Redmond's secrets.'

He waved Keedy off and the sergeant left the room. In less than a minute, there was a tap on the door and Marmion expected Detective Constable Gibbs to report for duty. Instead, it was a uniformed policeman with the news that a woman had arrived to speak to the inspector.

'What's her name, Constable?'

'Mrs Hogg, sir.'

'Show the lady in.'

The policeman went out and returned a few seconds later with a tall, shapely, handsome woman in her thirties. Her features were clouded with concern. Left alone with Marmion, she was anxious to know if anyone had yet been arrested for the murder.

'Oh,' she said, drawing back, 'do forgive me, Inspector. I haven't even introduced myself. I'm Gillian Hogg.'

'Hogg was Mr Wilder's real name, wasn't it? Are you related to him?'

'Yes and no – that's to say, I used to be and, in some ways, I still am.'

'You're confusing me, Mrs Hogg.'

'It's quite simple,' she said. 'I was Simon's first wife.'

CHAPTER FOURTEEN

As she washed up the breakfast things, Ellen Marmion swung to and fro between regret and apprehension. Guilt dogged her. She was profoundly sorry that she'd unloaded all her worries on to her husband the moment he got through the door. After a long day at work, Marmion had arrived home just before midnight to be greeted by an exhaustive account of Ellen's latest anxieties about their son. It had only increased his frustration at being unable to confront Paul himself because of his commitments at work. All that Marmion could do was to soothe his wife and offer advice. When she recalled how tired her husband had looked and sounded, Ellen blamed herself for keeping him away from his bed for so long and resolved to be more considerate next time.

Apprehension swiftly displaced regret. She'd reached a point when she had to admit that she was deeply afraid of her son, fearful of what he would do or say and unable to exert any influence on him. Ellen looked back with a shudder at the long list of people – family members included – who'd been offended by Paul's behaviour. She wondered who would be his next victim. And yet, she reminded herself, he had been much more subdued since his meeting with Mavis Tandy. Ellen had feared that talking to her about life at the front would intensify

Paul's nightmares and lead to even more erratic behaviour. Surprisingly, however, Mavis seemed to have had a calming effect on him, leading Ellen to wonder exactly what had happened between them and to feel snubbed when he refused to tell her.

Paul had been remarkably quiet during breakfast but at least there'd been no sign of his bad temper. Ellen was grateful for that. What she couldn't understand was why he was spending an inordinately long time in the bathroom. When he eventually came downstairs again, she had her answer. He'd taken even more care with his appearance than on the previous day. He'd shaved, combed his hair with meticulous care and put on his best suit. His shoes had been polished to a high sheen. He was no longer the slovenly son, lounging around the house all day and prone to tantrums.

'You look very smart,' she said, brushing a speck of dust off his shoulder.

'Thank you.'

'Are you going somewhere important?'

'That's my business.'

'Yes, yes, of course – I didn't mean to pry.'

'I don't know what time I'll be back.'

'I see.'

'Don't make any meals for me.'

'Where will you eat?'

'I'm off now.'

'Wait,' she said, touching his sleeve. 'Is there anything you need?'

He looked indignant. 'What do you mean?'

'Well – money, for instance. I can lend you some, if need be.'

'I've got everything I want.'

'You only have to ask, Paul.'

'I can manage on my own.'

And without a word of farewell, he turned on his heel and left the house.

The unexpected arrival of Gillian Hogg had introduced a whole new dimension to the investigation. Since she was clearly so uncertain and overwrought, Marmion first offered her a seat then called for some tea to be made. When he described how the investigation was going, he chose his words with care. No reference was made to the hideous injuries sustained by Wilder because he wanted to shield her from the full details. Gradually, she began to relax. As her pinched face resumed something like its normal shape, he could see how attractive she was and was bound to wonder why any husband would cast her aside. Only when the tea arrived, and she'd had her first few sips, was she able to talk about herself.

'This won't get into the newspapers, will it?' she asked, nervously.

'That depends on what you tell me, Mrs Hogg.'

'It's very private.'

'All I'm interested in is information that will help me catch the person or persons I'm after,' he assured her. 'Anything you tell me of a personal nature will be respected as such.'

'Thank you, Inspector.'

She needed another sip of tea before she was ready to plunge in. When she did so, she spoke rapidly, looking over her shoulder to make sure nobody else was listening. Gillian was trembling.

'You'll wonder why I haven't come forward until now,' she began.

'I'm just glad that you *have* seen fit to contact us.'

'When I heard the news, I was petrified. I just couldn't move or think. The horror of it all was just too much to take in. Can you understand that?'

'It's not an unfamiliar reaction, Mrs Hogg.'

'I kept torturing myself with the thought that I might have done something to avert what happened but' – she spread her arms – 'how was I to know?' Gillian braced herself before her revelation. 'Simon was with me that night, you see.'

Marmion sat up with interest. 'Can you give me a precise time?'

'He left me sometime between half past nine and ten o'clock.'

'And where were the two of you at the time?'

'We were in my flat, Inspector,' she explained. 'Actually, it's *our* flat. It's still in our joint names. It's in Archer Street.'

'That's close to Shaftesbury Avenue,' he said. 'Mr Wilder was spotted there around ten o'clock by three different people. What I need to know is where he went afterwards. Did he tell you?'

'I'm afraid not – but I can tell you where he *didn't* go.'

'Well?'

'This must go no further,' she warned. 'I don't want anyone to know that I told you this – especially one particular person.'

'You can trust me, Mrs Hogg.'

'This is going to sound like malice on my part but that's not what it is at all.'

'I'll remember that.'

She looked him in the eye. 'Simon didn't go straight home, Inspector,' she said, 'because he didn't feel welcome there.'

'Is that what brought him to you in the first place?'

'We're good friends. In view of what happened, that may seem strange but it's the truth. We met and married when we were both struggling to make a living on the stage and we soon realised that it had been nothing more than an infatuation. Oh, that's not a complaint,' she went on. 'While it lasted, it was wonderfully exciting. It was like being in a state of permanent inebriation.'

'That's something I've never experienced,' he admitted. 'I've always had a sober disposition. Are you saying that you parted from Mr Wilder amicably?'

'It suited both of us,' she said, crisply. 'My career was taking me more and more outside London and Simon already had his eye on someone – or, to be more exact, Catherine had her eye on *him*. She'd been waiting in the wings for some time.'

'I gather that she's a wealthy woman.'

'I could never compete with her on those terms. Where I did have the whip hand over her was in the simple matter of caring for Simon. I loved him and listened to him. That's why we remained friends. Whenever he had a problem, he couldn't discuss it with Catherine, he always turned to me.'

Marmion was intrigued by the glimpse of a new aspect of the murder victim.

'And what sort of problems did Mr Wilder have, exactly?' he asked.

Keedy arrived at the house to find that Allan Redmond was not there. He was, however, as a kindly neighbour pointed out, very close at hand. Keedy only had to walk around the corner to the tennis club and there was Redmond in his tennis kit, looking fit and agile as he played a much older man. His service was so powerful and well directed that his opponent had difficulty getting his racquet on the ball, let alone returning it over the net. On the other hand, when the older man served, the ball was hit back hard every time and Redmond controlled the subsequent rally. In the end, the older man lunged forward and stretched for a ball that dropped tantalisingly over the net. He let out a yelp of pain. Clutching one thigh, he hopped on the other leg and signalled that the match was over.

After watching Redmond sympathise with the man, Keedy moved in. Once again, the dancer behaved as if he was expecting the visit and had no objection to it. There was a piece of sticking plaster on his temple. He touched it gently.

'This is what you've come about, isn't it?' he asked, amiably. 'I daresay that Odele told you about our little tussle.'

'You always seem to choose opponents who offer little resistance,' said Keedy, indicating the player now limping off court. 'Your friend was no match for you and neither was Miss Thompson.'

'I dispute that, Sergeant! She brained me with a flower vase.'

'That was after she caught you trespassing on her property.'

Redmond smirked. 'I just dropped in to discuss old times.'

'You went there to threaten the lady because she brought you to our attention. I'm beginning to see why she did so now.'

'Odele likes to cause mischief. That's all she was doing.'

'You caused more than mischief, sir. She was shaking with fear.'

'I don't believe that for a second,' said the other. 'She's as hard as nails. You have to be tough in an overcrowded profession like ours. Those gushing tears and the cries of terror were for *your* benefit, Sergeant. Odele has taken a fancy to you. She likes strong and handsome young men.'

'Not when they attack her, she doesn't.'

Redmond fixed him with a challenging stare. 'Does she want me prosecuted?'

'In my opinion, she *should* do.'

'Answer my question.'

'No,' conceded Keedy. 'Miss Thompson decided against it.'

'There you are, then,' said the other, triumphantly. 'Odele is a real fighter, I'll admit that. We often came to blows when she and I were

188

close friends. An argument would flare up, there was an unholy struggle, then we settled our differences in the most pleasurable way.' He beamed at Keedy. 'It was worth taking any amount of punishment for that.'

For a brief moment, Keedy felt the warmth of her body again and the softness of her lips upon his. He tried to dismiss the memory and concentrate on his job.

'I need to speak to you again, Mr Redmond,' he said, seriously.

'You *are* speaking to me, old chap.'

'I'd rather do it when you're properly dressed.'

'You're about my height and build,' said Redmond, sizing him up. 'I've got some spare kit at the house. I don't suppose you'd fancy a game of tennis before you put the thumbscrews on me, would you?'

'I'm sorry you take this so lightly, sir.'

'It's in my nature.'

'You are now officially a suspect in a murder inquiry.'

'That's nonsense. I'm the victim of Odele's twisted sense of humour.'

'Are you ready, Mr Redmond?'

Keedy pointed to the exit. After exchanging a long, hard look with him, the dancer twirled his racquet expertly in his hand then led the way off court.

There had been many times in his police career when Harvey Marmion was reminded that he had led a very conventional life. He now had another to add to his collection. As Gillian Hogg talked about her past, he realised that his own had been remarkably uneventful by comparison. Having run away from boarding school at seventeen, she'd been more or less disowned by her parents and had subsisted by taking on various jobs and by relying on the hospitality of friends. The one thing that her school had inculcated in her was a love of drama and she gravitated towards the West End, accepting the most menial employment if it got her through the doors of a theatre. Gillian eventually worked her way up to a post as an assistant stage manager that led, in turn, to fleeting appearances onstage. When she finally got a part in her own right, Simon Wilder, the former Stanley Hogg, was in the cast. They were lovers within a week.

What staggered Marmion was the ease with which they'd reached the decision to divorce. In return for being allowed to keep their tiny flat in Archer Street, she had agreed to provide evidence of adultery on her part so that her husband appeared to be the injured party. Yet, at the same time, she revealed that he had been unfaithful to her on a number of occasions. Shockingly, Gillian had accepted his infidelity without complaint. No woman of Marmion's acquaintance would behave like that. During his courtship of Ellen, he'd been roundly chastised by her if he so much as looked at another woman, however innocently. Yet here was a wife who condoned adultery as a normal and acceptable part of marriage.

'To put it simply,' said Gillian with a touch of pride, 'I was the one person to whom he could turn in a crisis and, as you've heard, Simon had quite a few of those. He came to me the other night to complain yet again of Catherine's treatment of him. When she could no longer dance, she became hostile and resentful.'

'I can understand her resentment, Mrs Hogg, but why was she so hostile?'

'She could no longer work alongside him at the studio and keep an eye on him. When the cat's away . . .'

'Is that what was happening?'

'It's what Catherine *thought* was happening, so it amounted to the same thing. At first, she accused him of seducing Jane Lammerton.'

'That's a new name to me.'

'She was a beautiful young girl who came for dance instruction. Simon swears that he didn't lay a hand on her but Catherine had her kicked out and barred her from the studio. Then there was Odele.'

'I thought Mrs Wilder accepted Miss Thompson as her husband's partner.'

'It was only after issuing a dire warning of what would happen to him if he dared to lure Odele into bed. Catherine said that . . .' Gillian cleared her throat. 'She said that she'd make it impossible for him ever to make love to a woman again.'

Marmion thought about the injuries inflicted on the murder victim and he had the unsettling thought that the man's own wife might in some way be responsible. It was clear from what he was hearing that Wilder and his wife had been locked into an increasingly bleak marriage.

'After Odele, it was someone called Nancy Lane and, after her, it was another girl with a pretty smile. Simon faced accusation after accusation and the irony was that he hadn't touched one of them. The latest was Colette Orme. He showed me a photo he took of her and she looked angelic. I could see why he'd be tempted,' said Gillian, 'but not with Catherine bellowing threats in his ears. She was poisoning his life, Inspector.'

Marmion sat back and glanced down at the few notes he'd been making. Most of what Gillian had told him had been unrecorded and he would certainly not pass it on to Claude Chatfield, who'd be scandalised by the irregularities of her marriage to Wilder. Nor would he dare to tell his own wife about the kind of existence that the dancer and his first wife had led. It was so far removed from Ellen's experience that she wouldn't believe it.

'Did he ever take you anywhere?' he asked.

'No, Inspector, he always came to me at the flat. Sometimes he just wanted to scrounge a drink. He was often in the area.'

'So we were told. He liked to hang around theatres.'

'Simon was a realist. He couldn't go on dancing that well for ever so he knew he'd have to go back to acting eventually. It's not only a question of talent,' she said. 'Having the right contacts is far more important. That's why Simon tried to keep in with producers and managers. He'd need them some day.'

'So he never took you to Chingford?'

'No, he didn't.'

'That's where he was found, you see. We'd like to know why he was in that specific part of the district. What made him go there in the first place?'

'Perhaps that's not what he did, Inspector.'

'I don't follow.'

'What if he didn't go there of his own volition?' she suggested. 'Supposing that someone *took* him there – by force, probably?'

Not for the first time, Marmion was glad that Gillian Hogg had been impelled to come to him. The investigation had taken a promising change of direction.

The parish church of St Mary Magdalene was the oldest building in Gillingham and, though it had undergone many changes over the centuries, it was still an impressive sight. Set at the heart of the town, it was known as the Church on the Green because it was surrounded by an expanse of grass. It had taken Paul Marmion some time to get to Gillingham. Getting off the bus too early, he'd had to ask for directions then tramp for the best part of a mile. Mavis Tandy had been relieved to see him at last and had taken him straight to her father's church. As they sat together in a pew at the rear of the nave, Paul felt increasingly uncomfortable but Mavis was completely at home.

'Can you sense it?' she asked.

'What do you mean?'

'Well, the church is empty but I can feel a presence.'

'Of course,' he said. 'I'm here with you.'

'No, Paul, there's someone else and he's looking down on us.'

'Is he?'

'A church is never empty, you see. He's always there.'

Closing her eyes, she went off into a kind of trance. Paul had no idea what she was talking about but he didn't want to upset Mavis in any way. He closed his own eyes and savoured the gentle touch of her shoulder against his.

'Can you feel it now?' she said at length.

'Yes, I can, Mavis.'

Then he wondered if Colin Fryatt had told her the same barefaced lie.

Joe Keedy would have preferred it if the man had changed out of his tennis kit but Redmond insisted on having the interview as soon as they got back to the house. With the look of a natural athlete, he enjoyed showing off his physique.

'Most people think that tennis is a summer game,' he said, flopping into a chair, 'but I play it all the year round. The only things that would stop me are a violent thunderstorm or three feet of snow. What about you, Sergeant?'

'I've never played tennis, sir.'

'That's a pity. You have all the necessary attributes.'

'I lack the most important one,' said Keedy. 'I don't have a racquet.

Tennis was a sport that I never even considered because it cost money to play. Joining a club and buying all the equipment can be expensive. I preferred football. All you need is a patch of land and a ball.'

'Why did you go into the police force?'

'That's immaterial, Mr Redmond. We're here to talk about you.'

'I'm just trying to be sociable.'

'Well, I'm not,' said Keedy, warningly. 'Why did you go to Miss Thompson's flat yesterday?'

Redmond laughed. 'I'd call that a redundant question, Sergeant. You've seen Odele. Any red-blooded man would want to spend time in private with her.'

'You went uninvited.'

'I had a key and couldn't resist the urge to use it.'

'You went there to frighten her.'

'She was the one who frightened *me*. Have you ever been hit on the head with a flower vase? It damn well hurt.'

'So did the way you grabbed her by the arms.'

'Odele used to like that in the old days,' said the other with a nostalgic grin. 'It was the one sure way to end a lovers' tiff.'

'In this case, you meant it as a punishment because she gave us your name.'

'Well, it was rather naughty of Odele.'

'The last time we met, you gave me an account of your movements on the night when Mr Wilder was killed.'

'I had nothing to hide, Inspector. As you found out, what I told you was the plain, unvarnished truth. You checked my alibi and realised that I was innocent of the charge.'

'Do you still maintain that innocence, sir?'

'Of course I do.'

'Then why bother to harass Miss Thompson? You had no need to do that. Being questioned by the police was a nuisance but it hardly justifies what you did.'

'I just wanted to . . . express my displeasure.'

'Oh, you did more than that,' argued Keedy. 'You didn't just go there to register a complaint. Your intention was to bully Miss Thompson so that she wouldn't tell us anything else about you. Now why would you do that if – as you said a moment ago – you had nothing to hide?'

'Well,' said Redmond, easily, 'perhaps there *are* one or two things I would like to keep secret but that's true of every man, isn't it? What about you, Sergeant? I dare swear that you've had your share of little adventures that you'd rather not talk about. It's normal behaviour for a chap.'

'Murder is never normal, sir.'

'You've established that my alibi is sound. Why not leave me alone?'

'There are two reasons,' said Keedy. 'First, you gave yourself away when you threatened Miss Thompson. An innocent man wouldn't have needed to do that. But the second reason is the important one.'

'I can't wait to hear it,' said Redmond with a taunting smile.

'When we returned to Scotland Yard yesterday, we saw the post-mortem report. It's always difficult to be precise about the time of death. We know the exact moment when the body was discovered but the pathologist believes that Mr Wilder could have been killed as much as four hours earlier.'

'So? I was right here, watching the air raid.'

'Yes,' said Keedy, 'but what did you do immediately afterwards? I've been looking at a map of London, sir. Wimbledon may seem a fair distance away from Chingford but not if you have access to a car, and I couldn't help noticing on my first visit here that there was one in the garage.'

'It belongs to my parents.'

'Oh, I expect you have a key, Mr Redmond. If they let you use their house so freely, your parents would surely give you free use of their car. So it would have been more than possible for you to leave here well after the air raid. You could have driven to Chingford,' Keedy went on, watching him carefully, 'stabbed Mr Wilder to death then returned here. That could all have happened quite easily within the time-frame given to us in the post-mortem report. What do you say to that, sir?'

Redmond's taunting smile had frozen solid.

Paul Marmion had been misled. The fact that Mavis wanted to see him two days in a row gave him the idea that she had become very fond of him but her primary interest was still in someone who was killed at the battle of the Somme. Paul had to repeat the same story time and again, always assuring her that Colin Fryatt had her photograph in his pocket as he fell. Gory details that Paul would never dare to mention to his mother and sister were drawn out of him by Mavis. She was determined to know everything.

'What do you think of Gillingham?' she asked.

'I like it.'

'Have you been to Kent before?'

'Only when I sailed to and from France – but Colin always said how nice Kent was.'

'What did he say about Gillingham?'

'He told me that he loved it because it was where *you* lived,' said Paul, putting words into his friend's mouth that had not actually been spoken.

His lie had the desired effect. Mavis emitted a long sigh of pleasure and grabbed his hand impulsively, thanking him for telling her something that she would treasure. They were walking beside the river in the morning sunshine. Paul was desperate to put an arm around her or, at the very least, slip a hand into hers but there was no question of that while they were talking about a third person. Even though he'd been dead for some weeks now, Colin Fryatt's presence was still very much felt.

'I've been practising "Onward, Christian Soldiers",' he volunteered.

'That's wonderful.'

'I'm nowhere near as good as Colin yet.'

'He was a real musician. I could see that. He talked about learning to play the trumpet so that he could join a proper band. Colin would have been good at that. He was good at everything he turned his hand to.'

Once again, Paul choked back a contradiction. While he had his talents, Colin Fryatt also had some glaring weaknesses and, during their short time together, he'd managed to conceal them from Mavis. Most of what she believed had come from letters he'd scribbled to her in the trenches. Before she fell asleep at night, Mavis read each one of them again before putting them under her pillow.

'Can you play it for me now, Paul?'

'What?'

'"Onward Christian Soldiers".'

'Oh, I don't know it well enough to do that.'

'But you said you'd been practising.'

'Yes, I have but . . .'

'I know it won't be the same as Colin, so I'll make allowances.'

Paul was in a quandary. Wanting to please her, he knew that he could play the hymn passably well. Yet he was prevented from doing so, knowing that his version would be a pale imitation of the one she'd heard Colin play. Also, there was something that weighed more heavily with him – the words of the hymn appalled him. While they spoke of notional soldiers in a spiritual war, he'd fought in a real one and found Christianity totally irrelevant. It had neither inspired nor protected Paul. When shells were landing all round him and when machine gun bullets were zipping through the air, he felt utterly at their mercy.

'Please,' she said, almost pleading. 'I'd love to hear you play.'

'I'm sorry,' he replied, 'but I forgot to bring the mouth organ.'

The instrument suddenly felt like a ton weight in Paul's pocket.

Alice decided to take Joe Keedy's advice. Instead of refusing to let Iris Goodliffe into her social life, she should first see how she got on with her colleague when they were off duty. Alice therefore bided her time until they broke off to take some refreshment. Iris was as effervescent as ever, plying her with questions, telling her family anecdotes and breaking into giggles whenever she saw something remotely amusing. As they sat down together, she turned to a more serious subject.

'It was on the front page at last,' she said. 'They mentioned your father's name and quoted what he said about the murder. All over London, people are reading about Inspector Marmion. You must be very proud of that, Alice.'

'I'm more proud than Daddy ever will be. He hates publicity like that. He always urges the press to concentrate on the facts of the case rather than on him. But they never listen.'

'I'd love to see *my* name in a newspaper.'

'That depends on what it's in there for,' said Alice with a laugh. 'You wouldn't be so happy if you were accused of soliciting or if you'd been named because you got drunk and ran naked down Tottenham Court Road.' Iris joined in the laughter. 'That actually happened, by the way. A middle-aged woman rolled out of a pub on a hot, sticky night, peeled off her clothes and staggered off down the road as if she was in some kind of race. When we caught up with her, she asked us the way to Euston.' Iris had a fit of giggles. 'Imagine how she must have felt when she saw *her* name in the papers.'

'You've met some funny people in this job, Alice.'

'It's opened my eyes, I'll admit that.'

They ate their meal and chatted away. The invitation came out of the blue.

'What are you doing this evening, Iris?'

'Nothing at all – what about you?'

'I thought I might go and see a film.'

'Which one?'

'I haven't decided. Would you like to come with me?'

Iris's face was a study in joy. It was over as simply as that.

Harvey Marmion was still at the police station when Keedy got back there. Detective Constable Gibbs stepped out of the room so that they had privacy. Each of them was eager to pass on news to the other. Bowing to his seniority, Keedy let the inspector go first and he listened agog at what he was told. Gillian Hogg's sudden intervention had indeed been illuminating. There was only one drawback for Keedy. Marmion talked about Wilder's promiscuity in a way that sounded like a sermon on fidelity and his future son-in-law didn't like the feeling that he was, by implication, being warned. The new evidence, however, was fascinating.

'A few days ago, we didn't have a single suspect,' Keedy pointed out, 'yet, in the course of one morning, we found two more.'

'Mrs Wilder deserves to be investigated, Joe, but I don't think she'd have actually killed him. She'd have found someone else to do that.'

'Do you have any idea who it might be?'

'None at all – and Gillian Hogg couldn't suggest a name either.'

'But she did tell you enough to throw suspicion on to Mrs Wilder.'

'Oh, yes – what she told me tallies with a number of things I'd noticed about the lady. Mrs Wilder is cool and calculating. If she *was* indirectly involved in the murder, it won't come as a rude shock to me. But you tell me about *your* suspect,' urged Marmion. 'Did Redmond try to charm you again?'

'He tried and failed.'

Keedy's report was shorter but no less interesting. He described how he'd finally got Redmond on the defensive and how the latter had tried to bluster his way out of his predicament. Having put some real fear into the dancer, Keedy had left.

'But I didn't go far,' he explained. 'I had a feeling that I'd lit a fire under Redmond's arse so I got the driver to pull over a block away from the house. My instinct was sound. He hadn't even bothered to change. Redmond came rushing out of the front door, opened the garage and backed the car out. Then he tore off down the road at speed. I proved one thing,' he concluded. 'Redmond *can* drive that car.'

'Well done, Joe. Will you tell Miss Thompson about your visit?'

'No,' said Keedy, awkwardly, 'there's no need for her to know that I even saw Redmond. She wasn't prepared to bring charges against him, so that's that.'

'It might be worth having another word with her.'

'Why?'

'You could get confirmation of what Mrs Hogg told me. If he and his second wife were effectively living separate lives, Miss Thompson would certainly know about it. See what you can dig out of her.'

Keedy was not happy with the assignment but he could not evade it without an explanation and he refused even to think of telling Marmion about the way that Odele had behaved when they were alone together.

'When are you going to see Wilder's bank manager?' he asked.

'I was just about to leave when you came back.'

'It's only a short walk down the high street. I'm glad that *you're* going and not me. I've always been in dread of bank managers.'

'If you remain solvent, they'll be as nice as pie to you. Well,' said Marmion with a smile of satisfaction, 'we've had a bonanza. You came back with an increased suspicion of one suspect and I was handed another suspect on a plate.'

'What comes next – a confession of guilt?'

'Let's not be greedy, Joe.'

'We can but hope. At least, we've made enough progress to keep Chat off our backs. He might actually be pleased with us for once.'

Marmion laughed. 'I don't believe in miracles.'

They were about to leave the room when the door was suddenly flung open and Claude Chatfield walked in with a gleam in his eye.

'Ah,' he said, 'I've caught you together so you can both hear the good news. I've discovered a suspect that neither of you even considered. His name should go straight to the top of the list.' His smirk oozed with self-congratulation. 'I had a feeling that I'd have to come here to do your job for you.'

CHAPTER FIFTEEN

Audrey Pattinson read the newspaper report yet again as if expecting new details to emerge about the murder. None appeared, however, and her hopes were dashed. The killer was still at liberty. That's what alarmed her most. Inspector Harvey Marmion was once again quoted, asking for anyone with information that might be germane to the inquiry to come forward, If the police were still seeking the assistance of the public, Audrey feared, they had made little progress. When she heard her husband descending the stairs, she put the newspaper quickly aside and went out into the hall.

'What time will I expect you back, Martin?' she asked.

'I don't know.'

'Will you be dining at your club again?'

'I haven't decided.'

Taking his hat from the peg, he stood in front of the mirror while he put it on. Pattinson was immaculately dressed and his black shoes shone like glass. His attention to his appearance was one of the first things Audrey had noticed about him and it had made her more conscious of the way that *she* dressed. When her husband walked into a room, he made an immediate impression. She, by contrast, melted into invisibility. Without being asked, she took the clothes brush from the stand and used it on his shoulders and lapels. All that she got was a curt nod.

'What are you going to do today?' he asked in a voice that betrayed no real interest. 'Will you just mope in here?'

'I don't know.'

'Go out and get some fresh air.'

'I may well do that, Martin.'

'Moping won't bring him back. You have to accept that.'

'I know.'

He opened the door and, after brushing her cheek with a feeble imitation of a kiss, he went out. Audrey watched him stroll purposefully along the road then she closed the door behind him. She went back to the newspaper for another doomed search then let her mind drift back to happier times when she'd played the piano for a man she considered to be the finest dancer in the country, and watched him develop the talents of his pupils. It all seemed an age ago now.

Brought abruptly out of her reverie by the sound of the doorbell, she needed a moment to compose herself before going to see who it was. Standing outside with a hopeful expression was Colette Orme. She was relieved when invited in.

'I wasn't sure if I should come, Mrs Pattinson,' she said.

'You're very welcome, Colette.'

'I don't think your husband is quite so pleased to see me.'

'He's not here at the moment so you can forget about him. How *are* you?'

'I'm still the same. What about you?'

Audrey nodded. 'The pain just won't go away.'

They went into the living room and sat down. Colette first of all thanked the older woman for calling in to see her when she did. It had been a great comfort. What she really prayed for, she said, was the arrest of the person who'd hacked Simon Wilder brutally out of their respective lives and left them barren as a result. Audrey sought to offer reassurance.

'Your life may seem empty now, Colette, but you have a bright future ahead of you. You must keep on.'

'That's what Dennis keeps saying.'

'Mine is a different story,' said Audrey, sadly. 'I'll never find that degree of pleasure again. Mr Wilder was unique. When I played for him, he made me feel as if I was important.'

'You *are* important, Mrs Pattinson,' said Colette, squeezing her arm. 'Without you, the studio wouldn't have been the same. I enjoyed dancing with Mr Wilder to gramophone records but I haven't forgotten all those times when you played for us.'

'Thank you, Colette.'

'But I'm not here to brood about the past. I need some advice.'

'I can recommend a couple of good dance schools.'

'This is not about me,' said Colette. 'It's about my brother. I'm worried that he's drinking far too much.'

'What does your father say?'

'Daddy doesn't mind because he's fond of a glass of beer himself. Sometimes he takes Dennis to the pub with him.'

'Your brother is old enough to make his own decisions,' said Audrey, gently.

'That's exactly what he said when I challenged him about it. And he's done so much for me that I hate criticising him. I have to keep biting my tongue all the time.'

'Does he get aggressive when he's drunk?'

'Oh no,' explained Colette, 'he just passes out. They had to carry him home last time and there have been a couple of times when he's fallen so deeply asleep at a friend's house that they've let him stay the night. I worry every time he goes out because I never know when Dennis will come back or what state he'll be in.'

'The question to ask is *why* he drinks so much.'

'He says he has to keep pace with his old army friends. Like him, they've all been wounded at the front. One of them – Peter Seymour – lost both legs. Compared to the others, Dennis didn't get off too badly.'

'Perhaps he drinks to forget his disability, Colette.'

'No, it's not that. He copes very well on his walking stick.'

'He pretends to for your benefit, perhaps, but it must irk him that he can't live a normal life.'

'But that's exactly what he intends to do, Mrs Pattinson. He does exercises to improve his bad leg and he doesn't spend all his time talking about the war. Whenever he can,' she went on, 'Dennis goes off to see his girlfriend.'

'What does *she* think of his drinking habits?'

'Oh, he doesn't touch a drop when he's with Harriet. Her father won't have strong drink in the house. Dennis is as sober as a judge there.'

'So he goes from one extreme to another.'

'Yes, I suppose that he does in a way. What can I do, Mrs Pattinson?'

'Well, I don't know that I'm the best person to ask,' said Audrey, modestly. 'Unfortunately, I never had children so I can't speak with authority. But one way you might get your brother to moderate his drinking is to say that you'll tell his girlfriend.'

'That would be cruel.'

'The question is – would it work?'

Colette was dubious. 'I'm not sure. I'll think about it. But I'm so glad that I caught you alone,' she went on. 'You're the only person I can really talk to about Mr Wilder. You *understand*, Mrs Pattinson. I could never speak to Mrs Wilder in the way that I can to you. Have you been in touch with her?'

'Yes,' replied Audrey, 'I went to offer my condolences. I wanted to ask if I could play at the funeral but I never had the opportunity. What about you, Colette?'

'I saw her for a few minutes,' said the other, still embarrassed by the memory. 'I didn't feel at all welcome. Mrs Wilder used to be nice to me at one time but she's very cold now.'

Audrey drew back from making a comment. She'd known Catherine Wilder much longer than her visitor and knew how capricious she could be. But she was too loyal to a woman who'd been glad to employ her at the dance studio and with whom she'd been on friendly terms at the start.

'There are so many things I'd *like* to ask her but I can't somehow.'

'We must always remember that she's a grieving widow. She's lost a husband as well as a business partner. It will take time to get used to it.'

'How long will it take *us* to get used to it, Mrs Pattinson?' asked Colette in a voice dripping with pathos.

Audrey reached out to pull her close and hold her tight.

'The rest of our lives,' she murmured.

Claude Chatfield was cock-a-hoop. The roles were reversed for once and he relished the fact. Ordinarily, he stayed in Scotland Yard and issued orders. It was left to detectives like Marmion and Keedy to gather evidence and hunt down killers. Now, however, instead of merely delegating, the superintendent was in a position to divulge significant information that he'd collected by his own diligence. It was a moment in which to luxuriate and Chatfield did just that.

'His name is Godfrey Noonan,' he said, chest inflated with self-importance, 'and you should have found out about him by now.'

'Who is he, sir?' asked Marmion.

'He is – or was – Wilder's agent. They had a successful partnership for years until Wilder sued him for non-payment of fees and for fraudulent accounting. Noonan was filled with righteous indignation at the charge, apparently, but he was completely routed in court. Wilder won the case and substantial damages.' Chatfield grinned. 'They did not part on the best of terms.'

'When did all this happen?'

'Four or five years ago, I believe.'

'It's surprising that Mrs Wilder didn't mention this gentleman.'

'I don't think the lady would ever refer to him as a gentleman, Inspector. By all accounts, Noonan is something of a rough diamond. He made his clients call him "God", so that gives you some idea of the sort of man he is. Once I'd lighted on his name, I did some digging into his past. He hated losing the court case because it brought him a lot of bad publicity and cost him some of his other clients. Report has it that he's a man who nurses grudges and gets his own back, no matter how long it takes. Quite naturally, he's been sick with envy at the way that Wilder's career reached new heights since they parted. Noonan has been unable to have a share of the money or of the glory.'

'All this is very interesting, sir,' said Keedy, 'but it doesn't convince me that he's definitely our man. While Mr Noonan should be interviewed, he mustn't take preference over our other suspects.'

'You didn't let me finish, Sergeant,' chided the superintendent. 'I took the trouble to look at a list of Noonan's clients and one name jumped out at me – Tom Atterbury. Could the two of them be in league together?'

'It's conceivable,' admitted Marmion. 'We must add God, as he likes to be known, to our growing list of suspects. When the sergeant interviewed him again, one of them moved closer to the top of that list this morning.'

'Oh?' Chatfield rounded on Keedy. 'Who might that be?'

'Allan Redmond, sir.'

'I thought you'd discounted him.'

'New evidence came to light.'

'I can't wait to hear it.'

Keedy reminded him about the assault on Odele Thompson and how different Redmond had been at their second meeting. The longer he went on, the more irritated Chatfield became as he realised that the candidate he'd put forward as the killer had a legitimate rival in Allan Redmond. Seeing his discomfiture, Marmion exploited it.

'Did you happen to notice if Mr Redmond is a client of Noonan's, sir?'

'He is not,' grunted Chatfield, 'but Atterbury is. That's telling.'

'I've met both of them,' said Keedy, 'and my guess would be that Redmond is far more capable of committing a murder than Atterbury. He's younger and stronger, for a start. I watched Redmond playing tennis and he has a fearsome forehand. With a knife in his grasp, he could easily have inflicted the injuries we saw on Wilder.'

'Noonan could also be involved,' insisted Chatfield, 'if only tangentially.'

'You may be right, sir.'

'I *am*, Sergeant.'

'Then you've done us a favour, Superintendent,' said Marmion. 'In bringing this man to our notice, you may have explained something that puzzled me. Let me walk yet another potential suspect past you.'

'Who is he?'

'It's a lady, sir – Catherine Wilder.'

Chatfield snorted. 'That's a ludicrous suggestion.'

'I thought that until I met Wilder's first wife. She gave me an insight into his domestic life that made me look at the woman afresh. Hear me out,' he added as the superintendent tried to respond, 'and you may change your mind.'

Marmion gave him an attenuated account of the conversation with Gillian Hogg, taking care to omit details of Wilder's promiscuity that he'd been ready to pass on to Keedy. He knew that he was making headway when Chatfield stopped shaking his head in disbelief and clicking his tongue. By the end of the report, he was forced to accept that Marmion's judgement was not as awry as he'd imagined.

'Don't you see what this means, sir?'

'Frankly, I don't,' said Chatfield, sullenly.

'It answers the question the inspector put earlier,' said Keedy. 'If Wilder's former agent is such an obvious suspect, why didn't Mrs Wilder give us his name?'

'It may well be,' continued Marmion, 'that she'd put the legal dispute with him out of her mind, but there is another possible explanation and it marries *your* theory to mine, Superintendent.'

'Stop talking in riddles.'

'The reason Mrs Wilder made no mention of Noonan might be that the two of them were acting in collusion? Atterbury could be part of the conspiracy.'

Chatfield rallied. The suggestion that the agent could, after all, be guilty made him feel that his research had been vindicated. He went through the list of suspects in his head – Tom Atterbury, Martin Pattinson, Allan Redmond, Godfrey Noonan and Catherine Wilder. The people who seemed to knit most easily together were Atterbury and Noonan, two men with strong motives to want Wilder permanently removed. If they had been assisted – or even suborned by – the victim's wife, they would have been given accurate information about their target's movements. It took the superintendent a few minutes to reach his conclusion.

'Find me a link,' he decreed. 'Find me a link between Mrs Wilder and one or both of these men. Then they can go off to the gallows together.'

Expecting her brother, Catherine Wilder opened the front door to greet him. But it was not Nathan Clissold standing there. It was the rotund figure of Godfrey Noonan in one of his more flamboyant suits. He swept off his hat and smiled at her.

'Hello, darling,' he said, grandiloquently. 'May I have a moment of your precious time?'

All of the national newspapers were available in the reading room at the club. Martin Pattinson went through each one of them to see what they said about the murder in Chingford. One of them carried a photograph of Inspector Marmion while another featured the postman, Denzil Parry, standing beside the spot where he'd discovered the body. Speculation was rife. The crime was described variously as a random attack by drunken thugs, the work of a foreign spy, an act of revenge by someone in Wilder's past, the wicked deed of some sinister devil-worshipping cult and a simple case of mistaken identity. Pattinson observed that the murder was still not given the prominence it merited.

Having earlier been overshadowed by details of the air raid the same night, it was now given far less column inches than the accounts of the latest surge by British troops in France. As a former soldier, Pattinson read those with interest as well.

When he'd finished, he went through into the lounge and saw a familiar figure in one of the high-backed leather chairs. After an exchange of greetings, he sat down beside his friend. A waiter was summoned and drinks were ordered. Pattinson's friend leant across to him.

'I was hoping to see you in here today,' said Tom Atterbury.

Marmion's visit to the bank did not take long. What he was really hoping to find was a safe-deposit box in which Simon Wilder had kept things of a private nature that might contain clues as to the identity of his killer. The inspector was disappointed. According to the manager, Wilder had no cache of documents hidden away and no secret bank accounts. Because he was keen to protect the confidentiality of his dealings with Wilder, the manager was not prepared to divulge all the information he held and Marmion did not press him. His primary interest had been in the possible existence of a safe-deposit box that would help to solve the crime.

It was time to look elsewhere. With Chatfield's orders still ringing in his ears, therefore, he got back into the car and asked the driver to head for central London.

Keedy was not looking forward to another meeting with Odele Thompson but it was unavoidable. He not only had to tell her about his encounter with Allan Redmond, he wanted to bring up the name of Simon Wilder's former agent. Keedy warned himself in advance to be on his guard. Given the slightest encouragement, Odele could not merely become a nuisance. She could represent a serious threat. It was not the first time that he'd aroused female interest during a murder investigation. When he and Marmion had investigated the untimely death of a young art student, Keedy had been helped by a friend of the deceased who worked at the Slade School of Art as a model. Indeed, when the sergeant had first seen her, she was posing in the nude and he couldn't help admiring the generous contours of her body. She, in turn, began to admire him and make covert advances to Keedy. He recalled the difficulty he had in shaking her off. Odele, he feared, might not be so easily dispatched.

In the event, she was not waiting to ambush him. When she opened the door, he could see that she'd been crying. Invited in, he noticed that she'd been drinking as well. Odele read the question in his eyes.

'Yes,' she told him, 'I am grieving but it's not because Simon is dead. It's because of the consequences. I've just been going through my diary and seen all of the exhibition dances that will have to be cancelled. The ones at large halls were particularly lucrative. It's all gone, Sergeant,' she said with a vivid gesture. 'What would you do if the income on which you were relying suddenly dried up?'

'I'd go back to my old job, Miss Thompson.'

'And what was that?'

'I helped with embalming at the family firm of undertakers.'

It was such an unexpected answer that she forgot her troubles for a moment and burst out laughing. Odele then dried her eyes and apologised for moaning about her lot. She offered him a glass of gin but Keedy declined it and launched straight into the purpose of his visit.

'I went to see Mr Redmond,' he said.

She was cynical. 'I'll bet he refused to admit he'd laid a finger on me.'

'No, he didn't do that, Miss Thompson. His claim was that you started it. He had some sticking plaster on his head where you hit him.'

'He struck the first blow and I just lashed out.'

'His version was slightly different.'

Odele became truculent. 'Do you believe *him* instead of me?'

'That's not the point at issue.'

'It is to me.'

'I wanted to know why he came here in the first place. If he was innocent of any part in the murder, he wouldn't have reacted in such a guilty way. There was no need at all for him to bother you.'

'Allan is like that. He's one of Nature's botherers.'

'He's also a very good tennis player. I watched him on court.'

'I'm still hoping to watch him *in* court, Sergeant. He's got blood on his hands, I'm sure of it. Allan Redmond came here to shut me up.'

'Luckily, he didn't succeed.'

'He's been dying to tear me away from Simon for ages. He thinks that we'd be a winning team on the dance floor. I quashed that idea when I hit him.'

'Did he really have to go to that extreme?'

'You'll have to ask him that when you arrest him.'

'I've told you before. We don't have enough evidence to do that.'

She pulled back a sleeve to show off her bruise. 'What do you call that?'

'That simply proves that he assaulted you.'

'Allan has all the instincts of a killer.'

'Then why didn't Mrs Wilder name him as a suspect?'

'That's her business.'

'She felt that a more likely suspect was Tom Atterbury.'

'Catherine *would* do.'

'Why is that?'

'She and Tom used to dance together at one time. It was a disaster. Catherine said that he set her career back several years. That was before Simon came on the scene. I named Tom Atterbury because I felt that he was capable of killing another man if he was roused,' she asserted. 'But Allan would have got to the victim first.'

'How do they get on together?'

'They don't.'

'Yet they sound like birds of a feather.'

'They're both birds of prey,' she said with feeling, 'I can tell you that.'

'Let me ask you about someone else,' he said, changing tack. 'What do you know about a man named Godfrey Noonan?'

'He's the most crooked agent in London.'

'Have you ever been a client of his?'

'I'm not that stupid, Sergeant. Everyone knows what a shark God is. Simon learnt that. He had to take him to court to get the money he was owed.'

'If he's such a crook, how does he stay in business?'

'I can see that you don't know much about the theatrical world,' she said. 'It's a place where hustlers and cannibals like God can thrive. He gets results. There's no question about that. Somehow his clients are always in work – though he charges them an exorbitant commission.'

'What would Mrs Wilder think of him?'

'Ask her.'

'We may well do that,' he said. 'Oh, there is one thing I meant to ask. Soon after I left Mr Redmond, he jumped into a car and drove off. I'm wondering if he might have been going off to a cottage he mentioned.'

'It's more than likely.'

'Do you happen to know where it is?'

'I certainly do,' she said. 'When Allan and I first met, he took me there to . . . further our acquaintance.'

'I'd be very grateful for the address, Miss Thompson.'

A slow smile spread across her face and she put her hands on her hips.

'What are you prepared to do for it?'

He was finally making some progress. Paul Marmion had just spent a whole hour in her company and she had not mentioned Colin Fryatt once. Mavis Tandy now seemed more interested in Paul himself and in his future.

'Will you go back to work in the civil service one day?' she asked.

'I doubt it.'

'Why is that?'

'It will seem deadly dull after what I've been through, Mavis.'

'Does that mean you'll stay in the army?'

'I've got to make a full recovery first.'

'And when you do – what then?'

He was about to say that his first priority was to go back to France to kill as many Germans as he possibly could, but he had second thoughts. Having got her off the subject of Colin Fryatt and the ongoing battle of the Somme, he wanted to keep her away from it. Instead, therefore, he was non-committal.

'I'll . . . look around.'

'What about the police?'

His lip curled. 'That's the last job I'd take.'

'But your father's a detective inspector,' she said. 'Didn't you tell me that *he* started off in the civil service as well?'

'That was different.'

'You also said you'd like to do something where you could wear a uniform and have plenty of action. The police force would give you both.'

'So would the fire service,' he countered. 'So, for that matter, would the Salvation Army. My uncle sees lots of action in the East End. He's been attacked more times than he can count.'

'But he's trying to *help* people.'

'When they're drunk, they just want a fight.'

'Is that how *you* feel when you've had too much beer?'

'I make sure that I never do,' he claimed. 'I hate to lose control.'

'I'm so glad to hear you say that, Paul,' she said, touching his arm.

They were standing beside the river, watching a barge chug past them. The journey to Gillingham was starting to pay dividends for him. Mavis had a genuine interest in him now. He was not simply there as someone's friend.

'Why don't you want to be a policeman?'

'Because you're never there,' he replied. 'My mother is always complaining that she hardly ever sees Dad. He gets called out whenever there's an emergency.'

'Haven't you been following his latest case in the newspapers?'

'No – why should I?'

'He's your father, Paul.'

'I've got my own life to think about.'

'But he's trying to catch a brutal killer. Doesn't that interest you?'

'The only thing that interests me at the moment,' he said, venturing a compliment, 'is *you*, Mavis. I've had such a lovely time.'

She smiled broadly. 'That's good. I was afraid that I'd bore you.'

'Oh, no. You're the most interesting girl I've ever met.'

'How odd!' she cried. 'That's exactly what Colin said to me.'

* * *

217

Harvey Marmion arrived at the office in Soho to learn that Godfrey Noonan was away on business for a while. The agent's secretary was a scrawny, tousle-haired woman in her fifties with an empty cigarette holder between her lips.

'How long is he likely to be?' asked Marmion.

'Mr Godfrey should be back fairly soon,' she replied. 'He went to Chingford but didn't expect to stay there long.'

'In that case, I'll come back later on.'

'Who shall I say called?'

'I'm Detective Inspector Marmion from Scotland Yard.'

'Very well – I'll tell him.'

She showed no surprise that a policeman was anxious to meet her employer. She simply wrote down Marmion's name on a grubby pad then addressed herself to the typewriter. He left to the clatter of keys. The office had already told him a lot about Noonan. Situated above a seedy restaurant, it was small, cluttered and festooned with theatre posters. Since it was so close to Archer Street, he decided to kill time by calling on Gillian Hogg. The address was easy to find but, to reach her top-floor flat, he had to climb up a veritable Matterhorn of steps. Fortunately, she was at home and, with some reluctance, she invited him in.

The flat was almost exactly the same size as the office he'd just left but it was excessively well organised and brightened by wallpaper that featured exotic birds. Even for one person, space was very limited. How she and Wilder had managed to live there together, he could only guess. A framed photograph of him stood on a table. She noted the interest he showed in it.

'What can you see, Inspector?' she asked.

'It looks like Mr Wilder in younger days.'

'He took it about three months after we'd married.'

Marmion was jolted. 'How could he take a photograph of himself?'

'Look at it more closely.'

He bent over to peer at it and spotted a vague shape on the shelf beside which Wilder was standing. Only one explanation seemed possible.

'He was standing in front of a mirror,' he guessed. 'When he developed the photo, he somehow managed to get rid of the camera – most of it, anyway.'

'Well done, Inspector!'

'I was told that he was a clever photographer.'

'Simon was an expert,' she said, 'but do sit down. Can I offer you anything?'

'No, thank you,' he said, choosing an upright chair. 'It's pure accident that I'm in the area. I came in search of a Mr Noonan.' Her face darkened. 'I can see that you know him.'

'I know him and avoid him like the plague. God is a menace.'

Marmion chuckled. 'I hope that you don't say that on a Sunday.'

'Simon had the most terrible trouble with him.'

'So I hear. What about you?'

'Oh, I had my problems with him as well,' she said, sourly. 'He lured me in with all kinds of false promises, one of which was that he was always happy to help his clients with loans if they hit a fallow period. When I hit a rocky patch early on in my career, I needed some cash to tide me over. God provided it. What he didn't tell me until I came to repay it was that there was a fair amount of interest to add.'

'He seems to have upset a lot of his clients.'

'He knows how to butter up the important ones, Inspector, the people who always land starring roles. We lesser talents were the ones to suffer and, since he tied us hand and foot with punitive contracts, it was difficult to break free.'

'I look forward to meeting him.'

'Take a peg for your nose.'

Marmion was seeing a new side to Gillian Hogg. At their first meeting, she'd been, for the most part, restrained and well spoken. There was anger in her voice now. He sensed that he was about to hear more about Godfrey Noonan.

'I got his measure when I tried to repay that loan,' she explained. 'I didn't have the full amount. "God is merciful", he told me and gave me a fortnight to find the money. But he wasn't prepared to wait for two weeks. That night, he called at the digs where I was staying and said that he was prepared to be paid in kind. Can you think of anything more disgusting?' she went on. 'That pig of an agent expected me to go to bed with him. And I wasn't the only victim. When I talked to some of the actresses on his books, most had been propositioned by him.'

Once started, she was happy to reel off more examples of the agent's duplicity and exploitation of his clients. She had got rid of Noonan and found another agent. Thanks to him, she went on to meet Wilder.

'You know what happened from then on, Inspector.'

'Yes, Mrs Hogg,' he said, unable to hide his disapproval. 'After a relatively short marriage, you decided to part from your husband and agreed to furnish evidence for him to divorce you.'

'Strictly speaking,' she said, 'it was a male friend who did that. Overcoming his distaste for the opposite sex, he allowed himself to be photographed with me in a compromising position. It's the only time in his life that he got close to a woman and it won't happen again. Simon was able to claim that the photo had come into his possession whereas he was the one who took it in the first place.'

'You're lucky that that never came to light in the divorce court.'

'You sound critical.'

'I uphold the law, Mrs Hogg. You and your husband flouted it.'

She gave a shrug. 'That's water under the bridge now.'

Marmion was compelled to revise his judgement of her. When she'd spoken to him in Chingford, she'd presented herself as the former wife of a man she supported through the difficulties of his second marriage. Evidently, the portrait was incomplete. He had the strong feeling that Wilder did more than just call in when in need of a sympathetic ear. The dancer came to enjoy pleasures denied him at home and Gillian was happy to offer them. As a wife, she'd found their relationship imposed too many limitations. The new role of his mistress was much more to her taste.

'Will you be at the funeral?' he asked.

'Nothing would keep me away, Inspector.'

'What about consideration for Mrs Wilder?'

'Catherine never showed *me* any consideration,' she said, acerbically. 'She's snubbed me in public a number of times. As far as she's concerned, I don't exist.'

'Did she ever have any connection with Godfrey Noonan?'

'As a matter of fact, she did.'

'Could you enlarge on that, please?'

'He and Catherine worked hand in glove at one time.'

CHAPTER SIXTEEN

It took Keedy some time to extricate himself from Odele Thompson's flat with the address he needed and he vowed to keep well clear of her in the future. While she'd contributed some useful information to the investigation, he told her, it didn't entitle her to a closer relationship with him. Even though he'd pointed out to Odele that he was engaged to be married, he still felt strangely vulnerable and couldn't understand why. He therefore tried to focus solely on his work. His next task was to track down Allan Redmond at his cottage in Hertfordshire but he needed a car to do that. Claude Chatfield had returned to Scotland Yard in one vehicle and Harvey Marmion had used the other to get himself driven to Soho. Keedy, therefore, had to travel to central London by public transport. It was a tedious journey until the moment when an idea popped into his mind. All of a sudden, he began to enjoy the trip immensely.

Since he knew the exact route of Alice's beat, he was able to work out roughly where she would be at the time he finally got off the bus. Instead of reporting to Scotland Yard, therefore, he sneaked off to intercept her for a short while. It was, he felt, the antidote he needed to the threat of Odele Thompson. Keedy had guessed right. Alice and Iris

Goodliffe were in precisely the area he expected to find them. The very sight of her cheered him up. She, in turn, was overjoyed.

'Where did you spring from, Joe?' she asked, excitedly.

'It would take too long to explain.'

'Oh, this is Iris . . .'

During the introductions, Iris shook his hand warmly and looked up at him.

'It's good to meet you at last, Sergeant Keedy,' she said. 'I've heard so many wonderful things about you.'

'Don't believe everything that Alice tells you,' he said.

'I only told her the truth,' insisted Alice.

'She said how tall and good-looking you were,' said Iris, 'and how you always dressed smartly.' After beaming at him vacuously, she became aware that she was in the way. 'Oh, I'm sorry. You didn't come to see me, did you? Why don't I walk on a bit, Alice? You can catch me up.'

'Thanks, Iris.'

As soon as the other woman left, Keedy stepped in to give Alice a kiss.

She was pleased. 'What have I done to deserve that?'

'I'll tell you sometime.'

'Tell me now, Joe. And explain how you managed to slip away from a murder investigation. Does Daddy know that you're here?'

'No, he doesn't and he must never find out.'

'How long can you stay?'

'Only a few minutes – I just had to see you.'

'Why? Has something happened?'

'Yes,' he admitted and, though he'd intended to say nothing about Odele, his tongue ran away with him. 'I had to interview the murder victim's dancing partner at her flat. She began to . . . show an interest in

224

me so I had to tell her that I had a fiancée. It was embarrassing. To be honest, I was glad to escape. Then I just felt the urge to see you.'

Alice was piqued. 'Did you give her any encouragement?'

'No, of course I didn't.'

'Are you sure?'

'Yes, I am,' he replied, hurt that his word should be questioned.

'Women don't do that sort of thing unless they sense something.'

'This one does.'

'Was it the first time?'

'Alice—' he protested.

'Was it? I'd like to know.'

'Then the honest answer is that it wasn't. She . . . made it clear that she was interested in me when she came to the police station.'

'And how did she do that?'

'It was . . . in her manner.'

'So even though you *knew* she had designs on you, you went off to be alone with her in her flat.'

'I *had* to go there. Your father sent me.'

'You could have taken somebody else with you.'

'Yes, I suppose that I could have done that.'

'But you didn't do that, did you? Why was that?'

'Look . . .'

She folded her arms. 'It's a simple question, Joe. Why was that?'

'I didn't come here to be interrogated,' he said, sharply.

'There are certain things I deserve to know.'

'I wish I hadn't even mentioned Odele now.'

'Is that her name – Odele?'

'Calm down, Alice. You're getting this out of proportion.'

'I've spent all that time, telling Iris what a lovely, honest, reliable man I have in my life and you go off with this Odele person.'

'I didn't "go off". I had to get an address from her.'

'And you gave her the wrong signals in the process.'

'No,' he said in exasperation. 'I didn't give her *any* kind of signal.'

'I always trusted you, Joe Keedy.'

'And you were right to do so.'

'I wonder . . .'

They were both throbbing with anger. Alice couldn't quite understand how they'd reached that position and she was unable to stop herself from making it worse.

'I'm beginning to think that Paul may be right about you.'

'What the hell has your brother got to do with it?'

'He said that you were too old for me and too fond of other women.'

Keedy spluttered. 'Then he can mind his own bloody business.'

'Joe!'

'I'm sorry to swear but I'm not having Paul saying things like that.'

'But there's a grain of truth in them. Before me, there were—'

'That's all in my past, Alice. Once I'd committed myself to you, no other women interested me.'

'Until you met Odele, that is.'

Keedy had to rein in his temper. Conscious that they were being watched by Iris Goodliffe from a short distance yards away, he wanted to bring the argument to an end. In his desire to see Alice, he'd foolishly managed to give her a reason to be jealous. They both needed time apart to cool off.

'I shouldn't have come,' he said, bluntly.

'It would have been better if you hadn't.'

'I didn't mean to upset you, Alice.'

'Iris is waiting. I'll have to go.'

'Let's not part on a sour note.'

'You were the one who introduced it.'

'That's not true at all,' he said, hissing the words at her. 'I came here because I wanted to see you. I thought you'd be pleased. Obviously, I was wrong. And as for your brother,' he added, eyes flashing, 'you can tell him that I want a word with him. Just because he's suffering from shell shock, it doesn't mean that he can spread lies like that about me.'

Hurt and inflamed, Keedy marched off.

Paul Marmion had enjoyed his day with her. Mavis Tandy was a good listener and an interesting person in her own right. When it was time to part, he didn't have to ask her if he could see her again because she put that question to him. She suggested that they might meet halfway between London and Gillingham so that neither had such a long journey. As she waited to wave him off at the bus stop, he reviewed the visit and decided that she really liked him now. It was only a matter of time, he hoped, before he'd replace Colin Fryatt in her affections and become her boyfriend with all the licensed pleasures that would mean. Meeting her had made such a difference to him. Paul had someone completely outside the family in whom he could confide. He'd told Mavis things that he'd never mention at home and she'd been both supportive and understanding. His only regret was that he couldn't see her more clearly. Mavis was still very largely a fuzzy outline to him.

When the bus eventually came, he was sorry that he had to leave. There was, however, an unexpected thrill. At the very moment when he was about to step onto the vehicle, Mavis grabbed him by the shoulders and planted a kiss on his lips. The warm glow inside him lasted all the way home.

* * *

Before he even met him, Marmion was ready to dislike Godfrey Noonan intensely. Everything he'd heard about the agent was to his discredit. When he finally confronted the man, however, his aversion was tempered by curiosity. There was something oddly engaging about Noonan. He was a fleshy individual of middle years in a striking houndstooth check suit and a red, spotted tie that matched a florid complexion. His large, mobile eyes looked out from beneath a wholly unconvincing ginger wig. Seated in a swivel chair that creaked ominously every time he moved, he seemed to occupy over half of the office. Marmion was glad that his secretary had stepped into the adjoining room to give them privacy. Three people in the limited space would have produced serious overcrowding.

'I gather that you went to Chingford today, sir,' began Marmion.

'That's right, Inspector. Had I known that you wanted me, I could have presented myself to you there.'

'What took you there, Mr Noonan?'

'I had to visit a friend.'

'May I know who it was?'

'Is that absolutely necessary?' asked Noonan.

'I can't force you to tell me.'

'Then I certainly won't do so. You've come about this wretched murder, haven't you? Simon was a good friend.'

'That's not what I heard, sir.'

Noonan gave a hearty laugh. 'Ah,' he said, 'you're talking about the court case. I have no regrets about that. Simon was quite right to sue me. It was all the fault of my accountant, actually. I'm pleased to say that he's no longer in my employ.'

'You and Mr Wilder had an acrimonious parting, I gather.'

'Balderdash!' he exclaimed, slapping a thigh. 'I'm never acrimonious.'

'He ceased to be a client of yours.'

'That was unfortunate but, in the circumstances, it was inevitable. I helped Simon through some very lean years, you know. It would have been nice to get a slice of his increasing fame.'

'I believe that you represent Tom Atterbury.'

'I represent lots of talented artistes,' said Noonan, expansively, 'and I have a long list of clients waiting for the chance to be one of God's Chosen People. That's what they call me, you see – I'm God.'

'How did Mr Atterbury and Mr Wilder get along?'

'They were friendly rivals, Inspector.'

'As it happens, I met Mr Atterbury and he was far from friendly. When we asked him where he was on the night of the murder, he deliberately misled both my sergeant and me.'

Noonan eyes protruded. 'You think that dear Tom is a *suspect?*'

'Everyone who stands to gain from Mr Wilder's death needs to be looked at, sir. That's part of the reason that I came to see you.'

'Well, you can take my name off the list immediately. I was not even in London. I was watching a play in Manchester. I can give you the name of the hotel where I spent that night, if you wish. In any case,' he went on, jabbing his spotted tie, 'what do I stand to gain from Simon's death?'

'You might get satisfaction – to put it no higher than that.'

'I mourn the loss of any genius, Inspector, and that's what he was,'

'So why did you attempt to defraud him?'

'I can't be blamed for the errors of my accountant.'

'You can be blamed for employing an incompetent in the first place.'

Noonan laughed. 'How right you are, Inspector,' he said, 'but we all make mistakes when we try to judge someone's character. For instance, *you* might be making one right now.'

'Why do you think Mr Atterbury should not be suspected of murder?'

'I know him too well.'

'The neighbours used to say the same thing about Dr Crippen.'

'Are you telling me that Tom Atterbury is about to poison his wife and run off with another woman?' Noonan's laugh was a guffaw this time. 'Clearly, you haven't met Naomi. She's Beauty Incarnate. Tom and Naomi are destined to win the British Dance Championship this year.'

'That's a feat made easier by the withdrawal of the favourite.'

'Tom and Naomi were the *real* favourites, Inspector. Take my word.'

'I was told that the strongest challenge would come from Mr Redmond and his partner.' Noonan wrinkled his nose. 'The gentleman is not a client of yours, I fancy.'

'He's neither client nor friend. I detest the man. But he should definitely be listed as a suspect. Allan really *did* stand to gain from Simon's murder.'

'Yet, according to you, the champions who'll definitely be crowned at the event are Mr and Mrs Atterbury. If Redmond wanted to improve his chances of success, surely he should have killed *them* instead.'

The comment was enough to silence Noonan and to wipe the flabby smile from his face. Marmion suddenly felt very unwelcome. He pressed the agent on the subject of Tom Atterbury but got very little new information out of him. When he shifted his attention to someone else, however, Marmion had more success.

'I understand that you know Mrs Wilder very well,' he said.

'That was years ago, Inspector. We've drifted apart since then.'

'Do you regret that?'

'Deeply – Catherine is a lovely woman.'

'Did you fall out when her husband took you to court?'

'No,' said Noonan, 'it was before that. We had . . . differences of opinion.'

He went on to confirm some of the things that Marmion had gleaned from his visit to Gillian Hogg. As well as representing actors and dancers, Noonan had been a shrewd investor in productions at West End theatres. He could sense the winners and detect the stink of potential losers. Before she married Wilder, Catherine was another enthusiastic investor in forthcoming shows and actually appeared in some of them as a result. Between them, she and the agent had turned a sizeable profit.

'Catherine felt that she was better off without me,' said Noonan, tolerantly. 'I had no quarrel with that. We've both made sound investments since, though I did warn her against buying that hall in Chingford.'

'It's been a Mecca for ballroom dancers.'

Noonan sniggered. 'You won't find much ballroom dancing in Mecca, I'm afraid. In the Middle East, they're more likely to be doing war dances.'

'You take my meaning, sir.'

'I do, Inspector, and they did make the place pay well, I grant you that. But there were ways they should have taken of increasing their profits.' He scratched his double chin. 'Who put you on to me?'

'It was my superintendent who first mentioned your name, sir.'

'You've also had help from one of my enemies. That's why you're asking me these questions. Who was it – some useless actor I refused to handle? Or was it some rancorous little darling who claims that I put a hand on her thigh?'

'I came here because of your link to Mr and Mrs Wilder.'

'You've heard all there is to hear on the topic.'

'Not quite, sir – you haven't solved one irritating little mystery.'

'And what's that?'

'I've spoken to Mrs Wilder more than once and we've talked about various people in the dance world. Given the fact that you and she were once commercial partners, isn't it remarkable that she never once spoke your name? I don't claim that she still worships God,' said Marmion, pointedly, 'but you'd think she'd remember someone as unforgettable as you.'

While she could not hear what was being said, Iris Goodliffe had seen that Alice and Keedy were having a heated row. She knew better than to ask what it had been about. For the best part of twenty minutes, they walked on in silence. There were a few incidents to deal with and that spared them the awkwardness of talking together. It was Alice who finally spoke up.

'Thank you, Iris.'

'I'm saying nothing.'

'I'm sorry you had to see that.'

'You don't have to apologise,' said Iris. 'And you don't have to tell me anything. But you were right about Sergeant Keedy. He *is* tall and good-looking.'

Alice winced. 'We had a silly disagreement, that's all.'

'I have those all the time with my sister.'

'It was my fault.'

'I'd never admit that. I always blame Evelyn.'

'Do you mind if we talk about something else?'

'No,' said Iris. 'We haven't decided what film to see tonight.'

'You choose.'

'We want something we both like, Alice.'

'What's on at the moment?'

Iris laughed. 'Oh, I can tell you that.'

She reeled off a list of films they might see and they discussed their respective appeal. Fortunately, they seemed to have similar tastes. Iris was in her element, offering all kinds of suggestions and recalling favourite films from her mental scrapbook. Alice threw in the occasional comment but she was not really listening to her friend. The argument with Keedy had worried her, creating a rift that went alarmingly deep. It had all happened so quickly and she was partly responsible. They'd never spoken to each other like that before. When they did have disagreements, they made sure that they took place in private. Alice was desperate to repair the damage but she had no idea whatsoever how she should go about it.

'I loved him in his last film,' said Iris. 'I've always wanted a man who could sweep me off my feet like that.'

'So did I,' murmured Alice. 'And I thought I'd found him.'

Having been given the allotted car at Scotland Yard, Keedy asked the driver to take him to the address in the Hertfordshire countryside. The long journey gave him time to reflect on the abrasive meeting with Alice. Though he blamed himself for raising the subject of Odele Thompson, he was still shocked by the sudden jealousy he'd unwittingly provoked. She'd accused him of things he hadn't done – or even thought of doing – and it was hurtful. As for the remark made by her brother, it made Keedy livid, all the more so because she had used it as a weapon to stab at him. He'd seen very little of Paul since the latter had come out of hospital but always asked Marmion about him. His only concern now was to meet him face to face and demand to know why he'd made such a comment to his sister.

Keedy was back in a situation he'd known before. Whenever he'd fallen out with one girlfriend, he'd immediately begun to search for a new one on the principle that that was the best possible way to get over his loss. He found himself doing that now, thinking about various attractive women who'd crossed his path recently and wondering what would have happened if he'd struck up a friendship with one of them. It was only a matter of time before Odele Thompson came to mind and he had to admit that she'd aroused flickers of temptation in him. If he was a free man, he decided, he wouldn't have ignored her innuendoes and rejected her advances. Odele had the vitality of a professional dancer and a lack of inhibition that was exciting.

The car reached a junction and came to an abrupt halt as another vehicle shot across its path. Keedy was, literally, catapulted out of his reverie. He was shocked that he'd even thought about other women. Alice knew and accepted that he had had a past littered with romances. They'd agreed to put it behind them and made a series of promises to each other. Keedy began to feel remorse. At the same time, he couldn't easily forgive the way that she'd attacked him. What had happened between them was more than a lovers' tiff. It had shown that, for all her protestations, Alice still didn't trust him. Since he was likely to meet a number of women in the course of his work, there would always be grounds for suspicion on her part. It made him feel shackled.

Meanwhile, he had a job to do so he began to chat to the driver.

'How much longer will it take us?'

'I don't know, sir,' said the man. 'It's the other side of St Albans.'

'Can you go any faster?'

'I'll do my best.'

The car surged forward and Keedy settled into the back seat. In making the journey, he was relying on pure instinct. When he'd seen

Allan Redmond leaving the Wimbledon house in a rush, he knew that he'd frightened the man into precipitate action. That was often indicative of guilt. Yet there was no guarantee that he'd fled to his country cottage. The drive across Hertfordshire could turn out to be a waste of time. Redmond might equally well have gone to ground elsewhere or even, it now occurred to Keedy, have decided to leave the country altogether. In that event, the dancer would instantly become the prime suspect and an angry Claude Chatfield would demand to know why the sergeant hadn't arrested the man when he had the opportunity. Keedy could already hear the superintendent's rasping voice.

'Come on, man,' said Chatfield, rapping his desk with his knuckles, 'you've been in this job long enough to develop your instincts. Is he or is he not our killer?'

'No, sir,' replied Marmion. 'Mr Noonan is not.'

'Are you certain of that?'

'I'm certain that he didn't *commit* the murder. You only have to look at him to see that. He's too fat, slow and short of breath. Noonan is also too fond of quality tailoring to risk getting a spot of blood on his clothing. On the other hand,' Marmion went on, 'he might well have incited someone else to kill Wilder.'

'So it *was* worth interviewing him?'

'Yes, sir, and I'm grateful to you for bringing him to our notice.'

'Mrs Wilder should have done that.'

'I mean to ask her why she didn't do so, Superintendent. When he told me that he hadn't had anything to do with her for years, I didn't believe Noonan for a second. I think he'd spoken to her earlier today.'

'How do you know that?'

'Why else would he go to Chingford?'

'One of his clients might live there.'

Marmion smiled. 'Godfrey Noonan would be highly unlikely to drive ten miles to see clients, sir. *They* come to him. He'd save on expenses that way and he'd also maintain his image as their God. When they need his services, they have to worship *him*.'

'Yet you say that he operates from some shoddy premises.'

'Don't be misled by that. He's clearly a wealthy man.'

'So he could afford to *hire* a killer.'

'You could say the same of Mrs Wilder, sir.'

When he delivered his report to Chatfield, he omitted all mention of Gillian Hogg. Having caught her unawares at her flat, Marmion's view of her had been adjusted. She was no longer the nice, quiet, altruistic woman he'd first thought and she hadn't been entirely honest with him at their earlier meeting. His view of Godfrey Noonan, however, was unlikely to change. The agent could be added to the long list of likeable rogues Marmion had encountered. Noonan was an affable, venal, ruthless, exploitive, larger-than-life character of a kind that could only exist in a theatrical environment. He was the exact opposite of Claude Chatfield, a decent, hard-working, law-abiding, dedicated, sober, joyless man whose God existed in the Roman Catholic Church and not – as in Noonan's case – in the shaving mirror.

'I'm *certain* that he went to see Mrs Wilder,' said Marmion. 'That's why he refused to say what had taken him there. Had it been a meeting with a client, he'd have had no reason to hide it from me.'

'I take your point,' conceded Chatfield. 'And though it has its charms, I don't think that Chingford would draw anyone out of an office in Soho unless he had a very specific reason to go there.'

'You asked for a link between Noonan and Mrs Wilder, sir.'

'That's true, Inspector.'

'Now you have it.'

'What about Atterbury?'

'He could be involved but . . . I'm not sure about that.'

'You and the sergeant both found him shifty.'

'We also caught him lying to us, sir, but dishonesty isn't enough in itself for us to accuse him of murder. I'd like to have him followed. It's the one way to find out if he's involved in a conspiracy with Mrs Wilder and Noonan. Will you sanction that?'

Chatfield pursed his lips. 'We have very limited resources.'

'Surely we can spare one man to shadow him?'

'Let me think about it.'

'It's what I'd advise, Superintendent.'

'I'd advise it myself if I had enough detectives at my disposal. I'd have each and every one of our suspects followed. But we have to put our men where they can be of most use. I'll mull it over.'

There was no point in arguing. The decision lay with Chatfield and all that the inspector could do was to hope that it was the right one. His main concern was to get back to Chingford so that he could question Catherine Wilder. He rose to his feet.

'I'll be off, sir.'

'Keep in touch by telephone.'

'You won't forget my request regarding Atterbury, will you?' Chatfield shot him a belligerent glance. 'No, no, of course you won't.'

Ellen Marmion kept reminding herself of her husband's advice. She was wrong to feel afraid of Paul. While they had a duty of care towards their son – all the more so in view of his injuries – they also had parental rights. One of them was to insist on being told what was going on in his life. They couldn't help him properly until they understood his real needs. To that end, Ellen had been steeling herself for the next encounter with Paul. Since he'd been distant with her at breakfast, she decided to be more assertive. The problem was that she had no opportunity to try the new tactic. Her son had been gone for five or six hours.

When he finally returned, Ellen was ready to ambush him.

'You've been gone a long time, Paul.'

'Yes, I know.'

'Mrs Belton saw you getting on a bus. Where did you go?'

'I just went for a ride.'

'You didn't stay on the bus all that time, surely?'

'No, I didn't,' he admitted.

'Why are you so afraid to say where you've been? You can't just shut us out of your life like this.'

'I went to see someone. Is that a crime?'

'It was that friend of Colin's again, wasn't it? She lives in Gillingham. Mrs Belton told me that the bus was going to Kent.'

'Well, you can tell that old busybody not to spy on me.'

'She saw you quite by accident.'

'Mrs Belton is always watching somebody,' he said, angrily. 'Look what happened to that son of hers, Patrick. She kept him under lock and key all day and never let the poor lad out of her sight.'

'There was a reason for that,' she argued. 'She'd already lost two sons at the front. Lena Belton didn't want Patrick to be killed as well. He was all she had. She thought that she was protecting him from being called up.'

'Well, it didn't work and it serves her bloody well right!'

'Paul!'

'No wonder he ran off to join the navy.'

'You ought to feel sorry for Mrs Belton. She was only doing what she thought was best. Since Patrick ran away, she's been all alone.'

'That's what happens to mothers who try to control their children every minute of the day. They can't live someone else's life for them,' he said with sudden passion. 'You should remember that. I'm over twenty-one now. I'm old enough to vote and to fight for my country. Don't you think that it entitles me to some freedom? Why must you keep asking what I'm doing and where I'm going? It's maddening! For Christ's sake – can't you see that?'

Charging up the stairs, he ran to his room and slammed the door after him. Ellen, meanwhile, was quivering with pain. The new tactic had failed abysmally. Her son had comprehensively shut her out of his life.

They got there just in time. The cottage was in a small village that comprised a pub, a church, a pond, a green and a few clusters of dwellings. For someone who wished to get away from the maelstrom of London, it was an idyllic place, tranquil, unspoilt and surrounded by rolling countryside. They'd had difficulty finding it and Keedy's driver had taken a couple of wrong turns along the way but they had at last got there. Redmond's car was standing outside the cottage. They drew up beside it. Redmond himself soon appeared with a suitcase. Keedy climbed quickly out of the police car to confront him.

'Are you going somewhere, sir?' he asked.

Redmond's jaw dropped. 'What the devil are *you* doing here?'

'I just dropped in for a chat – the way that you did at Miss Thompson's flat.'

'Ah, I see. That bitch, Odele, gave you my address, didn't she?'

'Unlike you, she was ready to assist the police, sir.'

'That's exactly what I did, Sergeant.'

'No,' said Keedy, 'it's what you very cleverly gave the impression of doing. After I left the house, I waited around the corner. I had a feeling that you might do a flit and – lo and behold – here you are!'

'This is my cottage. There's no law to stop me coming here, is there?'

'None at all, Mr Redmond, but you might have done us the courtesy of telling us where you were going.'

'The decision was made on the spur of the moment.'

'It was made the second you realised that we'd rumbled you. I could read your mind, sir. That's why I lurked around the corner. I knew that you'd bolt.'

'I fancied a break in the country, that's all.'

'So why are you leaving all of a sudden?'

'I'm going to stay with friends.'

'May I have their name and address, please?'

'No,' retorted Redmond, 'you damn well can't. You've no right to chase after me like this. I'm an innocent man in a free country. Now leave me alone.'

'Unfortunately, I can't do that,' said Keedy, levelly. 'When we identify a suspect in a murder inquiry, we like to make sure that he or she doesn't vanish into thin air. And that,' he went on, looking at the suitcase, 'is what you seem on the verge of doing.'

'I'm going to friend's, I tell you.'

'Do they live in this country or abroad?'

The question stunned Redmond. He needed a moment to regain his composure and adopt the happy-go-lucky air of a gentleman of leisure. Putting the suitcase down, he pretended that he was ready to cooperate.

'I'll be staying in Brighton with friends,' he explained. 'Their names are Jay and Tiffany White and, if you take out that little notebook of yours, I'll give you their address. Will that content you, Sergeant?'

Keedy held his ground. 'No, sir,' he said, 'I'm afraid that it won't. What I want is for you to hand over your passport.'

'I don't have it on me.'

'Oh, I think that you do. Hand it over or I'll have to search you.'

He stepped forward and reached out. Redmond shoved him roughly away.

'Keep your hands off me, you oaf,' snarled Redmond, losing his temper, 'or I'll knock your block off.'

'Assaulting a police officer is an offence, sir.'

'I refuse to be pushed about by anyone.'

'You're the one who did the pushing, sir.'

Keedy lunged forward without warning and grabbed him by the shoulders. Redmond immediately began to fight back and a brawl developed. The driver got out of the car to lend assistance but it was not needed. Redmond was strong and fired by rage but he had none of the skills that Keedy had mastered. When they grappled, punched, twisted and turned, the sergeant was always in control. In the course of the struggle, he pulled his opponent's coat halfway off him and something fell from the pocket. With a final effort, Keedy swung him round, pulled his arms behind him and snapped the handcuffs onto his wrists. Redmond continued to yell in protest.

Keedy bent down to retrieve the object that had fallen to the ground.

'Well, well,' he said, holding it under Redmond's nose, 'it seems that you *did* have your passport with you, after all.'

CHAPTER SEVENTEEN

Having been driven to Chingford a number of times now, Harvey Marmion decided that the scenery did not improve with the passing of time. He was taken through a bewildering array of London suburbs, some of which bore the indelible marks of Zeppelin air raids. Small children were playing in the rubble or re-enacting the moment when a British pilot brought one of the monstrous aircraft crashing to the ground. Privilege and poverty were on display at varying points. Marmion went through areas where the houses were large, detached and in a good state of repair; and he also drove past slums where ragged toddlers walked about on bare feet, and where gaunt women huddled on street corners to exchange gossip and voice complaints. War had imposed strict rationing on the populace. Food was scarce and some items were now unobtainable. There were fleeting moments in his journey when Marmion wondered if the German blockade would eventually starve the whole country to death. It was already having a visible effect.

The car drew up outside the Wilder house and he got out. He was pleased to find Catherine at home but less thrilled to see that her brother was there as well. Nathan Clissold stood protectively close to his sister.

'We still await news of an arrest, Inspector,' he said, meaningfully.

'You'll have to be patient a little longer, sir,' returned Marmion.

'I ran out of patience days ago.'

'Then you would make a very poor detective, Mr Clissold. Most of our work consists of waiting and watching. In the fullness of time, we get our reward.'

'Do you have anything at all to report?' asked Catherine.

'Yes, I do, Mrs Wilder. We've been busy.'

Marmion gave them a highly selective account of the information so far gathered. Though the name of Gillian Hogg was once again omitted, he did mention his visit to Godfrey Noonan. He paused for a response from Catherine but none came. She maintained the same blank mask throughout.

'I'm surprised that you didn't tell me about Mr Noonan,' he said.

'What is there to tell, Inspector?'

'He's crossed your path and that of your husband.'

'That was years ago.'

'When did you last see him?'

'I can't remember.'

'He came to Chingford this morning. I wondered if he'd called on you.'

'My sister just gave you your answer,' said Clissold, intervening. 'Noonan is an excrescence. He ought to be locked up. Once you get a crook like him out of your life, you don't let him back in again.'

'Have you ever met him, sir?'

'Only once – and that was more than enough.'

'Yet your sister got on well with him at one time. They invested in plays together. I gather that it was a profitable enterprise.'

'Those days are long gone, Inspector,' said Catherine, brusquely, 'and so, thankfully, has God.'

'That's a singularly ironic name for him,' said Clissold with a snort. 'He's one of the vilest devils I ever met.'

'So he didn't come here today,' said Marmion. 'Is that right, Mrs Wilder?'

'He'd have no reason,' she replied.

'Did you know that Tom Atterbury was one of his clients?'

'Yes, I did.'

'Why would an intelligent man like Mr Atterbury put his trust in Godfrey Noonan if – as your brother claims – the agent is an unashamed crook?'

'He's a crook who can find his clients regular work,' she said, flatly. 'That counts for a lot if you happen to be unemployed.'

'You mean that people overlook his shortcomings, as you once did?'

'Why are we talking about Noonan?' said Clissold, fussily.

'I should have thought you could have worked that out, sir. He once lost a battle in court with Mr Wilder. It was bound to leave him embittered. He'll be weeping no tears over the turn of events.'

'You consider him to be a *suspect*?'

'Given what happened, I'd have expected Mrs Wilder to do the same. Yet she never even thought to tell us about Mr Noonan. Why is that?'

'I've had other things on my mind, Inspector,' she said.

Though her head was bowed and her voice solemn, Marmion didn't get the impression that she was in mourning for the death of a murdered husband. From the start, Clissold had expressed no real grief over his brother-in-law's fate and there was no hint of his doing so now. Both he and his sister seemed curiously disengaged.

'I put forward the names of two possible suspects,' Marmion reminded her, 'and you discounted that of Allan Redmond, saying that a more likely person was Tom Atterbury.'

'That's right.'

'Can you tell me why?'

'He's been insanely jealous of Simon's success,' she replied.

'Would it make him stoop to murder?'

'It might, Inspector, but I'm not saying that it did. Tom would need someone to egg him on and his wife would be more than capable of doing that. Under her sophistication, Naomi is a wildcat. You wouldn't believe some of the things she said and did to me when I was dancing in competition against her.'

'So Mrs Atterbury could be an accomplice?'

'She'd be more than that. Tom jumps to her command.'

'Instead of bothering my sister at a sensitive time,' said Clissold, 'you ought to be interviewing Atterbury and his wife.'

'Thank you for your advice,' said Marmion, drily, 'but I came here for two specific reasons. One was to ask if Mr Noonan had been here and the other was to request something from Mrs Wilder.' He turned to her. 'Having seen examples of your husband's work, I realise that he was an excellent photographer. I assume that he had a darkroom somewhere in the house.'

'Yes, he did,' she admitted. 'Simon was always pottering about in there.'

'I wonder if I might see it, please.'

It was well into evening before Keedy returned to Scotland Yard with his prisoner. During the drive from his cottage, Redmond had threatened him with legal action, ridicule in the press and even violence. When he failed to rouse the sergeant, he eventually gave up and brooded in silence. He recovered full voice, however, when he was locked up in a holding cell. Pleased with the arrest, Keedy hoped for a rare compliment from the superintendent. It was not forthcoming.

'We have insufficient grounds to hold him,' said Chatfield.

'He attacked a police officer, sir.'

'Did he inflict any injuries on you?'

'Well, no . . .'

'So what form exactly did this attack take?'

'When I tried to search him, Redmond pushed me away.'

'Did you have any reason to search him?'

'Yes,' said Keedy. 'I was certain that he had his passport on him.'

'Did you ask for *permission* to search him?'

'That would have been pointless, sir.'

'So you tried to manhandle him.'

'Redmond is a murder suspect, sir, and he was acting in a suspicious manner. He was about to leave the country.'

'You don't know that, Sergeant.'

'Why else would he carry a passport?'

'Some people like to have it with them as a form of identification. It doesn't mean that they are about to jump on the next ferry. Besides,' added Chatfield, 'where would Redmond go? There's a war on. He's hardly likely to cross the Channel to France or Belgium, is he?'

Keedy was nonplussed. 'I never thought of that, sir.'

'Look before you leap, Sergeant.'

'But he was making a run for it, Superintendent.'

'That's how it may have looked but you've no proof that that was his intention. He might just have wanted to get away from London for a while and I don't blame him. This is a dangerous place to be with air raids increasing in severity.'

'We can't just release him, sir,' said Keedy, aghast.

'Yes, we can,' said Chatfield, peremptorily. 'We'll charge him with assault on a police officer and bail him. We need every cell we've got for *real* criminals.'

'Redmond *is* a real criminal. I'm almost certain he killed Mr Wilder.'

'Where's your evidence?'

'He provided that by trying to flee.'

'I'm sorry, Sergeant Keedy, but you're working on supposition rather than on incontrovertible fact. Don't misunderstand me. I admire your enterprise and I congratulate you on tracking him down the way you did. However,' he went on, 'you didn't find the evidence we need to arrest him on a charge of murder.' He raised an eyebrow. 'And there's something else that needs to be borne in mind.'

'Is there?'

'Like you and the inspector, I wondered why Mr Redmond had managed to avoid conscription so I made a few discreet inquiries about him this afternoon. He has powerful friends, Sergeant. To begin with, his father is a Member of Parliament and there are other members of his family in influential positions.'

'I don't care if he's the son of the prime minister,' asserted Keedy, 'Nobody is above the law, sir.'

'That's an admirable tenet but it's not entirely true.'

'Are you going to let Redmond get away with killing someone?'

'No, I'm not. If that's what he did – and we can prove it in court – then he'll feel the full rigour of the law. At present, however, all we can do is to give him a strict warning, charge him with a much lesser offence and send him on his way.' Keedy was struggling to hold his temper. 'Go on, Sergeant – say it.'

'I've nothing to say,' grunted the other.

'Let it be a lesson to you. Don't be too hasty to accuse someone of something unless you have unshakable evidence that they're about to do it.'

'There's a second lesson to take away as well, sir.'

'Is there?'

'Yes,' said Keedy, quivering with vexation, 'and it's this. Even if you do your duty and make what you believe to be an important arrest, you may get no support at all from a senior officer.'

'Are you daring to *criticise* me?' yelled Chatfield.

'I'm sure that you're only doing what you think best, sir, but I am shocked that you're frightened by the fact that Redmond has political contacts able to exert a lot of pressure on his behalf. I always believed that you'd take on anybody.'

Before the superintendent could master his rage and offer a stinging reply, Keedy walked out of the door in disgust and stormed down the corridor.

Colette always knew when her brother was going to see his girlfriend. Dennis Orme shaved for the second time in the day, combed his hair, put on his best suit and radiated pleasure. If he was going for a drink with old army friends, it was not the same at all. He made no effort to be at his best for them. When she heard him coming slowly down the stairs, she went out to see him off.

'Where are you taking her to this evening?'

'I'll let Harry decide that.'

'Her name is Harriet,' she scolded, 'and I'm fed up with reminding you.'

'She likes me calling her Harry,' he said, cheerfully.

'Well, I don't. It's a man's name.'

'So?'

He reached for his hat and put it on at the rakish angle he favoured. Colette watched him with a fondness tinged with anxiety. They were close as siblings and his injuries had brought them even closer. As a result, she didn't like to keep secrets from him.

'I went to see Mrs Pattinson,' she confessed.

'How is the old duck?'

'Dennis! Don't call her that.'

'Well, that's what she is, isn't she? I like the woman. She's kind and caring, unlike that misery of a husband. How can she put up with him?'

'Listen to me,' she said, seriously. 'I went to see her because of you.'

'Me? What are you talking about?' The sad look she gave him was answer enough. 'You had no right to tell her about *me*, Colette. It's nothing to do with her.'

'I wanted advice.'

'Well, I can give you that,' he said, angering.

'You drink too much, Dennis, and it worries me.'

'Why? You don't have to pay for my beer.'

'It will damage your health.'

'It's the only thing that improves it – that and seeing Harry. It helps me forget the pain, Colette. After a pint or two of beer, I feel that I can do *anything*. It's better than any medicine.'

'I don't want you to stop having fun with your friends,' she explained. 'I'd just like you to drink less, that's all. When I tried talking to Daddy about it, he just laughed and told me not to bother. But Mrs Pattinson said I was right to be worried. How do you think Harriet would feel if she discovered that you were more or less carried home after a night at the pub?'

'Keep her out of this,' he insisted. 'Harry must never know.'

'You can't hide it from her for ever, Dennis.'

'That's my business.'

When he limped gingerly towards the door, she grabbed his walking stick from the umbrella stand and offered it to him.

'You're forgetting this.'

'I'm going to try to manage without it.'

'But you *need* it, Dennis.'

'It's only a short walk and I can support myself on the wall as I go. It's all part of a ruse, you see. When I've got the walking stick, I look like a cripple and, in any case, it gets in the way. If I go without it, Harry will have to let me take her arm.' He chuckled merrily. 'That's my ruse. I want *her* to be my stick from now on.'

Climbing into the rear seat of the car, Keedy barked an order then lapsed into a sullen silence. As they headed back to Chingford, the driver didn't dare to speak to him. Behind him, throbbing with fury, his passenger was reflecting that it had been the worst day in his career as a policeman. He'd been put in an embarrassing position by Odele Thompson, tried to revive his spirits by speaking to Alice and managed instead to have a fierce row that was exacerbated by the news that her brother had told her not to marry him. Acting on initiative, he'd cornered a murder suspect before the man could disappear and overpowered him before making an arrest. Back in London, he'd been ordered to release the prisoner on bail because he had family members in a position to rap the knuckles of Claude Chatfield. After a bitter argument with the superintendent, Keedy had to endure the mockery of Allan Redmond as the latter was set free. Taken as a whole, the day had been nothing short of a catastrophe.

By the time he reached his destination, he'd added a more worrying setback to the list. Now that he'd calmed down, he could see how disrespectful he'd been towards Chatfield. While he didn't regret anything he'd said, Keedy feared that there would be repercussions. Demotion was a distinct possibility and he might even be put back into the uniform branch. For a man who'd sedulously worked his way up, that would be a humiliation. The only thing worse was dismissal.

Rushing into the police station, he went into the room from which they'd been conducting the investigation. Marmion was checking some notes. He looked up but had no time to welcome his colleague because Keedy blurted out a question.

'Have you heard from Chat?'

'No, I haven't.'

'Has he left a message for you?'

'Why do you ask?'

'Has he?' Marmion shook his head. 'That's a relief, I suppose.'

'What's going on, Joe?'

'The heavens have opened and it's raining shit all over me. I'm sorry,' he went on, 'I didn't mean to be coarse but that's exactly how it feels.'

'At a guess, you've had the gloves on with Chat.'

'Yes – and he was the one who delivered the uppercut.'

Marmion pulled out a chair. 'Sit down and tell me all about it.'

Keedy preferred to stay on his feet so that he could pace about the room. He explained what had happened and how infuriating it had been to release Allan Redmond from custody. In refusing to support him, Chatfield had made him look ridiculous. That was why he'd struck back at the superintendent.

'I could be facing the sack,' he said with a sigh.

'Chat can be vindictive, Joe, but he's not stupid. He knows that you're the best sergeant we have. Getting rid of you over a few hot words would be nonsensical. No, your job is safe but he'll want to make you pay somehow.'

'He's already done that, Harv. It made my blood boil. Have you ever been forced to release a prisoner who should stay under lock and key?'

'Oh, yes, it's happened to me a couple of times. The worst case involved a burglar I'd caught red-handed. I was told that police procedure hadn't been followed properly – although it certainly had. I not only had to let him go scot-free, I was ordered to apologise to the bastard.'

'I escaped having to do that.'

'Then you got off lightly. Yes,' he added as Keedy flared up, 'it may not have felt like it at the time but you'll come to see, in due course, that it wasn't quite so terrible, after all.' He studied his colleague carefully. 'There's more to it than trading blows with the superintendent, isn't there?' Keedy nodded. 'Then stop prancing around like a scalded cat and tell me.'

Keedy sank into a chair. 'I met Alice.'

'How could you? You're supposed to be on duty.'

'It doesn't matter how we met, I just wish that we hadn't. It ended in a blazing row. Don't ask me what it was about because that's personal but . . . well, we parted in a huff. The worst of it was that she told me what Paul said to her.'

'Oh, that . . .'

'Ellen must have told you about it. Why didn't you pass it on?'

'I didn't want to upset you, Joe.'

'I'm not upset, I'm seething. When Paul was in the army, he wrote to say how glad he was that his sister and I had become engaged. Now he's telling her to get rid of me because I'm too old and . . . you know the rest of it.'

Marmion felt uneasy. He'd had reservations about the match from the very start and, in some ways, his son's comment had mirrored his own view. Yet he'd come to accept that Alice was entitled to make her own choice and he'd been impressed by the way that Keedy had treated her. Now, however, there'd been a rift. He tried to sympathise with the sergeant. At a professional and personal level, Keedy was reeling from a blow. He needed advice and support.

'Keep away from her for a while,' he counselled. 'Alice is like her mother. They both have a temper if you catch them on the raw. Let her come to you before you go looking for her.'

'It's Paul I want to go looking for,' resolved Keedy.

'Leave him alone, Joe. Just ignore what he said.'

'How can I?'

'It's the most sensible thing to do.'

'I don't feel very sensible at the moment.'

Marmion clapped him on the back and turned the conversation back to the murder inquiry. He talked about his second meeting with Gillian Hogg and his first one with Godfrey Noonan. When he described the agent, he made Keedy laugh.

'It's true,' he said. 'Noonan was wearing a wig that looked more like a ginger rabbit. It had a life of its own, I know that. When he turned his head away from me, the wig stayed facing me. I was tempted to ask him what he fed it on.'

'Is he someone to watch?'

'I think so. And so is Mrs Wilder. I'd bet my pension that he came to Chingford to see her yet neither he nor she would admit it. Noonan is one of those greasy characters who couldn't tell the truth if he tried.'

'Why should he want to speak to Mrs Wilder?'

'Use your imagination.'

'Was Noonan *hired* by her?'

'I think that they could be in cahoots somehow.'

'He stands to gain his revenge but what's the motive for her?'

'We know that she and Wilder were living separate lives. Perhaps she became aware that he was getting consolation in the arms of his first wife. That would have incensed her.'

'Any wife would be upset if her husband had eyes for another woman,' said Keedy, 'but would she want his eyes removed along with his balls?'

'Mrs Wilder is not any wife. She's been a performer, used to devising effects in public.'

'Is that what you call castration?'

'It's symbolic, Joe.'

'Mrs Wilder may have ordered the murder but she certainly didn't do it herself and neither – from what you say – did that agent. So who was the actual killer?'

'It might have been Redmond, I suppose.'

'He's involved *somehow*. I'm sure of that.'

'My mind is turning more towards Atterbury. Ideally, I'd like him put under surveillance but Chat bleated about shortage of resources and said he'd "think about it". We know what that means.'

'It's a pity. Putting a shadow on Atterbury might be useful.'

'Forget it, Joe. It will never happen.'

The taxi drew up outside the house and they got out. Atterbury paid the taxi driver then took out a key. He used it to open the door of the house and ushered Pattinson inside. A man was standing in the shadows on the opposite side of the road. He took out his notebook and put the time of day in it. Then he settled down to keep vigil.

Though she'd suggested they went to the cinema that evening, Alice Marmion couldn't possibly stick to the agreement. She was in too great a state of emotional upheaval. As soon as her shift ended, she invented an excuse, promised that they'd go another night then apologised to Iris Goodliffe and raced off to her flat. In the privacy of her room, she was able to give full vent to tears and recrimination. She felt no better as a result. What should have been a brief, delightful encounter with Joe Keedy had somehow degenerated into a row about the very nature of their commitment to each other. How they'd allowed it to happen she didn't know, but her discomfort had been made worse by the fact that they had bickered in front of Iris. The unstinting praise that Alice had used when describing Keedy to her colleague had seemed hollow.

After going over it a dozen times, Alice decided that she had to confide in someone and the best person was her mother. She dried her eyes, changed out of her uniform and caught the next available bus. The journey was taken up with a rehearsal of what she was going to say. When she actually got to the house, however, the words were promptly forgotten. She simply burst into tears.

'Whatever's happened?' asked Ellen, embracing her.

'It's Joe . . .'

'Has he been injured?'

'Yes, Mummy, but not in the way you mean. We've both been injured.'

Ellen held her until the sobbing slowly ebbed. She then took her daughter into the kitchen, made a pot of tea and let Alice do the talking. It was a very garbled version of what happened but Ellen caught the gist of it. Alice first blamed Keedy, then herself and finally came round to the view that she was the real victim.

'It blew up out of nothing,' she wailed.

'That sometimes happens.'

'We just . . . lost control.'

'I can see that.'

'Did you and Daddy ever . . . ?'

'Oh, yes. We had a lot of arguments along the way.'

'How did you get over them?'

'We both came to see how unfair we'd been to each other.'

'It's not as easy as that in this case.'

'Oh, it was never easy, Alice, believe me. I'd sometimes sulk for a week or two but we always made up in the end. You and Joe are both strong-willed. When you have an argument, neither of you is ready to give ground.'

'But why did we have the argument in the first place?' asked Alice in despair. 'I was thrilled when he suddenly turned up out of the blue, even more so because I could show him off to Iris. She's heard me go on and on about him. What must she think now?'

'That doesn't matter,' said Ellen. 'Forget Iris. This is about you and Joe. Have you ever had a row like this before?'

'We have spats all the time but they mean nothing.'

'Have you accused him of looking at other women?'

'Yes, but I was only teasing him.'

'So what was different this time?'

'It was his response,' said Alice, lower lip trembling. 'In the past, he's just laughed. This time he really took offence.'

'Joe didn't *have* to tell you about this other woman.'

'I know.'

'It wasn't as if he was trying to deceive you.'

'But it's something he should have told me in private,' said Alice, 'and not when I'm on duty with another policewoman. It popped out as if Joe wanted to get it off his chest.'

'I'd take that as a good sign.'

'So why did I behave so badly?'

'It takes two people for an argument,' said Ellen, philosophically. 'There's something between you that has never really been sorted out.'

Alice nodded. 'I just wish I knew what it was.'

There was a long, heavy silence. They drank their tea and simply enjoyed the pleasure of being together. While she was upset to hear of the rift, Ellen was glad that Alice still felt able to turn to her. When her daughter had insisted on having a flat of her own, her mother had at first been hurt. Time had softened her pain. She'd now come to accept that Alice had a right to her independence even though it meant that she saw so little of her. But her daughter was there now and she was in need of sympathy.

'Is it *my* fault, Mummy?' asked Alice.

'No, it isn't.'

'That's what Joe will think.'

'There are faults on both sides and he'll know that. But you must remember something,' Ellen went on. 'When he saw you, he was sneaking away for a few minutes from a murder investigation that's putting a lot of pressure on him. It's the same with your father. He's all tensed up when he gets back here. His mind is still on his work.'

'I'd like to believe that was the case with Joe but it wasn't.'

'What *do* you believe?'

'I believe that . . . he may be unhappy about our engagement. He's always been like a rock until now but the rock was crumbling today. Joe is wondering if he really wants to marry me and – if you want to know the truth – I'm no longer sure that he's the right husband for me.'

'What did I say?' asked a voice.

Shocked to realise they'd been overheard, the two women turned to see Paul Marmion standing in the open doorway. He was grinning with satisfaction.

'You've come to your senses at last, Alice,' he said. 'Get rid of him.'

During the time they'd been away, Detective Constable Gibbs had handled any information that came in. People often took days before their memories were jogged or before they felt they might have something significant to report. Keedy sifted through their statements.

'This is the most promising,' said Keedy, holding up a sheet of paper. 'A man named Wainwright claims that he saw someone, who answers the description of Simon Wilder, walking along Old Church Road around midnight.'

'How well could he see in the dark?'

'Wainwright had been walking his dog for some time so he'd have adjusted to the dark. Also, he works as an engine driver. You need good eyesight to drive a train.'

'Does he specify an exact place in the road?'

'Yes,' said Keedy, 'and it's not far from where the body was found.'

'We need to talk to Wainwright,' decided Marmion, lifting another report from the table. 'It looks as if I might need to see him myself, Joe. You appear to be needed elsewhere.'

'Do I?'

'Yes, there's a request from Odele Thompson for you to call at her flat as a matter of urgency. There's something she wants to tell you.'

Keedy pulled a face. 'I've heard it before!'

'She doesn't mind how late it is when you get there.'

'Then she's out of luck. Why don't *you* go and see Miss Thompson while I have a word with Mr Wainwright?'

'That sounds like the answer.'

'It will be a false alarm, I warn you. She'll have nothing new to tell us.'

'You never know.'

They spent another hour assessing all the information gathered and linking it to existing intelligence. There'd been a number of putative sightings of Wilder – or someone very much like him – and they'd all happened in the same area. It was encouraging. They were slowly narrowing down the possibilities of where he'd actually been on the night when he was killed.

By late evening, when they were both starting to yawn, they split up to make separate inquiries, meeting up afterwards to compare stories on the drive back to Scotland Yard. First to recount his interview, Keedy turned out to have had the more productive visit.

'Wainwright was insistent that it had been the murder victim,' he said. 'He remembered how the man glided along the pavement, almost as if he was dancing.'

'Then it *was* Wilder!'

'I was right about his eyesight. It was very keen because it needs to be.'

Marmion sighed. 'Ah, he was one of those, was he?'

'There's no doubt about it. Wainwright takes his dog for a walk on certain nights and usually goes to a park – so do courting couples, of course. That's what interests him. He's a voyeur.'

'I despise people like that, Joe. The trouble is that they're difficult to catch peering through the bushes. At least he's done something useful this time.'

'He recalled something he'd forgotten to put in his statement,' said Keedy. 'He noticed that the man was carrying something that looked like a camera.'

'It was *him*,' said Marmion, decisively. 'It had to be Wilder.'

'How did you get on with Odele – Miss Thompson, that is?'

'To be honest, I didn't. She was livid that I turned up and not you. She'd put on a silk robe for your benefit. It was very eye-catching. She told me that Allan Redmond had offered her all kinds of blandishments to leave Wilder and team up with her, but that was not really news. When I told her you'd arrested him, she gave a whoop of joy.'

'What did she do when she heard I'd had to release him?'

'She was full of sympathy for you, Joe.'

Anxious to get off the subject of Odele Thomson, the sergeant went through the list of suspects once again and they discussed each one of them. They were so immersed in their debate that they didn't realise they were back at Scotland Yard until they felt the car slowing down. Keedy glanced out of the window with dread.

'I know that Chat is expecting the both of us,' said Marmion, 'but I suggest that you slope off and leave me to handle him.'

'I ought to face the music.'

'Let me do that on your behalf. You're off duty, Sergeant – disappear!'

Keedy didn't need to hear the order repeated. After thanking Marmion, he got out of the car and walked away from the building. The inspector, meanwhile, made his way inside and headed for the superintendent's office. He found the door wide open. Leaning against the edge of his desk, Chatfield was waiting impatiently.

'Where is Keedy?' he asked.

'I sent him home, sir. He was not well.'

'Did he tell you what happened between us?'

'He's very sorry and sends his apologies.'

'I'd have more respect for him if he tendered them in person,' said Chatfield with a growl of displeasure. 'I will not stand for insubordination.'

'Sergeant Keedy was disappointed, sir.'

The other man stood upright. 'How does he think *I* feel?'

'He knows that he shouldn't have walked out like that and he expects that he will be disciplined. All I ask is that you postpone it until we crack this case.'

'And are you any nearer to doing that?'

'We think so, sir. We can now put Wilder very close to the murder scene.'

As Marmion delivered his report, the superintendent's ire slowly turned to interest and then to a guarded optimism. Eventually, he forgot about Keedy's misconduct altogether.

'So you're concentrating your inquiries on three people.'

'That's correct, sir – Mrs Wilder, Noonan and Atterbury.'

'The sergeant is doubtless still claiming that Redmond is the killer.'

'He's coming round to my point of view, sir,' said Marmion. 'I just wondered if you could see your way to do the same.'

'I'm not sure that I follow.'

'Let me put a man on Tom Atterbury.'

'I'm sorry, Sergeant, I can't allow you to do that.'

'Then we're missing a vital opportunity.'

'The reason I can't let you put a man on Atterbury,' said Chatfield, airily, 'is that I've already done so. I know a good idea when I hear it, Inspector.'

He'd shifted his position throughout the evening in case he was spotted, crossing the road and venturing ever nearer to the house he was watching. When the front door opened, two men came into view and exchanged a handshake. He was close enough to hear Tom Atterbury speaking to his visitor.

'Goodbye, Pattinson,' he said, 'and thank you again.'

CHAPTER EIGHTEEN

After a sleepless night, Alice Marmion could only pick at her breakfast and she heard very little of the banter of the other women at the table. She felt completely unready for a day's work when she walked down the street to the bus stop. People looked at her differently since she'd become a policewoman. She'd always collected admiring glances in the past and, on one occasion, had aroused a man's interest so much that he stalked her and tried to molest her. Luckily, Keedy had come to her rescue, one of many examples when she was profoundly grateful to him. Men now tended to look at her with a mingled caution and disapproval, shy of approaching her and wondering why she should try to do a job for which they considered her to be ill fitted. For the most part, Alice's uniform made women curious and they were much more likely to speak to her.

As she stood in the queue, she simply wanted to be left alone but the old woman next to her tried to engage her in polite conversation. When the bus came, it was so full that only three people were allowed on. Neither Alice nor the old woman was among them. It was at least twenty minutes before another bus was due and Alice realised that she was behind time. The old lady, meanwhile, complained bitterly and said that her age entitled her to be let on the bus first. She kept up the tirade until another vehicle eventually came.

Squashed into a seat at the front, Alice was at last left alone to look back on what had been an uncomfortable visit home. Having gone in search of sympathy, she'd ended up arguing with her brother and telling him that he ought to keep his opinions to himself. What irked her was that Paul seemed to be enjoying her plight. The more he derided Keedy, the more she came to his defence and reminded herself just how much she missed him. Her mother had been thrust into the position of a referee who'd lost her whistle. All three of them had finished up yelling at the top of their voices.

Alice was tortured by regret. She was sorry that she'd quarrelled with Paul, sorry that she'd upset her mother in doing so and sorry, most of all, that she had no idea where she stood with Keedy. Would he apologise or would he simply decide that they had no future together? As long as he was with her, he was forced to reject any overtures from other women. Odele was a case in point. What would he have done if he hadn't been engaged to Alice? Did he feel trapped? One thing was certain. Keedy was such a handsome man that there'd be other Odeles to tempt him in the future. How could Alice possibly compete with them?

When she finally arrived for work, she was low, depressed and extremely weary. Alice was not robust enough to withstand a broadside from Inspector Gale.

'What time do you call this?' she demanded.

Alice yawned involuntarily. 'I'm sorry. The bus was late.'

'*You* were late, not the bus. If you rely on public transport, you should always allow for contingencies. Catch an earlier bus than the one you intended. Think ahead, girl and – for heaven's sake – stop yawning at me!'

Alice put a hand over her mouth. 'I couldn't help myself.'

'Sergeant Keedy is behind this, isn't he?'

'No, no, he isn't.'

'He kept you out late last night and you had virtually no sleep.'

'That's not what happened at all, Inspector.'

'I'm not blind,' snapped the other woman. 'Look at you. You're half-dead. What kind of an advertisement is that for the Women's Police Force? When you put that uniform on, you have to be at your very best.'

'Yes, I know that.'

'Then why do you turn up looking as if you're about to keel over?'

Alice drew herself up to her full height and tried to shake off her fatigue. Being dressed down by the inspector was the final indignity. Her pride was wounded. The one consolation was that Iris Goodliffe was not there to witness her disgrace. The inspector continued to berate her until she ran out of unpleasant adjectives.

'You can give Sergeant Keedy a message from me,' said the older woman. 'You're to be allowed plenty of time to rest between shifts. He ought to know that.'

'This is nothing to do with him, Inspector.'

'That's an arrant lie.'

'I'm late because the bus I usually catch was full.'

The inspector rolled her eyes. 'How many times have I heard that excuse?'

'It's the truth,' protested Alice.

'Shut up and listen to me.' The inspector glowered at her. 'I don't like excuses, I don't like unpunctuality and I won't tolerate lies. You're not fit to be seen in public like that. You've let me down and you've let yourself down. That's the message you must give to Sergeant Keedy. If he keeps you out till all hours and sends you to work looking like this, I'll have no alternative but to dismiss you on the spot.'

Alice felt as if the whole world was suddenly against her.

The presence of the driver made it impossible for them to have a private conversation. Joe Keedy therefore had to hold back the question he was dying to ask until they reached Chingford and went into the room that had become their temporary base.

Alone with Marmion at last, he was able to speak freely.

'Something happened, didn't it?'

'Yes, Joe, it did.'

'Well?'

'I managed to get a stay of execution for you. Chat will have to discipline you but at least he's agreed to wait until our work is done here.'

'I'm not worried about Chat,' said Keedy, irritably. 'It's Alice I was talking about. Something's happened. I can tell from your manner.'

'It's true,' admitted Marmion. 'Alice came home yesterday evening to see her mother and . . . Paul interrupted them.'

'There's more to it than that, surely, and I want to know what it is.'

Marmion was in a cleft stick. While wanting to appease Keedy, he drew back from revealing the full details of a family squabble. He'd returned home the previous night to hear about the way his children had ended up hurling insults at each other. Alice had eventually gone back to her flat, leaving her mother to have a separate argument with Paul. Once again, Marmion had rued the fact that he was not there to impose some kind of control, supporting Ellen, speaking sharply to his son and comforting his distraught daughter. The domestic upheaval was still at the forefront of his mind when he picked up Keedy in the police car. As a consequence, the sergeant had sensed that something untoward had occurred.

'Don't keep me in suspense,' said Keedy. 'Tell me what happened.'

'Paul made some remarks about you and Alice took offence.'

'What sort of remarks?'

'That's irrelevant. The fact is that they had a row and Alice defended you to the hilt. That really is all I'm prepared to say, Joe.'

He was rescued from the need to continue the conversation because the telephone rang. Marmion picked up the receiver. From the pained expression on his face, Keedy could see that he was talking – listening, rather – to Claude Chatfield. When he put the instrument down, the inspector was pleased.

'Chat's idea has borne fruit,' he explained.

'Which idea is that?'

'He put a tail on Tom Atterbury.'

'That was *your* idea,' said Keedy, indignantly.

'I'm happy to let him think that it's his, Joe. For once, he did actually take my advice and it's given us a lead.'

'What happened?'

'One of our lads was deployed to watch Atterbury's house. He came home in a taxi with another man and they both went into the house. When the visitor later left, Atterbury was heard to say his name.'

'Was it Pattinson, by any chance?'

'It was, indeed.'

'I knew that those two were connected somehow.'

'I must remember to thank the detective on duty outside. All that he had to go on was Atterbury's address and our description of him. There was a warm handshake as Pattinson left. They were obviously close friends. In the man's report, said Chat, they were described as "thick as thieves" but that's probably because he couldn't spell "conspiratorial" properly.'

'I'm not sure that I can.'

'It's time to call on Atterbury again, I think.'

'You didn't finish telling me about Alice.'

'Yes, I did,' said Marmion, resolutely. 'We're at work now. Our private lives don't exist until we come off duty. Right,' he went on, 'do you want to renew your acquaintance with Tom Atterbury or would you rather pay a courtesy visit to Odele Thompson?' Keedy gave a mirthless laugh. 'That settles that, then.'

Audrey Pattinson never had a chance of seeing the newspaper until her husband had finished reading it. As they sat at the breakfast table, he turned a page and ran his eye down it. Audrey ignored him. She had long grown accustomed to meals eaten in silence. For once, however, her husband had something to say to her.

'There are details of the funeral in here,' he said. 'Wilder's body must have been released to the family.'

'When is it, Martin?'

'You can see for yourself when I've finished with the paper.'

He carried on reading and left her fuming with an impatience she dared not show. Audrey still nursed hopes that she'd be able to play the organ at the funeral but there'd been no approach from Catherine Wilder. She realised that she had to put herself forward if she had any chance of being given a task that she would cherish. It was another twenty minutes before Pattinson folded the newspaper and set it down on the table. As he rose to go, she had her request ready.

'Martin . . .'

'What do you want?'

'I'm going to call on Mrs Wilder this morning. Since my work at the dance studio has finished for good, I might as well return the key to her.'

'Yes,' he agreed, 'she'll want it back and you don't need it. The key is in my room. I'll bring it down.'

'Thank you, Martin.'

'But since you won't be playing dance music any more, you might as well get rid of all that music. I hate listening to it. You can play Chopin instead.' He wagged a finger. 'No German composers, though – you know why. I'm not having my wife paying homage to the enemy.'

When he left the room, Audrey pounced on the newspaper immediately and flipped through the pages as she searched for the obituary column.

Arriving at the house, they rang the bell and waited side by side. Tom Atterbury soon opened the door. Displeased to see them, he realised that they would not have come together unless they had something important to tell him. Ungraciously, he invited them in. Marmion and Keedy left their hats on the stand and followed him into the living room.

'Do you have news?' asked Atterbury. 'Have you caught him yet?'

'No, sir,' replied Marmion, 'but we feel that we're closing in on the killer.'

'Who is he?'

'It's too early to put a name on him.'

'Or on *them*,' added Keedy. 'Two or three people may be involved.'

'As long as you don't think I'm one of them,' said Atterbury, scowling. 'I was insulted that you should even consider me as a suspect.'

'We have to look at everyone who appears to have a motive for

269

murder, sir. In your case, we were told, you were very envious of Mr Wilder's success.'

'I wasn't envious of it, Sergeant. I felt it was undeserved.'

'Why is that?'

'Simon had a modicum of talent, that's true, and when he danced with his wife he was able to look much better than he really was. Yet somehow they managed to persuade everyone that they were Britain's equivalent of Vernon and Irene Castle. Are you familiar with those names?'

'We are now, sir,' said Marmion.

'My wife and I are much more like the Castles.'

'We'll take your word for it.'

'A lot of people have said the same thing, Inspector. When I dance, I am often compared to Vernon Castle.'

'If you saw *me* dance,' Keedy put in, 'you'd compare me to *Windsor* Castle.'

'I've been talking to a friend of yours, sir,' said Marmion.

Atterbury was wary. 'Oh, who is that?'

'It's your agent, Mr Noonan. He speaks highly of you.'

'And so he should – I put a lot of money his way this year.'

'He seemed to think it was the other way around.'

'Agents are a necessary evil, Inspector. No matter how good you are, you need someone to ferret out work and to make deals. Godfrey does all that very well.'

'I thought his clients called him God.'

'I draw the line at that,' said Atterbury. 'It only feeds his vanity.'

'I wouldn't have thought it needed feeding,' said Marmion, coolly. 'We discovered that Mr Noonan and Mr Wilder had been at daggers drawn in the past.'

'Ah, so that's what brought you here to pester me again, is it? Yes, it's true. Godfrey did lose a court battle to Simon and the wound still festers.'

'Is your agent the sort of man who'd want to get his revenge?'

'He's already got it, Inspector. My wife and I are the embodiment of his revenge. Had he lived, Simon and Odele would have been knocked off their pinnacle by us at the British Dance Championships. That's the kind of revenge that Godfrey savours – an act of murder on the dance floor.'

'But you and your wife couldn't be certain of winning,' said Keedy.

'Oh, yes, we could.'

'There are other leading contenders. Mr Redmond is one of them.'

'Allan is a wonderful dancer,' conceded Atterbury, 'but he's let down by his partner. That's why he kept trying to seduce Odele Thompson away from Simon. She and Redmond would make a formidable pair.'

'I admire your confidence, sir,' said Marmion.

'It's the most important element in dancing.'

'Let's turn to another friend of yours – Martin Pattinson.'

'He's hardly a friend, Inspector. We happen to be members of the same club, that's all. We're on nodding terms, nothing more.'

'So you've never invited him to your home?'

Atterbury frowned. 'Why on earth would I do that?'

'You tell *us*, sir.'

'Then I can say categorically that Pattinson has never been here.'

'Your memory is very poor, sir,' said Keedy. 'We have information that places Mr Pattinson in this very house yesterday evening. You spoke his name as he left.' Atterbury was rocked and Keedy smiled. 'I see that you remember, after all.'

'So let's have no more prevarication,' said Marmion.

271

As the truth dawned, Atterbury looked from one to the other. Conflicting emotions made him unable to say a word for a few moments. When he finally spoke, the veins stood out on his temples.

'You *dared* to have me followed?' he roared.

'It seemed like a wise precaution, sir.'

'You had no right to do that.'

'I think you'll find that we have every right. It's a useful way of checking people's honesty. Yours was found wanting yet again.'

'How dare you!' shouted Atterbury. 'You'll be hearing from my solicitor.'

'He'll tell you exactly what I can,' said Marmion. 'When war broke out, the government rushed through emergency measures. One of them was the Defence of the Realm Act. We call it DORA. Your solicitor will know that DORA gives the police sweeping powers that include tailing someone suspected of having committed a felony. In short, Mr Atterbury, if I put six detectives outside this house to watch it night and day, the only thing you can do is to protest.'

'This is intolerable.'

'It's the law, sir,' said Keedy, 'so why don't you stop pretending that you and Mr Pattinson do nothing more than nod at each other, and tell the truth.'

'It was the truth,' insisted the other. 'Pattinson and I are acquaintances and not real friends. As it happened, he did come back here from the club. If you had a man watching the house, he'll have told you it was a relatively short stay.'

'But why did he come here at all?'

'I invited him in for a nightcap.'

'Did you discuss what happened to Mr Wilder?'

'No – why should we?'

272

'I don't think you're being entirely honest, sir,' said Marmion. 'The sergeant has already caught you lying about the time you got back here on the night of the murder and we've just seen you wriggling away from the truth once again.' He gave him a smile of encouragement. 'Why don't you start cooperating with us for a change? It will be to your advantage in the long run.'

Atterbury distributed a furtive glance between them before moving away.

'I need a drink,' he said.

Audrey Pattinson sat at the piano with a pile of dance music in front of her. It was very dear to her and she couldn't bear the thought of throwing it away when it held so many wonderful memories. On the other hand, she knew that her husband would open the piano stool to check that it was no longer there. Gathering it up, therefore, she took it upstairs to her bedroom and hid it in a drawer under some stockings. Even though she could play all the melodies without sheet music, she was determined to keep it as one more minor act of rebellion against the man who dominated her life. Picking up the satchel she routinely took with her to the studio, she pulled out another sheaf of music and put it in the drawer. She then looked into the satchel again and gave a yelp of surprise.

Something was missing.

Tom Atterbury had poured himself a whisky and soda before he even thought to offer a drink to his visitors. They declined the offer and waited for him to take a first gulp. Fortified by the alcohol, he gave his statement. He'd met Pattinson at the club, he said, and they'd had such a pleasant conversation that he brought him back to the house for a nightcap. It was the first time that Pattinson had been there and he was unlikely to go again. Atterbury's dancing commitments were such that he'd be out of London for a while and unable even to get to his club. It was a place to which he resorted when his wife, Naomi, was away. Had she been at home the previous night, he'd never have dreamt of bringing Pattinson back.

'Why do you say that, sir?' asked Marmion.

'The fellow is rather dry and humourless. Naomi wouldn't have taken to him.'

'Yet you did.'

'Only that once,' asserted Atterbury.

'We met Martin Pattinson and thought him very much a man's man. I suspect that his wife has a lot of long, lonely evenings.'

'That's *her* problem, Inspector.'

'It may not have been a problem,' suggested Keedy. 'Neither of us had the feeling that Mr Pattinson was sparkling company. His wife might have been glad to be left alone with her piano. She must be an excellent musician if Mr Wilder relied on her so much.'

'Pattinson was singing her praises when he was here.'

'And that's all you did, was it – just have a quiet chat?'

'What do you think we did, Sergeant – talk about the murder we plotted?'

'You're being sarcastic, Mr Atterbury.'

'Can you blame me?' asked the other, sipping a second whisky before going on the attack. 'You each interview me separately. You have me followed. You corner me this morning and try to trip me up all the time. Why don't you simply accuse me of killing Simon and put me behind bars?' Setting his glass on the table, he offered both wrists. 'Come on, put the handcuffs on me,' he sneered. 'Then see what happens when my solicitor gets me released. We'll sue you for false arrest.'

'That's debatable, sir,' said Marmion, easily. 'As it is, we've no desire to meet your solicitor at this stage. The person who interests us is your agent.'

'Godfrey?'

'When did you last see him?'

'It was a day or two ago.'

'What sort of a mood was he in?'

'Godfrey is always in a good humour, Inspector.'

'Would you call it a mood of celebration?'

'What would he be celebrating?'

'The presence of you and your wife in his list of clients,' said Marmion. 'He assured me that you would have been crowned champions even though you'd be competing against Mr Wilder and Miss Thompson. Now that they are no longer in the running, your triumph is even more likely. Isn't that something to celebrate?'

Atterbury was circumspect. 'What are you trying to get me to say?'

'I just want you to answer a simple question, sir.'

'Go on.'

'How well do you know Godfrey Noonan?'

Gillian Hogg was reading a play for which she was about to audition. When there was a tap at the door, she opened it to discover a small, bedraggled boy standing there.

'There's a gintlemun darnstairs as wants to speak wi' yer,' he said.

'Did he give his name?'

'Naw,' said the boy, 'but 'e give me a tanner to say 'e's too old to climb all them bleedin' steps.'

Having delivered his message and earned his sixpence, the boy scampered off. Gillian was curious. Marmion had been able to climb the stairs without difficulty so he was clearly not the caller. Taking her key, she locked the door then tripped down the stairs with a nimbleness born of years of practice. As soon as she stepped out into the street, a hand grabbed her by the neck and forced her against the wall.

'What have you been saying about me?' demanded Godfrey Noonan.

Timid at the best of times, Audrey had to summon up every ounce of her courage before she called at the house. Catherine was surprised to see her but nevertheless invited her in. Audrey was daunted by the sight of her brother. He had the same air of authority as her husband. During the introductions, she gibbered.

'What can we do for you?' asked Catherine.

'First of all,' said the visitor, holding up a key, 'I want to return this. If the studio is to close, you'll want the key back.' She handed it over. 'I suppose that there's no chance you'll want to reopen it and run it yourself.'

'I can't even think about that.'

'Decisions of that importance can't be rushed,' said Clissold.

'No, no,' said Audrey. 'I understand. By the way, I saw the announcement in the paper about the funeral.'

'Yes,' replied Catherine, 'we were just going through the order of service.'

'Did Mr Wilder leave any instructions for you?'

'Of course, he didn't,' said Nathan Clissold, 'because he thought he had years to live. Why should he start making stipulations about his funeral?'

'He promised me, you see.'

'Promised you what, Mrs Pattinson?'

'Well, perhaps "promise" is too strong a word but he was so pleased with my accompaniment that he told me he wanted me to play the organ at his funeral.' They grimaced. 'There were witnesses there – Miss Thompson was one and Colette Orme was another. They'll support me.'

'I'm sure that Simon might have said something along those lines,' said Catherine, quickly, 'because he was always making extravagant promises that he couldn't possibly keep. I learnt that to my cost. It's very kind of you to offer but we will be using the church organist for the funeral.'

'It's a man's job,' said Clissold with crushing finality.

Audrey was downcast. 'I've played at funerals before.'

'And you may well do so again – but not in this case.'

'Oh . . .'

Audrey felt thoroughly rejected. Having been so close to Wilder, she hoped she'd earned some rights with regard to him. Catherine and her brother had robbed her of that illusion. Before she left, she had one last request.

'Might I know which hymns have been chosen, please?'

'We haven't decided yet,' said Catherine.

'You'll have to wait and see,' added Clissold.

'Is that all?'

Catherine was issuing a challenge rather than seeking information. She made no bones about the fact that she wanted the older woman to go. Accepting defeat, Audrey nodded a farewell then left a house in which she'd spent so many happy hours when Wilder was alive. His death had put it out of bounds to her and the closure of the dance studio had deprived her of the one thing that gave her life pleasure and direction. All that she could look forward to now was a continuation of the domestic tyranny under which she'd been kept since the day she'd unwisely married.

Since Paul Marmion had an appointment that day with the army eye specialist – and since Mavis Tandy also had commitments – they were unable to meet. They had therefore agreed on a time and place for the following morning. Paul fretted at the delay but at least he was in a more conciliatory mood when he came downstairs.

'I'm sorry about last night,' he mumbled.

'You're not as sorry as I am,' said Ellen, sharply. 'Because of you, we all lost our tempers and said things we shouldn't have said.'

'I only told Alice the truth.'

'There are times when it's unkind to express an opinion.'

'I wasn't trying to be kind. I was being honest.'

'Well, you upset your sister and you upset me. I hope you're proud of that.'

He shuffled his feet. 'I didn't mean to upset anybody . . .'

The words came out easily enough but Ellen didn't really believe them. In the past, she'd loved her son uncritically and, in the wake of his injuries, she'd dedicated herself to nursing him back to full health. Recent events had made that more difficult than it had first seemed. His physical health had improved markedly but there were flashes of anger and sheer bloody-mindedness that frightened her. Paul appeared to take pleasure from distressing his mother and his sister.

'It's got to stop,' she affirmed.

'What has?'

'You can't go on like this, Paul.'

He mimed innocence. 'What have I done wrong?'

'You must consider other people's feelings.'

'I always do.'

'Alice and I were having a private conversation. You didn't need to butt in.'

'I agreed with what she was saying.'

'You reduced her to tears again,' complained Ellen.

'That's nothing new. We always argued as kids.'

'You're both grown-ups now. You have to behave responsibly. Alice realises that but you obviously don't.' He gave a non-committal shrug. 'If Joe ever gets to hear what you said, he'll be hopping mad.'

Paul straightened his shoulders. 'I'm not afraid of him.'

Ellen gave up. She felt that he was being deliberately obstructive yet again. Changing her tack, she tried a more sympathetic approach.

'What time is your appointment?'

'It's at eleven o'clock.'

'Would you like me to come with you?'

He almost laughed. 'Why should I want you to do that?'

'I came with you the first time you went to the specialist.'

'My sight has got much better since then.'

'I thought you might like some company,' said Ellen, 'that's all.'

'A minute ago, you were telling me to act like a grown-up,' he snapped, 'yet now you're treating me like a child who needs to hold his mother's hand. I can look after myself. You don't have to take me anywhere. I make my own decisions now.'

Ellen's heart constricted yet again. She was losing him.

After the visit to Atterbury's house, they got into the car and were driven back to Chingford. Marmion and Keedy had each reached the same conclusion.

'He's lying,' said the inspector.

'I don't think we heard a syllable of truth.'

'We gave him a fright, anyway. That justified our call on him.'

'What surprises me,' said Keedy, 'is that he and Pattinson are friends. What could they possibly see in each other?'

'If people have a common objective, they make light of differences. And they both had a good reason to get rid of Wilder.'

'Atterbury did because he detested a rival. It's not the same with Pattinson. He may have resented the amount of time that his wife spent at the dance studio but all he had to do was to snap his fingers and she'd have come to heel.'

'That's true.'

'So what was his motive?'

'It's not entirely clear,' admitted Marmion, 'but I sense that he's the kind of man who doesn't really need one. He spent most of his life as a soldier, remember. The army does strange things to people. We're finding that out with Paul.'

'He needs a good clip around the ear,' said Keedy, angrily.

'That's not the answer, Joe. We need to understand why he's behaving in that way. By the same token, we need to find out why Pattinson might be in an unlikely partnership to commit murder.'

'Which one of them carried it out?'

'Atterbury has to be favourite.'

'Even though he has an alibi, I wouldn't rule out Pattinson.'

'Does he deserve another visit?'

'I think he does, Joe. It will be interesting to see if he readily confesses that he went to Atterbury's house last night. If he doesn't,' said Marmion, 'then we can start to apply a little pressure.'

* * *

When she got back to the house, Audrey Pattinson was so downhearted that she slumped down on the sofa and put her hands to her face. During her time at the Wilder house, she'd felt utterly rejected and made to feel as if she was peripheral to the life of a man she'd seen almost every day for the last few years. It was as if Simon Wilder was being snatched away from her in death and that disturbed her. Though she had wanted to play the organ at his funeral, she could see that it would have been a test of nerve. In a fraught situation, she might have been overwhelmed by emotion and let down a man she'd loved deeply. To some extent, therefore, it was a relief that she was not even considered for the task. Yet that didn't lessen the pain of rejection or the muted hostility shown towards her by Catherine and her brother.

The sound of the front door opening brought her abruptly out of her gloom and she stood up to greet her husband. Pattinson came into the living room and glanced immediately at the piano.

'Did you get rid of that dance music?' he asked.

'Yes, Martin, I did.'

'Good – I never liked listening to you playing it.'

'But you encouraged me to work with Mr Wilder.'

'I learnt to regret that.'

'Wait,' she said as he turned away from her. 'There's something I need to ask.' He faced her again. 'I seem to have mislaid my notebook.'

'It's unlike you to be so careless, Audrey.'

'I'm *not* careless. I always keep it in my satchel. But when I looked for it earlier, it wasn't there.'

'It must have slipped out somehow,' he said. 'It might even be at the studio.'

'I don't think so. I always check my satchel before I leave.'

'We all make mistakes.'

'Are you *sure* you haven't seen it?'

His eyes blazed momentarily but he was interrupted by the doorbell. He went to open the front door and returned a short while later with Marmion and Keedy. They exchanged greetings with Audrey.

'If you wish to speak to my wife again,' said Pattinson, confidently, 'she'd prefer me to stay. Wouldn't you, Audrey?'

'Yes,' she said, as if by reflex.

'Actually,' said Marmion, 'you're the one we'd like to interview, sir. Are you happy to have Mrs Pattinson present while we do so?'

'No, I'm not,' said the other, glancing at Audrey. She left the room at once. 'Sit down, gentlemen,' Pattinson went on. 'Though I'm not sure how I can help you.' They each took their seats. 'I saw very little of Mr Wilder.'

'What about Mr Atterbury?' asked Keedy.

'Who?'

'Tom Atterbury – he's a professional dancer.'

'I don't consort with people of that kind, Sergeant.'

'Are you saying that you've never heard of him?'

'Oh, I've heard the name,' admitted Pattinson, freely, 'because my wife has mentioned it a few times. Mr Atterbury was one of Mr Wilder's rivals. Beyond that, I know nothing whatsoever about him.'

'So you didn't realise that he was a member of your club?' said Marmion.

'Is he? I never knew that.'

'And you've no idea where he lives?'

'Why are you asking me these questions, Inspector? The person you need to speak to is my wife. She knows far more about Atterbury than I do.'

'I dispute that, sir.'

'I doubt very much if she knows where Mr Atterbury lives,' added Keedy, 'but you certainly do.'

'What a preposterous accusation!' exclaimed Pattinson.

'We have evidence to support it, sir.'

'I've never even met the man.'

'Then why did you go to his house yesterday evening?'

Pattinson was shocked. He paled slightly but soon recovered.

'Do you deny it?' asked Marmion, taking over.

'What's all this about evidence?' demanded the other.

'Mr Atterbury aroused our interest, sir. We put him under surveillance and, as a result, know that you went back to the house with him. There's no point in lying. We've already spoken to Mr Atterbury and – after a flurry of denials – he confessed that the pair of you met at the club.'

'Aren't two people allowed to have a private conversation any more?' asked Pattinson, bitterly. 'Are the police taking *that* right away from us as well?'

'Can I take it that you now admit the pair of you spent time together?'

'What's wrong with that, Inspector?'

'Nothing at all, in theory – so why try to pretend it never happened?'

'That's none of your business.'

'It is if it has a bearing on the murder, sir.'

'Mr Atterbury is a suspect,' explained Keedy. 'When he has a secret meeting with someone else, we take note of that person. Why did you go to the house, sir?'

Pattinson glowered. 'I don't have to answer that.'

'You're within your rights to refuse.'

'And we're within our rights to continue this interview at Scotland Yard,' said Marmion, 'where we can explore your reason for withholding information from us.' He rose to his feet. 'The car is outside . . .'

'Wait,' said Pattinson, weakening. 'Look, all that happened is this. I didn't really know Atterbury but I got talking to him in the bar at the club. He seemed a pleasant enough fellow so I agreed to go back to his house for a drink.'

'But the two of you were in a bar,' observed Keedy. 'Why take a taxi back to Mr Atterbury's house when all you had to do was to place an order with the barman there and then?' Pattinson glared at him. 'Was it because you were afraid of being overheard in a crowded room?'

'You give the impression that it was the first time you'd met Atterbury,' said Marmion. 'Was that the truth, sir?'

'Yes, it is,' insisted Pattinson.

'Did you realise that he was the dancer mentioned by your wife?'

'Yes, I did.'

'And did you tell him of your association with Mr Wilder?'

'No,' said Pattinson. 'That never arose.'

'So what did you find to talk about?'

'We talked about all kinds of things, Inspector. Heavens above, man, can you remember everything you've said when you've had a few drinks? We were . . . passing the time together. Is that a crime?'

'It begins to look like one when you deny it ever happened.'

'That's easy to explain.'

'Really?'

'Yes, it is. The fact of the matter is that I'd had far too much whisky and felt rather ashamed of it, so I tried to block it out of my memory. As a rule, I'm very abstemious.' The detectives glanced meaningfully at the well-stocked drinks trolley in the corner of the room. 'So I gave myself a stiff reprimand and put the whole incident out of my mind.' He sat back with relief as if he'd just engineered his escape. 'That's exactly what happened.'

'Thank you for making it clear, sir,' said Keedy.

'There's just one slight problem,' said Marmion. 'You've given us a frank account of the visit to Mr Atterbury's house but, for some reason, it doesn't dovetail with the story that *he* gave us.' He sat down again. 'Which one of you is lying?'

CHAPTER NINETEEN

Sir Edward Henry went down the corridor in unaccustomed haste, knocked on the door of an office then opened it without invitation. In his hand, he was brandishing a newspaper as if waving a desperate flag on a desert island to a distant vessel. Claude Chatfield was on his feet at once.

'Have you seen this?' demanded the commissioner.

'Regrettably, I have.'

'How could it have happened?'

'I don't know, Sir Edward, but the moment I read it, I came in search of you.'

'I only got here ten minutes ago,' said the other. 'I had breakfast with the Home Secretary. We had, as you may well imagine, rather a lot of things to discuss. When I got back here, the morning newspapers were waiting on my desk and this headline jumped out at me. POLICE CONFIRM BODY WAS BUTCHERED.'

'We confirmed nothing of the sort, Sir Edward.'

'Then who was responsible for the leak?'

'I've already set a search in motion,' said Chatfield, 'and I'll make a point of tackling the reporter who wrote the story.'

'That will be pointless. They never reveal their sources.'

'It's the other papers we have to worry about now.'

'You are quite right, Superintendent,' said Sir Edward, putting the newspaper down. 'I've had two editors on the phone already. They accused me of giving an exclusive to the *Daily Mail* whereas what really happened is that someone was offered a hefty bribe by the paper and they took it.'

'He'll be dealt with when we find him.'

'The damage has already been done, alas.'

'Unfortunately, it has,' said Chatfield. 'When they heard that somebody had been stabbed to death, the residents of Chingford would have felt justifiably nervous. Now that they know the victim was castrated and lost both eyes, they'll be howling at us for letting a monster prowl their streets.'

'They'll be wondering who the next victim is.'

'They've no call to do that, Sir Edward. The killer doesn't need to strike again because he's got what he wanted. Simon Wilder was a specific target who was destined to be mutilated in a specific way. Why that was, I don't know, but the people of Chingford – the men, particularly – needn't be shivering in their shoes.'

'You're going to have a very rowdy press conference today.'

'I can handle that,' said Chatfield, arrogantly.

'How much more are you going to tell them?'

'What is there left to tell?'

'You could release the names of suspects, I suppose.'

'Inspector Marmion has advised against that and I agree with him. Tell people that they're under suspicion and you forewarn them. We have to move by stealth, as I did in the case of Mr Atterbury.'

'Oh – what did you do?'

'I put him under surveillance and he was seen in the company of another of our suspects. Marmion was going to interview both men today.'

'Does he think that they are the culprits?'

'He rates them as strong possibilities, Sir Edward.'

'What about that other dancer? I've forgotten his name.'

'It's Allan Redmond. He's the son of Ewart Redmond, M.P.'

'Then it behoves us to operate with extreme care. Members of Parliament can exert great power and cause embarrassment for us.'

'That's what I tried to impress upon Sergeant Keedy. He moved far too soon to arrest Redmond on what I thought was flimsy circumstantial evidence. I ordered the prisoner's release.'

'Does that mean he's *not* the killer?'

'Far from it, Sir Edward,' said the other. 'It means that we stay within the bounds of the law and are seen to do so. Keedy was overzealous. I've told him to refrain from confusing instinct with proof. It's possible that Redmond *is* the killer, or at the very least is in league with him, but I still had to let him go. That will make him feel safe and he'll be off guard as a result.'

'What does the inspector think about Redmond?'

'Marmion has him down as a prime suspect along with Tom Atterbury and Martin Pattinson. There's also another name in the running, Sir Edward. It's that of Godfrey Noonan, a disreputable agent with a score to settle against Wilder. It may not be a coincidence that Atterbury is one of his clients.'

Sir Edward stroked his moustache. 'So we have four suspects in all.'

'Actually, we have five.'

'Who's the other one?'

'Marmion thinks he should look closely at Mrs Wilder.'

'She'd never be party to such bestial behaviour, surely,' said the commissioner in disgust. 'Castration and gouging out eyes – this is a man's work.'

'The man could have been egged on by a woman. Think of Lady Macbeth.'

'Is Mrs Wilder in the same mould?'

'Only time will tell, Sir Edward.'

It was still only a matter of days since her husband's murder but Catherine Wilder had already got used to his absence. Having gone through the motions of being a broken-hearted widow, she was now waiting to get the funeral out of the way and to shift the attention off herself. Cards and letters were still arriving in large numbers, expressing sympathy and saying what a supreme dancer her husband had been. The vast majority of them were from women, many of whom he'd taught. Catherine felt no obligation to carry on her husband's work. When a back injury ended her own career, she had to look elsewhere for fulfilment and it was not in the world of dance.

'Well,' said her brother, putting a sheaf of papers into his briefcase. 'I think that we've sorted everything out now.'

'Thank goodness for that.'

'I'll go and speak to the undertaker.'

'Please do, Nathan. I'm so grateful for your help.'

'You can come with me, if you wish.'

'I'd rather leave it to you. I'd only be in the way.'

'Is there anything else we need to discuss?'

'No,' she replied, 'but I would value your help again tomorrow.'

'Ah, yes, you're going to see Simon's solicitor. I'd certainly like to be there to lend my support. Solicitors can be cagey. I talk their language.

He won't even try to slip anything past you while I'm there.'

'That's very reassuring.'

She gave him a light kiss on the cheek then walked into the hall with him. He put on his hat, opened the door and went across to his car. She waved him off and stood there until the vehicle was out of sight. Catherine then closed the door and went straight upstairs to change out of her dark dress to put on something more colourful. As she sat in front of the dressing table mirror, she kept one eye on the clock on the bedside table. Time was running out. Her brother had stayed longer than she'd hoped but he was safely out of the way now.

When she heard the chug of an engine and the swish of tyres, she went to the window and saw the taxi drawing up outside the house. A few minutes later, she was being driven towards central London.

Marmion sat at the table and pored over Simon Wilder's appointments book. Though he had been through it many times, another study of the contents always provided fresh information. Keedy, meanwhile, was on the telephone to Claude Chatfield, making an overdue apology for his behaviour when they last met and being rewarded with a frosty silence at the other end of the line. He put the receiver down and ran a worried hand through his hair.

'Chat is determined to make me suffer,' he said.

'You deserve it, Joe.'

'He insists that I deliver my apology in person.'

'That sounds reasonable to me.'

'He'll probably want me in a kneeling position.'

'Don't forget the sackcloth and ashes.' Marmion tapped the book. 'I've been taking a look at this.'

'*Again?*' said Keedy. 'You must know the contents off by heart.'

'I still haven't plumbed its full depths. For example, I spotted something today that I've never noticed before.'

'What is it – something in invisible ink?'

'It's almost invisible, Joe, and that's why I missed it. Take a look at this page for me,' he said, offering him the book. 'What do you notice about it?'

Keedy held the book and studied it. 'All I can see is a list of names.'

'Look again.'

'I am looking again and I still see nothing but the same names.'

'What about Colette Orme?'

'She's here. She had her lesson and paid her fee.'

'Is that all you see?'

Keedy's scrutiny was more careful this time. 'No, it isn't,' he said. 'There's a very faint mark beside her name. Something in pencil has been rubbed out.'

'Well done – you're improving.'

'It looks like a small tick.'

'That's exactly what it is. Now turn over the page.' Keedy did so. 'Look at the name of Grenda Hayward. Do you notice anything?'

'Yes,' said Keedy, crossing to the window and letting more light fall on the book. 'It's the same tick rubbed out again.'

'I've counted five in all,' said Marmion, 'and I've only gone back over the last year. Five female dancers have been picked out for some reason.'

'We can both guess what that reason was,' said Keedy with a cackle. 'Wilder is making a note of his conquests.'

'Oh, I don't think it's that easy, Joe.'

'Why not?'

'Colette Orme is among them. She may have been entranced by Wilder but I don't think she gave herself to him – or to any other man,

292

for that matter. There's a refreshing innocence about her that you won't see in . . . well, in Odele Thompson, for instance.'

Keedy frowned. 'Do you have to bring *her* up?'

'She proves my point. If anyone was likely to fall for Wilder's charms, it was the woman who spent so much time being held by him on the dance floor. I think it's fair to say that *you* established she was not a blushing flower. She admitted that she'd been Redmond's lover at one time.'

Keedy was perplexed. 'You're very mystifying today.'

'My point is simple. There's no tick beside Odele Thompson's name.'

'So?'

'Whatever it signifies, it's not a conquest in bed. If that's what the tick meant, she'd probably have a dozen or more beside her name.'

'I'm beginning to see what you mean,' said Keedy, thoughtfully. 'These ladies were picked out for another reason altogether. Whatever can it be?'

'There's only one way to find out, Joe.'

'I'm blowed if I see what it is.'

'We talk to one of the dancers who earned herself a tick, and one who didn't, but we have to be very discreet. It may be that this young lady didn't realise she was chosen for a particular purpose. I don't suppose you'd like to canvass Odele's opinion, would you?'

'No,' replied Keedy, putting the book down firmly on the table.

'Then I'll reserve that delight for myself. You can talk to someone else.'

'Who is it?'

'It's his star pupil – Colette Orme.'

Colette Orme had no idea what to do. Needing help and advice, there was nowhere she could turn. Her father would not supply it and, although he was always at her beck and call, neither could her brother. She realised that she had been floating on a cloud of promises, none of which could now be kept. Simon Wilder, her mentor, friend and inspiration, had promised her fame as a dancer and his continuous support throughout her career. His murder had revoked those promises. He'd made other commitments to her as well but, as she discovered when she spoke to his wife, they would never be honoured. Colette felt abandoned, bereft and frightened.

The one person who might help her was Audrey Pattinson but she was wary of appealing to her. Though they were good friends, there were some things she'd concealed from the pianist because she didn't know what the older woman's reaction would be. And yet she'd been given a cordial welcome when she called at Audrey's home and their shared love of Wilder had brought them closer together. Colette was impaled on the horns of a dilemma. She could either hope that, in time, there'd be no revelations to embarrass her; or she could approach Audrey and risk losing her respect and her friendship. It was an almost impossible choice to make.

After brooding on it obsessively, she forced herself to leave the house.

As she let Marmion into her flat, Odele Thompson expressed her disappointment.

'I was rather hoping that Sergeant Keedy would come,' she said.

'You'll have to put up with me as his substitute, I'm afraid.'

'Oh, I didn't mean to be rude, Inspector.'

'I understand, Miss Thompson.'

'It's just that I . . . enjoyed talking to him.'

'Sergeant Keedy enjoyed talking to you as well and he sends his regards. As it is, he has another interview to conduct. I chose to visit you.'

'I don't really have anything more to say so your visit is pointless.'

'It may not be.'

They sat down and Marmion told her about the sequence of ticks in Wilder's appointments book. She asked for some of the names that he'd picked out and he rattled them off from memory.

'I know them all,' she said, 'and each one is young and very pretty. Grenda Hayward could turn any man's head and you've seen how beautiful Colette Orme is.'

'Why did he single them out?'

'It's not for the obvious reason,' said Odele. 'I'm not claiming that Simon was a saint, because he certainly wasn't. But his taste ran to ladies of a very different kind. Catherine would have spotted the signs if he'd started chasing any of the pupils you've listed and she'd have challenged him.'

'So what's significant about the names I gave you?' asked Marmion. 'Are they simply young and attractive? Is that what links them?'

'Not really, Inspector. If those were the two factors he picked out, there were other names he could have ticked. Annie Lakin is a case in point. She's the most gorgeous of the whole lot yet she wasn't in your list. And I can think of one or two others who'd fit the category of young and pretty.' She laughed. 'There was a time when *my* name might have been included.'

'It still could be,' he said, gallantly.

She inclined her head. 'That's very kind of you, Inspector.'

'Anyway, I won't intrude any longer. Thanks for your help, Miss Thompson.'

'I didn't really give you any.'

'Yes, you did. You clarified my mind.'

'I wish that someone would clarify mine. Since Simon died, I've been in a state of total confusion. I just can't think straight.'

'Perhaps you could answer another question for me,' he said. 'The sergeant may have asked this before but you might have a different answer this time. When we wanted names of potential suspects, you suggested those of Allan Redmond and Tom Atterbury.' She nodded. 'You put Redmond first but Mrs Wilder wasn't sure that either of those gentlemen were possible killers.'

'Then she doesn't know them as well as I do.'

'Of the two names, Mrs Wilder thought that Atterbury was the more likely one to be involved. Why did she pick him out?'

Odele's face was puckered with concentration for a long time then her eyes lit up as if she'd just made an unexpected deduction.

'I can make one suggestion, Inspector . . .'

When the taxi dropped her off at the Charing Cross Hotel, she paid the driver and went into the building. There was no need to ask for a room number at reception. She already knew it by heart. Catherine first checked that nobody was watching her then she took the lift up to the third floor and stepped out into the corridor. Once again, she made sure that the coast was clear before setting off briskly along the plush carpet. When she reached a room she'd been in on a number of previous occasions, she rapped on the door with her knuckles. Seconds later, the door was opened and she stepped into the room to be embraced by the man waiting for her.

'You're late,' he said, locking the door.

'My brother stayed longer than I expected.'

'You're here now, anyway. What's been happening?'

'I'll tell you afterwards.'

Allan Redmond grinned broadly and led her towards the bed.

* * *

Joe Keedy wondered if he'd made a mistake. In refusing to visit Odele yet again, he'd given into the distant fear that she'd make advances to him again. Yet there was no guarantee that she'd do that and, in any case, he was more than able to resist her overtures. When he'd told her that he was engaged, he was simply using the truth as a defence weapon. Keedy was now uncertain if that weapon still existed. The argument with Alice had opened a gap between them and he was unsure how to bridge it. Then he'd heard from Marmion about a family row the night before when Paul had urged his sister not to marry Keedy. The news had annoyed the sergeant intensely but he was also reassured because Alice had reportedly sprung to his defence. They had, in effect, been reconciled. In that frame of mind, he'd have been fortified against any overtures that Odele might make. He began to regret avoiding her.

When he reached Colette's house, he was told by her brother that she was not there but was expected back soon. Dennis Orme invited him in and offered to make a pot of tea. Keedy did not wish to put someone with a disability to the trouble.

'I can do most things on my own,' said Orme, brightly. 'I just take a little longer than most people.'

'Inspector Marmion told me how much you'd helped your sister's dancing career. Most brothers wouldn't have done that.'

'If you'd seen her dance, *you'd* have wanted to support her. I loved watching her sail around the dance floor with Mr Wilder.' He pointed to the photograph of Colette. 'There she is, Sergeant. Dad and I are so proud of her.'

Keedy was struck by how attractive and graceful she looked. He also admired her bravery in wanting to dance for a living in front of an audience. His own attempts at dancing were very limited and not fit for public scrutiny.

'I'd love to be able to dance like that with Harry,' said Orme. When he saw Keedy's look of amazement, he chuckled. 'Harry is my girlfriend, you see. Her real name is Harriet. My sister hates me calling her Harry but it's what we both like. Who knows?' he went on, patting his knee. 'I may be able to shuffle around with Harry one day. She's strong enough to hold me up.'

'You're a lucky man.'

'That's what I keep telling myself. I'm still in one piece, I've got the best girlfriend in the world and my sister is going to dance on the stage in the West End.' He got up. 'Well, if you don't want a cuppa, I do. As for Colette, she won't be long. She'll be back in no time at all.'

Audrey Pattinson had been pleased to see Colette again and was glad that her husband was locked away in the room where he had his military museum. It meant that the two women could talk in private. Colette told her story haltingly, not knowing if she'd get sympathy or condemnation. Audrey listened with a blend of surprise and alarm but she made no comment until her visitor had finished.

'Do you think I was wrong to do it, Mrs Pattinson?' asked Colette.

'It was an unusual request,' said Audrey, quietly.

'But there was no harm in it.'

'I daresay it seemed like that at the time.'

'Mr Wilder did make that promise, you see, and I was counting on that. But when I spoke to his wife, she more or less hurried me out of the house.'

'How much did you tell her?'

'I didn't really have time to tell her anything,' said Colette, 'and I certainly wouldn't have confided in her the way I just did with you.'

Audrey sat up. She tried to put aside her qualms and find a way of soothing her visitor. In choosing the older woman as her confidante, Colette was placing great faith in her and Audrey was touched by that. She searched for words of comfort.

'All that you can do is to watch and pray,' she advised. 'Your anxieties may be completely unwarranted. Mr Wilder's promise may have been kept somehow. The whole thing may blow over and you'll go on to another phase of your life.'

'There *is* no other phase without him, Mrs Pattinson.'

'For me, there isn't, Colette. I've gone back to being an anonymous old lady who likes to play the piano in her spare time.' Audrey chewed her lip. 'And I'm afraid that there'll be a lot of spare time to fill from now on. But you,' she added with a smile, 'are still at the beginning of an exciting journey. One day I'll be able to watch you performing onstage and remind myself that I played a part in your career.'

Cheered by her words, Colette was in a more positive mood when she left the house. Within a few yards, however, the doubts and fears reasserted themselves.

Alice Marmion did her best to put her problems aside and do her job properly. On patrol all morning with Iris Goodliffe, she had a number of incidents to deal with. For the most part, they were minor matters that could be solved with a stern word to naughty children or with some practical assistance to old people in distress. Aware of her friend's situation, Iris was very tactful, inventing a new topic of conversation whenever the current one was exhausted. During a break, Alice thanked her.

'I wish that it was the other way round,' said Iris, chirpily.

'You wouldn't think that if you were in my position.'

'Yes, I would, Alice. It would mean that at least I *had* a boyfriend.

And if he looked anything like Sergeant Keedy, I'd be kicking my heels with joy. My sister says that I'll never find a man of my own because of my manner. According to Evelyn, I put men off. Do you think that's true?'

'No, Iris, I don't. You just haven't met the right one yet.'

'I've met dozens of right ones,' admitted Iris. 'They didn't happen to think *I* was the right one for them. I'd better resign myself to being left on the shelf.'

Alice stopped herself from saying that she'd felt the same but she now had faith that the breach with Keedy could be repaired. In defending him against her brother's criticism, she'd emphasised all of his virtues and felt ashamed that she'd attacked him in front of someone else. What had been faintly glowing embers of love had slowly become a fire that was now starting to burn inside her. She wanted him more than ever and dared to believe that he still wanted her. The exact moment of reconciliation, however, would have to be postponed because their lives were not synchronised. A vicious murder was keeping the two of them apart.

'When will you see him again?' asked Iris.

'Chance would be a fine thing.'

'Must work always come first for Sergeant Keedy?'

'I can wait, Iris. That's what my mother does. I can take lessons from her.'

'I'd wait for someone like him. To be honest, I'd wait for *any* man.'

Though Alice laughed, she felt sorry for her friend. Iris's social life was more or less non-existent. She had nowhere to go and nobody to see. To lift Iris's spirits, and to prevent herself from spending the whole evening preoccupied with her sorry plight, Alice came up with a suggestion.

'Why don't we do something together after work?'

'Oh, I'd love that. What will we do?'

'Given the choice,' said Alice, 'I'd like to make a wax effigy of Gale Force and stick pins in it.' Iris chortled merrily. 'We can go to that film we missed last night. I just want an evening when we let our hair down and have some harmless fun.'

The first thought that went through Keedy's head was that the photograph did not do Colette Orme justice. In the flesh, she looked much prettier and had a glow about her that was arresting. Dennis Orme introduced the sergeant then hovered to see if he was needed. When Colette realised that she was to have a conversation about the murder victim, she asked her brother to leave them alone. She and Keedy then sat down opposite each other. He spoke softly.

'There's a question I need to ask you, Colette,' he began.

'I've already answered the inspector's questions.'

'Something else has come to light. We're hoping that you can help us.'

'I'll try.'

'You were clearly Mr Wilder's best pupil.'

'Oh, I don't know about that,' she said, modestly. 'I may have been one of the better dancers but Mr Wilder told us that he didn't believe in having favourites.'

'We've seen the record of the lessons he gave you. To spend that amount of time on the dance floor, you have to be dedicated. Your brother has been telling me how fit and lithe you keep yourself.'

'I only did what Mr Wilder told me. He went running every morning.'

'Did you know a pupil named Grenda Hayward?'

'Yes, I know most of the people who had lessons at the studio. Grenda is a nice girl. We used to walk home together sometimes.'

'What about Winifred Gleeson?'

'I never got on with her,' said Colette, 'and neither did Grenda. She was too fond of boasting how good she was, yet we could both dance rings around her.' She peered at him quizzically. 'Why are you asking me about them?'

'We noticed something in Mr Wilder's appointments book, Colette. There was a tick beside five names. You, Grenda and Winifred were three of them. We just wondered if you could explain why you were all picked out like that?'

She was clearly baffled. 'I don't know, Sergeant.'

'Was it because Mr Wilder was putting you in for some kind of examination? I know that you can win medals to show what standard you've reached.'

'I've got all my medals on display in my room.'

'What about the others?'

'Grenda Hayward passed all her exams but Winifred failed. She said it was the fault of the judges but we know the truth. Miss Thompson said she'd never be as good as the rest of us.'

He was curious. 'What is Miss Thompson like as a dancer?'

'Oh, I think she's marvellous!'

'Was she as good as Mrs Wilder?'

'In some ways, she was; in other ways, no, not at all.'

'What is her main virtue?'

'Odele Thompson has the perfect figure for dancing.'

'Yes, I suppose that's true,' agreed Keedy, wishing – as an image of Odele gatecrashed into his mind – that he'd never brought up her name. 'You must have learnt a lot from simply watching her.'

'I did, Sergeant.'

'Let's go back to the appointments book.'

'Mr Wilder used to fill in the amount we paid at the end of each lesson.'

'Our interest is in those ticks, Colette. Can you think of *any* reason at all, why he should single out five of his pupils, you among them? Don't hurry. Take plenty of time to think it over. Out of all the people he taught, five of you were given some sort of preference. Why was that?'

Colette shook her head but it was without any real conviction. A hunted look had come into her eye and she began to fidget. Keedy bided his time.

'I really don't know,' she said at length. 'I have no idea why Mr Wilder ticked our names. That's the truth, Sergeant. I can't help you.'

The visit to Odele Thompson had not been entirely unproductive. Marmion had seen hints of the vivacity that she'd turned on for Keedy's benefit and he'd asked a question about Allan Redmond that had made Odele say something that she hadn't even dared to think before. As a result, Marmion asked to be driven to the Wilder house. When he rang the doorbell, he had a long, fruitless wait. A second ring was no more successful. He was about to move away when Grace Chambers, the next-door neighbour, returned from the shops.

'Hello, Inspector,' she said. 'Is nobody in?'

'It doesn't look like it, Mrs Chambers.'

'Well, it is Friday, I suppose.'

'What does that mean?'

'It was Mrs Wilder's day for going up to the West End. A taxi very often called for her on a Friday morning.'

* * *

Reclining on the bed, Allan Redmond smoked a cigarette and admired Catherine Wilder's naked body as she came out of the bathroom.

'I thought you were supposed to have a bad back.'

'It's only a handicap if I try to dance with any real vigour.'

'You can certainly do other things with real vigour,' he said, patting the bed. 'Come here.' Catherine sat down beside him. 'I have to tell you, Mrs Wilder, that you have revolutionised my Fridays.'

'I could say the same of you, Allan.'

'Is there any chance of your staying the night?'

'No,' she replied, 'it's too dangerous. Besides, I have to get back. Letters and cards are still pouring in. I have a part to play in Chingford. I can't miss a cue.'

'Fair enough – I won't stay either.'

'Where will you go?'

'Back to the friends I told you about in Brighton. All I have to do is to walk out of here, take a taxi to Waterloo and hop onto a train.' He pulled her close and kissed her. 'We haven't talked about the funeral.'

'I didn't come here for that,' she said, reprovingly.

'Do you want me there or don't you?'

'I'd love you to be there, Allan,' she said, stroking his cheek, 'but I don't think it would be very wise. People would think you were gloating and the last thing you must do is to draw attention to yourself. Keep your head down in Brighton.'

'When can we see each other again?'

'When this is all over – and when the police stop pestering the life out of me. They'll give up, eventually. All that we have to do is to wait. Meanwhile . . .'

'Meanwhile,' he said, stubbing out his cigarette in the ashtray on the bedside table, 'I have a tempting proposition to put to you, Mrs Wilder.'

* * *

Back at the police station, they were able to describe their respective visits. Harvey Marmion's account provoked an immediate protest from Keedy.

'Allan Redmond and Mrs Wilder?' he asked in disbelief. 'They're like chalk and cheese. I can't see them ever getting together.'

'It was Miss Thompson's suggestion.'

'Then why didn't she mention it earlier?'

'I don't think her mind was properly focussed then, Joe. The main reason for naming Redmond as a suspect was that she wanted to give him a fright. Until today, she'd never linked him with Catherine Wilder.'

'Odele is wrong.'

'What about these regular Friday trips to the West End?'

'There are all sorts of explanations for that,' argued Keedy. 'Mrs Wilder goes to Harrods or visits an art gallery or attends a concert or simply goes to see friends.'

'What if it's one particular friend?'

'Then his name is not Allan Redmond. He hasn't even bothered to stay in London. When I caught him outside his cottage, he seemed to be making a run for it. Left to me, he'd be cooling his heels behind bars.'

'That reminds me, Joe. You still have to apologise to Chat.'

'I'll do so through gritted teeth.'

'Get it done this evening before he takes you off this case.'

Keedy was horrified. 'He'd never do that, surely.'

'It depends how much you upset him. Anyway,' said Marmion, settling back in his chair. 'How did you find Colette Orme?'

'I liked her a lot and I liked that brother of hers. He's one of those people who have the most amazing resilience. Nothing is allowed to get him down.'

'If only I could say that of Paul. Sorry . . . do go on.'

Keedy told him about his interview with Colette and how her manner had changed towards the end of it. Certain that she knew more than she was prepared to tell him, he'd drawn back from being more forceful in his questioning.

'She's such a delicate creature,' he said.

'Yes,' said Marmion, 'and she's in a very fragile state. From her point of view, it must look as if her whole world has collapsed. Wilder was a second father to her.'

'He certainly didn't take advantage of her. Hey, wait,' he went on, snapping his fingers, 'maybe *that's* the answer. The women whose names he ticked are the ones he *didn't* try to seduce. They had protected status.'

'That's a bit far-fetched, Joe.'

'It's no more far-fetched than putting Redmond into bed with Mrs Wilder.'

'They both had a viable motive.'

'Independently, they did,' said Keedy. 'It's just such an unlikely pairing.'

'We know that she treated her husband badly.'

'We only have his first wife's word for that, and you said that she was less convincing when you dropped in at that flat of theirs.'

'Gillian Hogg had an axe to grind, that's true.'

'So did the killer.'

'Well, it wasn't her, I know that. So who are we left with – Atterbury, Pattinson, Noonan, Redmond and Catherine Wilder. In other words, we've ticked five names, Joe. That's exactly what Wilder did in his appointments book – five significant names.'

'He rubbed out the names. Which ones do *we* rub out?'

'I think we should keep all of them under suspicion. We still don't know if we're dealing with someone acting on his own or with one or more accomplices.'

'Atterbury and Pattinson would act together.'

'What about Noonan and Atterbury?'

'You met the agent,' said Keedy, 'so you're the best judge. The two people I refuse to believe planned and executed the crime together are Redmond and Mrs Wilder. I'd keep *him* top of my list but I'd be tempted to cross her off it altogether.'

'Nobody gets crossed off until this murder is solved,' said Marmion, firmly. 'The one thing we may have to do, of course, is to add other names to the list.'

They took great care not to be seen together. Catherine Wilder left first, making her way to the ground floor before leaving the hotel. She only had to wait a few minutes before she was able to get into a taxi. Allan Redmond, meanwhile, had a bath before dressing, taking the lift downstairs and settling the bill. He took a taxi to Waterloo station and wallowed in frothy memories all the way to his destination.

Audrey Pattinson was disturbed. While she was glad that Colette Orme felt able to come to her with her problem, she wished that she had not heard what the girl had to say. It troubled her at a deep level. Yet there was nothing she could do beyond expressing her sympathy. Audrey was still going repetitively through the details of her conversation with Colette when her husband came into the living room. His arrival broke her concentration. Pattinson held up a large notebook.

'I had a feeling that you'd mislaid this somewhere,' he said.

She got up at once. 'Where did you find it?'

'Never you mind – the fact is that you can have it back.' Audrey almost seized it from his grasp. 'Don't snatch it, woman. It's not as if it's any use to you now.'

'It's a souvenir, Martin, a cherished souvenir.'

'Then you ought to take more care of it.' He clicked his tongue in disapproval. 'You're slipping, Audrey, and it's not the first time. I think you need to buck yourself up. Don't make me have to say that to you again.'

He went out abruptly and left her clutching the book as if it was a missing baby that had somehow been found alive and returned to its mother.

CHAPTER TWENTY

Ellen Marmion's contribution to the war effort consisted of knitting socks and gloves for the soldiers at the front. While it was something she could do equally well at home, she preferred to be part of a circle. It enabled her to stave off loneliness and to enjoy the company of other women. Some of them had sons or husbands in the army and one of them had lost a brother at the battle of the Somme. All of them had felt the impact of the war and it forged a bond between them. After a morning with her knitting needles, Ellen had a snack with a couple of the other women then made her way home. Minutes after she got there, her son let himself into the house with his key.

'How did you get on?' she asked.

'He said there was a slight improvement.'

'That's encouraging.'

'What he couldn't tell me was when I'd be able to see properly again.'

'It may never happen, Paul,' she said with a philosophical sigh.

'It's *got* to happen,' he said, trying to convince himself. 'I want to be normal again. I want to live a normal life.'

'You have a normal life and you should be grateful. You were spared when others died or came back with terrible wounds.'

He almost sneered. 'The hospital chaplain used to say that.'

'He was right.'

'It didn't feel right at the time. I was in pain all over and I was completely blind. I had to rely on other people for just about everything.'

'That's all in the past now, Paul. You're getting better. At least, your eyesight is,' she added, meaningfully.

He bridled. 'Don't start all that again.'

'It's your attitude, Paul. You seem to go out of your way to be disagreeable.'

'I said I was sorry about last night.'

'What use is that to your sister? She was still shaking when she left here.'

'Then I'll apologise next time I see her,' he said without enthusiasm. 'Will that do?'

'No, it won't,' returned his mother. 'You obviously won't mean what you say and, in any case, can you imagine that Alice will want to come anywhere near this house after the way you attacked her?'

'I just gave her some advice, that's all.'

'It was unwanted advice.'

'Aren't I allowed to have an opinion of my own?' he whined. 'When I was younger, you and Dad always encouraged me to speak out. Now you want to shut me up because I don't agree with you.'

'You're entitled to have your own opinions, Paul. That's your right. But you ought to have the sense to see when you're upsetting someone very much.'

'Alice should be able to cope with criticism.'

'I'm not only talking about your sister,' said Ellen, reasonably. 'You upset me as well. And you've said odd things to some of our neighbours. They've stopped me in the street and asked if . . . well, if there's anything wrong with you.'

'I got wounded on the battlefield,' he shouted, 'that's what's wrong with me!'

'You don't have to yell.'

'People ought to be told what's going on over there.'

'They *have* been told,' she reminded him. 'Millions went to see that film about the battle of the Somme. We went and you came with us. It told the truth about the war for the first time. We *saw* what you had to go through, Paul. To be honest, it made me shudder but it also made me proud that you had the courage to fight for your country.'

His head drooped. 'I don't feel very courageous at the moment.'

'What *do* you feel?'

He shook his head in puzzlement. For a moment, he seemed much younger than he really was and suddenly vulnerable. All the latent anger had drained out of him. He even let his mother put a gentle arm around his shoulder.

'I don't know,' he confessed. 'I really don't know *how* I feel.'

Starting at the point where the victim's body had been found, they walked in the direction of the road where one of the witnesses claimed to have seen Simon Wilder on the night of the murder. There were serried ranks of houses on either side of them. When they reached a side street off Old Church Road, they stopped.

'This is where Wainwright remembers spotting him,' said Keedy, 'though we've no guarantee that it was Wilder, of course. It was just a guess, really.'

'He's the best witness we have so far, Joe.'

'One man and his dog are not going to solve this crime.'

'But they might help us to do it,' said Marmion. 'As you pointed out, an engine driver would need good eyesight and that camera was a telling clue.'

'He only said that it *looked* like a camera.'

'Then it probably was. Don't forget his hobby. Wainwright likes watching couples enjoying a private moment in the park. He's an owl, Joe. He can see in the dark. In other words,' he went on, turning around, 'Wilder was probably going to a house between this point and the murder scene.'

'That's a hell of a lot of houses and our officers visited each one of them. Nobody admits to seeing or letting Wilder in that night.'

'They'd hardly do so if they were actually involved in the murder.'

'None of our five suspects lives in this part of Chingford.'

'His wife would be the closest.'

'No,' said Keedy, forcefully, 'I think we should forget her altogether. I can't say that I took to the woman but that might be because of the situation she was in. We've seen it before. When someone is told that their nearest and dearest has been murdered, they behave in peculiar ways.'

'I'd rather keep Catherine Wilder on our list. There's just something about her that rings bells. Gillian Hogg said that she had a heart of stone.'

'You can't expect an ex-wife to like the woman who replaced her.'

They walked back in the direction from which they'd just come. There was plenty of traffic and a number of pedestrians were about. Marmion became pensive.

'That camera interests me,' he said.

'We can't be certain that that's what Wilder was carrying.'

'He was a photographer as well as a dancer. That clinches it for me, Joe. But why would he be carrying a camera in the dead of night?'

'We may never know.'

'The last time I went to the house,' recalled Marmion, 'I asked Mrs Wilder if I could look at the darkroom. You've seen how big the place was. I was expecting a sizeable room but it wasn't much more than a boot cupboard. When I asked her why a professional photographer didn't have better facilities, she said that her husband found it perfectly adequate. Then she and her brother more or less hustled me out of there.'

Keedy grinned. 'They'd be useful as bouncers at a sleazy nightclub.'

'Oh, I don't think that either of them would deign to go near a nightclub, Joe. Clissold is something of a toff and his sister would find it infra dig.'

'I don't agree. I reckon that she and Wilder used to perform at nightclubs in the old days. In that game, you go wherever you can find an audience. She may turn up her nose at such places now but she couldn't do that when she and her husband first started dancing together.' He looked across at Marmion. 'Have you ever been much of a dancer?'

'Ellen and I used to go to church socials when we first married.'

'It's something Alice and I have never done. She's always talked about it but, when we actually have some leisure time together, there's never been a dance on.'

'That's a pity. You'd be good at it.'

'I'd be hopeless, Harv. I've got two left feet.'

'You could always get Odele Thompson to give you lessons,' said Marmion with a wicked grin.

Keedy almost choked. 'Lessons in *what*, though?'

Colette Orme spent the afternoon working in a haberdashery shop. It was one of the many jobs she'd taken in order to save up money to buy the dresses and the dancing shoes she'd need for her career. During a quiet period, she was left alone to reflect that her professional career had disappeared before she'd even embarked on it. Without the support and instruction of Simon Wilder, she'd lost her confidence. In his arms, she'd compete with anyone on a dance floor. It was unthinkable that she'd ever find another partner. When she'd first joined the studio, she'd been given a lot of help by Catherine Wilder and she was inspired when she saw husband and wife dancing together. Since she'd effectively retired, however, Catherine had been less helpful and more critical of her. As Colette had found to her dismay, she was more or less exiled from the house now. The expected closure of the studio was the death blow to her high expectations.

Concern about her future was matched by apprehension about her past. While she kept telling herself that she'd done nothing wrong, Colette was dogged by guilt. She'd sought advice from Audrey Pattinson and achieved a measure of calm while she was with her. Once she was on her own, however, the old anxieties splashed over her like a waterfall. Added to them was the fear that she might have lost a good friend in Audrey. The older woman had listened to her plea but she'd also been startled by what she'd heard. Colette was starting to regret that she'd turned to her.

'Can you hear me, young lady?' asked a sharp voice. 'I'd like some of that ribbon. Do you think you can stop daydreaming and serve a customer?'

Colette hadn't even heard the woman come into the shop. Completely flustered, she mouthed an apology and vowed to keep her mind on her job from now on. It was too painful to think about anything else.

* * *

314

The dance studio had been much more than a place of work to Audrey Pattinson. It was her sanctuary. She could escape from the tensions of her domestic life, play the piano to her heart's content and watch those who came for instruction improve and blossom. It had given her life a validity she'd never experienced before. At a stroke, she'd lost her escape route, her chance to play dance music and her contact with almost all the people who came to the studio. She'd been part of a community that had now fractured irreparably. It was time to look elsewhere.

Meanwhile, she fled to another place of sanctuary. Since she was on the organists' rota at the parish church, she was entitled to practise there whenever she wished. Audrey therefore sat in front of the instrument and played a succession of her favourite hymns, reaching every corner of the church with booming chords. Since she knew the music by heart, she played with her eyes closed, vexed by a thought that lanced through her mind. Efficient, well-organised and fastidious, she never mislaid things. There was no way that she had let her notebook go astray. After the last time she'd been the accompanist at the studio, she remembered distinctly that she'd put it into her satchel with the sheet music. Yet it had unaccountably disappeared.

It was her husband who'd found and returned it, taking the opportunity to administer a verbal reprimand. Where had he discovered it? How had it got there? When did it actually vanish from her bag?

'Who took it?'

In addition to that of Colette Orme, there were four other names ticked by Simon Wilder. Taking two each, the detectives split up and tracked down the young dancers. When they later met up again at the police station, Keedy announced that he'd drawn a blank. Neither of the women he'd interviewed had the slightest idea why they had been singled out. One of them, in fact, had made such little progress that she'd abandoned her dance lessons altogether. Marmion had also returned empty-handed. The first person on whom he called was so distraught at Wilder's death that she could barely speak. His second call produced a different result.

'Her name was Grenda Hayward,' he explained.

'I remember that name. It's so unusual.'

'She thought it was Anglo-Saxon but she wasn't certain. Anyway, I got her chatting about her sessions with Wilder before I sprung the question on her and her manner changed in a flash. She went from being quite open with me to the very opposite. Grenda guessed what that tick was for, Joe. The problem was that she refused to tell me what it was.'

'That's more or less the reaction I got from Colette Orme.'

'Why did Wilder rub out those ticks, I wonder?'

'It's too late to ask him now,' said Keedy.

There was a tap on the door and Gibbs entered to tell them that they had a visitor. When he heard that it was Gillian Hogg, Marmion asked for her to be shown straight in. She soon appeared.

'Perhaps you can enlighten us, Mrs Hogg,' said Marmion after he'd introduced Keedy to her. 'I have Mr Wilder's appointments book in front of me. He ticked five names, all of them young female dancers. Why do you think he'd do that?'

'Perhaps they showed exceptional promise.'

'That's not the answer,' said Keedy. 'I talked to a girl named Rosie Hilton and she admitted straight away that she'd been hopeless on the dance floor. All five ticks were rubbed out, by the way.'

'Whatever Simon had in mind,' she suggested, 'he decided against it. That's the only thing I can think of.'

'That had occurred to us.'

'Was he a person who tended to change his mind?' asked Marmion.

'Oh, no,' she said. 'Simon made instant decisions and stood by them. That's how we came to get married, after all. However,' she continued, 'that's not what I came here to discuss. I've been wondering how you got on with God, Inspector.'

'I'm glad I came to you beforehand. It prepared me.'

'Was he as crafty as ever?'

'I wouldn't like to share that office with him, I know that. Mr Noonan is an ebullient character and doesn't let you get a word in. I'd hate to talk business with him. People must offer his clients work just to shut him up.'

'Did you mention my name to him?'

'No, I didn't.'

'You must have said something that made him think of me, Inspector.'

'Why do you think that?'

'He paid me a courtesy visit at the flat.'

Marmion was staggered. 'Mr Noonan walked all the way up those stairs?'

'He sent a messenger to tell me that a man wanted to speak to me. When I got to the bottom of the stairs, the man turned out to be God, as in Godfrey. He grabbed me by the throat and demanded to know what I'd told you.'

'I'm sorry if I landed you in trouble, Mrs Hogg.'

'Did he threaten you?' asked Keedy.

'Oh, yes, he told me to keep my mouth shut in future, only he used more decorous language. I've never seen him so riled up like that. It's the reason I wanted to report it,' she said. 'He *frightened* me.'

* * *

317

Evening found Godfrey Noonan relaxing in the one chair big enough to accommodate him at the home of a client. After adjusting his wig, he downed the best part of a glass of whisky then smacked his lips.

'This is good stuff,' he said, approvingly. 'It's the best thing ever to come out of Scotland – but that may not be saying much.'

'You're being unfair, God. I have a soft spot for Scotland.'

'Then you can keep it.'

'By right, we should be drinking vintage champagne.'

'We'll do that after the Championships. We'll have something to toast then.'

'It's a foregone conclusion.'

'It is now, anyway.' Noonan sniggered. 'Simon Wilder is unavoidably detained elsewhere.'

'I'd have beaten him even if he and Odele *had* competed. I had a secret weapon to deploy.'

'Yes, I've met Naomi many times.'

'I'm not talking about my wife,' said Atterbury. 'My secret weapon was a man named Martin Pattinson. We belong to the same club. I learnt by chance that his wife was Simon's accompanist.'

'What a wonderful discovery that must have been!'

'There's more to it than that. Pattinson loathed him almost as much as I do because his wife was besotted with Simon, so much so that she kept a notebook in which she recorded all the routines he created.'

'That was Simon's strength – his choreography.'

'It was masterly. I know that because Pattinson stole his wife's book and let me copy out whatever I wanted. Let's face it,' he went on, 'Simon is never going to put those clever figures into his waltzes, quicksteps and foxtrots, is he? So I might as well make full use of them. That's the way to ensure you win,' he boasted. 'You put a spy in the enemy camp.'

'You're a man after my own heart, Tom.'

'Rumour has it that you don't possess one.'

Noonan rocked with mirth. 'Then rumour, for once, is right. Oh,' he went on, 'isn't this as close to perfection as we're likely to get? Simon has been deprived of his crown and his bollocks, so the field belongs to Tom and Naomi Atterbury. All the effort we made together is at last paying off.' He emptied his glass and held it out. 'Since you ask, I would like another.'

Whenever she spent time in church, Audrey Pattinson was, as a rule, at once calmed and inspired. This time it was different. She left the building in a state of rising anger. Having played her way through a dozen or more hymns, she should have felt the warmth of an inner faith. Instead she felt determined and combative. Deprived of precious aspects of her life, Audrey had nothing left to lose. For the first time in their marriage, she would have the audacity to challenge her husband.

He was doing the crossword in the newspaper when she stormed in and didn't even bother to look up. Furious at being ignored, she struck out at once.

'Why did you take my notebook?' she demanded.

He lifted his head. 'What's that?'

'You stole the notebook from my satchel.'

'No, I didn't,' he retorted. 'You let it go astray somehow.'

'I *never* lose things, Martin, and you know it. I'm very punctilious. It's an article of faith with me. That notebook went into my bag on the day that Mr Wilder was murdered and it came into this house.'

'You have it back now, Audrey, so there's no need to make a fuss about it.'

'You took it, didn't you?'

'No,' he replied, putting the newspaper aside, 'of course, I didn't.'

'There's nobody else in the house.'

'It must have dropped out of your bag.'

'You're lying.'

He was roused. 'Don't you dare speak to me like that!'

'I want the truth,' she said, undaunted.

'The truth is that you lost it.'

'You can say that until you're blue in the face but we both know it's a lie. The only way that notebook could disappear was if you took it so that you could accuse me of being careless.'

'This is laughable,' he said, now on his feet. 'Why should I want a notebook filled with squiggles and numbers?'

'There you are – you obviously looked inside it.'

Pattinson blustered and gesticulated for a few minutes but his wife refused to back down. Ordinarily, they never had arguments because his authority was never even questioned. This time, however, Audrey was no longer afraid of him and he couldn't understand why. Piqued at her resistance, he eventually changed his story and even produced a faintly apologetic smile.

'Calm down, my dear. This is not worth getting so upset about. As it happens,' he went on, pretending to recall something that slipped his mind, 'I may have borrowed it a couple of days ago. I was interested. I'd never looked inside it before and wanted to know why you always had your nose in that notebook.' He forced a laugh. 'I *still* don't know because I couldn't understand all those symbols and abbreviations. It was like a book on algebra to me. There,' he added as if pacifying a small child with a piece of chocolate, 'now we can forget the whole thing. I borrowed it, forgot that I had it then found it again. You know the truth of it now, Audrey.'

'I've known the truth of it for years, Martin,' she said, still simmering. 'But I never had the courage to do anything about it before.'

Spinning on her heel, she went out of the room and climbed the stairs with an urgency that belied her age and her normal passivity.

When they returned to central London, it was too late for Marmion and Keedy to call on Godfrey Noonan. They therefore went straight to Scotland Yard and presented themselves to the superintendent. Marmion gave an account of developments during the day and elicited little more than an occasional nod or sniff of disappointment from Claude Chatfield. Remaining silent, Keedy was rehearsing his apology.

'So,' said Chatfield, 'the solution to this crime is hanging from the slender thread of a man with a dog who may or may not have seen Mr Wilder on the night when he was murdered.'

'You're being too pessimistic, sir,' said Marmion.

'Well, you can hardly expect me to dance around the office with undiluted joy. I've spent most of the day fending off awkward questions from the press about the nature of Wilder's injuries and why we seem to have made no visible progress in this investigation.'

'I'm sure you handled them with your usual expertise, sir,' said Keedy in a gesture of appeasement. 'We're very grateful for the way that you keep the press off our backs so that we can get on with the important job of detection.'

Chatfield ignored him. 'What about this agent, Inspector?'

'We'll call on him tomorrow morning, sir,' said Marmion.

'He sounds like a credible suspect, working in conjunction with Atterbury.'

'That's a line of inquiry we're pursuing with gusto.'

'I didn't hear much gusto in your report.'

'Keep listening, sir.'

After grilling Marmion for a few more minutes, Chatfield dismissed him then turned a glaucous eye on Keedy. The sergeant had his apology ready but was unable to deliver it because of a salvo of stinging questions.

'Why did you join the Metropolitan Police Force?' asked Chatfield.

'I wanted to be involved in the fight against crime.'

'And what were you taught from the very start?'

'I was told that obedience to a superior officer was essential.'

'Would you call yourself obedient?'

'Yes, I would, Superintendent.'

'Do you understand the importance of a structure of command?'

'Of course, I do.'

'You are answerable to those above you. Is that agreed?'

'It is, Superintendent.'

'Is it your place to contradict them?'

'No, sir.'

'Is it your right to walk away from one of them without permission?'

'It's wholly wrong and reprehensible, sir,' said Keedy, getting in what he thought was the best sentence he'd devised. 'It was unacceptable.'

'That's why I refuse to accept it. You are in trouble, Sergeant.'

'I realise that, sir.'

'But so is this investigation,' said Chatfield. 'Before I subject you to the appropriate disciplinary procedure, therefore, I intend to let you continue until this case is solved. After that . . .'

Keedy pursed his lips. 'I'll accept whatever punishment you choose, sir.'

'You'll have no choice. Don't you dare insult me again with an act of gross disobedience. Find yourself a dictionary and look up the word "contrition". That's what I want to see – true contrition.' He pointed to the door. 'Clear off, man!'

Cowed and chastened, Keedy was out of there in a split second.

Marmion returned home earlier than expected. Ellen gave him a warm hug then told him about the events of the day. Up in his bedroom, their son was playing a medley on the mouth organ. It was almost plaintive. Ellen had supper ready for her husband but he decided to postpone the meal.

'I'll have a word with Paul while I get the chance,' he said.

'Try not to have an argument.'

'I want to *stop* him arguing, Ellen.'

'So did I, so did Alice and so did your brother but he didn't pay attention to any of us. Tread carefully.'

'Leave him to me.'

Fatigue was starting to set in after a long day at work but Marmion shrugged it off and went upstairs. When he knocked on his son's door, the music stopped at once.

'What do you want?' yelled Paul.

'I want to talk to you, son.'

The door opened. 'Oh, I didn't realise it was you, Dad.'

'Can I come in?'

'Yes, yes . . .'

Clad in his pyjamas, Paul stepped back so his father could enter the room. Marmion looked at the souvenirs on the wall, mostly dating from the time when his son had played football. On the mantelpiece was a photograph of the whole team.

'How many of you are left?' he asked.

'If you count me, there's only five.'

'I'll certainly count *you*, Paul, because you were the captain.'

'We'd never win a match with only five players.'

'Do you miss the game?'

'I miss it like hell.'

'You'll be able to play it again one day, Paul.' His son shook his head. 'Yes, you will. You were far too good to give up – too good and too young.' He glanced at the mouth organ. 'We heard you practising. It was "Take Me Back to Dear Old Blighty", wasn't it?'

'Yes, it was one of our favourites.'

'Are *you* happy to be back in Blighty?'

'It's better than dodging the Boche. At least,' said Paul on reflection, 'that's what I thought at the time. I'm not so sure now.'

'Your mother tells me you've made a new friend.'

'She was Colin's friend, really. Mavis wrote to me.'

'I'm glad you were able to offer her some comfort. I'm only sorry,' said Marmion, pointedly, 'that you can't manage to do that for your own family. Why do you think that is?'

Paul needed a full minute to assemble his thoughts into words.

'I don't know,' he admitted. 'I try to say something nice to people but it comes out really nasty. I can't seem to stop myself. There's all this anger inside me and it just takes over.'

'Are you angry with *us*, Paul?'

'No, no, you're my family. I wanted to come back from France as a hero but you've had to put up with this half-blind curmudgeon who doesn't fit in any more.'

'You'll *always* fit in here,' his father assured him.

'Thanks, Dad . . .'

Marmion crossed the room to study the photograph. Paul was seated in the front row with a football on his lap. Beside him, chest inflated, was his best friend.

'Colin was not much of a player, was he?'

'He tried his best.'

'He was only in the team because of you, Paul. Whatever you did, Colin Fryatt had to do. That's no bad thing for a lad like him. You were a leader and he was just a follower. Without a friend like you, he'd have struggled.' Marmion grinned. 'The one thing he could do better than you was to play that mouth organ.'

'It's not as easy as it looks.'

Marmion turned away from the photograph. 'I'm sorry, Paul.'

'What for?'

'I'm sorry I wasn't able to give you more of my time. Your grandfather was a policeman, yet – even when he was on night shifts – he always found an hour to spend with me and my brother. I never managed that with you and Alice.'

'You're a detective,' Paul reminded him. 'Grandad was never more than a bobby on a bicycle. He didn't have the responsibility you have. Catching dangerous criminals is more important than kicking a football about in the park.'

'I wonder about that sometimes.'

'It is, Dad. The whole country is watching you so you have to concentrate on your work. I read the morning's paper for once today. It's not very kind to you and Joe.'

'We're only human. We can't work miracles.'

'Is it true that the victim lost his . . . ?'

'Yes,' said Marmion, sadly, 'it is. Both eyes were gouged out and his testicles were lopped off. What sort of man would do that?'

'I reckon he must be an angry husband with an unfaithful wife.'

'That was our thinking as well but it raises another question.'

'What's that?'

'If a jealous husband is roused to *that* pitch of fury,' argued Marmion, 'why would he stop at killing the lover? Surely, he'd want to murder the wife as well.'

Though Paul was baffled, he was also curious. While he pressed for no details of the investigation, he offered various theories about the crime. He made sensible comments. Marmion enjoyed the simple pleasure of chatting at ease to his son. It was the longest they'd spent alone together since Paul returned from France. Only when he realised that supper was waiting for him downstairs did Marmion finally break off. Yet some kind of link between them had been established again. Unexpectedly, it had taken a murder in Chingford to bring them together.

Before the war, Alice would never have dared to go into a public house on her own or even with a female companion. Women who haunted pubs unaccompanied by a man were, for the most part, either prostitutes or habitual drunkards. The situation had changed dramatically. When a huge army was formed in 1914 to fight the Germans, hundreds of thousands of jobs were suddenly available. Since there were not enough men to fill them, women took their place, proving that they could do most things equally well and – for the first time in most of their lives – earning a proper wage for doing so. Old barriers disappeared and social conventions were revolutionised. The sight of two women drinking alone in a bar was no longer so shocking. When, after leaving the cinema, they went into a pub together, therefore, Alice Marmion and Iris Goodliffe hardly earned more than a glance from the men there. They were simply two more working women with money to spend.

The only shock was the one that Alice suffered. Until that evening, Iris had always seemed a likeable, good-humoured, well-behaved young woman who looked up to her colleague. That, it transpired, was the sober version. When she'd had a drink or two, Iris became raucous, giggly and relentlessly argumentative. Her voice rose by an octave or more and trebled in volume. Instead of deferring to Alice all the time, she protested loudly against everything that her friend suggested. The evening became increasingly uncomfortable and embarrassing. Alice couldn't wait to escape. By the time they stepped out into fresh air, Iris was so inebriated that she could hardly stand up. Alice had to support her all the way back to her flat then put her to bed. As she left the building, she vowed that she'd never spend an evening with Iris again when her friend was anywhere near alcohol.

The rows with Joe Keedy and her brother had been bad enough but they paled beside the endless disputes into which she was dragged by Iris. Boarding the bus, Alice felt exhausted. It was as if she'd walked into a pub with a good friend and walked out again with an intoxicated monster. A whole evening had been ruined. In trying to escape from bad experiences, she'd simply added another one to the list. Iris had become a menace and yet, as she was forced to admit, nobody else was to blame. It had been Alice's idea for them to go on to the pub after seeing the film.

Plunged back into dejection, she sat on the bus and gazed unseeingly through the window. Alice didn't have the bravado to look ahead to the following day when she would have to face a penitent Iris. It was a torment on which she refused to speculate. All that she could do in the future was to refuse every invitation that her colleague thrust at her. If it meant spending night after night alone, Alice was ready to accept that regimen. Engrossed in misery, she almost missed her stop and had to jump off as the vehicle moved away. She needed a moment to get her bearings. Alice was just about to set off when her way was blocked by the frame of a man. He'd emerged soundlessly from the shadows and stood directly in her path. Alice tensed, ready to fight him off or to scream for help.

Joe Keedy swept off his hat and stepped in to give her a welcoming kiss.

'Remember me?' he asked.

CHAPTER TWENTY-ONE

The car picked him up at the usual time then headed for Joe Keedy's address. When it got there, the sergeant was already waiting on the pavement. He clambered into the rear seat beside Marmion.

'You're keen this morning, Joe.'

'Today is the day, I'm sure of it.' He held up a thumb and index finger, half an inch apart. 'We're *that* close to solving this crime.'

'I see that you've woken up full of confidence and in a happier frame of mind.' Marmion gave a knowing smile. 'I fancy that there's a good reason for that.'

'There is,' confessed the other. 'We had a long chat last night.'

'Everything's settled down, has it?'

'We're back to where we should be.'

'That's good to hear,' said Marmion with relief. 'I wish I could say the same where Paul is concerned but there's still a long way to go yet. However, we did manage to have a proper conversation at last and he was . . . approachable. That's an improvement in itself. The main thing is that I was able to reach him.'

'Ellen must have been grateful for that.'

'She was overjoyed.'

Keedy rubbed his hands together. 'Where do we start?'

'Before we go to Chingford, we're making a detour to Islington.'

'Why are we going there?'

'Mr Noonan won't be at his office this early,' replied Marmion, 'so I thought we'd surprise him on his own doorstep. I managed to find out his home address.'

'After what I've heard about him, I'll be interested to meet him. But I thought that Mrs Hogg said that she wouldn't press charges.'

'That doesn't mean we let him get away with intimidation. We need to scare him a bit – and to find out just how close he is to Tom Atterbury. Their names keep sticking together in my mind.'

'Don't forget to add Martin Pattinson,' said Keedy. 'He and Atterbury were seen together. They could both be working with the agent.'

Marmion was not persuaded. 'I can see Noonan and the dancer conspiring,' he said, 'but the agent and Pattinson would make very strange bedfellows. They're poles apart, as you'll soon find out.'

'We've come across odd partnerships before.'

'That's true. Everything is possible.'

'What sort of a welcome will we get from Noonan?'

'It will be a very frosty one.'

'You said that he was overflowing with amiability.'

'Not when he's hauled out of bed by two detectives,' said Marmion. 'Brace yourself for some bad language, Joe. He'll vent his spleen.'

Though she was not entirely sure what her husband had said to him, Ellen could see that it had had a calming effect on Paul. He was pleasant and forthcoming over breakfast that morning. He even rose to some gentle teasing.

'You might as well throw away those knitting needles.'

'Why?'

'We've already got enough socks and gloves at the front. In fact, I had so many pairs of socks given to me that I'd need to be a centipede to wear them all.'

'We're simply trying to make a gesture, Paul.'

'I know – and we appreciate it.'

'It's so difficult to know what we can do to help.'

'Try knitting some bulletproof vests.'

He laughed ironically. Ellen knew that his mood could not be ascribed wholly to a conversation with his father. Paul was going out for the day and it was easy to guess with whom he'd be spending it. She made the mistake of mentioning the name.

'You're seeing Mavis today, aren't you?'

'I might be,' he grunted.

'Where are you meeting her?'

'Don't know.'

'Haven't you arranged a place?'

'Not yet.'

'How will you know where to find her?'

'Who cares?'

'Why are you being so evasive?'

He lapsed back into the studied silence that she'd come to know and fear. Ellen was intruding again yet, she told herself, it was her right as a mother to know something about her son's movements. She pressed on.

'I was wrong,' she admitted. 'When she first wrote to you, I was worried that Mavis would be a bad influence on you. I thought she'd make you talk about the war and bring back all those terrible memories you've tried to put behind you. But I was wrong, Paul. Since you're so eager to see her again, she's obviously become a good friend. Is that right?'

'It might be.'

'Does she talk about Colin a lot?'

'Sometimes.'

'She must miss him a great deal – and so must you.'

He got up from the table. 'I'll go and get ready.'

'Paul . . .'

'Yes?'

'You could always invite Mavis here, you know. We'd love to meet her. Why don't you bring her to tea one day?'

'Because I don't want to,' he said in a tone bordering on ferocity. 'Mavis is my friend, not yours. She's the *only* thing I've got that's mine and I want it to stay that way. Can't you understand? I'd never bring her here. Mavis is *mine*.'

Ellen felt as if she'd been poleaxed.

It was a day of decisions for Audrey Pattinson. She'd already made the one that had a bearing on her own life. It was now time to advise someone else to reach a decision. Dennis Orme opened the door to her.

'Oh, hello, Mrs Pattinson – come on in.'

'Thank you.'

'Colette is upstairs. I'll give her a call.'

Audrey went into the living room and waited. She soon heard Colette tripping down the stairs and was grateful that her brother left them alone to talk in private. When the door was closed, she sat beside Colette on the sofa. Their mutual discomfort was almost tangible.

'I'm sorry I bothered you like that, Mrs Pattinson,' said Colette, shamefaced.

'No, no, you did the right thing.'

'Did I?'

'It must have taken a great effort on your behalf.'

'I've been worried sick.'

'It's a trouble shared now,' said Audrey, 'and that makes it easier to bear.'

'I just don't know what to do.'

'That's why I'm here.'

'I thought you were cross with me,' said Colette. 'When I called at your house yesterday, you were very funny with me. We'd always been friends before.'

'We still *are* friends, I hope. And I wasn't really cross with you, Colette. I was a little stunned by your revelation, that's all. It was such a surprise. It's taken me a little time to work things out in my mind but I've done that now.' She put a hand on Colette's knee. 'Do you know what I think you must do?'

Godfrey Noonan had just finished breakfast when they called at his house. He was outraged at being caught in a lurid silk dressing gown. Without a wig to hide it, they could see that his bald head was covered with freckles. After being introduced to Keedy, he kept them standing in the hall.

'Couldn't you bloody well wait until I got to the office?' he demanded.

'No, sir,' replied Marmion. 'We're investigating a murder and have to follow up leads whenever they crop up. There's a secondary reason for seeing you today. We had a visit from Mrs Hogg yesterday.'

Noonan looked blank. 'And who might she be?'

'She's the lady you tried to intimidate, sir,' said Keedy.

'I've never intimidated a lady in my life, Sergeant.'

'You threatened her outside her flat.'

'Really? Where was this?'

'You know quite well, sir,' said Marmion. 'It was in Archer Street. It seems that you grabbed her by the throat and issued a warning.'

'That's a serious allegation. It amounts to slander.'

'I take it that you're denying the accusation, sir.'

'I certainly am, Inspector – with every fibre of my being.'

'Given the choice between believing you and believing the lady,' said Marmion, coolly, 'I'd have to choose the lady. What about you, Sergeant?'

Keedy nodded. 'Mrs Hogg would be my choice as well, sir.'

'Can she produce any witnesses?' asked Noonan, slyly.

'You made quite sure that she was unable to do so, sir.'

'So it's a question of my word against Gillian's.'

'How did you know her Christian name, sir? You pretended you'd had no idea who she was a moment ago.'

'There are so many women in my life,' said Noonan with an oily grin, 'that I don't remember them by their names, only by their respective attributes.'

'Then you should remember Mrs Hogg,' said Marmion. 'She's the one with the bruises on her neck. You put them there.'

'Prove it in court.'

'We don't have to,' said Keedy.

'As it happens,' resumed Marmion, putting his face close to that of the agent, 'the lady does not wish to press charges. We just wanted to mark your card, sir. Stay away from Mrs Hogg. Is that clear enough for you? Stay away or we'll be back.' He had the satisfaction of seeing the agent swallow hard. 'Right,' he went on, taking a step back, 'we can move on to the main reason we have for coming here. When did you last see Tom Atterbury?'

* * *

The postman brought another sheaf of letters and cards. Hearing them drop through the letter box, Catherine Wilder went to pick them up then adjourned to the living room. She used a paper knife with an elaborately carved handle to slit open the envelopes. Some of the letters were long and moving but they had little effect on Catherine. Nor did the cards produce anything but mild interest. Unable to mourn, she could not share in the mourning of others. The final card was quite unlike the others and it lifted her out of her indifference. It was sent by the friend with whom she'd spent an idyllic afternoon at the Charing Cross Hotel. The message excited her.

A thousand thanks for yesterday. It won't be long now.

Allan Redmond hadn't needed to sign his name.

Throughout the journey, Paul Marmion imagined how they'd pass the day together. Mavis was his now. The farewell kiss she'd given him as they parted had sealed the fact. Colin Fryatt may have brought them together but he was no longer there. Life belonged to the living, Paul reminded himself, and he intended to make the most of it. They'd chosen Dartford as their meeting place. Neither of them had been to the town before so they could explore it together. That treat, however, was at the very back of Paul's mind. He had other hopes and ambitions.

Mavis was waiting at the bus stop to greet him. It was an encouraging sign. As he stepped down onto the pavement, she lunged forward to embrace him and he felt the seductive touch of her breasts against his chest.

'Where shall we go?' he asked.

'Let's just walk.'

'Can we find somewhere a bit private?'

'We'll do whatever you want to do, Paul.'

It was beyond any doubt now. She was definitely his.

* * *

Whenever he was in his miniature museum, time passed imperceptibly. Locked away from interruption, Martin Pattinson cleaned his weaponry and polished his medals, rekindling memories of his army days. He'd been happily engaged in there for hours that morning. The first time he heard the noise, he paid it no heed. The second time, however, it was much louder. It sounded as if something heavy was bumping its way downstairs. He unlocked the door and went to investigate. What he saw made him gasp in astonishment. His wife was standing in the hall with two large suitcases beside her.

'What are you doing?' he asked.

'I'm going to my sister.'

'But you don't need two suitcases to do that. All that you usually take for a weekend is the small valise.'

'I'm not going for the weekend, Martin.'

'Oh – how long will you be gone, then?'

'I won't be coming back,' she said, calmly.

He was stunned. 'You can't just walk out of here.'

'I should have done it years ago.'

'But we're married, you're my wife, we made pledges to each other.'

'You never kept a single one of them, Martin,' she told him. 'Taking my notebook was the final straw. You stole it then lied about it. I don't want to be in the same house as a man who does that sort of thing.'

'I apologised,' he gibbered. 'There's no need to get so upset. At least sit down and discuss this properly. You owe that to me, Audrey.'

'I owe you *nothing*.'

There was such a blend of quiet rage and determination in her voice that he was startled. Audrey had never dared to speak to him like that before. Throughout their marriage, she'd been a model of obedience, accepting his authority without question and asking permission to do what she wanted to do. Now she was about to walk out of his life indefinitely. The implications frightened him. He tried to threaten, cajole, persuade and even beg her but it was too late. His wife was deserting him.

'This is madness, Audrey,' he howled. 'You must see that.'

'All I get here is misery. I won't spend another minute under this roof.' She heard the sound of a car pulling up outside. 'That will be my taxi.' He moved to stand between her and the door. 'Out of my way, please,' she said.

'Give me one more chance, Audrey. That's all I ask.'

'Out of my way!' she yelled.

Pattinson was beaten. He stood meekly aside.

The detectives felt that their mission had been accomplished. In catching Noonan unawares – and without his wig – they'd been able to warn him to keep away from Gillian Hogg in future. Marmion had really shaken him. When they'd interrogated him about his relationship with Tom Atterbury, they learnt that the dancer was one of his favoured clients. Since they both lived in Islington, the two men often saw each other. Noonan claimed that he hadn't met his client since the murder but they didn't believe him for a second. Before they left, they told him that they were watching him closely and that, when further evidence emerged, they'd need to take a statement from him at Scotland Yard. The agent had quailed visibly.

'We got to him before he'd put his armour on,' said Marmion. 'He'd have been much more of a handful at his office.'

'Noonan's a big man. When he grabbed Mrs Hogg, he must have hurt her.'

'He won't do it again, Joe.'

'Should we ask Chat to put a tail on him?'

'It's too late for that. Atterbury will have told him about being followed. That will have put Noonan on guard. The best time to tail someone is when they haven't the faintest clue that they have a shadow. Noonan will *think* that we've got him under surveillance, however, and that will make him sweat.'

'I see what you meant about him,' observed Keedy. 'He's hardly a natural ally for Pattinson. One is a loud-mouthed showman and the other is a tight-lipped army man whose wife is afraid of him.'

'He and Noonan are in different worlds.'

'Are you saying that Atterbury and his agent were acting independently?'

'That's how it looks to me.'

They were back at the police station in Chingford, enjoying a cup of tea and discussing their visit to Islington. Keedy was still bubbling with optimism but Marmion was characteristically wary. They were interrupted by Gibbs, who came in to tell them that a young woman was anxious to speak to them. He showed Colette Orme into the room and Marmion gave her a warm welcome.

'Thank God!' said Keedy under his breath. 'I thought Odele was on the prowl again.'

Of all the people that Catherine Wilder didn't want to see on her doorstep, Odele was probably the first. Respecting each other as dancers, they'd never managed to convert that respect into friendship. Catherine was too embittered by the loss of her career to welcome anyone who took her place. The mere sight of Odele Thompson dancing with her husband had come to be a source of unceasing resentment. When they met again now, there was a brittle exchange of greetings. Catherine stood aside to let her visitor into the house.

'You've had a lot of cards,' said Odele as they came into the living room. She scanned the displays on the mantelpiece and on the piano. 'I can't see mine.'

'It's there somewhere, Odele.'

'Is everything organised for the funeral?'

'Yes, thankfully – my brother has taken charge of that.'

'You look as if you're bearing up well.'

'Nights are the worst. That's when all the memories ambush you.'

'Yes,' said Odele, grimly. 'I've had nights like that.' Glancing in the mirror, she adjusted her hair slightly. 'Inspector Marmion called on me,' she went on with a mischievous grin. 'I'd have preferred that good-looking sergeant of his but I think that he's hiding from me so the inspector came instead.'

'What did he want?'

'Apparently, he's spotted something in the appointments book. Simon had put a tick beside five names with a pencil then rubbed them out. The inspector asked me if I knew what those ticks meant but I didn't. I wondered if you might know.'

'I never saw any ticks and I checked the book at the end of every week when I totted up the takings. Can you remember which names were ticked?'

Odele listed three of them but took time to recall the other two. Like her, Catherine couldn't understand why those particular dancers had been singled out. It was Colette Orme's name that interested them. Aware that Wilder had given her preferential treatment, they speculated on what would happen to the young dancer in the future. Catherine dismissed her chances of having a professional career but Odele felt that losing her mentor might actually toughen Colette and give her the urge to go on alone.

'What she wants, of course,' said Odele, fishing for information, 'is for the studio to stay open.'

'There's no hope of that,' said Catherine, tartly. 'I intend to sell it. Believe it or not, I've already had one offer – though I turned it down flat. God came to see me.'

'What did he want?'

'He said he'd do me a favour by taking the studio off my hands. His offer was so insulting that I sent him packing. Whatever happens, he's not getting his grubby paws on the property.'

'That would be a ghastly prospect!'

'It won't ever happen, I promise you. Look,' she said, nudged into a reluctant hospitality, 'since you're here, can I offer you anything?'

'I wouldn't mind a cup of tea, Catherine.'

'Since we lost our servant to the war effort, I've had to do some of the chores myself. But my tea is perfectly drinkable.'

'Thank you . . .'

Instead of sitting, however, Odele took a closer look at the cards. Hers was clearly not among them and its omission was deliberate. It was one more slap in the face from Catherine. Most of the people who'd sent their condolences were known to Odele but some were complete strangers. The card she found most illuminating was tucked away in the middle of the display on the piano. When Catherine finally came back with a tea tray, Odele held up the card.

'Dear old Allan!' she said with a smirk. 'His writing doesn't get any better, does it? He always sent me a card afterwards as well.'

Paul knew that she wanted him. He could sense it in the way that she looked at him. Desperate to reach out to her, he was unable to do so because there was always somebody about. They visited a tea shop and he was rewarded with the brushing of her knees against his. It appeared to be accidental but he believed it was deliberate. Mavis was dropping hints. The biggest hint of all was that she never once referred to Colin Fryatt. It was as if he'd never existed in her life. Paul had totally eclipsed him. Though his vision remained blurry, he could see enough of Mavis to think that she was really beautiful. He loved the tilt of her chin and the way her hair bobbed whenever she moved her head. What he wanted above all else was the feel and the taste of her. The urge built up inside him like a machine slowly gathering speed.

They were strolling down a road when his chance finally came. Dark clouds had been forming all morning. The first spots of rain dropped on their faces. Seeing that a shower was imminent, they looked around for cover.

'Let's go into that church,' she suggested, pulling him by the hand.

'It's going to teem down any minute.'

'We'll be safe and dry in there.'

Paul would never have dreamt of sheltering in a church but he was with a vicar's daughter. It was the obvious place of sanctuary to Mavis. She turned the iron ring that lifted the latch and the heavy, studded door opened on squealing hinges. They stepped into the gloom of the nave. Mavis led the way down the aisle then sat in a pew, patting the place beside her. Paul sank down gratefully, rubbing his shoulder against hers. Evidently, they were quite alone. Mavis began to point out some of the architectural features in the chancel but he was no longer listening. Paul's interest was solely in her. His moment had at last come.

Putting an arm impulsively around her, he kissed her full on the lips. Though Mavis responded spiritedly, it was not in the way that he'd hoped. Pushing him roughly away, she wiped her lips with the back of her hand.

'What are you doing?' she cried. 'This is a church.'

'We're alone, aren't we? That's all that matters.'

'Oh, no, it isn't.'

'Come on, Mavis,' he said, caressing her breast. 'I want you.'

She pulled away from him. 'Take your hands off me!'

'I thought it was what you wanted.'

'Well, it isn't. You've disgusted me, Paul.'

'Wait,' he said, pulling her down again as she stood up. 'Don't you like me?'

'I did like you – until now.'

'Colin said that you were a pushover.'

She was outraged. 'That's not true.'

'He told me that you let him do whatever he wanted.'

'I did no such thing.'

'He boasted about it to everyone.'

'Colin wouldn't do that. He respected me.'

'According to him, the pair of you went the whole way.'

Mavis let out a scream of protest. Instead of trying to push past him again, she went to the other end of the pew, rushed up the side aisle and fled through the door. Paul went after her but he knew that it was a waste of time. As she ran off down the road, his legs refused to go after her. Colin Fryatt had lied. To gain a false reputation among his sniggering army friends, he'd made ridiculous claims about his girlfriend. Paul had been deceived into believing him. He wanted the favours that Colin was supposed to have had. Instead of having a compliant young woman in his arms, however, he'd tried to molest a virgin and he'd done so – of all places – inside a church. It was unforgivable. A sense of profound shame coursed through him like electricity. It was intensified by the disillusion he felt with his best friend. Taking the mouth organ from his pocket, he flung it away with contempt.

Then he went slowly back inside the church and knelt down at the altar rail. For the first time since he'd been wounded in action, Paul prayed as if he actually believed that someone was listening.

The estate agent was a cadaverous man in his fifties with a well-cut suit that Keedy immediately coveted. Acting on information supplied, tearfully, by Colette Orme, the detectives had gone to an office in the high street. Marmion explained that they were interested in a particular rented property.

'Nobody was at home when one of my men called there a few days ago,' he explained. 'According to a neighbour, the house is rarely occupied. We'd like to know who rents it from you.'

'One moment, Inspector,' said the man, opening a drawer and taking out a ledger. 'My memory is that the rental agreement was made through a third party.' He flicked through the pages until he found the one he wanted. 'Yes, here we are. It was made on behalf of a gentleman named Philip Clandon.'

Keedy was dismayed. 'Are you *sure* that was the name?'

'It's the one I have here, Sergeant. What name were you expecting?'

'Simon Wilder.'

'Yes,' said Marmion as the estate agent blinked in recognition of the murder victim, 'now you understand our interest in the property. I take it that you have a spare key.'

'Yes, yes,' gabbled the man, standing up. 'I'll get it for you.'

With the key in their possession, the detectives jumped back in the car and were driven to the address they'd been given. Keedy was bewildered.

'Colette must have been mistaken,' he said.

'I don't think so, Joe. Nobody would make a mistake over something as important as that. She's been tortured by the memory of it.'

'Then why isn't the house in Wilder's name?'

'He didn't want anyone to know he was renting it.'

'Somebody must have recognised him going there.'

'Not if he took care to visit the house after dark when nobody was about.'

'Who is this Philip Clandon?'

'We'll soon find out.'

Perched at the end of a terrace, the house was small, squat and unobtrusive. A thick bush in the tiny front garden shielded the lower part of the property. Marmion and Keedy got out of the car and let themselves into the house. When they entered the living room, they came to an abrupt halt. Expecting to see conventional furniture, they were instead confronted by a photographic studio. The whole of one wall was covered by a painted backdrop of white clouds flitting across a blue sky. In front of it was a chaise-longue. A decorated screen stood in one corner with a couple of flimsy robes draped over it. In another corner was a trolley loaded with bottles and glasses.

'That's how he did it,' said Keedy, noting the alcohol. 'He got them drunk first then persuaded them to pose for him.'

'They were *already* drunk, Joe. They were intoxicated with the idea of being a famous dancer. Colette was a typical example. She was in thrall to Wilder. When he told her that she was engaged in producing something artistic, she believed him, and it must have been the same with the others.'

'Is that all he did – take photos of naked women?'

'We'll soon see. Let's look in the darkroom.'

'How do you know there *is* one?'

'There has to be,' said Marmion. 'A photographer of his standing would never put up with that glorified cupboard at his other house. He'd want much more space and he'd want it where Mrs Wilder knew nothing at all about it.'

It didn't take long to search the small house. The darkroom was upstairs at the back of the property. To block out any light, a black blind had been drawn down over the window. The place was filled with photographic paraphernalia. Marmion's eye went straight to the album in the corner. It contained a succession of nude or scantily dressed young women in artistic poses. There were far more than the five who'd been singled out in the appointments book. The most recent model was Colette Orme, posing nude on the chaise longue and smiling invitingly at the camera. Marmion closed the album in embarrassment.

'We've seen enough,' he said.

'Wilder obviously wanted a private treasure trove.'

'There's more to it than that, Joe. The girls were tricked into believing that they were taking part in an artistic enterprise. Colette Orme admitted that. Wilder got her to adopt a number of balletic positions. When he showed her the photographs afterwards,' said Marmion, 'she made no objection at all. He promised her that they were for his eyes only.'

'So that was his game – he made copies for circulation.'

'Men of a certain sort would pay well for the photos in that album. They wouldn't be looking at them for artistic merit. What they were after was the sheer excitement. Do you remember the money found in Wilder's safe?'

'Yes,' said Keedy, 'it might have come from the sale of the photos.'

'Mrs Wilder didn't even know it was there yet she controlled all of their joint earnings.' Marmion looked around. 'This was his little factory, turning out photos for lonely men to gloat over. I feel so sorry for Colette and the other dancers. They all thought they were pupils of a genius. They had no idea that they were the victims of a repulsive pornographer.'

'So who *killed* him?'

'Wait a minute, Joe.'

'Was it Atterbury or Redmond? Did they discover this secret den?'

'*Wait*, I said.' Eyes closed, Marmion held up a hand to silence him. 'I'm in a darkroom of the mind. I'm developing a photo there and I'm waiting for the image to become clearer. Here it comes, very slowly . . .' He opened his eyes and grinned. 'Yes, I can see his face at last. It's not the one I expected but that doesn't matter one bit. We've identified the killer of Simon Wilder. Let's go and get him.'

Colette Orme walked home in distress. Having to confess to another woman what she'd done was humiliating but the meeting with the detectives was far worse. As she explained what Wilder had talked her into, she finally realised how cunning he'd been, first plying her with praise, then drinking wine with her and gradually luring her into a position where she could deny him nothing. Unaware that others had visited the photographic studio, Colette had been thrilled at the thought that she was the chosen one. It was their secret, she'd been told, a bond between the two of them that drew them ineluctably close. If anything happened to him, he'd promised, the photographs would be returned to her in an envelope. Wilder had not touched her at all that evening, assuring her that he respected her too much to do that. What he had done was to make her feel special. When she'd left the studio, she'd been walking on air. As she trudged home now, she had feet of lead.

She was jerked out of her introspection by the sound of an argument.

'I just want to know why, Den, that's all.'

'It's none of your business.'

'We haven't seen you for weeks.'

'And you're not going to see me ever again.'

'Why – what have we done wrong?'

'Bugger off!'

'I thought we were *friends*.'

What Colette witnessed next was not an act of friendship. Her brother, Dennis, had been arguing with a stocky young man with one arm and a face pitted with scars. He showed no pity. Raising his walking stick, Dennis belaboured him unmercifully, driving him away. As he stumbled past Colette, the man was swearing volubly.

Colette was appalled. 'Dennis – what have you done?'

'Shut up and get inside the house.'

'I heard what he said.'

'Forget him, Colette.'

'Was he one of the friends you went drinking with?'

'It's none of your business – now get inside.'

'Why are you so angry with me?'

He had no chance to reply. The police car came hurtling around the corner and juddered to a halt outside the house. As soon as he saw Marmion and Keedy climbing out of the vehicle, Orme retreated into the house and slammed the door behind him. Colette was confused.

'What's going on?' she asked.

'We need to speak to your brother,' said Marmion. 'Do you have a key?'

She took one from her pocket. 'Yes, it's here.'

'Thank you,' said Marmion as she handed it to him. 'You wait outside.'

347

He unlocked the front door and let Keedy go in first. Hearing noises from above, the sergeant went slowly up the stairs. When he reached the landing, he could go no further. Orme was standing there with a pistol in his hand.

'Stand back!' he ordered. 'I know how to use this.'

'Then why didn't you shoot Simon Wilder with it?'

'That bastard would have died too quickly. I used the butt to knock him out then gave him what he deserved. Do you know what he did to my sister?'

'We've just been finding out, sir.'

'And we understand why you were upset,' added Marmion, coming up the stairs. 'Mr Wilder made copies of a photograph that was taken of your sister. You must have become aware of it somehow.'

'It was my own *friends*,' shouted Orme in disgust. 'One of them had bought it from someone and was showing it around. It was Colette. They were looking at my sister and saying what they'd like to do to her. I couldn't stand that so I walked out on them for good.' He gestured with the gun to make Keedy step back a pace. 'Wilder was behind it. He'd taken photos of Colette before – proper photos, not the kind *they* were goggling at. So I went after him and I bided my time. He was never going to look at my sister with her clothes off ever again because I took out his eyes. And he was never going to *use* her for his . . . That's why I cut off his balls as well. Don't ask me to feel sorry for him. It's what he *deserved*.'

'Put that gun down,' said Keedy, gently.

'Stand back.'

'It's over now, Dennis. There's no escape.'

'I'm warning you,' said Orme, pointing the weapon at his face.

'Think of your sister. Is this how you want her to remember you?'

'I only did it for Colette.'

Marmion had paused on a step. 'And how does killing her instructor help your sister's dancing career?'

'You keep out of this, Inspector.'

'What you did was done in a blind rage.'

'I won't tell you again.'

Orme pointed the gun at Marmion this time. Seeing his chance, Keedy dived forward and knocked Orme off his feet. There was a fierce struggle on the floor with neither man getting the upper hand. Marmion dashed up to the landing to help Keedy but he was too late. The gun went off with a fearsome bang and both men froze in position. There was a long, agonising pause.

'Are you all right, Joe?' asked Marmion, worriedly.

Keedy rolled off the dead body. 'He shot himself,' he said, gazing in horror at the blood all over his jacket, 'and he ruined my best suit.'

Claude Chatfield was delighted that the murder of Simon Wilder had finally been solved though disappointed that the killer had escaped the hangman. Puritanical by nature, he was shocked by some of the aspects of the case and was anticipating some awkward questions at the imminent press conference. Meanwhile, he congratulated his detectives on their success.

'Thank you, sir,' said Marmion, 'but the real praise should go to Sergeant Keedy. He risked his life by tackling an armed man.'

'That won't be forgotten,' promised the superintendent.

'I hope that it exonerates him.'

'An act of bravery is always commendable, Inspector, but it won't blind me to the fact that the sergeant behaved disgracefully towards me in this very office.'

'I apologised for that, sir,' said Keedy.

'The matter is not yet settled.'

'I'm ready to take my punishment.'

'This is hardly the ideal moment,' said Chatfield. 'I'm just about to introduce you to the press as the heroes of the hour. How would it look if I told them that I was just about to discipline you for insubordination? It would seem petty of me. For the time being, Sergeant, you are safe.'

'Thank you, sir.'

'I'd like to add my thanks as well,' said Marmion. 'Nothing should take away the sergeant's lustre at a time like this.'

Keedy saw a chance to use flattery, 'You deserve some of the plaudits as well, Superintendent,' he said. 'I was so convinced of Redmond's guilt that I brought him back here in handcuffs. Wisely, you had him released from custody.'

'You didn't appreciate my wisdom at the time,' said Chatfield.

'I'll take care to do so in future, sir.'

'That's heartening. Going back to the murder victim, why did he rent that house in the name of Philip Clandon?'

'Mrs Wilder had the answer to that, sir,' said Marmion. 'She and her future husband met when they were acting in a comedy by Bernard Shaw. It was called *You Never Can Tell* and the character played by Mr Wilder was a certain Philip Clandon. He decided to use the name again.'

'I have another question for you, Inspector, and it's one that will surely be directed at me in a short while, so I'd be grateful for an answer. What put you on to this fellow, Orme?'

'It was his dedication, sir.'

'Dedication?'

'Dennis Orme was intensely proud of his sister. He'd made great sacrifices for her. He'd do anything to further her dancing career. Then he saw a nude photograph of her being passed around his drunken friends in a pub and something snapped inside him. He wanted revenge against the man who took the photo.'

'I thought he was disabled.'

'He was stronger and more mobile than I thought,' said Marmion. 'When I first met him at the house, he put on a show of struggling along on his walking stick. As the sergeant found out, however, he could certainly defend himself.'

'Yes,' said Keedy, 'he was powerful. I had to fight for all I was worth.'

'The irony of it all is that the sister he idolised is the one who'll suffer most now. Her dancing career is in ruins and she'll be haunted by what her brother did. When she got back to the house, Dennis Orme was having an altercation with one of the people he used to go drinking with. Orme had cut himself off from them. On the night of the murder, he'd told Colette, he'd got so drunk that he'd slept at the house of a friend. In fact, of course,' said Marmion, 'he was stalking Simon Wilder.'

Chatfield looked at his watch. 'Time to go, gentlemen,' he said. 'Tomorrow morning, your names will be all over the newspapers and I can tell you now what the most popular headline will be.'

'So can I, sir – DANCE OF DEATH.'

351